KISS

of

DEATH

LP LOVELL

Cover Designer: Charlotte Johnson

Editor: Wallflower Editing

Kiss of Death is a complete story. Una's backstory is in MAKE ME, a short novella at the end of the book. Warning; it is very dark and at times disturbing. If you'd like to read it first, go to page 573. If you'd like to dive right in with the twisted romance of Nero and Una, keep reading.

KILL ME

Kiss of death #1

LP LOVELL

CHAPTER ONE

Una

Bumping my bike over the curb, I allow it to roll down the small embankment into the treeline. Kicking the stand down, I take off my helmet and rest it on the fuel tank, then pulling the hair tie from my hair, sending long, white-blonde strands cascading down my back. The scent of the woods wraps around me, the pine trees, the earth, the moss. After the confines of the city, it's a welcome reprieve that revitalises me. The city is too loud, the cars, the people, it both overwhelms and numbs my senses. Out here, I can hear everything and nothing, because silence reigns, disturbed only by the occasional chitter of a bird.

Pulling my hood up over my head, I start jogging up the road, clinging to the shadows as I approach the house. To the mansion of some guy with a fuck lot of money, I know better. This is the fortress of Arnaldo Boticelli, the underboss of the Italian Mafia. Not many outsiders will ever see the inside of those walls, and I am always an outsider. It's why they hire me.

I wait until the guards change; taking advantage of their small moment of distraction to make for the six-foot high stone pillar that sits to the left of the enormous metal gate, just in the shadow of the guardhouse. Gripping the ledge, I haul myself up, launching straight over the top and landing on the other side in a silent roll. I pause, waiting, listening. My senses are attuned, picking up the slightest sound and movement. I can tune it all out or allow it all in. The faint panting of a dog and the clumsy footfalls of heavy boots are all I hear. Thirty seconds is all I have to get to the house. I run over the dark lawns, but the closer I get, the riskier it is. The mansion is like a modern palace, made of glass walls that allow light to spill out across all that surrounds it. There are at least three snipers on the roof along with four guard patrols circling the perimeter and six directly surrounding the house.

Scanning the house, I spot one of the upstairs guest rooms has a window that is ajar. The enormous pane of glass is tilted from a central pivot, and the room behind it is cast in darkness, one of the few that isn't lit up like a Christmas tree. The guard below the window seems distracted, bored. Making a break for it, I sprint into the light cast across the lawn and outflank him. My feet whisper across the grass as I run up behind him, jumping and wrapping my thighs around his hips in order to leverage my arm around his throat. He staggers for a moment and slams back into the wall, winding me as he tries to pry my arm off his throat. I squeeze harder, using everything I have to crush his thick neck. And then he goes down, hitting the ground with a soft thud. I land lightly on my feet beside his unconscious body, my chest heaving with the effort.

Now…I just need to scale the building and slip in the second-storey window. Easy.

4

Arnaldo's house is a fortress of marble and glass, all of which I know is bullet proof. Pressing my back to a wall, I peer around before ducking back in. Two guards stand outside the double doors that lead to Arnaldo's office. Yanking my hood further down until it shadows my eyes, I take a deep breath before stepping out from behind the wall. The guards snap their attention to me, and I pop just a little more sway in my hips as I approach them. They both reach for their weapons and I drop to the ground, ripping the pistols from my thigh holsters and pulling them up in front of me. The triggers give way under my index fingers and the guns release with a silenced pop. Both of them grapple for a second, reaching for the small darts protruding from their necks before they simultaneously slide down the doors. Darts so aren't my style, but then it doesn't go over well to come into a client's house and kill their personal guards. I press my boot against the arm of one of the guys, shoving him to the side so I can open the door. My boots sink into the thick carpet and I push the door closed behind me.

Arnaldo looks up from his enormous desk and smiles, steepling his fingers in front of him. Of course, he was expecting me. I told him I was coming. Two of his guards stand like silent vigils behind him, their backs straight and their assault rifles pointed at me. I keep my face lowered towards the ground, ensuring that the hood casts my face in shadow.

"You going to shoot me, boys?" I ask, a cocky smile playing over my lips. When in the worst situations, I often find a smile can save you. Everything in life is about perception. What you do doesn't matter, only your opponent's perception of what you will do. Smile when they expect you to cower, play the helpless woman when they expect you to come out all guns blazing. An unpredictable enemy is the most deadly, after all.

"Una," Arnie greets me in his thick Italian accent before clicking his fingers and signalling for his men to leave. He knows I won't talk with them here. The door clicks shut, and he smiles, gesturing for me to sit. "Thank you for agreeing to meet."

I narrow my eyes at him. I'm already aware of the man behind me, but I'm waiting to see if he'll move. Arnaldo is the one who gives it away, his eyes shifting infinitesimally before meeting mine again. Smiling, I tilt my head to the side at the same time as I drop the tiny silver blade from the thick cuff around my right wrist. It's the size of a large hairpin, but as sharp as a razor and weighted to have a reasonable throwing range. My hand flics out behind me as I keep my eyes fixed on Arnaldo. I hear the blade drive home, burying itself into the wood of the door. The mob boss's lips curl into the shadow of a smile and his eyes pinch at the corners.

"You missed." The voice behind me is rough and deep. He approaches from behind, and I fight to stay still when I feel him brush entirely too close to me. Circling in front of me, he stops, our bodies barely an inch apart. The aim is to intimidate and it amuses me. He's tall, a lot taller than me, but where most of the men Arnaldo keep seem to be bulky, this one is athletic. His shoulders are broad, but taper into a narrow waist. Honed muscles lay over his lithe frame, the result of discipline and work. Some women see a man like this and think him attractive, but I'm beyond such base notions. I think him dangerous. He stands casually, his hands in the pockets of the expensive suit that wraps around his body like a glove. He radiates power like a beacon, it unfurls, curling around me and sucking all the air from the room. My curiosity wins out and I tip my head back, dragging my eyes up his chest until they reach his face. He looks like one of those guys you see in a magazine. Full lips, chiselled jaw, high cheekbones, and hair that's just slightly too long to be professional. Everything about him screams entitled, rich, pretty boy, until I look in his eyes. They're the colour of a well-aged whisky and almost completely unreadable, ice cold. I fight to keep a smile off my lips, because everything about him screams challenge. His eyes narrow and I see the tight restraint, the leash he puts himself on, because there's an edge to him, something cold and dangerous with a ruthlessness to rival my own. He catches me off guard for the smallest of moments, but it's enough, because he's seen my face. I'm not entirely upset at the notion, because it means I might have to kill him, and this one would make for an exciting adversary.

Reaching up, I brush my finger over the shell of his ear, coating my finger in the blood pooling from the small knick. "I never miss." His eyes hold me captive as I lift the finger to my lips and suck, tasting the coppery tang of him. He doesn't flinch, doesn't move. "If I wanted you dead, you'd be dead." His expression never wavers, never gives away even a hint of what he's thinking. He's both intriguing and infuriating.

"Bacio della morte," he says in fluent Italian, his tongue caressing the words like a lover.

Kiss of death. It's what the Italians call me.

"Sei spaventato?" I reply with a smirk. *Are you scared?* I can't help but bait him, though I doubt this one fears anything. You know what they say, there's a fine line between bravery and stupidity. He'll find it's a very fine line indeed when dealing with me.

Tilting his head to the side, a stray lock of dark hair falls across his forehead. The move reminds me of a predator weighing its prey, which is laughable. His eyes hold mine long past the point where normal people would start to feel uncomfortable. The way he looks at me almost has me wanting to look away, to back down. *Me!* I never back down from anyone, because to do so is to perceive a threat. No one threatens me. Who is this man? He embodies power, wears it like a man who was born with it, and yet, I do not know him, which means he does not assume power. Curious. Everyone can be read like facts off a sheet of paper, their fears, their hopes, their strengths, their weaknesses…if you know what to look for, they'll tell you everything. He's telling me nothing, giving away nothing, and it has me intrigued. I stare into his eyes, pushing, probing, looking, and yet he stands like a wall of iron in front of me, impenetrable and steadfast.

Eventually, I tear my eyes from his and walk past him dismissively. An uneasy feeling crawls through my gut at having my back to him, my instincts warning me that this one is dangerous, but survival and domination are as much about the bluff as anything else. To acknowledge him as a worthy adversary in itself lends him power that I am not willing to give, because I am the danger here, and if he makes a move, regardless of who he is, he will soon learn why.

I round the desk and Arnaldo hefts his weight from his chair, pulling me into a hug and kissing both my cheeks. The Italians have their ways and they get upset if you piss in their cornflakes, so I play along, despite the fact that the brush of his skin against mine has long ingrained instincts roaring to the surface. I liken it to a lion throwing itself against the bars of a cage, overcome with the primal instinct to kill. But I have forged a prison of tempered steel that keeps my monster firmly locked up, chained and hidden from the world until I need her. He pulls away and I release the breath I'd been holding. Arnie's a bear of a man, who always smells of cigars and whisky, but he's a loyal client, and I value loyalty.

"Arnie, it's been a while," I say casually. He sits back down and offers me a drink he knows I won't take, followed by the chair he knows I'll refuse to sit in. I've worked with him for four years. He knows well enough.

"I'm happy to say I haven't needed your services of late." I move, leaning my back against the wall, off to the side of Arnie's desk.

I glance at tall, dark and handsome. He's standing in the same position, only now he's facing us. His hands are still in his pockets, giving the perception of casual relaxation, but nothing about that man is casual. He's aware, watching, waiting. A frown shadows his features as he assesses me.

"He needs to leave," I say, tilting my head towards him.

Arnie sighs and leans back in his chair. "This concerns him. Plus, I don't trust you not to kill me." He grins.

"Oh, Arnie." I smile sweetly, slipping my fingers beneath the thin hood and pushing it back off my face. "It's cute that you think anyone could protect you if I wanted you dead." His face becomes serious as I move to his desk, swaying my hips with every step. "Don't worry. I'd want at least twenty for you." I wink. Like I said, this game is all about perception. Confidence is a must, and charm goes a long way. I'm not one for bullshit. I'd happily never interact with a client face-to-face, but Arnie is one I make an exception for. Even he must remember his place though, because mob boss, cartel leader, motherfucking president…death doesn't discriminate, she sells to the highest bidder.

CHAPTER TWO

Nero

The way she walks, the way she speaks, the way she toys with Boticelli has me more interested than I should be. I know little about her, but I can tell one thing, she can't be controlled. The stories about her are well known, the Russian assassin who took out Salvatore Carosso, a key player in the Mexican Cartel. If I saw her on the street, I wouldn't look at her twice. And that, I realise, is why she's so good. On the outside she looks like a pretty little thing full of empty threats, but one look in her eyes has me weighing her very differently, because there's nothing there. No emotion, no doubt, no conscience.

She approaches Boticelli's desk, and I watch the muscle in his jaw twitch at her thinly veiled threat, and yet, he says nothing. He does nothing. She has the underboss of the Italian mob biting his tongue like a whipped dog. The corner of my lip twitches as I try not to smile. He's scared of her. His eyes dart to me, as though I'll save him. I won't He's a means to an end, but I have fuck all loyalty to him beyond what he can do for me. It's her I need. She hops up on the edge of his desk, facing me and crosses one leg over the other, swinging her boot back and forth as if she doesn't have a care in the world. She braces her hands behind her, stretching her lean body out and thrusting her chest forward. The material of her top pulls tight over her chest, and my eyes trace the length of her body. White-blonde hair falls down her back in waves, making her milky skin appear even more pale. Yeah, I can see why she's so good, because if I didn't know who she was, I'd be all too willing to sink my dick in her. She's like killer Barbie. She's perfect.

"Fine. You want to talk in front of him, do, but…" She swings her gaze towards me, narrowing those unusual indigo coloured eyes at me. "Betray me, and I will find you."

There are two types of people in this world, those who threaten and those who promise. I always appreciate people who make promises. Her eyes lock with mine, and I stare back at her wordlessly. Little does she know that to speak of this situation would damage me a lot more than it would her. She'll find that out soon enough though.

"Okay." Arnie huffs impatiently. "This is your mark."

He hands her a file and she opens it, skimming over the page before closing it and discarding it on the desk beside her. "Three," she says simply.

The boss narrows his eyes. "Three million? He's a capo."

12

She tilts her head back and then rolls her neck to the side, looking at him with a bored expression on her face. "He is not just a capo. He's Lorenzo Santos. I need time to get close to him, and time is money, Arnie."

Fucking Lorenzo. He's an idiot with his dick in his hand. She'd only have to look at him and he'd blindly follow her to a slit throat.

Arnaldo grins like a shark and picks up the half smoked cigar from the ashtray on his desk. He takes a lighter from his pocket and flips the top, allowing the flame to kiss the blackened end of the cigar. He puffs on it a couple of times and exhales a heavy cloud of smoke.

"Getting close won't be a problem. That's what Nero here is for." He jerks the cigar towards me and ash falls on the desk, scattering across the wood. Una's eyes lock with mine, focused, studying. "Santos is throwing an engagement party in two week's time and you will be his date." The boss adds.

She knows just as well as I do that security that night will be even tighter than normal. She might get in, but she sure as shit won't be getting out. It's a suicide mission. And a test. Arnaldo thinks that our interests are one and the same, that this is a simple takeover. It's not, but for now, I need him on my side. More importantly, I needed him to put me in contact with the best hitman money can buy...or hitwoman. Una Ivanov. She's elusive and completely impossible to contact unless you're in the know. Arnaldo is in the know. The pieces are on the chessboard, I just need to put them into play.

She inhales deeply, her nostrils flaring. "Fine, but it's still three mil."

She hops off the desk and walks towards me. Her hips sway delicately, her body moving like liquid art. Coming to a halt in front of me, she lifts a hand, trailing perfectly manicured nails over my jaw. I wrap a hand around her wrist, halting her movement. I don't trust her for shit. A smile curls the corners of her blood red lips, and I squeeze her wrist hard enough to bruise her porcelain skin, hard enough that I know with a tiny bit more pressure I could break the delicate bones. Her eyes flash with something, but she never flinches, never moves, never stops smiling. We simply stare at each other.

"What was your name again?" Her expression shifts, interest shining in her eyes.

"Nero."

"Nero...?" I hesitate and her smirk widens into a full grin. "I will find out, so save me the time and the addition to Arnie's bill."

I have no doubt she will have my life story in a matter of hours. "Verdi," I say. She gives no reaction, no response at all.

"A nobody," she says quietly. "Curious."

"A nobody." I agree. I plaster a smirk on my face and release her wrist, trailing my fingers over her arm. She stiffens for the briefest second, but I catch it.

She presses her body against mine and her breath blows over my jaw, her eyes dropping to my lips as she tilts her head to the side. I'm sure many a man has been lured to his death by that tight body and those full lips. I'm not one of them. I keep my eyes on hers, waiting.

"And yet here you are, cosied up to the boss," she whispers, cocking an eyebrow. "High stakes for a nobody." Clever girl. She bites down on one side of her bottom lip. "I like you, Nero." She smoothes her palm over the front of my jacket, before slipping away from me. "I think you'd be hard to kill, and I do so love a challenge." She smiles and winks before she walks to the door leisurely, as though she has all the time in the world.

Pausing, she pulls her hood up again, until only her white-blonde hair spills over her shoulder, and then she's gone.

The game is officially in play.

TWO WEEKS LATER

Inhaling the smoke, I hold it, allowing it to burn my lungs before I release it. I'm about a mile away from Lorenzo's house, parked in the driveway of an empty house with a real estate sign outside. Una is precisely three minutes late.

I look up when a black Mercedes comes hurtling down the street. It slows and pulls into the drive beside my car before the engine cuts out. It takes me a second to realise who it is, because her long, white-blonde hair is now dark brown and skimming her jaw line. The door opens and Una's lithe frame unfolds from the car. Her body is covered in a red dress that masks any trace of her skin and yet clings to every single curve she has. If her aim is to distract and seduce then I can't imagine she'll have a problem. The woman is a siren. Death wrapped in a bow.

"Nice dress." I push off the hood of my car, throwing the cigarette on the ground.

She barely even spares me a glance. "Smoking will kill you," she says, moving to the passenger side.

"I'd say it's the least of our worries right now." I open the driver's door and slide into the leather seat.

She gets in and closes the door behind her. "Speak for yourself. Risk is calculated and directly related to your level of skill."

"Arrogance will get you killed." I reverse out of the drive, fishtailing the car onto the road with a flick of the steering wheel.

She lets out a short laugh. "I'm the best, Mr Verdi. It's not arrogance, simply fact." She takes a small mirror out of her bag and checks her lipstick. The red matches her dress and contrasts

16

dramatically with her pale skin. "I don't take jobs that will get me killed."

"So you have a plan to get out?" Arnaldo told me before not to ask questions and let her do what he hired her for, but this isn't Arnaldo's show, no matter how much he might think himself the puppeteer. I wish I could be the one to end Lorenzo, so I could smile over his dying body and watch his worthless life drain from him. But I need to remain distanced from this.

"You read the file I sent?"

"Yeah, but there wasn't much to go on." She sent me a file detailing her fake identity as well as vague details about said identity. That's it. "You're aware of the heightened security?"

I glance at her when she doesn't respond and see the corner of her lips curled up, sinking a small dimple into her cheek. "There was as much as you need to play your part. Don't question my methods, and I won't question why you want your brother dead." I turn my attention back to the road, tightening my grip on the steering wheel and clenching my jaw. Of course she would find out that Lorenzo is my brother. I feel her gaze touch the side of my face, but deliberately refuse to look her way.

"Half-brother," I say through gritted teeth. "And I have my reasons."

"You make the mistake of thinking I actually care."

"I need to know how this is going to play out. I can't be culpable." My voice lowers until it's barely above a growl.

She sighs dramatically. "We walk in together. Shortly after we arrive, I'll slip away. Your brother will follow me, job done. You won't see me afterwards so don't wait around."

"You really think you're going to make it out?"

She laughs, a light tinkling sound that contradicts her completely. "I know I am. You should worry about yourself. The girl you brought to the party kills your brother…that won't go down well for you."

"I have that under control." I hate my brother and he hates me, but he's the capo and I'm a good enforcer. Our feud isn't publicly known. As far as everyone is concerned, I'm the loyal brother, willing to kill for Lorenzo. The only ones who know any different are my closest guys, Tommy, Gio and Jackson. I suspect Lorenzo has kept it the same; after all, rifts in the family make it look weak. But then, he never was the sharpest, so I could be wrong. By the time anyone is brave enough to voice their suspicions, I'll be capo. They're scared of me now; they'll be terrified of me then.

When I pull up to the house there are a line of cars waiting to get up the driveway. The parking is on one of the lawns outside the gates, and people are waiting on foot as Lorenzo's soldiers pat down guests upon entry.

Una smooths a hand over her wig and throws the door open. Reaching out, I grab her arm to stop her, but before I can she rips away from my grasp and slams the same arm across my throat. My Adam's apple hits the back of my throat and I choke for a second, my vision dotting. It takes me a couple of precious seconds without oxygen to move. My instinct is to grab the back of her head and smash it against the dash, but that wouldn't do much for her face, and I need her intact for this job. Instead, I grip her wrist and squeeze, hard enough to shove her an inch away from me. She may be fast, but she's tiny and I'm infinitely stronger. She pulls her arm away from me, tucking it back against her side. Her nostrils flare, pupils dilated. Her fists clench and release repeatedly as she tries to gather control of herself.

"I need you right now, but do that again and I'll put a bullet in that pretty little head of yours," I growl, trying to leash my temper. I don't like surprises, and I certainly don't like being bested. Cracking my neck from side to side in an attempt to dislodge the ache deep in my throat.

She turns to face me, those indigo eyes locking with mine. Something shifts between us, the threat of violence pulsing like a living thing. "If you value your life, do not ever touch me when I'm unawares."

"What I was attempting to do was to warn you that they will frisk you. If they find even your handy blade there, it will fuck everything." I point at the thick silver cuff around her wrist.

She turns away, perching on the edge of the seat. "That information really wasn't worth getting injured for," she drawls, that hint of a Russian accent creeping in where she usually hides it so well.

I laugh. "Duly noted." She thinks she's bulletproof because she incites fear. She has no power here because she relies on the most basic animal instinct. Survival. People will do whatever they have to in order to survive and so fear becomes a valuable ally. I learned a long time ago that surviving is not living, so I will either get what I want or die trying. I always get what I want.

CHAPTER THREE

Una

We approach the gate, waiting in line with the other guests. Nero slides his hand around my waist, resting it on my hip. I grit my teeth but make a concerted effort to keep my gaze forward and a smile on my lips. I'm a killer, but above all else, I'm an actress. I can be anyone, assume any role or identity given to me, because killing someone is the easy part. It's getting close that's the problem, and trust me, when you go after the kind of people I do, you want to be close before you take a shot at them. They have a habit of dodging bullets and shooting back. His fingers wrap around my hip, gripping me more firmly.

"You're brave," I growl under my breath. His fingers twitch and the heat from his palm seeps through the material of my dress, branding my skin.

He huffs a laugh. "Maybe I just have complete faith in your ability to be professional."

"Hmm." I smile at one of the guards who glances my way as he's patting down the woman in front of us. I trail my hand up my body until my fingers cover his, gently wrapping them around his hand. I squeeze and he lets out a low grunt. "How professional do you think you'll be when I break your hand?" I hiss, smiling sweetly at him for the sake of our audience.

He leans in, smirking as he brushes a finger over my cheek. "Now, now, *Isabelle*. You'll make me hard before my pat-down." He leans in close until his lips are at my ear. "I do so love a violent streak in a woman."

And I do so love making men bleed. On a job I'm focused, in control, and yet, something about him makes everything in me want to rise to the challenge he constantly throws down simply by existing. To anyone looking at us, we must look like a couple that is so in love they can't keep their hands off each other. Perception is everything. I squeeze his hand harder and watch the strain flash across his face. He pulls back slightly, and I slowly release him, keeping my eyes fixed on him as his fingers trail over my hip, caressing the top of my ass.

The couple in front of us move away and we step up to the guards.

"Hold your arms out to the side," one says robotically to me. I do as told and take a deep breath as his hands sweep over my body. He moves onto Nero while the other guy runs a bug scanner over me. Of course it never goes off. I have all the tools I need to kill Lorenzo on my person, but nothing that could possibly be so easily detected or even so much as suspected.

When they're done, Nero smiles and wishes them a good day in Italian before placing his hand at the small of my back.

"Before you threaten to dislocate my shoulder, remember we're a couple, *Morte*. And trust me, the more I look like I want you, the more my brother will want you." His voice drops and though nothing this man says should affect me, it strangely does, just enough to draw my attention to the fact.

"Well, you Italian boys do like to keep it in the family."

He ignores me as we pass through the high stone walls that surround the garden courtyard at the back of the house. The property reminds me of a traditional Tuscany villa, with the terracotta tiled roof and the flowers growing up the side of the enormous house. As soon as we walk into the courtyard, people greet Nero. Again, his name doesn't hold much weight, and I can see that in the way people approach him, and yet that effortless power of his seems to win out. They quickly drop their gaze when he speaks, even older, Made men who owe him no such respect. It's not respect though, it's impulse, an instinctual reaction they can't help. Nicholai would love him. He'd rise in the bratva fast with that kind of ability. The Italians are stupid though. Ability means nothing against bloodlines. The last I checked, the fact that your father fucked your mother wasn't a reason to garner respect, but that is the Italian way.

As per the file, he introduces me as Isabelle Jacobs, an all-American girl he's 'dating', just until the family finds a well-bred Italian girl and demand he marry her of course. Traditions again. I'm treated as all women are treated in the mafia, like a pretty ornament whose sole worth is in my ability to spread my legs. In my line of work, I have found that the underestimation and quick dismissal of women works in my favour.

We've been here twenty minutes when I spot Lorenzo, and when I do, I find him already watching me. His fiancée is on his arm. She can be no more than twenty, and she looks terrified. Well, I'm about to save her from an arranged marriage. I hold

Lorenzo's stare for a beat, and when he doesn't look away, I flash him a small smirk before dropping my gaze as if I'm shy. When I look back up, his attention has shifted slightly to Nero on my left. The look in his eye is pure animosity. Nero has three older guys eating out of the palm of his hand, laughing and talking in Italian, another move to exclude me from the conversation. Of course, I understand every word they're saying. I pull away from Nero's side and he offers me a brief glance, a frown marring his features. I make a show of seeming pissed off and storm away. I approach the small open bar, pushing past the cluster of wives that are standing by it, delicately clasping their champagne glasses.

The waiter behind the bar smiles politely, resembling a little penguin in his tuxedo. "Vodka on ice," I tell him. He pours the clear liquid into the glass, the ice cracking under the alcohol as he slides it across to me.

"A woman who likes the hard stuff."

A slow smile pulls at my lips as I turn to face the owner of the subtly accented voice. Lorenzo isn't quite as tall as his brother and he certainly doesn't carry the air of power, despite the fact that he's capo. He has the same dark hair and deep brown eyes, the same chiselled cheekbones and jaw line, coupled with a set of lips that I'm sure make most women fall all over themselves. And yet, Nero is somehow just more in every way, speaking from a completely objective standpoint, of course.

"Always." I lift the glass to my lips and take a sip, locking eyes with him over the rim of the glass.

He turns, bracing his back against the bar and allowing his eyes to roam over the guests gathered in the garden. "How do you know my brother?"

"I fuck him." Titters erupt from the women behind me, and I smile. Of course he catches it. He was supposed to. "I see you're more the settling type. Congratulations." His eyes drop to my lips. "I do love a wedding." I lower my voice and allow my gaze to roam over his body while biting my bottom lip. The look in his eyes is one I recognize all too well. The pulse point at his neck beats faster and his pupils dilate. His breathing picks up ever so slightly and he shifts on his feet, probably because his pants are becoming a bit uncomfortable. "Although, you don't look thrilled at the prospect." I rest my elbow on the bar and pop my hip, accentuating the curve of my body.

"Hmm, well, this world is full of so much temptation," he says each word carefully. "And you deserve a better offer than my brother." He almost hisses the words, as if the very notion offends him. The more he talks, the more the differences between Nero and he become painfully clear. Admittedly, Nero had the advantage of knowing what I was from the moment he met me. But Lorenzo's naivety, his assumption that I am exactly what I appear to be…well, it's disappointing. Or perhaps I'm just that good. After all, I was crafted for this very purpose, to be a chameleon, to blend in and become whatever it is my prey wants me to be. Right now, he wants me to be the hot chick that his brother is sleeping with. He wants to fuck me and stick it to Nero. I step forward, closing the gap between us.

"So make me a better offer." I raise an eyebrow and focus on his lips, which slowly curl into a satisfied grin.

That's all it takes for him to pick up my glass off the bar and down the remaining vodka before turning and walking away. Glancing across the courtyard garden to where Nero is talking in a small group, I know his attention has been firmly on me this entire time. His eyes lock with mine, narrowing, as his jaw tenses. Ignoring him, I follow Lorenzo out of the courtyard. He slips through a side gate, whispering something to the guard standing there as he passes. The guard nods, and when I approach him with a sensual smile gracing my lips, he steps to the side without a word. I leave some distance between us as I trace Lorenzo's path up the stone steps that lead to a sunroom attached to the back of the house. Inside, various plants creep over the glass and the scents of different flowers assault me. The sound of running water trickles over my senses. Most people would probably find it soothing, but for me it triggers a short burst of images to flash through my mind. Hands holding me down, panic, choking, drowning, catching a breath only to drown all over again. Snapping my focus back to the task at hand, I crack my neck from side to side and take a deep breath to centre myself again.

Lorenzo hooks left, under a small archway that leads into what I assume is the main house. He walks up the stairs and along a corridor before he stops at a door. He glances over his shoulder, flashing me a small smile as the heavy oak door opens with a groan.

The room is small with a couple of leather sofas in the middle and a desk at the back. I'm registering every possible threat, anything I can use as a weapon in the event that something goes wrong, and most importantly, an escape plan. There's the door I came in through of course, but that leads back into the house, which may be heavily guarded. At the back of the office are two narrow glass doors that lead out onto a stone balcony. That's my most likely escape route at this point.

The latch of the door clicks shut with a heavy finality and the silence it leaves behind is deafening, as though the world itself is suddenly holding its breath, waiting for death to strike.

Hands brush over the side of my neck, but I don't flinch this time, because I'm ready. I'm in the place in my mind where the kill, the lust for blood, goes beyond any uncomfortable feelings he may elicit. It's a side of myself that I hide, that I'm ashamed of, but not because of some misplaced guilt. Do not give me credit that is not due. I'm ashamed because I'm better than that. I was trained to be impassive, the elite, silent warrior. Death is a job, a necessity, we neither like nor dislike it, it just is. But for me, in a world where everything is a map of grey existence, this is my only spike of colour. It's when I take the ultimate prize from someone else that I am given a gift, a moment of relief, a moment of bliss. And the possibility of that moment excites me.

His lips brush over my skin so lightly that the hairs on the back of my neck prickle to attention. "Would you like a drink?" he murmurs.

I turn to face him, deliberately placing myself barely an inch away from him. I'm careful not to lean in, not to incite anything. Yet. I need him to get that drink first. "I'll have whatever you're having." His eyes flash with lust, and yet he holds his composure as he steps into the corner and starts pouring from the crystal decanter. Keeping my eyes fixed on him, I slide the diamond ring off my right index finger and use my thumbnail to dislodge the stone. Sliding the ring into my clutch bag, I keep the small stone in my hand. When he turns around with the drinks, I'm sitting on the edge of his desk with my legs crossed. His eyes move over my body as he hands me the glass. I place it to my lips and take a swig of the well-aged amber liquor. The sharp, smoky taste dances across my tongue, and I narrow my eyes at him, daring him closer. The second I put the glass down on the desk beside me, he makes a move, stepping towards me and wrapping a hand around the back of my neck.

"You're a beautiful woman, Isabelle."

I smile. "So, you know my name."

He smirks. "Of course." His lips slam over mine so hard it takes me by surprise for a second, but just a split second. His glass is still clutched in his hand between us, and he's really making this too easy. I reach across the gap between us, brushing the edge of the glass and dropping the stone in his drink. It makes a small fizzing sound, but I grab the back of his neck and moan into his mouth, covering it easily. His tongue probes against my lips, seeking entrance, but instead I push him away. His eyebrows pull together in confusion.

"I think I need to finish my drink for what you're offering," I tease, scraping my teeth over my bottom lip and picking up my glass.

27

He huffs a low chuckle and lifts his own glass to his lips, taking a heavy gulp. I need him to finish it. Tipping mine back, I down the entire thing. He cocks a brow and takes another heavy gulp that leaves the glass almost empty. Good enough. And the effect is almost instant. He frowns and a soft cough works its way up his throat. I place my hands behind me on the desk and lean back. He coughs again, clutching at his throat.

"What…?" His gaze lifts to mine, and I see the exact moment when he realizes his error. He opens his mouth to shout, probably for a guard, but all that comes out is a choked sound. His chest heaves and a thin sheen of sweat coats his skin. His knees buckle, slamming into the hard tile floor with an unforgiving crack. And there he stays, a powerful man brought to his knees, left gasping and mumbling incoherently. I push off the desk and circle his prone form.

"Cyanide. Nasty stuff. It turns your own body against you, prevents your cells from absorbing oxygen." I tilt my head to the side, looking down at him. His eyes fix me in a glare that holds absolutely no weight given his current position. Dropping to a crouch in front of him, I grab his jaw, forcing him to look at me. "So while you're there, gasping for air, your body is suffocating from the inside." I smile and he stares at me as if he's going to survive this and hunt me to the ends of the earth. He wouldn't be the first to think so. The human mind is a strange animal and even at the last minute, when it knows it's lost, that the body it holds so dear is failing, it still hopes. The truth is, when pushed to the very edge of our survival, human beings are dreamers and fantasists by nature. No matter how much of a realist we are in life, death reveals all, taunting us with our own naïve brand of hope.

"Do you know who I am?" I ask, standing and moving around him slowly, leisurely. He doesn't answer, of course, what with the effort to breathe. "They call me bacio della morte." His eyes briefly flick to me before squeezing shut. "Arnaldo sends his regards." His teeth grit, and I know any minute his heart is going to give out. He pitches backwards and lands, sprawled awkwardly on the carpet. He's still breathing, but barely. His lungs are nothing more than a desperate quivering reflex of a failing body. Taking my lipstick and compact mirror from my clutch bag I apply a new coat, ensuring his messy kisses haven't smudged the last layer all over my face. The frantic beat of his lungs slows until only a few gasps remain, like a fish left out in the sun to die. And then it stops. His breath ceases and he slips into cardiac arrest. Dropping to my knees beside his body, I lean over him and wait for the tell-tale hiss of air leaving his lips.

"Prosti menya." *Forgive me.* I'm not a pious woman. I've seen too much evil in this world to ever believe in a god or anything greater than this hellhole of a life we have. This man did nothing to me; he's simply a job, a paid contract. He died because he was weak. I continue to survive because I am strong and do what I was trained to do. Kill. I ask forgiveness because although I have to do this, I shouldn't enjoy it nearly as much as I do.

As always, I press my lips against his waxy forehead. Just then, the door opens and I leap to my feet, widening my stance and crouching like a cat ready to strike. I release a breath when I realize it's Nero. "Fucking knock!" I snap.

He glances from me to his brother's lifeless body on the floor. "I'm sorry. They're coming for you."

Well, fuck. No sooner has he said the words than I hear the fast approach of several men. The stairs groan under their weight, and I know if I stay here, I'm dead.

I go to yank open the glass doors, but they're locked. I pick up the heavy leather chair behind the desk with the intent of smashing the glass, but a single gunshot goes off before I can.

"Go! Run!" Nero hisses, glancing down the corridor and clutching Lorenzo's gun in his hand. He shot the glass out. Throwing myself through the narrow gap, my dress catching on the jagged glass that lines the doorframe. I'm on the first floor, and it's not that high, but it's no walk in the park either. I won't die, but if I break an ankle, then I might as well have, because if I can't run, I'm dead.

Another gunshot rings out, this one coming so close to me that I hear the sharp crack as it breaks the air next to my ear. I'm all for making this look authentic, but I swear to god, if he shoots me... Springing up onto the balcony, I launch myself into the air. There's a moment of complete weightlessness before I hit the grass, dropping into a roll of torn red satin. The logical thing would be to make for the treeline and hop the fence over the property line, but that's exactly why I'm not doing that. Ducking against the building, I press myself into the brickwork directly beneath the balcony. The voices above me are shouting orders, baying for my blood. Nero is right there, instructing them to double the patrol on the fence line and not let anyone leave. Ripping off the wig and pulling the pins from my hair, I shake out my long strands. The dress is already ruined, but I grab the material of the bodice and pull it apart, shredding it down the middle until it pools at my waist, revealing a pale blue sleeveless dress beneath. I step out of the first dress and hook around the corner of the building. Balling up the red material and the wig, I make sure to hide them well at the base of a bush that sits against the house. As I make my way towards the gardens, I pull out a pair of sunglasses from my bag and slide them on. My step falters only for a second when six armed men in suits round the corner and start jogging straight towards me.

"Ma'am, this area is off limits," the first one says, his expression stern and unforgiving.

I glance at the gun in his hand and swallow heavily, taking a shaky step to the side. All for show, of course.

"Oh, I'm sorry. I seem to have lost my boyfriend." I push a tremor into my voice.

"Please go back to the party with the other guests." He says dismissively.

I smile sweetly, like the nice, dutiful girlfriend. They suspect nothing, because they're looking for a sexy, murderous brunette in a red dress, and in this dress, well, I could almost pull off sweet.

Rounding the sunroom at the back of the building, I slip back through the gap in the wall. Keeping my gaze fixed down as I pass the guard; although, this is a different guy from when I passed by earlier. When I step into the courtyard, the guests are visibly tense. The men are all looking on edge, not helped by the fact that none of them have any of their weapons to hand. For men like these, being without a gun is like being naked. The women huddle together nervously like the pathetic sheep they are, and I notice the strategic circle of men that surround them, as if they're some grand treasure they must protect. Everyone's attention seems to focus on me. That can't be good. A throat clears behind me, and I realize that it's not me they're focusing on, it's Nero. He stands behind me at the top of the steps that descend into the garden, the floral archway surrounding him and contrasting with the hard, dark lines of his face and body. I drop down a couple of steps, slipping out of sight of the gathered crowd.

"Ladies and gentlemen." His voice is a deep boom that I'm sure can be heard clearly by even those furthest away. "There is nothing to be concerned about, merely a small security issue." He smiles and it's so genuine, so confident, that even I find it soothing. "Please, let's enjoy the party while the guards handle it." He raises his full champagne glass, flashing a wide, perfect smile at the guests. There are a few murmurs, questions, confusion. He ignores it, necking the glass of golden bubbly liquid before descending the steps and wrapping a hand around my waist.

"Don't. People will ask questions," I hiss.

He smiles at someone over my shoulder. "No, they won't. I want them to see. Now smile." I smile at him.

31

"I need to get out of here," I say through clenched teeth.

He pulls me close, wrapping his arms tightly around my waist. "Touch me," he demands when my arms remain rigid at my sides. Complying with his request, I slide one palm up his chest, and the other around the back of his neck. His mouth drops to my neck, but he never makes contact. "They won't let guests leave until I say so." And he can't clear it too soon as he needs to avoid suspicion. "Dance with me. Act like you want me." I can hear the smile in his voice and it has me wanting to kidney punch him.

"I'd rather cut you," I say, smiling sweetly.

He takes my hand and a strange tingle buzzes up my arm, almost like electricity humming over my skin. I frown down at our intertwined fingers. He leads me to the small clearance in the middle of the patio where a string quartet are seated and playing the kind of music that Nicholai listens to.

He spins me and I pivot on my toe. I can dance. Dancing and fighting are one and the same, a pattern, the meeting of bodies, a liaison in which you must read your partner and either follow them or counter them. His hand presses into the small of my back, wrenching me against his hard body so abruptly that I lose my breath on a gasp. His full lips curve on one side and that shadow of a dimple sinks into his stubble-covered cheek. I follow every movement he lays down. Our bodies moving together like hot and cold water, fluid, different and yet exactly the same.

"I'm impressed," he rumbles against my ear.

"I'm offended," I reply. He huffs a low laugh and his warm breath blows against the skin of my throat. "Nero, I really need to get out of here."

He pulls back and looks in my eyes, his expression so hard, so resolved that he looks as though he would tear down entire

32

countries in this moment. "I won't let anything happen to you." His hold on me tightens, and I suddenly realize that I don't mind. Any touch is enough to make me want to kill, but…silence. The pounding need is just absent.

"I'm a big girl." Swallowing down the feeling of unease in my gut, I attempt to brush off his comment.

"You are, Morte." He spins me again, his grip firm and unrelenting as he moves me across the dance floor.

The worrying thing is that I believe him. I trust him when he says he'll protect me, even though I don't need his protection. Nero Verdi is the most dangerous man I've ever encountered, and yet, there's something about him. I can't put my finger on it, but I'm certainly not as guarded as I should be around a man like him. He throws me off and it's unsettling. After all, complacency will get you killed. I know that all too well.

CHAPTER FOUR

Nero

She relaxes in my arms and her fingers tighten, clinging to my bicep. When I walked into that room she was hovering over my brother like a beautiful avenger, a walking angel of death bearing down on her victim with the strangest expression, somewhere between blissful relief and anguish. The way she moves, the way she looks at me even now is that of a predator, a killer, a demon in a dress, and I'd be lying if I said she doesn't make my blood heat.

I glance over her head and see two guards jog up to a couple more on the gate, speaking into radios. I told them to handle it, whilst assuring them that I should go back to the party to give the illusion of normalcy. Of course, the guests will be told what actually happened, but right now, revealing the truth will not only incite panic but also look weak. The fact that the Italian Mafia sustained a hit within their own walls at an engagement party…well, that's just embarrassing, but Arnaldo planned for this. And really, if the truth comes out, Lorenzo will look like the weak one, killed because he was trying to fuck another woman at his own engagement party. I can't help but smile. His father would be rolling in his grave. But it's this very fact that will keep this entire thing quiet. People might whisper that it was my date who killed him, but no one will ever confirm it. Other than his direct security, I guarantee no one will ever know. Reputation means far more than justice in our world.

"They're searching the guests," Una breathes against my throat, her voice strained. I spin her, switching our positions. Sure enough, the guards are looking at the guests, searching bags, and I'm sure looking for a mysterious brunette. I doubt they'll look at Una, but they might. After all, she technically never came through the gate. If they check, we're fucked.

I spin her again and smile, hoping we look like the perfect couple. Keeping my eyes trained on the approaching guards, I watch them draw closer. The people around us start to slow, paying more attention to the guards as they fan out into the dancers. A flash of panic crosses Una's eyes, and I worry that she'll do something rash, like turn this party into a bloodbath.

"Sir," someone says behind me.

Shit. I grab the back of Una's neck and wrench her to me, slamming my lips over hers. She freezes, her nails digging into my shoulder. Trailing my hand down her back, I brush her ass as I caress my tongue over her bottom lip. This needs to look good, good enough to make people uncomfortable. She stiffens and tries to shove away from me, putting up a fight. Damn it. Right now, our fates are intertwined. If she gets caught then so do I.

Taking control, I thrust my hand into her hair and grab a handful of it, pulling the strands roughly. The second I do, she releases a sharp breath. her lips part, and breath dancing over my tongue. The ice cracks inch by inch until she's soft and pliant in my arms. Her fingers trail from my shoulder to the back of my neck, nails raking over my skin in a burning trail that has me hissing against her lips and pulling her tighter against my body. She tastes of champagne and danger, and everything about her has adrenaline slamming through my veins like a drug. The kiss becomes a battleground, the rougher I am, the more bruising my grip, the deeper she falls. There's nothing sweet or gentle in it, just brutal passion. She bites my lip hard enough to draw blood, and then swipes her tongue over the wound, making me groan. My cock is plastered against my zipper and heat rips over my skin in a wave. Finally releasing my grip on her hair, she staggers away from me, gasping for breath. Her wide eyes meet mine, those lilac-tinged irises swirling with confusion and lust. She looks horrified.

We stand in a sea of people, but all I feel is her. My skin prickles and I grit my jaw as need and desire pulse through my veins. Una is a tool, an assassin, the enemy. Anything. She is anything but what I'm seeing her as right now – someone I want to sink balls deep inside. The personal and the professional must always be kept separate in this business, especially when you're dealing with the kiss of death. Squeezing my eyes shut for a few seconds, I take a deep breath before turning and walking away from her. That kiss saved us, for now. I need to get us out of here.

I approach Romero, Lorenzo's second. He folds his arms over his chest and squares his shoulders, glaring at me in a way that promises retribution. To the outside world, Lorenzo and I were brothers. Only Lorenzo and I, along with our closest friends, knew the truth. We were bitter enemies, and I just won.

"We need to start moving guests out of here."

Jet-black eyebrows drop over equally dark eyes as he assesses me. "I'm going to kill you," he growls. I smile, noticing the vein at his temple throb.

37

I huff a laugh. "Would that you could. Your fearless leader is dead, Romero. Who do you think will take his place?"

He snarls, getting in my face. "You're a bastard. The family will never back you."

I laugh. "You're right, I am a bastard."

I bask in the knowledge that Lorenzo – my father's first born, his heir, his son, his greatest accomplishment – was fucking weak. And I, the unwanted bastard son, the result of my mother's infidelity, have won. I'd truly hate him if I weren't actually grateful. You see, Lorenzo had his love, and it did him no favours. No, Matteo Santos forged me. His hatred made me strong. His constant reminders of what I am made me smart. His physical blows made me a fighter. I learned from him that respect and power are not a birth right. He had the power of his name, but no matter how many times he beat me, I never felt an ounce of respect towards him. My sole purpose is to destroy his empire, piece by piece. I killed him, and now his son is gone. Sometimes, I wish I'd stayed my hand, so he could have been here to watch his son fall, so he could have died knowing that I would take over. I am a bastard, but it means nothing because I will take everything and more.

"Move the fucking guests out. Now," I growl.

Romero clenches his jaw, the muscles in his shoulders tightening dangerously. I want him to, I really do. Instead, he turns and walks away. A few minutes later the guests start to leave, and I don't see Una again. She disappeared like an apparition, a ghost on the wind.

CHAPTER FIVE

Una

I'm striding down a hotel stairwell, trying to look inconspicuous as I make my way to the underground parking deck. With my blood-stained dress and semi-automatic rifle, the elevator wasn't exactly an option. My phone rings just as I reach the underground level and I touch my earpiece.

"Not a good time," I growl.

"I've been trying to get a hold of you for the last week. So tell me, when is a good time?"

Nero.

"I've been off the grid."

"No shit."

There's something about him that manages to elicit a certain level of irritation, dare I say, anger. It's a skill; really it is, because I don't do angry. Anger is a useless emotion and only serves to blind reason.

"Look, is there a reason for this call?" I pant.

"Of course. I have a job for you."

"Have Arnie contact me."

He huffs a laugh. "Oh, Una. I think we're past that."

Really? This guy. "I don't," I say bluntly. The door at the top of the stairs crashes open, the sound echoing around the empty concrete stairwell. "Shit!" I have a good lead but I'd still rather get out clean. Someone fires a couple of rounds and they ping off the metal bannister next to me.

"You sound busy." I can hear the amusement in his voice.

"No shit," I growl, shoving through the door. "Text me a location. I'll be there tomorrow." I hang up and pick up the pace, sprinting across the parking deck. I jump in the Porsche parked under a broken light and slam my hand over the start button. The engine purrs to life and I ram my foot on the accelerator, making it spit and snarl as the tires shriek against the tarmac.

Leng's men burst onto the street just as I pull away from the hotel. That was close. Too close.

Pressing speed dial, I listen to the earpiece ring out with a dial tone. "Una." Olov answers on the first ring.

"I'm twenty minutes away. Be ready to leave immediately," I tell him, speaking in quick-fire Russian. He hangs up and I speed towards the private airfield on the outskirts of Singapore.

CHAPTER SIX

Nero

Flipping open the top of my cigarette packet, I take one out, placing it between my lips. I sit behind the very desk my father used to, the desk Lorenzo sat at until just two weeks ago. I'm the capo of New York. These are dangerous times though. I'm keeping my inner circle tight, only dealing directly with the three guys in this room. Jackson is pacing in front of my desk, clenching and releasing his fists repeatedly. Gio is leaning against the far wall with his arms crossed over his chest and a scowl fixed on his face. Tommy's he stares blankly at the opposite wall. His sleeves are rolled up, his forearms and the material of his white shirt painted in blood. The tell-tale splatter of a slit throat sprayed across his neck. He and Jackson were involved in a deal that went south earlier tonight, and one of his guys was taken out. It got messy. It was expected though. Any takeover will be met with a certain amount of resistance. People think they can move the goal posts, demand new terms, more territory, better prices. It's my job to make it clear that the only one who will be renegotiating here is me. Power is all about perception and fear. If I have to paint the streets with their blood to get my point across, I will.

"We should go back there and kill every fucking one of them." Jackson's gaze meets mine, every muscle tense with the need for retribution. He's a big guy, broad-shouldered and lethal if you're on his bad side. I lean back in my chair as I lift the lighter to my face. The heavy click of the silver zippo is the only sound in the room aside from his ragged breaths. I inhale, drawing the smoke into my lungs, letting it fill me, burning me from the inside out.

"No."

"Fuck!" he shouts, pushing away from the desk. "Levi is dead because of those motherfuckers!" I still, tilting my head to the side as I look up at him. He stares back at me for a long moment before swallowing nervously. I push up from the desk and slowly move around it. Everyone in the room seems to hold their breath. I stop only when I'm standing nose to nose with him. There's a pause, a tense moment where we just stare each other down. He's like a brother to me, but brother or not, no one questions me.

"You don't get to think, Jackson. You don't get an opinion," I growl under my breath. A muscle in his jaw ticks and it's enough to piss me off. Slamming a hand around his throat, I squeeze hard enough to make him choke. "You are a fucking soldier! Get out." Releasing him, he staggers away from me, heading straight for the door.

He pauses when a loud click sounds behind me, turning around with his hand already reaching for his gun. Gio moves away from the wall, gun already trained on the glass French doors that lead to the balcony. I turn around, squinting to see into the darkness on the other side of the glass. I can just make out someone in black, crouched down. The handle is twisted and the tiny figure waltzes into the room like she owns the place. A black hood hides half her face, but I'd know those red painted lips anywhere.

"Boys." Una smiles and then in the blink of an eye her gun is pointing at me, one bright red fingertip lingering over the trigger. She lifts her head enough that I can just make her eyes out. "Nero. Power looks good on you." She winks. "Send them out," she orders, jerking her head towards the three guys, two of which have weapons trained on her.

You could cut the tension in the room with a knife, that is until Tommy laughs. "I like her," he mumbles around his cigarette, as though she didn't have a loaded gun pointed at me, and absolutely no conscience to stop her from pulling the trigger.

I step forward, closing the distance between us. "Sociable as ever, I see."
Her smile widens and she cocks a brow. I'm pretty sure she's not going to shoot me, but truthfully, I can't predict what she'll do because she plays by her own set of rules.

"I don't play well with others," she says, a little pout forming on her lips. I keep closing in on her until the barrel of her gun presses against my forehead.

"You're not going to shoot me. A capo is worth, what? A couple of million?" Her head tilts, eyes tracing over me predatorily. "You don't work for free." I smirk.

Her eyes dance dangerously and she trails the gun from my forehead down over my temple. Her scent assaults me – vanilla and just a hint of gun oil. She glides the cool metal over my cheek and along my jaw. That tight body of hers is so close I can feel every breath she takes as her tits press against my stomach. That ruthless look is in her eye, the same one she wore after she killed my brother. That look, the gun on my cheek... it makes my dick hard. I have to bite back a groan when she leans in, brushing her lips over my jaw until she reaches my ear.

"Send. Them. Out," she purrs, ramming the gun underneath my chin hard enough to force my head back.

The barrel bites into my skin and a low laugh works its way up my throat. It's only when you're staring death in the face that you truly remember you're alive. My blood rushes through my veins, forcing adrenaline through my body. Smiling, I click my fingers, gesturing for them to get out. Tommy gets up and leaves without a backwards glance. That fucker doesn't give a shit. Jackson moves next, and Gio is the last, ever loyal, and far too serious.

"You can't put me down before I put him down," Una drawls, sounding almost bored, reading him without even sparing him a glance.

"Go, Gio." Maybe I should be more worried about her, but she's not going to shoot me. I know she's not.

He sighs and steps out of the room, closing the door behind him. I have no doubt he's lingering just on the other side. She clicks the safety on and holsters her gun at her hip before stepping back very deliberately. I drop into the chair behind my desk. For a long while she simply stands, surveying every inch of the room.

"So, you kept the ugly house."

"A show of power." I hate this house, but to the family here in New York, this is the capo's house. To reside in it is symbolic

46

of the power I now hold. I don't give a shit. I'd happily burn it to the ground with them all in it.

She approaches my desk and takes a seat in front of me, making a slow show of crossing one leg over the other as she trails one blood-red nail over her thigh. She pulls her hood back and the light touches her fully for the first time since she walked in here. Hers is a cold beauty, almost inhuman, because set into the youthful face of an angel is the hard severity of someone who has seen and done unspeakable things. There's an argument for everything, and I won't pretend I'm any better. I've done things that would make even the hardest of men flinch, but they were done in the name of something. Power, family, more power...take your pick. What Una does though...she fights for no one, not even herself. Let's see if I can change that.

"I have a job for you."

She laughs quietly. "I came here as a courtesy, Nero." She takes a knife out of a thigh holster and casually flips it through her fingers. "You helped me once. But you do not summon me. You do not hire me." She slams the knife in the antique wooden desk hard enough that her knuckles turn white around the hilt. "You are a capo," she spits, those violet eyes locking with mine.

I sigh. The problem with Una...she's the top of the food chain and she swims with sharks. She hasn't realised yet, I am a motherfucking shark, circling in the dark waters right beneath them all, waiting, biding my time. I explode out of my chair and have my hand around her throat in a heartbeat, slamming her down on the desk.

"You make the mistake of thinking that mere titles mean anything to me. I get what I want, and what I want right now, Morte, is you," I growl at her. A wide grin stretches her lips. It's the first time I've seen her genuinely smile.

"Nero, you say the hottest things." She shifts and wraps her legs around my waist. I cock a brow at her and then she locks her ankles together, tightening her thighs around me like a boa constrictor. When I readjust my grip on her throat, she bites her lip, as if she likes it. Her hips shift, and I bite back a groan as she yanks me even closer, squeezing me into the gap between her thighs. She narrows her eyes and her body trembles with the effort of trying to hurt me. My kidneys are screaming in protest, but my dick is begging to be inside her. I have a kamikaze cock. Her hips rock, the friction forcing a low growl from my throat. I pull her up from the desk by her throat, holding her only inches away from me.

"You are disposable to me, Una," I breathe. Her lips part, drawing my eyes to them, so full and perfect. I feel her strangled breaths on my face, her rapid heartbeat beneath my fingertips and most of all, I feel her pussy pressing against my cock. She laughs, breath wheezing past her lips. I fight with my own control as I walk the fine line between wanting to fuck her and strangle her. We remain locked together like that for a few seconds, and it's torture. Shit! I don't have time for this. Finally, I release her and push away from her body. Her legs unwind from around me and she coughs, sitting up and clutching at her throat.

"You have a firm grip."

I walk to the wall, bracing my forearm against it. I need her. I can't kill her, and as for fucking her…they don't call her the 'kiss of death' for nothing. Apparently, my dick didn't get the memo.

"I don't have time for this bullshit, Una!"

She lets out a tinkling laugh, so at odds with the killer she is. "I like you, Nero." I turn to face her, watching as she crosses her legs on the desk. "I respect you, and you've moved up in the world." She gestures to the room around us, the very room in which she killed Lorenzo. "But not enough that I work for you.

48

There's an order, a balance. You may not care for titles, but the world does. You may think I'm disposable, but let me assure you, there's only one Una Ivanov and my services are very much in demand."

"I'll pay you."

She smiles and drags her hand through her long blonde hair. "You couldn't afford me."

Taking a deep breath, I reach for the packet of cigarettes inside my pocket. I watch her tense, and suddenly, the blade she impaled in my desk is in her hand. I narrow my eyes. "If I wanted you dead, you'd be dead." I repeat the words she once said to me as I pull the cigarettes out.

She drops onto her feet, pulling her hood up and making her way towards the doors she came in through. "See you around, *capo*."

I take the unlit cigarette from my mouth and hold it, pausing. This is it, the pivotal moment where all my plans will either succeed or fail, because without her, it all falls to shit. "I know where your sister is." She freezes, and I put the cigarette back in my mouth, lighting it. By the time I take my first drag, she still hasn't turned around. I wait, watching the rapid rise and fall of her shoulders.

"I don't have a sister." Her voice is like thunder, rolling, building.

I fight a smile. I have her. "Anna Vasiliev, born March 6 1991."

Whipping around to face me, I see the indecision written all over her face, the confusion, the fracture. The cool calm and sheer indifference that make up Una Ivanov, crack and splinter. She might as well have exposed her jugular to me. Getting what you want from people is easy, you just have to find their

49

weakness. I'll admit, finding hers was difficult, until I had someone go to Russia and start digging. I've had to pay more money for information on her than I think I would have for the president. Of course, Una Ivanov isn't her real name. Nicholai Ivanov, boss of the Russian Bratva, gave her that name. He thinks of Una as his daughter, and named her so. The woman has powerful allies; I'll give her that. Her real name, Una Vasiliev. An orphan. Until she disappeared at age thirteen that is. I guess not many people would go out of their way to find an orphan. For the most part, she's a ghost.

I look in her eyes and see it, a spark, hope. She wants to believe me. She wants what I say to be true. I see the divide, the fight within her. Hope versus the rational, smart decision, because hope without reason is such a frail, weak emotion. But weakness is a part of human nature. Una barely seems human, always professional, measured, deadly. Will she be rational now, or will she find a slither of humanity? Heart or head? That is the question.

CHAPTER SEVEN

Una

My heart is hammering, the pulse in my throat pounding so hard I can barely breathe. Nero takes a slow drag of his cigarette, watching me like a hawk, looking for any sign of weakness. Little does he know, he might as well have liver punched me, because I feel paralysed right now. How does he know about Anna? No one knows about the sister I was torn away from when the bratva took me from an orphanage thirteen years ago. I spent years being trained, beaten, broken, only to be rebuilt into the embodiment of the perfect soldier. The bratva made me strong, they made me a warrior, they made me exactly what they wanted. Una Vasiliev died in that place, everything that she was stripped from her.

Except Anna, because I could never let her go, even when I wanted to, even when I knew my obsession with her brought me nothing but pain and unanswered questions.

I never mention her, and my silent search for her is my own. Finding Anna is near impossible. All the answers lie within the bratva, a place in which I have status and privilege, but if Nicholai realized I had a weakness, he'd search for her and kill her himself. And he'd genuinely believe he was doing me a favour, setting me free. Maybe he would be, but when I think of my sister, my innocent, sweet sister, a deep ache buries itself into my chest. Anna was never strong. She was sweet and good, and she depended on me. I shielded her innocent eyes from the ugliness of the world, corrupted myself, sold my soul off piece by piece, and I did it willingly, to keep her safe, to keep her pure. And that was just in the orphanage. My greatest failing in life is the inability to protect her. But now I can...if I could find her.

Do I believe Nero? I don't know. But just hearing her name fall from his lips has something inside of me shifting. A door that I firmly slammed shut when I was fifteen years old is now open a crack. Emotions are seeping out and I'm fighting to shove them back into that dark corner of my mind where Una Vasiliev lives, the young girl crying for her sister, hurting for all that she lost, for all that she had to do to survive. I feel. For the first time in a very long time, I feel something besides the cold detachment that comes with killing. I'd forgotten what anger feels like...to be so consumed, so utterly driven by that sole emotion. I'm angry at myself, but mostly I'm angry at Nero for using her against me, for cornering me, despite the fact that I know I would do far worse to get what I want. I feel threatened, and that's never good. Rolling my shoulders and closing my eyes, the icy rage locks around me, imprisoning me in its grasp. And the switch flips. I have no more control over it than the instinct to draw breath. When I open my eyes, my senses have sharpened, my vision becomes clearer, and I can sense every single breath he takes. Adrenaline courses through my veins. My mind perceives a threat, and my body is responding automatically. After years of training, it's no more than a reflex, like someone throwing you a ball and your arm moving to catch it. I'm ready to fight. Ready to kill.

"You found a name. Well done," I say. Even to my own ears I sound cold, efficient. Nero raises a brow. His eyes lock with mine and I see wariness there, but not fear, never fear from him. Silly. "What did you think, Nero? That you'd dig up a name and have me doing your dirty work like some pet?" A smile pulls at my lips. "I've been very nice to you until now, I really have, but do not lie to me. Do not piss me off. I will end you and never think of you again," I whisper.

His expression remains impassive, almost bored. Something in me delights in his unspoken challenge. He stands there, authority and power pouring off him in waves. The dark lord on the mafia throne. "I'm not lying. And you could kill me, but then you'd never know, would you?" Those deep brown eyes hold my gaze, and doubt starts to take hold of me.

What if he's telling the truth? Or maybe I just want to believe him. I hate that this is even a subject of discussion. I should just walk away now. I haven't seen Anna in over thirteen years; she should be nothing more than a ghost to me..

"This isn't a trap, Una. This is a simple exchange of favours," he says, his voice deep and melodic.

I move to the desk, bracing my hands against it with my back to him. "Fucking mafia with your favours." I don't like this. I'm untouchable, but right now I feel like I've torn open my own ribcage and am daring him to thrust a blade into my beating heart.

I glance over my shoulder. "What do you want?" I ask, and he smiles, blowing a long stream of smoke through his lips. I'm the starving lion lingering just outside the confines of a trap. Nero is dangling Anna in front of me like a piece of prime rib, and he knows I'm going to walk inside. I can't resist. I guess we all have our weaknesses, even me.

"Simple. You help me destroy my enemies."

Simple, he says. I know all about his antics in the last two weeks since I killed Lorenzo. Turns out, Nero is the bad boy of the mafia, and considering it's the damn mafia, that's saying something. Arnaldo appointed him capo in the wake of his brother's death, and now shit is hitting the fan. The Italians value family and honour above all else. Turns out Nero values neither. He's a ruthless fuck, but then I already knew that. I had him pegged the moment I met him. Still, decapitating Lorenzo's second was extreme and probably isn't in the team building and leadership manual. Nero Verdi has enemies coming out of his asshole. I have no desire to share them with him.

Turning to face him, I square my shoulders and tilt my head to the side. "I hear you have many enemies, *Capo*. What with killing your own brother for the throne." I tsk. "Nasty business, especially when you Italians value family so much."

A twisted smile pulls at his lips and smoke drifts around his face; rising and making him look like the devil himself. "Ah, but the question is, how much do you value *your* family, *Morte*?" He emphasises the word, purring it as though it were an endearment.

I grit my teeth. "What's the job?"

He approaches and pulls a piece of paper from the inside pocket of his jacket, holding it out to me. I take it from him, and he drops into the chair behind his desk. Unfolding the sheet of lined paper, I find four names scrawled one below the other.

Marco Fiore
Bernardo Caro
Franco Lama
Finnegan O'Hara

I recognise three of them and two of them are no street rats. Bernardo Caro is another New York capo, and Finnegan O'Hara…well, he's into everything and everyone. There are several hits on his head. I'm already thinking of my contacts, how I could get to them, who I should hit first… I slowly lift my eyes to him. He's watching me, one elbow resting on his desk and his index finger tapping over his bottom lip. I fold the paper and hand it back.

"I can't hit this many in one network." Three of those guys are Italian. It would draw too much attention, and in this business, attention is never good.

He shrugs, pursing his lips around his cigarette as he inhales. The end glows a bright cherry red and he flashes me a dark look. "Then good luck finding your sister." Smoke drifts between his lips as he speaks.

I clench my fists so hard that my nails break the skin on my palm. "You don't understand," I growl. "The way I work, I maintain a fine balance. I'm unbiased in my services, and therefore I have somewhat of a diplomatic immunity among the crime organisations. If I do this for you, I'm not leaving my name on it. It's bad for business." Not to mention that if someone decides I'm a threat or that I'm taking sides, it'll be open season on my head. I'll have no choice but to go back to Russia for protection, and I may never find Anna.

He shakes his head. "I need them to know it was you and not me."

"Does it matter? Someone has to hire me."

He smirks. "Plausible deniability."

This is suicide, but it's amazing what you'll do for the thing you want most. I've spent my entire life alone, an island surrounded by waters so deep and dark, no one could ever hope to cross them. But Anna…she walks on water. My boundaries don't apply to her, or the fantasy of her at least. Who knows who or what she's become now. "If I agree to this, it will take time," I say reluctantly.

"I've got time." His lips kick up at one side. "I'll pay you three for each one. Plus your sister. You work no other jobs until this is complete and you stay with me."

Jeez, I guess he's wealthier than I thought. Wait, what?

I tilt my head, narrowing my eyes. "Yeah, that's not going to happen. I'm not good with people."

He smirks. "No people, just me. I have a penthouse in the city."

I glare at him. "Why? I have an apartment in the city. Surely you know my sister is enough incentive for you to trust me."

He moves back to his desk, stubbing out his cigarette in the steel ashtray. His head remains tilted down as he flicks the butt away. "My reasons are my own. Take it or leave it."
Why would he want me in his house? That's where he's most vulnerable.

"I'll agree if you can give me proof." I swallow hard, trying hard to hide just how much this means. "I want proof that you have something on Anna."

"So you can find her yourself and sell me out?" We stare at each other for long moments, those whisky eyes of his, so hard, so calculating. Finally, he pushes his chair back and pulls open the bottom drawer. He takes out a photograph, holding it against his chest until I look up and meet his gaze. "If you betray me, if you cut and run, I will send this photograph to Nicholai Ivanov," he says coldly.

My expression must give away my fury, because he places the picture on the desk. Ignoring him, I rush forward to look at the photo. It's blurry and distorted; the image zoomed in from a distance. It's dark, but there's a line of girls, all of them bound at the wrists. Two men stand with guns, on either side of the women. In the middle of the image is a girl. She can be no older than eighteen. Her white-blonde hair hangs over her face, and I can barely make out her profile, but it's a face I would know anywhere. Anna.

"Where did you get this?" I whisper.

"This was taken three years ago in Juarez. A shipment of slaves were sold to the Sinaloa Cartel."

My blood runs cold and it feels like someone has wrapped a fist around my heart. "A slave? In the cartel?"

His lips press into a flat line. He says nothing, but his silence is answer enough. My fingers tighten on the edge of the desk, and I feel. I feel…everything. Emotion bubbles up my throat, and I bite hard on the inside of my cheek in an attempt to channel it, but I can't. My long dormant heart feels like it's breaking, splintering open and bleeding out. My mind flashes through memories, only instead of seeing them as myself, I imagine it's her. Men holding her down, laughing as they tear her clothing from her body, hands clamping around her delicate throat, nails raking over soft skin as they force her legs apart. Only she wouldn't fight like I did, and she wouldn't have a Nicholai to save her. My nails scream in protest as I grip the wood hard enough to bend them back. White-hot rage rips over my skin, and I want nothing more than to make the rivers of Mexico run red until I find her. Images blink behind my eyelids like a faulty film reel, and it makes me want to scream.

"Una!" Fingers brush over my jaw, and I flinch back as Nero tears me from the screaming in my mind. "Look at me." My heart is hammering, and I can feel the thin layer of sweat coating my skin. "Una, look at me." He repeats. Hands land on either side of my face, his grip strong and deliberate, forcing me to lift my eyes.

Meeting Nero's gaze, his perceptive eyes search mine. I'm frozen, stuck in a place between the past and the present, reality and nightmare. His thumb strokes over my cheek and it's like breaking the surface after being submerged in water for several minutes. I drag in a staggered breath, sucking the oxygen into my lungs. My focus snaps back into place almost instantly and I slam my palm against his chest with enough force that he moves back a step, his hands falling away from me. Backing up, I begin pacing around the desk, putting distance between us. Of all the people to have a relapse in front of...

"Do we have a deal?" His expression shutters once again.

My jaw hurts from gritting my teeth so hard. "I'll kill your people, but I want more than just your information on Anna." He lifts his chin. "I want you to help me get her back." It's a small price to pay. For her.

Whatever his plan, it must be important because he nods quickly. "Done." He puts the photo back in the drawer and slides it shut. "I have to handle something, and then I'll take you home." Great. I'd almost forgotten that I'm going to have to live with him.

Fifteen minutes pass, and when Nero doesn't come back I get annoyed and bored. I'm not some staff member he can just keep at his beck and call. Screw this. I leave the office and make my way through the house, ducking into doorways whenever I see any of his men. I manage to make it into the sunroom where I slip outside unnoticed. Making my way across the sloping lawns, I inhale the cool night air, allowing it to help calm my racing mind.

When I'm away from the house, I call Sasha. "Hello," he answers in Russian. I smile. Sasha is one of the few people I trust in this world. We grew up together, were trained together and shaped into what we now are. He's as close to a brother as I will ever get.

"Sasha, it's me." I slip easily into my native tongue, although it feels strangely foreign. I've been away for so long now.

"Una. Where are you?"

"On a job in New York." I don't say more than that and he doesn't ask. This is our life, this is what we do. Although, he'd be disappointed if he knew I was selling myself out right now, not to mention he'd tell Nicholai. I went to Nicholai's facility when I was thirteen after he saved me from being raped and sold as a whore. Sasha was there from the age of nine. I'm loyal to Nicholai because he's the only father I've ever known, but I see his flaws. He would kill Anna, and I know he would do it because he loves me. In many ways, I see his logic, I even agree with it. I just can't allow it, not when it's Anna. Sasha, on the other hand, has complete loyalty to Nicholai. He has no weakness such as a long-lost sister. I care for him like a brother and he cares for me too, but ultimately, he would betray me before he would breach Nicholai's trust. I have to be careful. "I need a favour."

"Oh?"

"But you have to promise me you won't breathe a word of this to anyone." The pleading tone in my voice is pathetic really.

"Fine," he says, reluctantly.

"I need you to locate where the Sinaloa Cartel keep their sex slaves."

He goes silent. "You do realise they keep thousands of slaves?"

I sigh and pinch the bridge of my nose.

"Are you looking for someone specific?"

"Yes."

He says nothing for long seconds and then releases a long breath. "Well, are you going to tell me who?"

"She won't be under the same name now. You're looking for a girl sold into the Sinaloa about three years ago. White-blonde hair, blue eyes."

He clears his throat. "Okay, I can't promise anything, but I'll have a look." The other thing Sasha specializes in is hacking. The dark web, bank accounts, emails, even CCTV footage. If there is a trace of Anna to be found, he'll find it. I admit, it's a long shot.

"Thank you." I hang up and drag a hand through my hair. We now live in an online world, and even the criminals have moved into a new era. Weapons dealers, sex traffickers, drug dealers...you can buy rocket launchers on the dark web. Gun traffickers have their own version of eBay. Just as they always have done, they have a dark and sordid underground, even within our own Internet. It's here that Sasha and I often find our prey. Don't mistake us for some kind of good Samaritan's though. We take them out for someone else who probably wants to take their place or whose own illicit trade is threatened. That's the way the world keeps turning, with those who have power garnering more on the backs of someone else. People like Anna are sold and traded like cattle, and for the most part, no one can touch the men who do it. Every so often though, someone like me crawls out of the woodwork. In many ways, I've been equally robbed of my life, but I have a purpose. When I find Anna, and I will find her one way or another, I'm going to slaughter anyone who had a hand in taking her.

Nero may know roughly where Anna is but I'm not about to sit back and let him take his sweet time in finding her, just so he can get what he wants from me. I'm no one's pawn. I need more information though. If Sasha can't find anything, then I'm left with Nero as my only hope of ever finding her. That doesn't sit well. I want to kill him and smile as I watch him bleed out, but I can't and I won't. He found Anna. Despite the unlimited resources at my disposal and a reputation that tends to make people talk, I couldn't find her. He succeeded where I failed. How? I've looked, but I guess I never really thought I would find her, and now that I'm faced with the possibility, now that I've seen her, she's suddenly more than just a fading memory.

My thoughts are interrupted when I hear footsteps brushing over the grass. The distraction is a welcome reprieve from my thoughts, and part of me hopes it's an attacker. I need a fight right now. I need the violence and bloodshed to remind me what I am. Listening, I blow out a breath that fogs around my face. Despite the days being warm in April, the nights are still cold here in New York. Of course, compared to Russia it's positively sweltering. I don't miss those freezing cold winters in that concrete fortress.

Turning as the footsteps get closer, I see one of Nero's guys approaching, the quiet one. His black suit blends into the darkness as though he were a part of it. His eyes scan the night as he approaches me, as though looking for any hidden threats. I keep my face tilted down, shielding it from his view.

"I'm Gio, Nero's second," he says, his voice a little too cultured for New York. He has all the traditional Italian features except for his deep blue eyes, and he's almost as handsome as Nero, but he lacks that ruthless edge that makes the capo more somehow.

"Does that mean I'm supposed to trust you?"

A humorless smirk cuts over his face. "It means he has my loyalty. And for now, so do you."

61

"You know I'm a threat to him."

"Nero doesn't need my protection. Trust me." I believe him. "Why are you out here?"

On a sigh, I scoop my hood off my face. He's Nero's second. I can't hide my face from him for the extended period of time this job is likely to take. "I'm not running if that's what you're worried about. I made a deal."

"A deal you're not happy with," he counters.

I tilt my head to the side and smirk. "Whatever gave you that idea?" I startle when two black shapes come barrelling down the sloped gardens towards us. My muscles tense but Gio doesn't move. When they're a few feet away I see they're dogs. Two black Dobermans circle his legs excitedly until he barks a command at them and they drop to a sit, one on each side.

"Nice dogs," I remark, watching the way they study me intently.

"They're Nero's. This is Zeus." He places his hand on the one on his right. "And George." He points to the one on the left. It's George who breaks his vigil, as though he can't contain himself. He jumps up and rushes towards me, his ears back and his little stump of a tail wagging. Smiling, I lean over and run my hands over his slick, black coat. "Real smooth, George," Gio huffs. "Some guard dog you are." Zeus stays where he is while George leans against my legs, begging me for attention.

"He called his dog George?" I look up at him, cocking a brow.

He shrugs. "Come on. I'll show you around."

I glance back at the ugly house sitting just above us on the hill. "I'm good. Where's Nero?"

"He's unexpectedly pre-occupied."

"Okay, either you take me to him or I'm leaving. And you can tell him that I don't wait around for anyone."

He turns and starts walking towards the house with a low chuckle. "This is going to be good."

Falling in beside him, we walk in silence. The smell of night lilies assaults me as we pass through the gardens. Roses adorn the flowerbeds, their crimson petals bleeding against the night. The dogs break away, running ahead of us into the sunroom at the back of the house. I pull my hood up as we enter. It makes me uneasy being around all these people, being seen. Gio leads me along a corridor until we come to a door that opens onto a set of concrete stairs. A burst of cool air drift up them as we descend into the basement, like icy fingers, reaching for us. At the bottom, he approaches an old, rusted metal door, then presses a code into a keypad, eliciting a loud click. With a rough shove he pushes the old door open, its hinges screaming in protest.

"Here you go." He stands back, gesturing me to move ahead of him. I don't like it, but I steel my spine and step inside, keeping my focus on him. Gio is the worst kind of dangerous. The first impression is that he's nice, intelligent, smiles easily and has an air of kindness to him. Everything about him makes you forget that he would put a bullet in your head quick as look at you if the situation called for it. I don't forget though. He didn't make it to Nero's second by being soft.

As I step through the door, a gruesome scene unfolds before me. The room is nothing more than a large, empty space with concrete walls and floor. A drain is set into the middle of the floor, which gently slopes in towards it. The entire room smells of blood and death, and the floor is stained with evidence of the acts committed within these walls. It reminds me of the facility I grew up in, concrete and blood. Directly above the drain is a body, suspended by the ankles via thick metal chains that hang

63

from a hook in the ceiling. The man is barely more than pulverised flesh, his face completely unrecognisable. The big guy that was in Nero's office earlier stands in front of him, his shirtsleeves rolled up and a set of brass knuckles clutched in his hand. Blood coats his fingers, spreading up his forearms and catching the edge of his shirtsleeves. Nero and the other guy that were in the office are off to the side. Nero leans against the wall, a cigarette hanging between his lips. He almost seems casual, but I know better.

"This is Tommy." Gio points to the guy straddling a chair right next to Nero and he lifts a hand, waving at me as he grins. He's the only one here who doesn't have the dark hair and olive skin. His green eyes, pale skin and chestnut hair give him away as something other than Italian. "And Jackson." He waves a hand dismissively towards the big guy. This is Nero's inner circle, I realise. Every capo, boss or leader has one. You have to. I have people I use for certain things. No one can stand completely alone. It's impossible.

Sighing, I move over to the wall where Nero's standing, prepared to watch them flex their muscles and treat the guy on the chain like a piñata. Nero's arm is a couple of feet away from mine where I brace against the cold concrete, but I'm abnormally aware of him. He stands in his silent vigil, king of all he surveys, and it's everything that he doesn't say or do that makes him so formidable. Nicholai always said that a man's weight is all in how he is perceived, and perception can always be altered. A man who makes threats, a man who is seen to commit violence is doing so because he feels he has to make a point. Nero wants me to take out his enemies. He's not making a point, far from it, he's deliberately trying to remove himself from it. He doesn't need to make threats or kill people, because he knows what he is and he's confident in his abilities. I can feel his eyes on my face but I ignore it, crossing my arms over my chest as I school my features into a bored expression. Truthfully, once you've seen one interrogation, you've seen them all.

Gio approaches the suspended man, circling him with his hands buried deep in his pockets. "Is he dead?"

Jackson cracks his neck to the side impatiently. He's the muscle, the most reckless of the three, the most easily riled or baited, I note. "It can be arranged."

"If we wanted him dead, I'd have used a bullet and saved your shirt," Gio lilts, his voice like velvet as he says the words quietly. "Wake him up."

Jackson picks up a bucket from beside him and throws water over the unconscious man. He gasps and jerks awake, thrashing against the chain like a fish on a line. Out of the corner of my eye I see Nero drop the cigarette and crush it under his shoe, driving a black mark into the concrete floor. He steps forward, the atmosphere in the room changing, as though the beating so far was just a warm-up and it's all about to kick off.

Tommy chuckles under his breath and twists his head towards me. "Hope you're not squeamish."

I say nothing. The only reason I'm even standing here is because I have to wait for Nero to give me his royal decree. I don't like to be kept waiting, and especially not when I'm waiting to go to his apartment...something I don't even want to do. So, I stand on the side lines, watching the boys' club strut around, weighing each other's balls. Although, I will say I'm curious. I want to see what Nero does that has them all waiting on baited breath, or perhaps even they don't know.

Nero stands in front of the man. His silence might as well be a gunshot in the room. Reaching inside his jacket pocket, he removes a pack of cigarettes, taking one to replace the one he just stubbed out. His movements are slow, methodical, deliberately unhurried as he puts the packet back in his pocket and takes out the lighter. The low click gives way to the bright orange flame dancing over the end of the cigarette until it glows a bright red. I notice every tiny, inconsequential detail, because he demands it, without ever speaking a word. He has a gift, and when he finally does speak, everyone listens.

"You should know, Mr Chang, that I always get what I want." He straightens the collar of his jacket, brushing away a non-existent piece of lint.

"Not this time!" the hanging guy rasps, though it's lost on a choked cough

Nero smiles; it's almost charming and certainly disarming. "You aren't walking out of here alive," he tells the man. Well, he's not going to tell him shit now. Don't get me wrong, he knows he's going to die, I'm sure, but hope will play tricks on the human mind. It's that fragile hope that has them spilling their guts, not a guaranteed death penalty.

"Fuck you!" The guy spits through swollen lips and broken teeth. He sways slightly as his weight shifts, and the chain lets out an ominous creak as the links grind together.

Nero sighs and then inhales on his cigarette. For the first time, I notice the way his full lips purse around it, his defined jawline flexing beneath a layer of dark stubble as he draws the breath. He turns away, giving a slight jerk of his chin to Gio, who immediately leaves the room. "One of my guys was killed in your ambush," he says, his tone completely neutral. "I think you sold me out." This time, the guy says nothing, and the only sound is the rasping of his breath. Sounds like a punctured lung to me. Nero shrugs. "Okay."

I'll admit I'm intrigued when Gio comes back in the room carrying a metal bucket. He places it at Nero's feet, where he leans down and takes out a bottle. Nero nods and steps back as Gio opens the bottle and pours it over the suspended man. It only takes a second for the smell to hit me. Gasoline. The liquid soaks the material of his jeans, cascading down his mangled body until he's coughing and choking, trying not to inhale it.

"What are you doing?" he asks, panicked.

Nero drops to a crouch, until he's almost eye level with him. "Getting what I want." He takes one final drag of the cigarette and throws it, straight at the guy's face. The ember catches and the flames tear over his body. His screams echo around the concrete room, accompanied only by the sound of the fire tearing over his skin. I'm no stranger to violence, but that's a nasty way to go. Gio moves and pulls something else from the bucket, but I can't clearly see past Nero who stands calmly, watching the burning, screaming man as if he were observing a bonfire. A hissing sound fills the room, and the flames die instantly. Gio stands to the other side of the smoking body, fire extinguisher in hand. They put him out? They set him on fire and then they put it out. Why? All I can smell is singed hair and burnt flesh, and the odour has me swallowing back bile.

Another bucket of water is thrown on him and again he jerks awake, only this time it must feel like he's imprisoned in the inner circle of hell. The scream that tears from his lips would have even the hardest of men recoiling. His skin is raw and mangled, literally as though it melted in the fire. He's completely unrecognisable, not that the round with the brass knuckles had done him many favours. Nero stares down at him.

"Painful, isn't it?" The man's unbroken moans continue. "Your lungs are incinerated from the inside, which means you're going to die. You have hours, maybe days, depending on how strong you are." He pauses, and still all the guy can do is moan.

Damn, I'd feel sorry for him if I could, but honestly, I'm simply enamoured by Nero right now.

"Give me a name and I'll give you a bullet. If not, I hope you enjoy your last few hours on this earth."

"Abbiati," he sobs, the word barely comprehensible.

"Thank you." Nero removes his gun and shoots the guy in the head. The body goes limp and blood gushes into the drain. It reminds me of an animal carcass hanging in a slaughterhouse.

"Gio, Jackson, I think Bruce Abbiati needs a little visit." Nero says darkly. "Be sure to send a message." He tucks his gun back into the holster at his chest and approaches me. "Apologies for the delay." Then he walks out of the room without a backwards glance.

Nero Verdi, for all of his refinement, is a monster; one with no boundaries. To watch a man burn, to hear his screams and not even flinch…well, that puts him on my level. As if he wasn't dangerous enough to me. He's every bit as unfeeling and ruthless as I am. But he's also smart and cunning, and intelligence is the most lethal weapon a man can possess.

CHAPTER EIGHT

Nero

The second we're in the car I can feel her unease. She sits in the passenger with her back ramrod straight and her fingers lingering over the knife holstered at her thigh.

"Why?" she asks.

"You'll have to be more specific."

"Why are you insisting that I stay with you?"

I stare through the windshield at the headlights cutting through the darkness. "I have my reasons."

"Well, sharing is caring."

My lips twitch as I look at her again and find her intense gaze on me. "I know enough about you to know that you're very capable with some extremely powerful contacts. Right now, we've entered into something that mutually benefits us. I get what I want, and you get what you want."

"Yes, and I agreed to the exchange of services, did I not?"

"Come now, Una, don't tell me that you wouldn't look for a way out of it the second you got a chance." She says nothing. "You might pay Arnaldo a visit, or try and find your sister yourself, not that you'd get far, but still."

I pull to a stop at a red light. "I fail to see your point."

Reaching out, I trail a finger down the sharp plane of her cheek, knowing full well that it makes her uncomfortable. I've never had women complain about my touch, never met a woman that didn't beg me for it. They all want a taste of a bad boy, a walk on the wild side. If only they knew exactly what they were climbing into bed with. Una's different. She's no normal woman, and she definitely doesn't see me as the fuckable bad boy. She sees me for exactly what I am and doesn't even blink. Her skin is like satin beneath my fingertip as I trace a line to the corner of her lip, before gripping her jaw. "You stay with me, then you can't run around plotting my demise in your spare time."

A slow smile pulls at her lips, even as her eyes flash with something dangerous. "You really think you can hope to hold me against my will?"

I smirk back at her. "Oh, it won't be against your will. Because the second you get away from me, I will give Nicholai the information I have on Anna." Her breath hitches ever so slightly, her pulse throbbing erratically beneath my fingers. I allow a full-blown grin to make its way across my features. "And for all of your bravado, I don't think you want that, do you, *Morte*?" I have her, hook, line and sinker. She's got nowhere to run but straight to me. I will become her saviour and her nightmare. I'll be whatever the fuck she needs me to be if she plays the role I need her for.

Her facial expression relaxes back into one of passive indifference and outright attitude. "Okay."

"Okay?"

She pulls her face away from my grasp. "I asked for the why. You gave it. I can appreciate a shrewd manipulator, Verdi."

Oh, we're on a surname basis now. I snort as the light turns green and I pull away.

"Of course, if you want me to do my job, then I'll need my gear. Not to mention clothes. We need to make a stop."

"Fine. Where do you need to go?"

The headlights glide across the metal roller doors of several storage units. Zeus and George sit bolt upright on the back seat, ears pricked as they stare out the windshield. I cut the engine and get out. We're in a particularly run-down part of Brooklyn. A chain-link fence surrounds the lot with two security lights on either side of the gate casting an orange glow across the concrete walkway that separates the two rows of units. Una slams the car door and starts walking, her figure casting a long shadow. There's a single security guard on the gate. This place is about as secure as a garden shed in the Bronx. What the hell is Una possibly using this place for? I scour the shadows, listening. All I can hear is the distant hum of traffic, interrupted by the occasional boat horn. I follow her, feeling the hard outline of my gun against my ribcage. My fingers itch to feel the weight of it in my hand, but I refrain. Call me paranoid but I've experienced one too many dodgy deals and subsequent shootouts in locations just like this.

The sound of one of the metal doors rolling up punches through the night air. I catch up to Una as she steps inside the open unit and flicks on a light. The back wall is lined with several metal lockers, not dissimilar to the kind you'd find in an auto shop. She takes a set of keys and unlocks one. Opening drawers, she starts removing various weapons, pulling out the clips on the pistols and checking them before sliding them back in.

"Hand me one of those bags, will you?" She points to the left-hand wall, where a couple of empty black holdalls are hanging. I had one to her and she puts god knows how many different guns in there, and then she moves on to the next drawer. Grenades. The next, knives.

"You done?"
She glances sideways at me before zipping the bag. "You know I have guns. And we're not taking down the pentagon."

She glares at me. "I like *my* guns."

"And the grenades?"

A small smile touches her lips. "Well, grenades are always handy." I shake my head as I toss the bag over my shoulder. She picks up a long steel briefcase from the corner, followed by one of the zipped duffels against the wall.

"I need that, too." She points at a black plastic case, which I pick up. "Okay, let's go." She rolls the metal door back down, snapping the padlock back in place.

"You know, you should probably find somewhere more secure to store your shit."

She walks past me. "Well, no one would store anything of value here, so no one bothers to break in." She shrugs one shoulder. She says that now.

I pull into the parking garage beneath my building and glance at Una. She hasn't spoken a word to me since we picked up her supplies, and honestly, I'm good with that. I really don't care much for her emotional wellbeing past her ability to kill. I get out of the car and open the back door, letting the dogs out. They walk to heel as I make my way to the elevator, sparing only a brief glance over my shoulder just to check she is, in fact, following.

Her footsteps behind me are so quiet it's almost unnerving. She takes 'silent as the grave' into an entirely new context.

The elevator doors open and I step in. She looks like a cornered animal when she slides in beside me, ready to bolt at any minute. She lingers slightly behind me, ever the strategist. I catch her blurred reflection in the brass doors, and even with that limited view I can see the tension in her shoulders. She's uncomfortable and fight ready.

I inspect the cuff of my jacket, adjusting the edge of my shirt. "I'm not about to jump you, Una."

"You'd be stupid to," she replies, her voice tight.

Well, isn't this going to be fun? Gio thinks I'm crazy bringing her here. He wanted me to leave her at the house, but I know there's no way she'd stay there. Well...she might, but not without slaughtering every man there who sees her face before we part ways. The tension in this small metal box becomes stifling, until I'm ready to either pry the damn doors open or point a gun at her head and tell her to stop with her shit. Luckily for both of us, the low ping rings out before the doors glide open. The dogs trot ahead, disappearing into the kitchen where Margo, my housekeeper will have left them food.

"The elevator only operates with a key, and the emergency exit has sensors and alarm systems on the door. So, if you run, I'll know." I look at her, making sure she sees how deadly serious I am. Honestly, I have no idea how to handle someone like her. I deal with men for whom threats and leverage will undoubtedly work. She's too calm, too accepting. It makes me suspicious. I've never had to supress someone of her skill, nor with her contacts. I'm pretty sure she could call in a favour from any big gun she likes, even Arnaldo. After all, I'm off the grid here, working on my own, and I have no doubt that she knows that. I'm just hoping that her sister is enough. True, she might be able to find Anna on her own, but I've had guys buried in the cartels for years. I'm her best bet. She steps away from me, moving to the floor-to-ceiling windows that surround the entire apartment, like a literal glass wall, imprisoning her here, high above New York.

"Your room is this way." I ascend the stairs to the second floor. The balcony style railing runs along the length of the apartment, overlooking the open-plan living space below. My step falters at the first door, the room furthest from mine, the one I had intended to put her in, but for some reason I keep walking, stopping at the one next to mine. I push the door open and hold my arm out in a sweeping gesture.

"You should have everything you need, but if not then tell me and Margo will get it."

"Margo?" Suspicion laces her voice.

"My housekeeper. I don't keep girlfriends."

She smirks. "You say that as though they're pets. Butterflies in a jar." She walks a few steps away and spins on her heel to face me. "You strike me as the sort to pluck the wings off pretty butterflies, Nero."

74

Una Ivanov. There's something about her that constantly taunts, teases and dares. I move further into the room, slowly closing the gap between us until I'm close enough to see her indigo eyes in the darkness. The easiest way to intimidate someone is to get in their personal space. It's a habit when trying to force someone to back down, but with Una, I find it has the opposite effect. She rises to the threat, making everything in me sit up and take note. I want to be indifferent to her, I need to be, and yet, everything she does captures my attention. How can it not? I've never met a woman like her, and I know I never will. There *is* no one like her. She's the best, the kiss of death herself. My eyes trace the outline of her full lips, and I suddenly remember *exactly* how they feel against mine, the lash of her tongue, the violent scrape of her teeth…

"Don't worry, I'll leave your wings well alone."

She smirks and tilts her head back to look at me. "You mistake me for something pretty and fragile, but I assure you, any wings I had were plucked a very long time ago," she says it casually, but I catch the briefest flash of sadness in her eyes. She doesn't say it for pity though; she says it because she hates to be seen as anything delicate. I shouldn't give a shit, but she's like a puzzle that I can't resist wasting my time on.

"Fine then, be an ugly caterpillar." She snorts and the briefest smile flashes over her lips, sinking a dimple into her porcelain cheek. A butterfly indeed, although her wings are made of steel and her touch may very well kill. Forcing myself to move away from her, I step out of the door.

"Nero." I halt when I hear her voice. "Uh…" she stammers over her words and it has me turning to face her. "You might hear things tonight. Don't come in here." Before I can respond, she slams the door shut.

CHAPTER NINE
Una

" *You will learn your place, Una. You are nothing and no one, an unwanted orphan. Say it!" The matron of the orphanage shouts in my face, spit flying from those thin, cruel lips. A cigarette hangs between her fingers and the smell of tobacco wafts around the room. Defiantly, I hold her stare, refusing to break. The rough wood of the chair bites against my bare thighs, exposed by the sundress I'm wearing. The leather belts that secure my wrists to the arms of the chair are worn, but they still chafe against skin, leaving my wrists raw. The matron likes to do this, to make sure the children here are well behaved and easy. I'm not. I know what they do with us, what they have planned. I refuse to accept this fate, and above all, I refuse to accept it for my sister*

"Fine. Remember you deserve this," she growls, before taking the cigarette and stamping it into my shoulder.

It hurts, it really hurts. And then that smell, burnt flesh and melting skin. It's the first time I've smelt it, but it won't be the last.

The scene then shifts, the matron's face blurs and morphs until I'm staring at Erik. Leather restraints give way to rough hands, and the wooden chair becomes a concrete floor. I know what happens here, and already my breathing is picking up, my heart thrumming so fast I can barely stop myself from having a full-blown panic attack. I thrash against the restraining hands but all it earns me is a swift slap across my cheek. My head reels back and a sting erupts across my skin.

Erik's body lands on top of me, his hot breath blowing over my cheek. "I'm going to break you," he hisses.

It's at this exact moment that the part of me that still had a scrap of faith in humanity shatters. Everything becomes a blur of torn clothing and adrenaline. I fight, lashing out at anything within reach. Somewhere in the chaos I become removed, and instead of experiencing it myself, I become a bystander, and the girl being held down becomes Anna. Only she doesn't fight, and Nicholai never arrives to save her. Tears track down my face, and I scream as I try to get to her, but I can't. It's as though my feet are set in concrete and all I can do is watch as my little sister shuts down and becomes nothing more than a fractured vessel in front of my eyes, her innocence stolen by monsters who have no right to take it.

Gasping awake, I drag in lungfuls of air. Tears track down my temples, while the tell-tale ache of a scream lodges in my throat. It takes me a second to remember where I am. I can't remember the last time I stayed in the same place for more than a week or two, and the constant travelling never ceases to disorientate me. Nightmares have plagued me for years. Well, they're not nightmares so much as memories. My entire childhood was one long nightmare, so I have plenty of material. This is new though. This is the first time Anna has become the focus of my torment. That wasn't a memory. I didn't break, but Anna would break. The thought is enough to make my blood run cold, and a tiny voice in the back of my mind begs me to hope, to hope that maybe that was not her fate. I should know better. There is no room in this world for hope, only cold reality.

The bright lights of the city below cast a faint glow throughout the room that throw shadows across the pale grey carpet. My pulse is still pounding, and my skin feels sticky with sweat, so I get up and silently move to the bathroom on the far side of the room. Without turning the lights on, I start the shower and strip before stepping under the hot water. Letting the darkness and water wrap around me, soothing the tension in my body. I should hate the dark, but I love it. It allows us to just be, to hide all the flawed, unsightly parts of ourselves. With the light comes the truth, the reality of our shitty existence. When I'm done, I step out onto the mat and wrap one of the thick towels around me.

After a nightmare I'm always left wide awake and unable to sleep, so I leave the bathroom and venture out into the apartment in the hopes of finding a laptop or data device of some description. To my surprise, I find all my stuff resting against one of the couches in the living room. George hops up from his bed in the corner, while Zeus studiously ignores me. Slinging the black duffel bag over my shoulder, I head back to my room, but pause when I hear a low whine behind me. George stands, watching me go with the most heartbroken expression on his face. How a supposed guard dog can be as cute as any lap dog I don't know, but he is.

"Come on," I whisper. He keeps his head low as he walks over to me and then follows me up the stairs, looking sheepish the entire time. "You're such a baby." I laugh.

Returning to bed, George curls up at the end while I dig

around in the duffel bag and find a laptop at the bottom. I have a couple of locations in the city just like the storage locker in Brooklyn, as well as others around the world. Guns, passports, money, a laptop and a change of clothes to hand are always needed. You never know when a job might go wrong, and of course there's the rogue scenario. Pissing off the wrong people might result in someone putting a price on my head. The second that happens I have to disappear and run for Russia, and it's not like I can just pop home and pack a bag before I do it. This life is one where you're constantly looking over your shoulder, but it's the only one I know.

Sometimes, I'm sent after targets who seem to straddle both worlds. Cartel bosses who have a wife and kids that they kiss goodbye every morning before they step outside and kill people, peddle drugs and sell whores. I know better than anyone how that always ends, with widows and orphans. But when I see them playing at having a normal life, it confounds me. I don't understand the motivation to *be* normal, to have the standard…the human compulsion to love and be loved is such a crippling weakness, and yet, even the worst of humanity still want such a simple thing above all else. No, I can't do normal. I like the rush, the thrill of not knowing whether today might be my last. It makes each kill that much better. Every time I go after a hit, it's kill or be killed, and every time I succeed, each time I win, it makes my grey world a little brighter. My entire life is a game of survival that I am determined to conquer.

Removing the brand-new laptop from the bag, I open it. In the side pocket of the duffel is a memory stick. There's nothing on it, of course, all the information I have on the many crime organisations I work with is on my person at all times. I grab my necklace, a simple silver leaf, about half an inch long. It looks inconspicuous enough, but it's actually a locket. Inside is a tiny memory card, the kind that goes in a cell phone. I pop it into a slot on the memory stick and insert it into the USB drive. Years of information starts downloading onto the computer drive.

Four names. Four hits. I work, pouring over information until the sun starts to bleed across the grey morning sky. I learn my targets, their connections.

Finnegan O'Hara is Irish and honestly, has a knack for pissing off a lot of people. He's IRA, high up in the Irish mob in Europe and owns most of the Irish ports. If the Italians want to run drugs through Ireland, which is the easiest export point on the continent, then they have to go through Finnegan. Someone was bound to gun for him eventually. Nero seems less restrained than a lot of the mafia that I usually deal with. It doesn't surprise me that he's taking him out.

The other three: Marco Fiore, Bernardo Caro and Franco Lama are all Italian, and I have no idea why he wants them.
I'm not aware of any feuds between Nero and any of them, but then I didn't even know who Nero was until I met him. Even now, I'm not sure how he fits into all this. Lorenzo and Nero were both the sons of Matteo and Viola Santos. Lorenzo took the name and yet Nero has his mother's maiden name, Verdi, a powerful family in their own right, but with no real weight here in America. Nero had his brother killed, which is about as dysfunctional as it gets. So is it simply a family feud? If so, it's escalated pretty far, and Arnaldo is aiding it, so what's his play?

Fuck, this is enough to give me a headache. Why do I even care? I never ask for a reason behind a job. Really, these are hits like any other, except that the payment is my long-lost sister, and my employer insists on me living with him. And of course, there's the fact that I'm quite literally laying my head on a chopping block, but again, do the reasons matter? The only reason I'm doing this is to get to Anna. It matters though, because it's right there, like an alarm going off in my mind. I rely on my instincts, and my instincts are telling me that Nero is not simply the stung son of a capo, out for revenge. There's more to this. What am I not seeing?

I've been here five days, and I've barely seen Nero. He remains in his office most of the time, while I spend all my time researching names, locations, contacts. A job like this takes a long time to put into play, and I'm still not sure how I'm going to pull it off. George sits at my feet, waiting for the crusts off my toast while I sit at the breakfast bar. I absentmindedly hand him one while skimming over the floor plans for one of Bernardo's nightclubs. The sun is just starting to rise, painting the kitchen in hues of pink and orange. I assume Nero isn't awake until I hear a faint rhythmical beat coming from somewhere in the apartment. Frowning, I get up and follow the sound, opening a door that is right next to the elevator. It's a gym, with a treadmill, heavy bag, various weights and machinery. It must be one of the biggest rooms in his apartment, and this place isn't exactly small.

Leaning against the doorframe, I watch as his feet pound the treadmill. I can see his side profile from where I'm standing, but he doesn't seem to notice me. He's topless, his shorts riding low enough on his hips that I can make out the line of muscle that sweeps down his side before meeting the V at the front. Each muscle flexes beneath his tanned skin as he runs. Sweat glistens over every inch of him, dotting along the back of his neck before falling between his shoulder blades. I grew up training with soldiers, mostly men. I see the male form as an asset. Muscles equate to strength, nothing more. But as I watch Nero, I note the graceful way he moves, the way each line and plane of his body blends into the next. He's beautiful. There really is no other word. His body is crafted into a weapon, a destructive force of nature. And just as the perfect blade takes time to make, to balance exactly, that body is the product of dedication and sweat. He slams his hand over the stop button and the treadmill slows rapidly beneath him until he comes to a halt.

"You're staring," he says without looking at me. He swipes a towel over his face and turns to face me, his chest heaving. "That's never good where you're concerned."

"I'm not planning on killing you. Yet." I step inside the room and lean against the wall.

He smirks as he steps off the treadmill and approaches. For the first time I see the tattoos on his body, script across his chest reads an Italian proverb, which equates to something along the lines of karma is a bitch. His right arm is covered to the elbow in an intricate sleeve, but I can't make out the details without staring. He gets entirely too close as he reaches for his water bottle on the shelf right next to me. I flatten myself against the wall, but still his scent wraps around me. Sweat mixes with his body wash and he's so close to me I could literally move my hand an inch and touch him. Damp hair falls over his forehead messily as he stares down at me.

"Maybe you just like looking." Lifting the water bottle, he places it to his lips and drinks, staring at me with amusement in his eyes. A drop of sweat rolls down his throat, and I can't help but track its path down his chest. Something foreign settles in my gut and my jaw clenches. He makes me uncomfortable and yet, I want to touch him. I want to know if he feels as hard and implacable as he looks. He knows it though, because he brushes a hand over my waist. When I tense, he smiles. He thinks he's simply making me uncomfortable, but it's so much more than that.

I grip his wrist. "Don't." I warn.

He leans in until his lips are at my ear. "Or what?" he dares on a dark whisper.

Placing my hand on his stomach, I dig my nails into his skin hard enough to push him back a couple of inches. His gaze meets mine, my breath hitching as his abs tense and roll beneath my fingertips.

No one could ever argue that Nicholai isn't a master in training his assassins. He used to tell me that some guy had trained a dog, taught it to salivate on command through simple conditioning. He would ring a bell every time he fed the dog, so the dog associated the bell with food. I was trained much the same way, conditioned into having set responses. We were deprived of human touch, of even the slightest form of affection. The only time we touched another person was during a fight, under raining fists rather than soft caresses. On the rare occasion we did receive some form of contact outside of the ring it was deliberately coupled with pain, usually an electric shock. Add into the equation a lethal set of fighting skills, and the nature of human survival, and you create a reflex killer. I will admit that reflex has saved my ass more than once; however, as I got older, things changed. Much of my job involves seduction, which I was also trained in. The result is a constant battle, the instinctual versus the necessary. My instinct is to tear Nero's arm from his body, but…I don't want to.

"I'm serious, Nero."

"And yet, you're touching me." His eyes dropping to my hand splayed across his stomach. He makes no move to step away, simply waits. I realize that I can't remember the last time I touched another human being voluntarily, not to aid a job, and not to kill them. I don't know what it is about him. He's not a soldier, not a brother in arms, or a boy I grew up with. He's not really a client, and he's certainly not a hit. He is… an anomaly, an exception, a strange ally. He confuses me whilst leaving me in awe of his savagery. He leans in closer and my nails dig into his skin. His powerful heartbeat pounds through his body, ricocheting up my arm. I blink and tear my hand away from him. Huffing a small laugh, he steps back very deliberately before leaving the gym.

I stand there, confused and extremely uneasy. Weakness. This is what weakness feels like. I think he likes it. He doesn't fear me, so he wants to challenge me, wants to see me snap. Well, this living situation is going to get awkward real fast. When I go back into the living area he's not there. When he appears again he's fully dressed in an immaculate dark grey suit, his hair damp from the shower.

"I have some business to handle, I'll be back later," he says briefly, whistling at the dogs who both leap up to follow him as he walks to the elevator.

"What? You'll be back later. Are you serious?"

He turns to face me, a bored expression on his face. "You're reminding me why I don't let women stay with me."

On a laugh, I grab one of his kitchen knives and launch it at him. It nicks his jacket before hitting the steel elevator door and clattering to the floor. He cocks a brow and lifts his arm, showcasing the neat slice through the expensive material.

"Your aim is shit," he growls, stalking towards me.

"It is. I was aiming for your chest." I shrug. "Your kitchen knives aren't very well balanced. But, now I have your attention, I think we need to rediscuss our terms." He ignores me and walks straight past, heading up the stairs. I follow. "You see, you're so quick with your threats – if I leave you'll go to Nicholai. All that shit." He walks into his bedroom, ducking into the walk-in closet. Again, I follow. "But if you go to Nicholai, he'll find Anna himself, and you'll have no leverage," I drawl, as if the entire notion is boring to me. At least then I could kill him. I stand in the doorway of the closet, watching him strip out of the damaged jacket and take an identical one off a hangar. "So…"

"So nothing," he snaps, the bite in his voice making me straighten and take note. He storms the space between us and grabs my jaw, forcing my head to the side until his lips are against my ear.

A fissure of fear settles in my chest, and I smile, feeling my heart hammer in my chest. I *feel*. Hot, angry breaths blow over my neck, and I shiver.

"Don't play games with me, Una. Don't try to negotiate or back me into a corner." His voice is deathly calm. "We both know that you want your sister a damn site more than I actually need you. But feel free to test me on it and see what happens." He releases me, shoving my face away from him and storming out of the room.

I stay there, feeling the rush of adrenaline in my system, revelling in the thrill of him. He scares me, and I like it.

CHAPTER TEN

Una

Tommy rocks up a few minutes after Nero leaves. Strolling into the kitchen with his hands in his pockets, whistling to himself. His chestnut hair is messy and although he's wearing a suit – of course – the jacket is unbuttoned and his shirt is open to the middle of his chest. I can also smell the whisky on him from here. Sitting at the breakfast bar with my laptop in front of me, I try to form a plan to take out Marco Fiore. Nero left me a file this morning at least. Like homework. Great.

"Apparently, you and I have a hot date." Tommy winks, pping up on a stool across from me.

"So you're babysitting me," I say without sparing him a glance.

He laughs, cocking his head to the side as he does. "Well, babysitting implies that you need supervision. I'd go more with watch duty."

I sigh. "Fine. Then you can be of use. I need you to tell me everything you know about Silk."

His eyebrows pinch together. "Marco's place?"

"Yes."

"It's a strip joint. He's there every Friday and Saturday."

Today's Wednesday. "Perfect."

"No, no, no." He shakes his head again and braces his elbows on the breakfast island as he leans forward. "You won't get him there."

Huh. So, Tommy is well aware of exactly why I'm here.

I smirk. "You do know who I am?" He stares blankly back at me. "I can get to anyone, anywhere." He shrugs and leans back in his chair. Returning my focus to my laptop screen, I study the street view outside Silk. "What about his strippers?"

"They're tight. Mostly Italian girls. It's not impossible but you might fail."

"Which fucks me for another route." I interrupt. I see him nod in my peripheral. "Security?"

He takes a cigarette packet from the inside pocket of his suit jacket. "Marco's a shady fucker. Keeps armed guys with him at all times." He takes a cigarette out and presses it between his lips as a raspy laugh works its way up his throat. "Mind you, I'd

88

be shady if I'd made an enemy of Nero," he mumbles as he holds the lighter up, cupping the flame.

"So he did do something to piss Nero off." I can't help but probe, even though every professional facet of me is screaming not to.

Tommy exhales a long stream of smoke, a small smile touching his lips. When his eyes meet mine, I know that he knows I'm pushing. He knows that I have no idea why I'm hunting Marco. And yet...

"He supported Lorenzo." He shrugs. "He's not a fan of Nero and well, I love Nero like a brother but he has a nasty temper on him."

"So I see." *Don't ask.* "How do you know Nero?" *Brilliant.*

He leans back in his chair, eyeing me warily. "We grew up together."

"You're not Italian." For a second I think I've struck a nerve but then he simply shrugs.

"Half Italian, half Irish."

"That's unfortunate lineage." I keep my eyes on the screen in front of me. The Italians and the Irish hate each other.

He laughs. "Yeah, I was the half-breed and Nero was the bastard."

"A bastard?" *Jesus, I just can't stop.*

He takes a long inhale on the cigarette. "So they say. Anyway, we were the outcasts, so we banded together, I guess."

"Well, Italians are all about their bloodlines," I mumble.

"Aye, they are." I get up and make two cups of coffee, placing one in front of Tommy. He takes a hip flask out of his pocket and pours a little in, winking at me as he does.

"I see why you're on babysitting duty now," I remark dryly.

He shrugs. I swear he's impossible to rile. Perhaps that's more the reason why he's here instead of say, Jackson. I'm pretty sure I could goad Jackson, put him down and walk out of here without a backward glance. I swear I can already feel the walls pressing in on me. It's not the physical fact of being here; it's knowing I can't leave. The sooner I get a plan together, the sooner I can get out of here and do what I do best. Tick tock.

Tommy gets a text late in the afternoon and immediately stands up, picking up his jacket off the back of the chair. I'm grateful that he's leaving. An email from Sasha popped up in my inbox half an hour ago and I'm itching to read it, hoping desperately that he has something on Anna. It's been five days. Drumming my finger on the edge of the keyboard, I nervously wait for Tommy to leave. He shrugs his jacket on and offers me a small salute before he turns and walks towards the elevator. The second the doors slide shut I pull up my email. Sasha's message has no subject, no text, simply a link to a website.

I click on it and a website pops up. It's a webcam site that has me swallowing back bile. It's all in Spanish and there are various windows, each depicting a video stream. I click on one and it shows a girl sitting on a bed. She's completely naked with her knees pulled up to her chest. Dark hair hangs over her face and she looks so broken, as if every shred of hope has been stolen from her. Normally, I wouldn't care. I'd put it down to yet another example of the shitty world we live in and move on, but the revelation of Anna's fate has flawed me. The girl hunches in on herself. A bullet would be kinder than this. Steeling myself, I keep clicking through the various windows, each one a different dingy, concrete room, a different stained bed, a different destroyed woman. Some of them are alone, others have men in the room with them, and some are being raped, their lifeless bodies being abused again and again. I stop when I see a girl with white-blonde hair. A man is standing in front of her, undoing his belt. She sits on the edge of the bed, her face down and her hands in her lap. He grabs her chin and forces her head back. The hair falls away from her face, and I see her.

"Anna," I breathe. All too quickly it hits me, my sister is in that place, my sister is one of those girls. I should turn the feed off, but I can't. The man backhands her across the face, and then he's on top of her, his jeans shoved down past his thighs as he forces himself on her and rapes her. Everything in me tears apart at the sight of it, and I want to look away, but I can't, because if she can endure it, then the least I can do is watch it. I wish she knew that I'm here, that I'm looking for her. The worst part is her acceptance. She doesn't fight, doesn't move, she's just given up. But wouldn't I? God knows how long she's been enduring this, over and over, day in day out. The longer I watch, the more broken I feel, until I'm right there with her, hopeless, desolate, destroyed. The pain washes over me like a tidal wave, a darkness so deep it's bottomless. Anna is in hell, and I feel like I'm right there with her, those images branded into my mind. I push to my feet and pace to the window. I want to find that man and rip his goddamn heart out of his chest. The desolation gives way to anger, and that's good. It's good. Anger is a much more manageable emotion to deal with. Startling, I reach for my knife when I sense someone right behind me. Nero's hand slams around my wrist and his eyes lock with mine as the point of the blade hovers inches from his chest.

"Honey, I'm home," he says dryly, his expression dark.

Yanking away from his grasp, I begin pacing again, trying to formulate a plan, contacts. I need to get into Mexico.

"I need to leave," I blurt. He sighs and walks over to the coffee table, glancing down at the laptop screen.

"It changes nothing."

"Are you fucking kidding me? My sister is in a dirty web brothel, being raped and beaten. I have to get her out."

He cracks his neck from side to side. "She's been there six months. She's been a sex slave for seven years. A couple more weeks won't kill her," he says, his expression nothing but icy indifference.

"You knew about this?" I whisper, pointing at the laptop. Why do I feel betrayed by that notion?

He quirks a brow. "Isn't that what we made a deal for? You kill my marks and I get your sister? As I recall, you haven't killed anyone yet." His lips set into a hard line, those dark eyes focused on me, radiating power and arrogance.

"That was before I knew where she was. I'm going for her myself." I shove past him, heading for the stairs.

"If you thought you could get her yourself, you never would have made a deal with me," he drawls. Pausing, I turn around. He hasn't moved and his back is still to me, his face twisted slightly to glance over his shoulder. "The same deal still stands, you leave and I go to Nicholai."

I rush him and he turns at the last minute, taking the punch that I land on his jaw. His head snaps to the side, and when he brings his gaze back to mine, hard, angry eyes have me taking a small step back. "You're disgusting." I spit.

"Ask yourself this, Morte... You found that website pretty quickly, considering you've been looking for your sister all this time." He rubs his hand over his jaw before slowly closing in on me. He stops when his chest is barely an inch from mine but makes no move to touch me. "Perhaps you didn't want to find her. After all, this *weakness* is what brought you right here to this very moment, at my beck and call. You could be forgiven for wanting to leave such things buried." He pulls away, staring

LP Lovell   KILL ME

at me with calculated indifference.

Is he right? Could I have tried harder to find Anna?

"I can't just sit in this apartment knowing what's happening to her." Everything suddenly feels too much. My skin feels tight and hot, and the walls feel like they're moving, creeping closer. I yank at the collar of my shirt, which feels as though it's suffocating me. "I need to get out."

He grabs my arm, and I lash out instinctively. His fingers slam around the back of my neck and he turns me, ramming me against the window with my arm twisted behind my back. His chest presses against me, and I can feel the rabid animal in me clawing to get out of her cage.

"Enough," he growls.

"I'm going to give you three seconds to let me go," I say calmly. Of course, he doesn't, and I jolt my head back, smashing him in the mouth. Dull pain explodes across the back of my skull, but I don't care. I lift my leg and kick off the glass, throwing us both a few yards across the room. I hear the sound of smashing as Nero hits the glass coffee table. I roll off him, completely unscathed after my broken fall. He remains dazed on the floor, and I take my chance. He's really leaving me with no options. If I stay, I risk Anna being in that place for weeks more, and one day more is a day too long. If I leave, he'll go to Nicholai and Nicholai will probably kill her. That leaves me with one option, kill Nero and run. Throwing myself on him, I straddle his waist and rain punches over his face. His lip is split from the head-butt and blood trickles over his chin. He's dazed, and I'll have to work with that. Nero is a lethal adversary, and I won't have many chances to get one up on him. I place my hand under his chin, gripping it firmly in my palm. Using the other hand I grasp a handful of his hair and twist. I pause for a second, summoning the strength needed to snap his neck. It's not as easy as it looks.

"I didn't want to have to kill you, Nero," I whisper. I truly didn't. Nero is not a good guy, but I'm not a good girl. His actions are heinous, but it's nothing I wouldn't do myself. I feel strangely connected to him, as if the darkness within us unites us somehow. How can you judge or persecute someone when they are, in effect, the reflection of yourself? I don't look at him and see his acts; I'm simply reminded of my own.

His eyes flash open and his hand slams around my throat, launching me to the side. The air leaves my lungs when my back hits the carpet and I scramble to get away, but his body lands on top of me, pinning me to the ground with his enormous weight. I fight him, attempting to buck him off and create enough space that I can get my legs around him. I can't. My nails rake over skin in the struggle, making him growl and wrap his fingers around my throat. He squeezes hard enough that I panic. My oxygen cuts off and my heartbeat rises.

Embrace death.

I hear the voice in my head, the voice of my training instructor. I can't though. My mind is too free, all the ingrained instincts I know so well are absent, and the need to survive is pounding away at me. Nero looms over me like every demon I've ever had, mocking and taunting me with my own weakness. His dark eyes watch as I flounder and fade. Black spots dot my vision. He's going to kill me.

CHAPTER ELEVEN

Nero

Her eyes roll back in her head and I force myself to let go of her delicate neck, despite wanting to snap her like a fucking twig. She sucks in a gasping breath and her eyes open, slowly focusing on my face. "You were going to fucking kill me," I growl at her.

She frowns. "And strangling me was what? Foreplay? Get off me." She tries for authoritative but it's pathetic, really.

Wrapping my fingers around her wrists, I pull them up above her head and pin them in one hand. I brace the other hand beside her head in an attempt not to press every single part of me against her, and that's not for her benefit, trust me. This shouldn't be hot in any way, but violent women have an effect on me, and it doesn't get more violent than her. Watching her gasp for breath, my hand wrapped around that slim neck of hers…the only thing that could make it more perfect is if I were balls deep inside her. She tried to kill me and I have a fucking hard-on for it.

"I'm not doing your fucking job," she hisses through clenched teeth, panting. Oh, she's got a mouth on her when she's pissed off.

Clenching my jaw, I bring my face close to hers, even though she refuses to look at me. Her head flails from side to side. "I took you for intelligent, Morte. You're acting like a kid trying to play hero to her sister."

She yanks against my grip, bucking her body in an attempt to break free. "You have no intention of getting her back, do you?" She fights again, but it's feeble really. She's long lost the advantage.

Grabbing her jaw, I force her to look at me. "I gave you my word, didn't I? Are you questioning me?"

"You're a liar," she says quietly. Her lips part, her tongue flashing across them for the briefest moment. I struggle to tear my eyes away from her mouth. My dick is rock-hard, and I know she can feel it. I don't care.

"I don't lie," I say absentmindedly. Her chest rises and falls heavily, pressing against me. When I meet her eyes again, they're on my mouth. Damn, she makes this difficult. Her teeth gently scrape over her full bottom lip and I fight with myself, because fuck knows this is the last woman on earth I should want to kiss, and yet, she's the only one I've ever wanted to put my mouth on this much. Women are nothing more than a moment of pleasure to me, but Una…well, Una would be a world of pleasure and pain. I want to fight her and tame her only for her to break free and do it all over again. I want to strangle her while I fuck her and then fall asleep, never quite knowing whether I'll open my eyes again, or whether she'll put a bullet between them instead. She's a challenge, the unattainable killer. I could list every reason why this is bad, but right now not a single one comes to mind. She reels me in like a magnet, and I fight it, but eventually…

Gripping her jaw, she gasps as I force her head back. There's a beat, a moment where our eyes lock, and it's the rage there that pushes me over the edge. Mercilessly, I slam my lips over hers. Her fucking mouth. How many men have kissed her and actually lived to tell the tale? For a second she freezes, and then her lips part and her tongue darts over my bloodied bottom lip. She moans into my mouth, the sound going straight to my dick. She tries to pull her wrists free and I release her, trailing my free hand over the curve of her waist, the swell of her hip, the toned length of her thigh with the blade holstered to it. When I drop my lips to her neck, her fingers wind through my hair, pulling me closer. Her pulse pounds beneath my lips, and when I bite down on her soft skin, she physically trembles. The vicious little killer softens, purring beneath my touch. Her hips shift and she rubs against my hard dick, forcing a low groan past my lips. She's dangerous and addictive, simply kissing her is a rush of danger, and I'm quickly reminded why when I feel the cool brush of steel at my throat. Clever girl. Smirking, I slowly pull my face from her neck and stare down at her swollen, blood-stained lips and too bright eyes.

"Last chance," she says, her voice wavering.

I cock a brow, daring her. She presses the knife into my skin, the sharp sting of the blade breaking through flesh. Warm blood trickles down my throat. "I'm asking you to trust me, Una." I keep my eyes locked with hers, hoping she can see that I mean it. "Trust. Me," I growl. She looks so vulnerable, so beautifully feral.

"Never."

I push my throat harder against her blade, hissing a breath through my lips as my mouth brushes against hers. "If you won't trust my simple ability to hold up my end of a bargain, then believe in my basic sense of self-preservation." I breathe against her. "I'd have to be a stupid man to screw over the kiss of death, wouldn't I?" She squeezes her eyes shut.

"Not if you kill me."

I smile and stare at her lips. "Well, now that would be a waste." Her eyes lock with mine and she seems to be searching for something. Finally, she takes a deep breath before the blade slips away from my neck.

"Fine, but if you fuck me over, there will be nowhere you can hide, Nero."

"Such a savage little butterfly." I smirk and push off her. She rolls to her feet and says nothing, simply walks past me and heads for the stairs. I have to give her points for effort and creativity. My dick is so hard it hurts.

Heading straight for my room, I strip as I go into the bathroom. The second I'm standing under the hot water of the shower, I fist myself and start stroking over the length of my dick. Squeezing my eyes shut, a scene forms in my mind. It's so hot and twisted. I picture Una, standing over Lorenzo's dead body. She looks at me and then bites down on her bottom lip, dragging her teeth over it as she releases the soft flesh. Hopping up on the desk, she slowly glides her skirt up until the material is bunched at her waist. No underwear, just endless milky soft skin and a bare pussy. She spreads her legs wide and I get a glimpse of perfection. Her hand drops between her legs and she starts to work one perfectly manicured finger over her clit. The noise she makes has me groaning and throwing my hand against the tile to steady myself. She takes two fingers and buries them in her pussy, moaning and writhing, whispering my name.

Pleasure courses through my veins and electricity rips over my body in a wave. A low growl leaves me as I come, watching it wash away down the drain.

This is what I'm reduced to, beating one out in the shower, because the deadly assassin I brought into my house tried to kill me. A beautiful woman with a homicidal streak has always been my weakness.

****

I wake to a blood-curdling scream that has me instinctually reaching for my gun before I realise it's just Una. I swipe a hand over my face and roll over, hearing another scream, and then another. Jesus. Is she being murdered? Getting out of bed, I leave my room, lingering outside her door for a second. She said not to go in there, but it's my damn apartment, and I need to sleep. This has been constant for days now. I push open the door and approach the bed. She's tossing and turning, and it looks as though she's fighting a battle in her sleep.

"Una." She doesn't wake, but the tight set of her body looks almost painful. I sigh and shove her arm. In the blink of an eye she's bolt upright and I'm staring down the barrel of a .40 cal. Of course. "Are you ever going to stop pointing guns and knives at me?" I sigh.

Her arm wavers an inch before she finally lowers it. She's left all the blinds open and the ever-present light from the city below illuminates the room. Dark shadows linger under her eyes and for once she has no smart remark for me. She drags a hand through her hair and leans against the headboard. "What are you doing in here?"

"I love to hear a woman scream, as much as the next guy, but if I'm not fucking her or hurting her, then it's just annoying." She glares at me.

"Again, you're the one that wanted me in your apartment, not me." God, she's never going to stop with that shit.

"Yeah well, I didn't expect the big bad killer to have night terrors." Her jaw clenches, her eyes flashing angrily. Apparently, that hit a nerve.

When I sit on the edge of the bed, she moves away from me, shunting to the other side.

"What are you doing now?" she snaps.

"Sleeping." I lie down on the bed, ignoring her. That vanilla and gun oil scent of hers wraps around me immediately.

"Here? You want to sleep here?" she asks, her voice hiking.

"Your whining I can sleep through. When you're whining you're not screaming bloody murder, so I'll take it."

"You're an asshole," she grumbles under her breath. Ignoring her, I close my eyes. "Nero, seriously…" She shoves me. "You are not sleeping in my bed."

"Actually, *my* bed." I have a moment where I marvel at what a normal conversation this is. I could almost be friends with Una if I wasn't me and she wasn't her, but even then, I'd still want to fuck her. Or maybe I wouldn't. It's her bloodlust that makes my dick hard.

"I'm starting to worry that you have no sense of self-preservation whatsoever."

I smile. "Is that a threat, Morte?"

"I don't threaten."

I smile wider. "Promises, promises."

She growls under her breath. "You're insane."

I'll get up in a minute, of course, but something about her temper makes me smile. She's right, I am insane. I have money, respect, power, women and a job that feeds into all my dark and violent desires. I have everything I want and need, and yet, Una makes it all feel boring. She's dangerous and unpredictable. She's everything I crave from life in one deadly package, and that might well make me insane, but if there's one thing I've learned in life it's to accept things for what they are.

The gentle trail of fingertips over my chest pulls me from sleep. I blink my eyes open, gathering my bearings as I look around the room before glancing down to find Una's cheek pressed to my bare chest. Shit, I actually fell asleep here. Her arm is thrown over my body and her fingers glide over my left pec, before trailing down my abs one muscle at a time. I swallow hard when her palm presses flat against my lower stomach, her fingers just brushing the waistband of my boxers. Her deep, even breaths are the only thing that stops me from throwing her down on this mattress and taking her. Instead, I grit my teeth and lie there, my dick throbbing as I stare at the dark ceiling.

CHAPTER TWELVE

Una

I feel the warm, solid chest beneath my cheek and listen to the strong, rhythmic heartbeat pounding like a steady drumbeat. Safety, familiarity, warmth…things I crave. Things I will never again have other than here, in my dreams with the boy I loved. It's been a long time since I dreamt of him. The weight shifts beneath me and my semi-dreamlike state starts to shatter. I don't want it to. Desperately, I try to cling to it, but the morning always comes eventually.

"Alex?" I croak, wrapping my arm more tightly around him.

"Guess again."

I jolt awake and the second I realise there's a body in the bed with me, I'm on the defensive. Reaching under my pillow, I grab my knife, before throwing myself on top of the hard body beside me. Nero doesn't even open his eyes but a wide grin works over his lips as I run the blade along his jawline. He slept in my bed! Anger has never been a problem for me. Emotions are simply a forced response born of attempting to appear normal to the outside world. But ever since he brought up Anna, I've been out of control. I feel too much. I would say it's just her, but I don't think it is. He has the ability to rile me where no one else ever has. He brings things out in me that I didn't even think existed. I feel like a ball of thread and Nero is just pulling and pulling, unravelling me. And eventually, all that will be left is a tangled mess, impossible to put back together again. He scares me, and I long for my cold indifference, my dark hole where nothing and no one can possibly touch me. His eyes flash open, ensnaring me instantly.

"Careful, Morte."

"Or what?"

He grips my hips and his body rolls beneath me, pressing his hard dick right into the apex of my thighs. Warmth unfurls low in my stomach, and I frown. One of his hands wraps around the back of my neck and he wrenches me forward until we're face-to-face, the blade between us. My heart pounds in my chest and I close my eyes for a second, listening to that rhythmic pulse hammering in my ears. Life. Electricity.

"Look at me," he demands. I meet that dark gaze of his, normally so calculating. The whisky colour of his irises swirl, morphing into a honey gold. Wrapping his fingers around my wrist, he squeezes hard and forces the blade away from his throat. I swallow heavily, dragging in much needed oxygen. It's like he's vacuuming all the air from the room with just a look. My mind flashes to that kiss yesterday. I only wanted to render him weak, but the brutal brush of his tongue, the way he takes without apology…I've never felt so out of control, and I've never wanted that lack of control so much.

His thumb brushes over the side of my neck just as I feel the sharp scratch of the blade over my collar bone. Perhaps I should feel threatened, but I don't. Everything slows and I smile as I stop thinking, and just feel. I feel the frantic rush of adrenaline and desire swirling and mixing into something so potent, it cripples me.

My entire being focuses on the exact point where his hot skin presses against the insides of my thighs, where the blade ominously lingers. His free hand glides over my thigh and I grit my teeth, fighting my quickening breaths. I tell myself to pull away, because part of me wants to walk this line with him. A gasp tears past my lips when his fingertips brush the seam of my underwear. His gaze brands me as he studies my every move, every tremble, every desperate breath. When his fingers slip beneath the thin material, my hand darts out, grabbing his arm and forcing him to pause. Cocking a brow at me, he twists my wrist, causing the blade, still clutched in my fingers, to drag over my chest in a burning line. My breath hitches and blood wells before spilling slowly over my skin. My grip on him softens enough that he brushes over my wet pussy, leaving me physically shaking as the opposing voices in my head reach a crescendo. The moonlight spilling through the windows plays over the smirk on his lips before he roughly presses two fingers inside me. My eyelids shutter on a ragged breath.

"Fucking look at me." His voice rumbles through the darkness and my eyes snap open.

He holds me hostage, watching me as he pulls his fingers out and then thrusts back in. My mouth falls open on a silent moan that hitches in my throat and everything slips away. Logic and reason cease to exist and all that matters is that he makes me feel this need; he makes me want him in this all-consuming way. Nero is danger and lust, rage and desire and I shouldn't like it, but I do. Our eyes lock as his fingers move inside me, sending me hurtling towards a precipice. The knife digs into a point in the centre of my sternum and heat tears through me as the thrusting becomes more aggressive. My core tenses just as a moan slips past my lips.

"Come for me, Morte." He groans and the intensity presses in on me until I fall apart, feeling his eyes on me and moaning incoherently as my nails claw over his skin.

I remain there, on my knees, my hands braced against his solid chest as I attempt to catch my breath. I've never felt anything like that, never felt so completely owned by someone. The knife disappears and he brings his fingers to his lips, smearing moisture over them before sliding them in his mouth. My heart stutters over itself, and I'm caught between being embarrassed and consumed with a debilitating want. I can't take my eyes off his mouth as his tongue flashes out over his lips. Then he pushes up off the mattress until our faces are a mere breath apart, his lips brushing over mine teasingly. His tongue strokes over my bottom lip until all I can taste is myself. His cock is pressing against me and it has me faltering, the trance slipping.

"I…" I start, but I have no words. Climbing off him, I rush for the bathroom, seeking some space, some clarity. I go to slam the bathroom door but he's there, blocking it.

"Don't do that shit," he says calmly, the desire I saw in his eyes only seconds ago replaced with a simmering anger.

"Get the fuck out, Nero," I snap.

"Who's Alex?" he asks.

What the fuck? The mention of his name has memories flashing through my mind in a burst of images. Brown eyes, an easy smile, safety, warmth, love, and then horror and heartbreak, death and destruction.

"Someone I killed."

Nero watches me through narrowed eyes and his jaw sets in a hard line. I don't want to talk to him about Alex, because in a strange way he reminds me of him. *It's the eyes; they have the exact same colored eyes.* That's where the similarity ends though. Alex was kind and good. Nero is bad and cruel. Alex was the light to my dark. Nero would be the pitch-black shadows that linger even in the darkness, calling to me, enticing me.

We stare at each other for a few seconds before I cock a brow at him. "I need to shower." The numbers on the bedside clock glow, showing that it's only five thirty in the morning, but I don't care. I'll take any excuse to get away from him.

"Tommy's busy today, so I'm taking you to a meeting with me," he says out of the blue.

I want to tell him to stick it, because I'm not one of his soldiers, but honestly, the thought of getting out of this apartment is far too good to pass up.

"Fine. Now, get out." He drags his eyes over my body without an ounce of shame and then turns and leaves. Sighing, I brace my hands against the vanity, staring at my reflection in the mirror. I jagged line runs from my collar bone to the centre of my chest, just above my tank top. It's just a scratch, and it's nearly stopped bleeding already.

I don't want to think about Nero and what just happened in there. It's more concerning to me that I thought he was Alex. That's disturbing on so many levels, but mostly because Alex was the only person who ever made me feel safe, an instinctual bone-deep safety, an implicit level of trust. Nero made me feel that same safety for just a few seconds, and I don't like it because it feels like he's taking something from Alex, something he has no right to take. Alex may be long gone, but he will always be that boy for me, he has always been 'the one'. Some people have a past, demons...mine ride on my shoulder constantly waiting for an opportunity to take a bite. I've done awful things, and truthfully, I tell myself that I did them to survive, because I had to, but there is no such thing as having to. There is always a choice. I chose to survive, whatever the cost, even when it cost Alex's life. What is the price of one human soul? Because I'm sure by now I don't have one. Any soul I do have left I'm willingly selling to Nero. If the devil were a person then it would undoubtedly be him.

I spend a couple of hours in my room, avoiding Nero. He's waiting in the kitchen with an espresso in his hand, wearing a suit that hugs every graceful line of his body. I wonder if anyone actually falls for his sophisticated façade. Don't get me wrong, he's intelligent and a shrewd negotiator, not to mention manipulative, but beneath all the cunning civilities he's feral and blood thirsty, the most basic of animal qualities. I've never felt that more than when his eyes were on me and his fingers in me, his name on the tip of my tongue. I want to be appalled by him, but the worse his is, the more captivated by him I seem to become. His eyes flick up briefly and he studies me while sipping on his coffee. A small frown line sets between his brows.

"If you even think about asking me to dress like that…" I point at him. "I'm going to cut you." His lips twitch and he wisely keeps his mouth shut. Pulling the clip out of my gun, I place it on the breakfast bar, loading three more bullets into it then clicking it back into place. I can feel his eyes on me.

"What?" I growl without looking up.

"This isn't really a gun kind of meeting."

Placing my gun in my holster, I lift my gaze to him. "It's that kind of attitude that will get you killed."

When we get to the parking garage, Tommy is leaning against a black Range Rover. He grins at me. "Una, you are looking ravishing today."

"Fuck off."

Laughing, he opens the back door of the SUV, but Nero places his hand on the small of my back, leading me away. I quickly shrug off his touch, glancing over my shoulder to see the dogs jump in the SUV.

"First babysitting me, now you have him chauffeuring your dogs." I snort. "What did he do to piss you off?" The lights on a black Maserati flash and I go to the passenger door.

Nero glances at me over the top of the car, his expression its usual unreadable mask. "It keeps him out of trouble."

I get in the car as he slides behind the wheel. "Better to find trouble than be driving dogs around."

The engine purrs to life. "In this city, there is nothing more dangerous than being Irish *and* Italian," he says quietly.

"You care about him."

"In order to lead you must be loyal to those who follow you. My guys work for me, and I protect them." He reverses the car out and puts it back in gear. "That's the mafia."

There's something about him that has me perplexed. The mafia would never truly accept Tommy. Like I said, they're all about bloodlines. And from what I know of Nero, he's not exactly popular in the mafia himself. Respected? Yes. Feared? Certainly. Liked? No. I still haven't worked out what his play on this entire situation is, and with my sister in the balance, I want to know.

"Is that what all this is about, the mafia?" I ask, feigning only vague interest. "Your loyalty to them?" The muscles in his jaw tighten and then spasm beneath his skin. He says nothing, so I ramp up the pressure. "You've managed to climb pretty high…for a bastard." The second I speak the words I feel the air shift, like the crackle of electricity in the atmosphere before a storm. Outwardly, he doesn't move. His gaze remains fixed on the road, but his posture tenses, his knuckles turning white on the steering wheel.

"Stop talking, Una," he says on a low growl.

I'm close. "I want to know what a bastard enforcer is doing with the underboss of the Italian mob. I want to know how someone of your stature was able to dig up my sister. How is it that you have your own brother killed and manage to walk into being capo?" The car slams to a halt before we even exit the parking garage, thrusting me forward against my seatbelt. We sit for a second, the engine idling, and neither of us saying anything. He turns that icy glare on me, pinning me to the spot.

"If I wanted you to know anything, I would have told you. I don't trust you, Morte."

"And you're not telling me anything, so I don't trust you."

He smirks. "Just remember that this situation is mutually beneficial. I don't give a fuck if you trust me, I don't need you to, you don't need me to. Simply trust in the fact that I have something you want and you have something I need."

"Lies. You don't need me. My bullet or yours, they both end the same way. You need someone to blame. I'm not sure whether I should be offended or flattered that I'm the one whose back you've decided to put a target on."

His eyes trace over my face, my lips, my throat. I feel like a rabbit caught in a trap, waiting for the big bad wolf to take a bite. "You're everyone's exception," he says simply.

"What?"

"Arnaldo, Nicholai, the cartel...they all turn a blind eye to you."

I lift my chin defiantly. "Because I'm neutral. I told you, I don't take sides."

"You're not taking sides now."

Oh, but I am. For Anna. And for all of me saying I don't trust Nero, weirdly, I think I do. Every rational fiber of me knows he's dangerous. Every ingrained piece of training is screaming that I know better. And yet...aren't we already allies in a twisted way? I killed his brother and essentially made him capo. He found my sister where I never could, and now we're here, bartering, tentatively trying to outmaneuver each other. The thing is, I trust him more *because* he's blackmailing me. I may not understand his motivations, but I know that he wants something and is prepared to give in exchange. It's a simple concept.

"And now my sister is in hell, but you won't help her until I kill your list, all of whom are practically untouchable."

"If there is one thing I have witnessed in this world, it's the lengths people will go to for love. Even death herself is affected by its illness," he says coldly.

"Are you going to tell me what you're doing to get Anna back?"

"No, just know that I can pull strings and reach people that you couldn't hope to yourself." He leans in, stroking a finger down my cheek. I tear my face away from him but he grips my jaw, dragging my face towards him. If I wanted to, I could break his wrist, but I don't. All I should feel is hate, and loathe his touch, but I don't, because when he touches me like this, I don't feel the usual ingrained instinct to kill. It's as though all my conditioning can be overridden by his cruelty. It's a strange thing, to never be able to tolerate human touch. And the second that I can, I crave it, no matter its form. Nero is this warped exception to everything I know, as though he is above the law of physics themselves.

"And now I'm your Russian dog, chained and leashed, doing your bidding," I whisper.

He drags me to him, brushing his lips over mine. "You're not a dog, Una. You're a dragon, a thing of myth and whispers." His teeth graze my bottom lip and a ragged breath falls from my lips. "You ask me what I want. It's simple. I want power. With you, I will burn everything to the ground." A maniacal smile works over his lips and that darkness of his calls to me on every level, to the monster that I am. His fingers squeeze harder, forcing my head back. I relish in the touch because it's hard and angry, passion laced with hate.

"How?"

"Power is nothing more than a game of strategy, a chessboard. You are my queen, Morte, the most valuable piece on the board."

"Queen protects king," I whisper. Or in this case, the queen is a body shield for the king.

"Queen takes all." His fingers dig into my cheeks before his lips press against mine, rough and brief before he shoves me away from him like an unwanted toy.

CHAPTER THIRTEEN

Nero

S tay in the car." I throw the door open. She gets out and I glare at her over the roof. "Was I speaking a foreign language?"

She cocks a brow. "I didn't leave your apartment to sit in your car."

"I didn't bring you with me for a day trip. I brought you because Tommy is busy –"

"Ah, yes, driving Zeus to his appointment with a tree to take a piss on."

"– and you can't be trusted on your own."

"So now I'm the untrustworthy one? As I recall, I came of my own free will."

"Fucking women, you're all the same, don't listen to shit," I grumble, turning my back and heading towards the stairwell.

"Careful, capo. I'm the one who brought the gun, remember?" She falls in step beside me, and low and behold, she has her gun strapped to her damn thigh.

"This is a government building."

"So, take the service entrance."

Stopping, I grab her arm, turning her to face me. She tenses and I smirk. I've learned with her, that it's the casual touches that make her uncomfortable. Grab her by her throat or grip her arm hard enough to break it and she's fine. Finger-fuck her, and it's tentative, but it seems pleasure can tamper her bloodlust. "This is not a tactical assault. I told you, it's not a gun affair. It's a meeting."

"I thought that was mafia code for kill someone." She raises both eyebrows as though this should be obvious.

"What? No." I shake my head. "Jesus. Look, lose the gun or wait in the fucking car." She rolls her eyes and unbuckles the holster from around her thigh, dropping to a crouch and sliding it across the parking garage floor until it comes to a halt beneath the car fifty yards away.

"Happy?" she scowls. I eye the cuff at her wrist. "Don't even think about it." She struts past me, hips swaying in a way that I don't think she's even aware of. Damn, her ass looks good in those pants.

I have a meeting arranged with Gerard Brown, otherwise known as the current Port Authority Chief. Of course, he doesn't realize it's me he's meeting with, simply the director of

Horizon Logistics, a legitimate company that, as it happens, I own. His secretary shows us to his office, eyeing Una the entire time. I don't blame her. Nothing about Una fits into normal society unless she's forced to. Give her a job, tell her she has to play the mayor's wife and she'll pull that shit off no problem, but in her natural state, people become wary of her. It's the same way an antelope can sense the presence of a lion. Their instincts tell them she's dangerous and yet they trust what their eyes see, that she's just a tiny, pretty little woman.

Gerard Brown is a middle-aged guy with a beer gut, an ill-fitting suit and a moustache that looks like he stole it from the set of a seventies porn film. That said, this is the man that controls all of the docks in New York City. Nothing comes in or out without his say-so, and it just so happens that Finnegan O'Hara has his say-so. Whether he knows about the nature of O'Hara's dealings, it's impossible to say.

"Mr Brown. Thank you for seeing me on such short notice." He holds his hand out and I shake it. His thick eyebrows pull into a frown, and he squints behind his glasses.

"I'm sorry, you'll have to forgive me, but I don't know your name. My secretary –"

"Was never told it," I finish for him, taking a seat in the leather chair across from him. He sits and places his palms flat on the desk, subtly glancing at Una where she stands with her back to the wall, placed exactly between the window and the door. "I am Nero Verdi."

His face pales and he leans back in his chair, trying to put as much distance between us as possible. "Mr. Verdi." He tugs at his collar and a thin sheen of sweat blossoms on his skin.

I cross my ankle over my knee and brush my pant leg with a smile. "I see my reputation proceeds me. Good. This should go quickly then." He squeezes his eyes shut and swallows heavily. "You have a working relationship with Finnegan O'Hara."

"Please. I don't want any trouble –"

"You handle his shipments, which means you know when the next one's coming in…when he's coming in. No?"

He shakes his head. "No, I don't know."

"What kind of chief doesn't know what's coming into his own ports?" I fix my gaze on him and he visibly flinches. This will be easy.

"Please, I don't –"

"You're boring me." Una sighs, pushing off the wall. She grabs him around the throat, shoving him back in the chair as she takes a seat on the desk. "When is he coming into the city?" Nothing. "I'm going to count to three," she says the words so sweetly. "One, two, three." The blade at her wrist drops into her hand and she grips it, driving it towards his face. He shrieks and braces. There's a beat of silence, a tense moment before he opens his eyes and finds the point of the blade poised millimeters from his right eye. She wraps her free hand around the back of his neck and pulls him towards her, cradling his head against her chest as if he were a small child. "You don't need your eyes to talk, Gerard," she whispers before stroking her fingers down his cheek. She then puts the blade away and hops down off the desk, returning to her spot by the wall.

I glance over my shoulder at her and adjust in my seat because my dick is uncomfortably hard. Damn, it's the way she handles everything, so calm, yet so psychotic. Turning back to face Gerard, I cock a brow at him. He's trembling and about to spill his guts, because if he doesn't, Una will cut his fucking eyes out of his head. I know it and he knows it.

Una bristles with attitude and impatience as I step into the elevator. Accordingly, I'm agitated and pissed off. My skin feels too tight for my body and my dick will not let up. My balls are starting to ache, bringing about a whole new meaning to blue balls.

The second the doors glide shut I turn on her, pressing my hand against the centre of her chest and shoving her against the mirrored wall of the elevator. Her eyes narrow but she makes no other move to stop me. "At any point, did I ask for your help?" I'm not really pissed off about it. I'm pissed off because I want to fuck her, but that's not rational.

She slaps my hand away from her chest, which just serves to eliminate the only thing between us. Her chest brushes against mine, the tension in this confined metal box becomes stifling. "The civilized bullshit doesn't suit you." She smirks, dragging her gaze from my eyes to my lips and back again. "Don't pretend you're not every bit as monstrous as I am, Nero." She strokes her hand down my chest, my stomach, skimming over my crotch. I clench my teeth and suck in a sharp breath. "You're worse."

Her lips barely touch mine and I have to bite back a groan. Fuck, fuck, fuck! For a second, I lose track of everything that isn't her, her tight body, her perfect lips, her lethal words. And then I manage to get a handle on it. Just.

"I am," I agree, stepping back and smoothing a hand down the front of my jacket. "But cutting people's eyes out..." I tilt my head to the side. "It's not the mafia way."

The elevator pings and the doors slide open. She strides past me. "You know the thing that pisses me off about the mafia?"

"I'm sure you'll enlighten me."

She stops next to the car, spinning on her heel to face me. "If

117

you're bad, just be bad. Why wear a white hat?"

Before I can respond, she drops to her knees on the dirty concrete of the parking garage and I lift a brow. She rolls her eyes. "Not likely," she grumbles before lowering herself to the ground and reaching underneath the car, coming back out with her gun. She climbs to her feet and fastens it back in place. Huh, I never realized how naked she looked without it until she put it back on. My vicious butterfly. My lethal queen.

CHAPTER FOURTEEN

Una

"So, Finnegan's going to be here in three days?" Leaning back in my seat, I pull one knee up, bracing my boot against the edge of Nero's expensive leather.

"Yeah, him and half an army of IRA guys."

The car winds through the streets of New York and the sun is just starting to drop between the skyscrapers, painting the sky in streaks of pink and purple. "Bernardo and Franco aren't in the city for another two weeks," I murmur.

"Okay, so we hit O'Hara, then Marco, and wait for Bernardo and Franco."

"Oh, it's 'we' now?"

"It's always been 'we'," he remarks quietly while turning the car at a junction. "You aren't doing this *for* me, Morte. You're helping me, so I help you. Remember that."

He's a bastard, he really is. His phone rings, the sound blasting from the car speakers loudly. He clicks a button on the steering wheel.

"Yeah?"

"Boss, I have a gentleman here who wants to talk to you. Seems the Los Carlos think they're getting an unfair deal." I think it's Jackson, and even I can hear the amusement in his voice. He's the only one of the three whose voice I'm not very familiar with.

"Where?" Nero asks.

"The club."

"On my way." The line goes dead and he turns the steering wheel hard, sending the car screeching down a side road.

"Trouble in paradise?" I drawl.

He looks at me and holds my gaze far longer than he should considering he's driving. "Par for the course, Morte."

The Los Carlos are a smaller gang here in the city, heavily involved in drugs and seemingly supplied by Nero. The Italians have always run the cocaine trade in New York and they probably always will.

Eventually, he pulls the car up outside of a dirty looking little club in Hunts Point, South Bronx. A couple of guys in suits linger just outside the door, guns in hand. When Nero gets out of the car they speak in quick fire Italian. This isn't my business and has nothing to do with why I'm here. I should stay out of it, and yet I find myself opening the door. Morbid curiosity has me climbing out of the car. I pull my hood up as I follow Nero to the door, and he makes no move to stop me.

Inside, it's just as much of a shithole. The floors are sticky and the walls and ceiling are so tarnished with nicotine they're stained a dull brown. Smoke seems to hang in the air as if it's a permanent feature. An old jukebox in the corner is playing some soul music quietly, and in front of us, sprawled across the black and white tile floor are two bodies. Both are Latino, and neither of them can be older than twenty. Jackson stands with his back to us, toe to toe with another kid. This one is maybe twenty-five at a push. He squares up to Jackson, gun in hand. Ten other guys are fanned out behind him, standing amongst the scattered tables and chairs that fill the bar. It looks like the scene of some cliché gangster film.

Nero pulls out a chair and takes a seat. Slowly reaching inside his jacket pocket, he takes out a packet of cigarettes, sliding one free. Everyone in the room has their eyes on him, watching, waiting. He places the cigarette between his lips and lights it. The heavy click of the lighter snapping shut is like a gunshot in the room. The guy across from Jackson starts to fidget and Jackson moves away, coming to stand behind Nero. The smirk on his face is part mocking and part genuine amusement. I remain completely removed off to the side of the room with my back to the wall. The safest place you can ever be is with a wall at your back, because people can't walk or shoot through walls.

Nero still says nothing and the tension in the room makes the young guy squirm. "Look, man, we want a bigger cut. Forty percent." He shifts his shoulders from side to side, acting the big man.

Nero leans forward, bracing his elbows on spread thighs. The cigarette hangs between his fingers, spilling ash onto the tiled floor. He couldn't look any more out of place here if he tried. So perfect in his expensive suit, immaculate and beautiful, dark

121

and deadly. Ten armed men face him and yet he never looks out of control. He never ceases to be the ultimate danger in the room.

Sighing, he gets to his feet and holds his hand out. Jackson wordlessly places a gun in Nero's waiting palm. They all reach for their weapons, but he remains relaxed, arrogant as he walks up to the kid and stares him in the eye before lifting the gun to his head. The kid opens his mouth, his eyes going wide...BANG. My fingers are wrapped around my gun, ready, waiting for the impending hailstorm of bullets. It doesn't happen. Yet.

"This is my fucking city!" Nero roars, eyeing them one by one. "And if you bite the hand that feeds you, I will put you down like a rabid dog." He points his gun at the ground and fires off two more shots at the dead body of their former leader. "Does anyone else want a bigger fucking cut?"

No one says anything. He hands the gun back to Jackson and straightens the cuff of his shirt. So civilized, yet so feral. "Now, if I have to come down to this shithole again, if I so much as hear a whisper of a problem..." He looks up, his expression speaking of destruction and war. "I won't kill you. I'll kill your wives, your girlfriends, your fucking children and your mothers." His voice gets steadily louder until it's like thunder, rumbling off the walls. "I suggest you don't test me." And then he turns his back and walks out.

Some people make threats, meaningless words and posturing. But Nero's soulless, and anyone can see it. When he says he's going to slaughter your family, you damn well believe him. Whoever said it wasn't better to be feared than respected? Somehow he achieves both.

"So was that the mafia way?" I follow him to the car. He simply glares at me and gets in. I snort. "I thought you guys were all about leaving the women out of it."

"I play by a different set of rules."

Indeed, he does. Nero Verdi will use whatever he has at his disposal to keep people in line, honour or ethics be damned.

"You know, it's situations like these where you should probably have your own gun," I say, fastening my seatbelt.

He starts the car. "Haven't you figured it out yet, Morte? I don't need guns. I only have to say the word and someone dies." And I can't help but be in awe of his sheer arrogance. To stand in the middle of ten guys and shoot their leader in the head. It's like he's invincible.

By the time we get back to the apartment, Tommy is already there, waiting. George runs up to me as soon as I walk in the door, whining excitedly. Taking a seat at the breakfast bar, I open my laptop, staring at the minimized window in the bottom left corner. Anna. Maybe it's just a twisted brand of self-torture, but I click it, opening up the box. She's lying on the bed, alone this time. Her too thin body curled in on itself. Seeing her so fractured makes my very soul hurt. I press my palm against my forehead and rest my elbow on the side, staring at the image of her.

"Una." I hadn't heard Nero come up behind me, which is all the proof I need that I'm not focused. Anna complicates things, but I can't see past her. He reaches around me and clicks a button, closing out the window. "Don't look at it," he says quietly. His body lingers so close, right behind me without touching. He brushes my hair off my shoulder, but again, his fingers never make contact with my skin. For a second, I find myself wanting his touch, but he steps back and all I hear are footsteps as he walks away. I need focus. Pain and blood, the promise of death. I need to remember what I am, to feel that cool indifference, the methodical application of force and consequence. I can't save Anna and I need to take it out on someone, or something.

I find myself in the gym, staring at the heavy bag. Plugging in my iPod, I blast heavy rock until the beat rumbles the floor beneath my feet. Cracking my neck from side to side, I go to town. The force of my bare fists colliding with the canvas of the bag quickly has my knuckles splitting. Blood coats the bag and my fists, but I don't care. I like the pain, the feeling of age-old scar tissue tearing apart again and again. I stop only when my body is soaked in sweat and my lungs are heaving for breath. A brush of contact on my arm has me whirling around, fists raised. Nero smirks, but the expression slips and his eyes narrow as he looks at my blood-stained hands.

"Tearing your fists up isn't going to get her back any faster," he remarks dryly. That uncomfortable feeling settles in my chest again, so I turn and hit the bag. Getting in three strikes before his arms wrap around me and he crosses my own arms over my torso, pinning them in place. I fight to get free, but just end up fighting myself. His breath blows over my neck in slow even draws. "Stop, Morte."

"Fuck you, Nero." My voice cracks slightly, frustration and helplessness seeping through.

He huffs a laugh and releases me. I whirl to face him and his eyes lock with mine for a beat before he slides his jacket off his shoulders and starts yanking at his tie. Dropping them to the floor, he then begins to unbutton his shirt. The material parts, revealing tanned skin over hard muscles. Tattoos appear beneath the veneer of his expensive suit.

"You want to hit something?" He spreads his arms wide. "Don't pretend you don't want a shot at me."

He moves, and I trace over the tight muscles of his stomach, bunched and ready. Clenching and releasing my bloodied fists, I mimic his movements. The corner of his lip twitches and an infuriatingly cocky smirk appears. I was always taught that if outmatched or outsized by an opponent, let them come to you. Defend, then attack. Right now though, I don't listen to any of it. The urge to take out every inch of my frustrations on Nero's perfect face drives me. I lunge and land a punch to his jaw. His head snaps to the side and he spits out a mouthful of blood.

"Feel good?" he asks on a grin.

"Not nearly enough." I hit him three more times and he let's me, before rearing back and nailing me in the gut. I cough and stagger back a step as I force my lungs to drag in a breath despite my paralyzed diaphragm.

He cracks his neck to the side and bounces on the balls of his feet, his arms hanging loose at his sides. "Don't think I'll go easy on you because you're a girl." We go toe-to-toe, catching each other with blows and ducking away. He grabs me around the throat and uses it to pull me close to him.

"So vicious, Morte," he purrs, his breathing heavy. I gasp for air and his eyes drop to my lips. He inches closer, until I punch him in the gut. Grunting, he lets go and hits me hard in the face. The taste of blood in my mouth elicits a laugh. I lunge towards him again but he swipes my legs out from under me, my back hitting the unforgiving floor of the gym. I roll onto my front, ready to push up, but he lands on my back, his entire weight pushing me into the mat beneath me.

One hand wraps around my throat from behind, whilst the other grips my hip. He's shameless in pressing his dick against my ass, rolling his hips against me. Lust and rage are so very close together, mixing and swirling into something explosive and raw. His lips brush over the side of my neck and hot, erratic breaths blow over my skin, making me shiver. "You done?" he asks in a patronizing as fuck tone.

Fuck him. I try to jab my elbow into him but can't do shit from where I am. He laughs and grabs both my arms, pinning them down beside my hips. His body shifts, and he slides away from me. Warm lips touch the exposed strip of skin at my lower back and I gasp, shaking beneath the brief contact. He flips me over and my skin erupts in goose bumps when his lips skate over my hipbone now. The bloodlust wavers for a second, giving way to an entirely different kind of lust. I grab a handful of his hair and use it to pull his face up. His eyes follow the length of my body, and the look in them has my resolve wavering. His palms inch over my stomach, pushing the material of my top up as he goes. My heart pounds, the rhythm getting faster and faster the higher his hands move. By the time his face is hovering over mine, I can barely breathe. Blood trickles from the corner of his lip and already his jawline is splotched in angry red marks.

When his lips crash over mine, he starts an entirely new fight. Teeth rake over my split lip and I hiss at the sting, gripping his hair and pulling hard. Winding his fingers around my jaw, he cranks my head back, forcing my lips to part wider for him. He doesn't just kiss me, he throws down a gauntlet, declaring war with every violent swipe of his tongue. I shove against his chest and he pulls back an inch. That's when I slap him, yes, I slap him like a girl. His head twists to the side before he very slowly brings his gaze back to mine. Those whiskey irises swirl dangerously and there it is; fear, reaching out with cold fingers. I smile and lean into its touch, relishing in the frantic pounding of my heart, the instinctual trembling of my body. Nero scares me and it's such a rare gift, one that no one else has ever given me.

Grabbing me by my throat, he wrenches me off the floor, tearing my shirt over my head before dropping me like dead weight. Then he's yanking at the button of my pants, dragging them down my legs. I barely get a chance to think about what that means before he's over me again, his hard body between my legs and his rough lips moving against mine.

He has me in a trance of sorts, caught somewhere between lust and rage. All I can feel is him, all I can think about is his hands on me, his tongue in my mouth, his raw brutality. I want to be on the receiving end of Nero. I need him at his worst, to make me fear him, and he gives me all of that and more, demanding and taking what he wants from me. Under his touch I feel alive. *I feel.* All my training, my past, my wariness of him, everything

126

I know I should do…it all disappears. All that matters is this exact moment. It's the kind of weakness that gets you killed, but I can't even summon the will to care.

I hear the clink of his belt buckle, feel the harsh grip of his fingers on my hips, the tearing of material. And then nothing but the hot press of his cock against me, pushing, threatening. Wrenching my hips up, with almost no warning, he slams inside me in one brutal thrust. All the air leaves my lungs, and my nails rake over the back of his neck, making him growl like the feral beast he is. My pussy clenches around him as shock waves ripple through my core. I've never felt so utterly invaded and it's both uncomfortable and welcome. His forehead falls to mine and I close my eyes, inhaling a staggered breath, breathing in the scent of his cologne, the hint of cigarette smoke.

A broken groan works its way up his throat. "You feel so fucking good, Morte." He pulls out and pushes back in, dragging a gasp from me. "So fucking tight," he growls against my mouth.

I want him to stop talking and just fuck me, so I press my lips to his. He groans into my mouth, slamming his hips into me, pushing me to the point of pain on every thrust. I like it, I need it. The pain is what drives me; the pain is what pushes me to the limit. The more he fucks me, the more rabid he gets until his fingers are digging into my skin and his kisses become bites. Everything about him savage and animalistic. He fucks me like he's trying to kill me, and I embrace the threat, daring him on as he wages sweet war on my body. I bite his bottom lip and my mouth fills with the metallic tang of his blood. My core starts to tighten, winding up and up until I feel like I can't take any more. One hand dives into my hair, wrenching my head back. His other hand slips between our bodies, where he pinches my clit at the same time he bites down on my neck, hard. I lose it. Screaming, writhing, shattering apart beneath him.

"I want to tear you apart," he growls, pinching my jaw between his teeth. The orgasm reigns on and on, slowly tearing

127

me apart before putting me back together again. My body falls limp, and he drives into me hard and fast three more times. Then his head falls back, and the sound that leaves his lips is so guttural, so primal, that it makes me shiver. The roped muscles of his neck pop out and then his abs tense as his body jerks. I've never seen a man look more vulnerable or more powerful than he does in this moment. He finally stills and pitches forward, bracing his hands on either side of my body as his chin touches his chest. A drop of sweat rolls down the center of his chest, winding between the angry claw marks that mar his skin.

It's only when my pulse slows and the aftermath of my orgasm fades that I start to feel uncomfortable. I just fucked him. And that's the last thing I need to be doing with Nero Verdi of all people. He just…he makes me burn for him. He feeds into every element of my nature, stoking the flames of my violence until it's an inferno. We're fire and gasoline, the perfect combination, the perfect disaster.

"*Now* do you feel good?" He cocks a brow.

Feigning indifference, I roll my eyes and shove him off me, climbing to my feet. I don't even bother putting clothes on. I just walk straight through the apartment and head to my room.

When I've showered, I lay in bed, staring at the ceiling. I don't even know what I'm doing anymore. It feels like everything I once was is slipping away, and I'm becoming something else entirely. I'm Una Ivanov, the kiss of death, ruthless, efficient, professional. It's like that person doesn't even exist here, in this apartment. I'm becoming someone who acts on impulse, without thought, driven by emotion and…cravings. That hardened mask I've worn for so many years now evades me, and I'm not sure I want it back. It's true that not feeling anything always kept me safe, focused, efficient, but it's like Nero pressed a defibrillator to my chest and shocked me to life, first with anger and hate, then with my love for Anna and the pain that followed, and now…now this lust that feels so wild and uncontrollable. Despite every ingrained bit of conditioning and any basic level of common sense that is screaming at me not to do it, I can't help myself. I have never felt more alive than when his lips are on me, his fingers threatening both pain and pleasure. I've never fucked a man because I wanted to, but with Nero it doesn't even feel like a choice, more like a need. But none of this changes the reality that I shouldn't even be in a professional relationship with him, let alone whatever this is. Nicholai would be so ashamed of me.

There's a soft knock at the door before it opens a crack. Nero walks in the room, wearing only a loose-fitting pair of tracksuit bottoms. His hair is wet from the shower, the strands swept back haphazardly.

"You'll need these." He holds up some bandages and approaches the bed. I sit up, crossing my legs as he takes a seat on the edge of the mattress. Reaching for me, he wraps his fingers around my wrist, pulling my hand towards him. A small frown line sinks between his eyebrows as he focuses on my hands, bandaging my ripped knuckles with strong but gentle hands. The gesture seems so at odds with everything he is. Bruises are already blossoming across his jaw in varying shades of purple.

"You should put some ice on your face."

His lips curl at one side, but his gaze never wavers from my hands. "That would just spoil your handiwork." When he's finished, he stands up and leaves. Just like that. I don't pretend to have a clue when it comes to…these things, but I've never been so confused. Perhaps we're just pretending that didn't happen.

CHAPTER FIFTEEN

Una

O'Malley's is an Irish bar in Woodlawn. The outside has tinted windows with dark green paint peeling off the frames and an old steel door that looks like it's seen better days. If I didn't already know that it was the epicenter of the New York Irish Mafia, I might have guessed. Although, right now, Tommy and I are just ignorant tourists stopping by an authentic Irish bar. When we step inside, I can practically feel how nervous Tommy is. I persuaded him to bring me here after Nero left early this morning. He wasn't keen and I know Nero would probably lose it if he knew we were here, but he asked me to do a job, and this is me doing it.

The guys sitting at the bar turn, eyeing us as we step inside. I flash them a grin and they slowly focus their attention on me. Tommy looks Irish, but I don't want them looking too closely.

If there's one thing to be said for mafia it's that everyone knows everyone else, and someone of Tommy's heritage will undoubtedly be memorable.

The barman braces his hands on the edge of the thick mahogany bar, a frown pulling his eyebrows together.

"Hi. Can I get a vodka on the rocks and a whisky?" I want them to think we're just two punters that have walked in off the street. Not that this place exactly attracts the average passer-by.

The man grunts some form of response before turning away and grabbing glasses.

"Ah, don't mind him, darlin'," one of the guys says in a thick Irish accent, flashing me a wink. He's a guy in his thirties maybe, with dirty blond hair and blue eyes that dance with humour. "Wouldn't know a good woman if she were to slap him upside the head. And you…" He flicks his eyes down my body, straightening the shirt of his collar with a cocky grin. "…are a mighty fine looking gal."

Slipping on the mask of a nice normal girl is as easy as putting on a jacket. Smiling, I lean my elbow on the bar. "My father always said, never trust an Irish boy."

"Ah, and why's that?"

"Because you'd charm the birds out of the sky," I reply, cocking a brow.

"Aye!" His friend laughs beside him, slapping him on the back. "This one would charm the knickers off a gal in a heartbeat."

The barman puts the drinks on the bar, and I hand him some money before turning away. "Nice talking to you." There's raucous laughter as I turn my back and it's decidedly less tense than when we walked in. We sit at a table in the corner, and I position myself with my back to the wall.

"I don't like this shit," Tommy grumbles, taking a heavy gulp of the whisky.

I sigh. "Keep your panties on. We'll sit. We'll drink. I'll go to the bathroom in a bit and scout an exit. Then we can go." I want to hit O'Hara here, because it's the last place he would expect, and the only place I know he'll come.

Tommy drums his fingers against his glass. Anyone looking at him would know, clear as day, he's agitated. I decide to speed things up and down my drink, before standing. The door at the back of the bar leads to a short passageway with ladies and gents toilets. I pass the bathroom door and follow the corridor that hooks right. Sure enough, at the end there is a fire exit, but it's locked, literally chained up and padlocked. Shit. Turning around, I freeze when I find the blond guy from the bar leaning against the wall, his arms folded over his chest and a wry smile on his face. A cigarette hangs from his fingers and he slowly brings it to his lips, narrowing his eyes as the smoke drifts up around his face.

"Ya lost?"

Shit.

I paint a smile on my lips. "I'm looking for the bathroom."

He jerks his head towards the corridor behind him. "Ya walked past it."

"Oh, thanks." I squeeze past him and he makes no effort to get out of my way. I can't work out whether he's onto me or if he's just trying to get in my pants. The second I get in the bathroom, I walk into a stall and bolt the door, bracing my back against it. The last thing I need is them taking too much notice of me. I need to come back in here when O'Hara is here, but then if this is anything to go by, I'm not going to go unnoticed regardless of whether blondie has made me or not. This is a mafia bar. They know everyone, see everything. Unless…

I open the stall and quickly wash my hands before stepping back outside. Sure enough, blondie is still in his spot, smoking his cigarette. I throw him a glance, making sure I lock eyes with him before open the door. I walk straight over to the bar.

"Do you have a pen?" I ask the barman. He hands me one, his surly scowl still firmly in place.

I grab one of the cardboard beer mats, the Guinness emblem all over it. I scrawl the number of one of my burner phones along with the name Isabelle onto the worn cardboard. I hand it to blondie's friend who watches me the entire time. "What's your friend's name?" I ask.

"Darren," he replies before taking a gulp of his beer.

I nod. "Give this to him, will you?

He chuckles, taking it from me. "I surely will, sweet thing."

I walk away and Tommy follows me to the exit. "What the fuck was that?" he hisses once we're outside.

"My in." We walk down the street, away from the bar.

"Nero's going to kill me."

"Nero wants O'Hara dead. He can suck it up."

CHAPTER SIXTEEN

Nero

I meet Gio at the docks and stand on the wharf, watching as police swarm around a shipment on dock twelve. The sun is starting to set and they're rigging up flood lighting to work by. It's a massive shipping container and admittedly, they could be looking for anything, but I don't believe in coincidences. They're settling in for a long night, and I have two hundred grand in cocaine coming in on that boat. It's just a matter of time before they find it. I'm out of pocket, there's no coke to go onto the streets, no revenue for me to send to the cartel. I want to know who the fuck ratted me out.

"Call Tommy, tell him to speak to his contacts at the precinct. I want to know where they got a tip-off."

Gio walks away from me, phone already in hand. Meanwhile, I call Jackson because I'm pretty sure I know exactly who it is. "Boss."

"I have a job for you…"

As soon as I step into my apartment, I see George sitting down right outside the gym. When I open the door, I'm greeted with Tommy's cry of pain followed by Una's laugh. She's on the floor and he's on top of her, his hands braced on either side of her small body. He's topless and she's wearing workout pants and a top that exposes her stomach. It would look intimate if she didn't have one leg looped around the back of his neck and her hand wrapped around her ankle, choking him out. Although, he doesn't look entirely upset with her crotch in his face.

"Tap out!" she shouts. His face has turned red and any minute now he's going to pass out. "Aw, Tommy." She ruffles his hair with her free hand as he loses consciousness. I've been trying to call him all damn day and he hasn't answered, and now I find him here, all over Una. She collapses back on the floor, her chest heaving as Tommy's limp body rests over her. My fuse is already burnt out today and the way her thighs are wrapped around him, his bare skin against hers… It has something hot and fast tearing through me. An irrational rage grips me, and I'm ready to shoot the fucker.

"I thought you didn't like being touched?" Even I can hear the accusing note in my voice.

Her eyes snap open and she lifts her head. "I don't."

Moving forward, I kick Tommy's unconscious body to the side. She lies on the floor while I stand over her, staring at her

136

exposed stomach, the swell of her breasts in that skimpy top. I clench and release my fists, wanting to fuck her and fight her, preferably at the same time.

"Looks like it." She glares back at me, lips pressing together in a tight line.

Tommy groans and slowly sits up, clutching his neck. "Fuck, Una, that hurts." She hops to her feet and shrugs, flashing him a wink and a genuine smile. Again, I don't like it.

I grab him by the scruff of his neck and drag him to his feet. "Where the hell have you been all day, Tommy, huh?"

His eyes go wide and his face drains of all colour. "I...uh, here, boss."

"I called you ten fucking times." I shove him away before I pound my fists into his face. I want to destroy everything in my damn path right now because I lost. Someone got one up on me. "Call the cops. I want to know who tipped them off about my shipment." He nods quickly. This is the one job I entrust to him, handle the cops, know what they know. He can be their best fucking friend for all I care as long as he gets me what I want, when I damn well want it. "Now get out," I snap. He rubs his hand over his neck, staggering towards the door. "And, Tommy... Don't touch her again." He nods and hurries away.

"What the fuck?" Una glares at me. When I don't answer, she rolls her eyes and walks out. When I step out, Tommy is lingering just outside the door pulling his shirt on. Una is heading towards the living area.

"Sorry, boss. I didn't realize..." He trails off. "I mean, it's not...I just let her kick my ass, that's all."

"Stop talking. Do what I pay you for."

CHAPTER SEVENTEEN

Una

I strip out of my workout pants, throwing them in the corner angrily. He's jealous. When the hell did we get into any kind of territory where jealousy was a factor? What is this, the middle ages? And Tommy, really? Shit. I go into the bathroom and start the shower. Gripping the edge of the sink I lean over it, trying to calm my erratic pulse as I wait for the water to become red hot. When I look up, I make out a dark figure in the foggy reflection of the mirror and turn around. Nero leans against the doorframe, his thick arms folded over his chest and a scowl on his face.

"Get out."

He completely ignores me, moving closer. "No." His body presses against mine, backing me into the counter. He towers over me, the soft material of his shirt brushing against my bare stomach as his fingers wrap around my jaw. His eyes are dark and turbulent, the threat lurking just beneath the surface. Tension radiates off him in waves that has my heart skittering in my chest like a startled animal. His mood is pitch-black tonight and I'd be lying if I said it didn't scare me.

"You don't let Tommy touch you." The low rumble of his chest vibrates against me.

I shove at him but he doesn't budge. "You're seriously jealous? You realize that's totally irrational?" He says nothing, and I shake my head. "Fuck you, Nero."

"Gladly, but I don't share, Morte."

"I'm not yours *to* share."

"You don't think so? Too bad."

His hand slips from my face, wrapping around the back of my neck before he slams his lips over mine. I rake my nails down the side of his neck and attempt to bring my knee up between his legs, but it does nothing. A low laugh rumbles against my lips before his teeth skim my bottom lip and his tongue demands entrance. My lips part and his tongue lashing against mine is nothing short of an assault. This isn't a kiss, it's a statement. I don't know how he can make me want to fuck him and slit his throat all in the same breath. That fog descends until all I can think of, feel, smell is him. He's toxic in the most addictive way. Releasing my jaw, he trails his fingers up my back, reaching for the clasp of my bra. With the briefest flick of his wrist, it comes loose and he drops his face to my chest. I gasp when his teeth clamp around my nipple, my fingers flying to his hair, needing more of his warm mouth on me. He works a burning trail down my sides until he's grabbing the material of my panties and sliding them over my thighs. A small voice in my head screams at me to stop this, but he renders me so weak. Gripping my waist, he lifts me onto the counter, and teeth sink into my neck as he wrenches my thighs apart. Tremors rip over my skin as I watch him watching me, those dark eyes igniting as he drags them over my naked body. He's still fully clothed, and I reach for the buttons of his shirt but he grips my wrist, pushing it away.

"I want to watch you shatter, Morte." I can see his dick tenting his pants from here, and yet he still makes no move to get undressed. Lips brush over my cheek before he pinches my jaw between his teeth. "I want to taste your tight little pussy." And then he drops to his knees in front of me, spreading my legs wide until my pussy is completely on display for him. A pained groan escapes his throat before he buries his face between my legs. My mouth falls open on a silent scream, and I grip his hair, pulling him closer. His hot tongue lashes across my clit; every nerve feeling like it's being electrocuted. His fingers dig into my thighs, holding me open to him, exposed. I can't feel anything but that exact pinpoint of pressure where his tongue meets me, and the hard scratch of his stubble against the soft skin of my inner thighs. Within seconds he has me moaning and writhing, rolling my hips against his face and begging him for something, anything. And then he stops.

"Look at me," he rumbles.

I drop my eyes to his, panting heavily as I watch him drag his tongue slowly up the length of my pussy. Oh god.

"Now tell me you're mine." A twisted grin lights his expression before he pushes his tongue inside me. It's too much and yet, not enough. Teeth clamp down on my clit, and I whimper, my body trembling, right on the edge. "Say it." He blows warm breath over my sensitive flesh. I clench my jaw, refusing to say the words he wants to hear. I haven't fallen so far from grace that I'll give him that.

He huffs a laugh and pushes to his feet, gripping my face in both hands. His lips are covered in my pussy and he slams them over mine so hard that his teeth click against mine. The salty taste of myself dances along my tongue as it meets his. And then he breaks away, taking a clear step away from me. "Like I said, too bad." He narrows his eyes and feigns a smile, but I can see the tension around his eyes. It mimics my own. I refuse to renege, even if my pussy is throbbing and my entire body feels like it might explode. He turns and walks out of the bathroom. Asshole.

I make a clear attempt to avoid Nero for the rest of the evening. Not that it's hard; he's been in his office ever since I got out of the shower. This situation has flipped in what feels like the blink of an eye. I went from the girl he was blackmailing to the girl he fucked and now, apparently, he thinks he has some kind of claim on me. Perhaps he does. I know I could never feel this unhinged for anyone but him. Nero Verdi is a rule unto himself, a complete anomaly to everything. He doesn't need to know that though. I've already exposed too many weaknesses to him; I won't give him any more.

I steal one of his shirts because I've run out of clean clothes and apparently he has no washing machine. Figures. Not like he's going to wash his own clothes. I hope it pisses him off, and then I hope he does something about it. Oh, how I'd love to make him bleed right now. Grabbing my laptop, I go to the living room, taking a seat on the uncomfortable couch. I throw myself into work, devising my plan to take out the three Italians on his list in the space of just one week. This situation with Nero is hurtling into dangerous territory very quickly. I'm losing control and I need to get this done and get out before I completely lose all semblance of sanity. I'm staring at my laptop screen when my phone rings. Not my normal phone, my burner.

I answer it. "Hello."

"Isabelle." That Irish lilt practically sings my false name.

"Darren. I thought you'd never call."

"Ah, but ya know, good things come to those who wait." I force a girly giggle.

"I'd rather you didn't make me wait. I'm free Friday night, take me out." It's forward, and normally I'd wait for him to make the moves but I'm winging it big time, and I set a precedent when I left him my number. I can only hope he appreciates forward.

He laughs. "Friday night isn't good, sweetheart."

I tut at the same time Nero walks in the room, leaning against the doorframe with his arms folded over his chest. A deep frown line is carved between his eyebrows making his expression hard and threatening. I stare him straight in the eye and smile smugly. "Shame. I'm not the kind of girl who likes to wait," I purr way too seductively.

He pauses. "I have this thing, but I could swing something before. Drinks?"

Good enough. "Perfect. I can't wait." I hang up.

"Who was that?" His voice is tight, layered with restraint. My eyes brush over his bare chest, and I have no doubt that's a deliberate move.

I glance back at my laptop and shrug. "A job."

"My job is the only one you need to worry about."

I slowly lift my gaze to him and cock a brow. "Your job is temporary, and once it's done, I will move on, and I will go back to doing exactly what I did before I ever heard your name, Nero Verdi." I say the words coldly, driving home the fact that he doesn't own me, and he never will. "But I do have a plan that will get it done."

He slowly moves across the room and halts in front me, his legs slightly spread and his shoulders squared as he stares down at me sitting on the couch. He's wearing only a pair of workout pants, his hands shoved deep within the pockets, making him seem deceptively casual, despite his intimidating stance. He really needs to give up on that shit with me.

Smiling, I lean back into the sofa cushions, crossing one leg over the other. His eyes tighten ever so slightly and the muscle in his jaw pulses as he traces the length of my bare legs, stopping where his over-sized T-shirt sits at mid-thigh.

"Well, you said you have a plan," he says, his voice demanding and impatient.

I sigh and make a deliberate effort to check my nail polish. "I do."

After a few seconds he growls, actually growls. "I don't have time for bullshit, Morte."

I glare at him. "Well, I've got nothing but time, seeing as I'm locked in this apartment." The truth is, I just like him angry. It's when Nero's at his best, his most exciting.

A breath hisses through his teeth, and I know I'm walking a fine line. Good. He removes his hands from his pockets and leans forward, gripping the back of the couch either side of me. Those dark eyes of his meet mine, his face barely an inch away. "Fucking talk." Pressing my fingers against his mouth, I push him away from me. His lips twitch under my touch and he nips at my fingertips. I yank my hand away and his teeth snap together. "Talk."

"I told you, I can't hit them all. Even if I take Finnegan separately, three kills in one network is too much. I can't do it."

His brows pull together and his face moves even closer to mine. "We had a deal," he barely breathes against my lips.

"I didn't say I wouldn't hold up my end," I snap. "But these guys aren't just any soldiers, Nero. Capos, enforcers, they travel in herds, armed herds."

"You're bacio della morte." His tongue caresses the words eloquently. "I wouldn't have sought the best if it was an easy job."

"Think about it, we'll get away with one. Two? Possibly, but the third is going to get spooked. Each one I hit makes the next harder. Surprise is my forte. I'll lose it."

He finally pushes away from me and sits on the edge of the coffee table opposite me, his thighs spread and elbows resting on them. Absently, he swipes his thumb back and forth over his bottom lip. "What do you suggest?"

"Call a truce."

His eyebrows shoot up. "A truce?" He laughs incredulously.

"Call a meeting. Get them all in one room. I'll do the rest."

He laughs again and shakes his head. "They won't fall for it."

"Why not?"

"Ah, Morte. Anyone in the mafia, anyone who knows me, or has even heard my name will know…" He tilts his head to the side and a wicked streak flashes across his eyes. "I don't make peace, I make war. I don't call truces when I can spill blood instead." A small tremor works over my skin and my stomach tightens at his words. I've known men like him my whole life and yet, there is no one like him. He's so utterly feral, so merciless. His arrogance annoys me; his manipulation infuriates

145

me, even though I'd do exactly the same if I were him. His savagery excites me, and his blood lust sings to me. The monster that he is calls to the one that I keep chained up, released only when I kill, but even then, leashed, restricted to clean kills and professional pride. Nero would paint this city red and set a throne from which to survey his blood-stained empire on the mountain of bodies. He wants power and he doesn't care how he gets it. He's right; no one would believe he wants peace, but of course there are two sides to Nero. There's the feral side that wants to bathe in blood, and then there's the sophisticated front he wears so easily. If faced with that side of him, they may just believe he's stepping up to his newfound responsibilities.

"Go to them as the capo. Pretend you have the collective interests at heart and that you're prepared to put aside differences for the greater good." He scowls at me as if the words offend him, and I roll my eyes. "Throw a few threats in there if you feel the need to get your dick out. You're Nero Verdi." I raise a pointed eyebrow. "You want power? Take. It."

"Ah, Morte, you should know better than anyone, I always take what I want." His eyes drop to my mouth as though pointing out that is what he wants right now. "And what will you do if I get them there?"

"Kill them all, of course. But first, we go after Finnegan."

He shakes his head. "We can't hit Finnegan tomorrow. The situation's changed."

"Changed how? We aren't going to get another chance any time soon."

He stares me down. "I said no."

"If he leaves the country, I'm not waiting weeks to hit him again, sitting here while you find every excuse not to get Anna."

"Not. Tomorrow," he growls.

146

Biting back a retort, I stand, needing to walk away from him. He might not be going after Finnegan but he doesn't know that I already have an in. I need this to happen. I need to finish this job and get Anna. What Nero does, I don't care.

CHAPTER EIGHTEEN

Una

My watch reads seven thirty. I said I'd meet Darren at eight. Tommy is sitting across the table from me playing solitaire while I pretend to be doing something constructive on my laptop. I've barely seen Nero for the last two days, and I get the impression he's tied up in mafia shit. He's permanently snappy, drinking like a fish and spending almost all of his time in the office. I don't care. While he's focused on other things, he's leaving me alone, which is good.

Wordlessly, I get up and head to my room. When I arrived here there were already some clothes in the walk-in closet. All of them are brand new with the tags still on. I pick out a simple black dress. God knows what he thought I would possibly need this for, but it's coming in handy now. I managed to order a pair of shoes online, and Tommy, of course, opened the package because I'm untrustworthy and likely to get bombs posted to the apartment or something. When he saw the shoes, he looked so confused. I explained that all girls like shoes and of course he just believed me, bless him. Slipping on the dress and the shoes, I check my face in the mirror, adding a layer of blood-red lipstick and dragging my fingers through my long white-blonde hair.

Tommy immediately looks up when he hears the click of heels on the kitchen floor. His eyebrows shoot up so far they're practically touching his hairline. "Uh, wow. You...you look amazing, but why are you dressed like that?"

With a smile, I pull the gun from behind my back. His eyes pop wide and he barely has time to try and scramble from the barstool before I bring the butt down hard on this temple. His eyes roll back and he goes down hard. I feel bad, but this is necessary. Nero wants to dictate how this job goes down but that wasn't part of this agreement. He hired me to do a job, and I'm going to get it done. For all of his bullshit saying we're in this together, we're not. As usual, it's me against the world.

I put the 9mm pistol in my handbag and swipe the key card out of Tommy's pocket before finding a pen and paper and scrawling a note to Nero. He's going to be so angry. The thought makes me smile.

Darren is sitting at the bar when I get to the place he wanted to meet. It's a new bar a few streets over from O'Malley's. The décor is all brushed steel and slate floors, very industrial. I hop up on the stool next to him.

"Is the vodka any good here?"

He turns to face me and his eyes immediately sweep the length of my body appreciatively, a slow smile pulling at his lips. "You look stunning. And I wouldn't know, I'm a whisky man." He's wearing fitted jeans and a grey shirt with no tie. Darren Derham – yes, I looked him up – is a good-looking guy. But he's also pretty high in the Irish mob on this side of the city. He works closely with Brandon O'Kieffe who's the capo equivalent in these parts. If I can get an in with Darren it's unlikely it will be questioned, but his position also means he's intelligent, cautious and anything but naïve. The benefit of being a woman is even the shrewdest of men never suspect anything, after all, how much harm could a girl possibly do? He orders me a vodka and the barman slides the drink in front of me. The ice clinks against the glass and he studies me as I lift it to my lips, taking a heavy swallow.

"So, Isabelle, what brings you to New York?"

I tilt my head to the side. It's a simple enough question, and yet…

"How do you know I'm not *from* New York?" I ask, adding a seductive smile to make sure it doesn't come off as defensive.

"The accent." He lifts his chin and picks up his whisky glass. "You're not American." Shit, he's good. I barely have any accent at all and you have to pay close attention to pick it up. All my instincts are telling me that I'm made, but I push them down. All I can think about is that I need to get this done. Nero makes me lose focus, but the fact is, I'm locked in that apartment, working for him in exchange for Anna, no other reason. And after his little pissing contest the other night, I don't trust his motivations anymore. No, I have my in. I'm going to see it through. It's a measured risk, for Anna.

So, I smile and feign an offended expression. "And there was me thinking that I'd mastered the New York accent."

He laughs. "Almost."

"Well, I'm just here for work," I tell him.

He nods. "Where in Russia are you from?"

I can feel my expression tightening with strain but I fight it, playing my role perfectly. "Moscow. My father was a lawyer there," I lie easily. "But I always wanted to come to America. Now, *you* can't even pretend to be from here," I tease.

He braces his elbows on the bar and smiles at me. "Dublin, born and bred. I came here for work, too." He downs the rest of his drink. The irony is not lost on me, two people in a normal bar, looking normal, pretending to *be* normal and trying their utmost to convince the other that they are indeed normal, yet he's in the mafia and I'm a hired killer.

We sit, both continuing our façade and exchanging pleasant conversation. We tell each other about the people we aren't, the people we might have been, I suppose. Slowly, I shift closer to him and when I place my hand on his thigh, he barely acknowledges it, comfortable with my touch. His hand lands over mine on his thigh and he leans into me, his lips so close I'm sure he's going to kiss me, but then his phone rings. He releases a frustrated breath and pulls away to pick it up. I quietly sip on my drink while he talks to whoever is on the other end. Now, Irish is English essentially, until two Irish people talk to each other and then it's just noise. I can't make out a word he's saying. He eventually hangs up and when he turns to face me again, I flash him a wide smile.

"I have to go." He sighs, and he doesn't look too happy about it.

I paint a disappointed expression on my face. "Oh, okay."

He stares at me for a long while and then pushes to his feet, pressing his body against my knees and running his knuckles over my jaw. The touch makes me uncomfortable. "I wish I could bring you with me, but unless you like a bar full of pervy Irishmen, I can't imagine it's your scene."

I shrug. "I happen to like pervy Irishmen."

He laughs. "I'll take that as a compliment." He drags his eyes over my body again. "Fine. But you asked for it."

Well, that was easier than I anticipated. Now, the next bit is considerably harder.

O'Malley's is packed tonight. Guys are hanging over the bar, drinking and laughing. Music blares from the jukebox and if I didn't know what this place is, the nature of these people, then it could be any local bar on a Friday night. Everyone smiles at Darren and some clap him on the back. Curious glances are thrown my way, but they last only a few seconds. There are a few women in here; most of them sprawled across one lap or another. Clutching my handbag close to me, I wish that I could have my gun in hand, ready. These are not the kinds of situations I put myself in. I plan and avoid unnecessary risks. Someone taps me on the shoulder, and I turn around. In the next second someone grabs my wrist, their grip too tight to be friendly. I tamper down my more volatile instincts and my eyes dart around, looking for Darren. He's gone.

"You're new," a voice says, quietly from behind me.

I glance over my shoulder at the dark-haired guy who is only inches away from me before looking at the guy to my left, the one with his hand clamped around my wrist. "You're hurting me," I whimper pathetically.

The guy behind me laughs. "If you'll kindly follow me." He passes me, yanking my bag from my grasp, before I'm pushed to follow him. This right here is why you don't go off half-cocked. Damn it.

I'm handcuffed to a chair and the dark-haired guy is pacing in front of me. Finnegan O'Hara. He must be in his forties, the salt and pepper of his beard and crow's-feet at his eyes the only sign of aging. He's a big guy, broad-shouldered and thick-set with an air about him that suggests he's capable of far more than just handling shipments. Two of his guys are on the door, the only exit, and there aren't even any windows in here. The floor beneath my feet is rough stone and the walls are concrete, reminding me of the facility I trained in, the Russian fortress buried in the snow. Both walls are lined with barrels and it smells like old beer; the cellar of the bar. I still don't know why they've brought me down here, so I'll play the frightened woman until they play their hand. A steady stream of tears flow down my face and my chest shudders with each breath. Men, even the hardest of them, don't like having to deal with emotional women and they will subtly focus their attention elsewhere to avoid having to deal with it. So, while his men stare straight ahead and he glances at the floor, I manage to drop the small silver blade from the cuff at my wrist into my hand. This bracelet may well be the most valuable thing I own. It's not an easy job, but I manage to get the end of the fine blade into the lock, wiggling it until I feel a small pop.

"Do you know who I am?" Finnegan asks, his expression serious.

"No." I shake my head. "Please let me go," I sob.

He huffs a laugh before turning on me and leaning over, gripping my forearms. I grind my teeth together, trying not to show my discomfort. "I know exactly who you are, Una Ivanov." My face goes blank and the tears cut off, my breathing returning to normal. There's only so much acting I can do. I've been made.

"How do you know my name?"

His lips twitch, and I hate that I'm on the back foot. I'm never vulnerable, but right now he has me on the ropes. "Nero Verdi has a reputation, but I have the contacts in this city," he drawls, his Irish accent more prevalent than Darren's. I narrow my eyes and say nothing. This is a leak on Nero's side. Fuck. "And my contacts are loyal to me. They trust me to protect them."

"If you know who I am, then you know what the cost of killing me is." I cock a brow, and I don't have to say a damn thing. When I said I was immune, I wasn't kidding. Am I an assassin? Yes. Am I technically fair game? Of course. But, and this is a very big but, I am like a daughter to Nicholai Ivanov. The mafias, for the most part, try and remain amicable and maintain peace where they can but the Russians…well, we're hot-headed by nature. No one wants a war with Nicholai. I've seen what he's capable of and he can make Nero look like Santa Claus.

He pushes away and takes a packet of cigarettes out of his pocket, pulling one loose and placing it between his lips. He lights it and stands a few feet away from me, blowing a long stream of smoke through his nose. "I have no fight with you or that mad Russian fuck." He spits on the ground. "But I have a fight with Nero Verdi and apparently, he's hired your services, so I have a job for you, Miss Ivanov. I want you to kill Nero Verdi for me. He won't even see it coming."

Oh, how the tables turn.

CHAPTER NINETEEN

Nero

My eyes land on Tommy's prone body the second the elevator doors open. I tuck behind the small protruding wall that divides the foyer from the kitchen and feel around underneath the side table next to the gym door. My fingers brush over the gun that's taped to the underside, and I yank it loose. George and Zeus run up to me excitedly, and I relax. If there were someone in the apartment still, then they'd let me know. It's why I have them. Going to Tommy, I crouch down, pressing my finger to his neck. He's fine, just unconscious. A nasty red mark is blossoming across his temple and it looks like he got pistol-whipped badly. I shake his shoulder and he groans, eyelids twitching before they finally open.

"Boss?"

I sigh. "Where's Una?" I know, without even having to ask, exactly where she's gone, but I want to hear him say the words. I want him to tell me that he let her fucking go.

"She, uh, she knocked me out," he says, dropping his eyes away from my scrutinizing stare.

I push to my feet. "Where is she?"

"I don't know."

"Fuck!" I brace my hands against the kitchen island and it's then that I notice the scrap of paper in the middle. Picking it up, I read over the scrawled words.

Nero.

Don't get your panties in a wad. I've gone to do my job. Don't wait up.

Una.

O'Hara. She's gone after fucking O'Hara, and he knows she's coming. Shit!

"What time did she leave?"

"About eight."

It's ten thirty.

I drop my head forward. "She's gone after O'Hara. Two hours is too long and he knows she's coming. She's probably dead." I say the words calmly, but I don't feel calm. I feel…aggravated, to the point that I want to rip this place apart.

"She might not be. She…I mean…" he stammers.

I twist my gaze towards him. "She what?"

He takes a seat across from me, resting his head in his hands. "She has this guy, Darren."

"You need to talk really fucking fast, Tommy," I growl.

"Look, she made me take her to O'Malley's on Tuesday," he says in a rush. "This guy tried to talk to her, so she gave him her number. She was going to use him as an in to get to O'Hara."

"Do you know any more about this guy?"

"Derham, I think she said his name was Darren Derham."

Well, this just gets better and better. "Find me details. I want family, a wife, a mother, anything you can find." I pick up my keys and take another gun out of the kitchen drawer. "I will deal with you later." That woman is incapable of listening to anything I say and now she's dragging Tommy into this shit with her. And me? I'm running headfirst after her for reasons I can't begin to explain even to myself.

******

Jackson pulls up in the alleyway just around the corner from O'Malley's. I called him on my way over because I sure as hell need backup and when it comes to fighting, Jackson's always handy. He gets out of the black SUV and eyes me with a tight expression before opening the back door. Moving beside him, I stare at the woman on the back seat, her stomach swollen and her face streaked with tears.

"I have no desire to hurt you. Call Darren. Now. Tell him where you are and that if he doesn't come alone, I'm going to kill you." A ragged sob comes from her. Fuck me, I don't have time for this shit. Jackson hands her a phone and she takes it, hands shaking as she follows my instructions.

"Darren!" she cries, her voice breaking. She draws several heaving breaths, tears and snot running down her face. "I'm in the alley one block over from the bar. He...he's going to kill me."

Snatching the phone away from her, I put it to my ear. The sound of dull music is in the background, as if he's in a hallway or a side room away from the main bar. "You have something I want, Mr. Derham. So, you are going to come and meet me, alone, or I am going to blow your pretty little girlfriend's brains all over the dirty fucking street." My voice rises and then I hang up, tossing the phone to Jackson.

"Point a gun at her head. You see any more than one guy walk around that corner, shoot her."

"Oh god." She starts whimpering and crying before she clasps her hands together and starts praying under her breath. I have no sympathy for that shit, and you know why? Because if you get involved with a mafia guy, this is to be expected. And if she didn't know he was mafia...well, that just makes her stupid. The mafia are all about protecting women and keeping them out of it, they create these rules that make them untouchable, rely on honor, and it works...until a bastard like me comes along. I don't have any honor and I'll use any means necessary to get what I want. If he wants to take what's mine, he can be damn sure I'll take what's his.

A few minutes later, a figure appears at the mouth of the alley. He's alone but his fingers are wrapped around a gun. "Who the fuck are you?" he asks, his voice strained.

"I'm the guy with a gun to your woman's head." I point towards Jackson who has his gun trained on the back seat.

"Darren!" she screams, and I see his eyes pinch slightly, his lips pressing together.

"What do you want?" he asks through clenched teeth.

I approach him and place my gun under his chin. He stares me straight in the eye. "I want Una."

"She'll already be dead."
I ram the barrel of the gun into his throat hard enough to make him gag and choke.

"You had best hope not, because at this point, her life is tied to dear Polly's here."

"O'Hara has her," he says through clenched teeth.

"Where?"

"The cellar of the bar."

"Thank you. You've been very helpful." I pull the trigger and a bloody gaping hole appears in his throat. He's seen Una's face, knows who she is. He's a liability. The girl starts screaming and it's loud enough to wake the dead. Jackson leans in the back of the car and then it's silent. He closes the door and opens the trunk, handing me a semi-automatic.

"Grab his feet." I pick up Darren's shoulders and Jackson gets his ankles. I don't have time to fix this now, so we just throw him in the trunk.

Only one guy guards the back of the bar. We duck down in the shadows behind a dumpster and watch for a second.

"Boss, we're walking into the Irish stronghold," Jackson says. I don't respond because I'm well aware. "Is she really worth getting killed for?"

Is she? I don't know. All I know is I want her back. I'm not ready for my vicious little butterfly to meet her end. If anyone is going to kill her, it will be me.

"We'll see, won't we?" I push to my feet. The guard turns to face us and Jackson shoots him, the muted pop from the silencer the only sound before he hits the ground. I'm hoping that they're all too drunk to pay too much attention and honestly, he's right, this is their stronghold. It's the last place they would expect a hit.

I fire off one round at the lock, yanking the old door open. I have no idea what I'm walking into, and I'm not sure I care.

CHAPTER TWENTY

Una

I don't work for free, Mr O'Hara. And honestly, I expect a certain level of professional courtesy."

He laughs. "I'm showing you it by not killing you."

I narrow my eyes, lounging in the chair casually. "Haven't you heard? I'm untouchable."

He moves closer. "No one is untouchable. So what will it be?

I throw my head back and laugh. "You'd be wasting your time." I spring up from the chair, taking him by surprise as I clasp the curved metal of the handcuff and rake the serrated edge over his neck. He staggers back a step, and I get a clear line of sight to the guard on the left of the door. I throw the slim blade in my other hand at said guard and it hits him in the side of the neck. Blood spurts from the small nick like a hosepipe being turned on. The other guard glances at his friend before pointing his gun at me, but I duck behind his boss who provides an ample body shield. Of course, O'Hara has recovered from my earlier swipe. It was only a flesh wound and although there's a lot of blood, he's annoyingly fine. The door flies open on a bang and the quick *pop pop* of silenced gunfire has Finnegan grabbing a handful of my hair and turning us to face the door. He forces me in front of him, ramming the barrel of his gun into the side of my neck.

"Nero." I barely breathe. He stands in the doorway looking like the devil himself come to mete out his wrath. His chest rises and falls raggedly and the muscles in his jaw pulse beneath the skin. Jackson lingers in the hallway just behind him. His gaze briefly touching on mine before he goes back to keeping watch.

"Well, well. I see ya finally found the balls to come after me yourself." O'Hara taunts, pulling my hair harder.

Nero tilts his head to the side slightly. "Oh, no. This one's all on Una," he says casually, but the meaning is all too clear, this is my fault.

"I can see why you'd want her back." O'Hara presses his face into my hair and sniffs. I scowl and try to shrug him off. "But this is a risk. Isn't that her job?"

Nero's gaze meets mine, dark and turbulent and promising nothing but pain and retribution. Something passes between us, a mutual understanding of necessary violence. Anyone else might hesitate, but I see the minute twitch of the muscle in his shoulder before he pulls the gun up. Grabbing O'Hara's right wrist, I shove it away from me, digging my finger hard into the nerve that runs through his forearm. I twist my body side-on as I do. Two bangs ring out, and then he's falling. O'Hara lands flat on his back, gasping desperately for air as a red stain slowly bleeds out across the centre of his chest. Nero comes to stand beside me and fires one shot at the dying man's head. He wordlessly walks straight out of the room. There is no time to hang around, so I follow him, and Jackson falls in behind me. I can practically see the anger swirling around Nero. For once though, it's warranted. I've always been meticulous and know that mistakes and rash action are what get you caught. Acting out of desperation could have gotten me killed. And Nero…I'm supposed to be taking out his target's so he's not associated with it, so why come after me? He's just implicated himself and for what? To play the white knight?

We walk a block over before he turns into a dark alleyway. A black SUV and the Maserati are parked under the cover of darkness. "Get in the car," he says without looking at me. He makes me feel like a chastised child, so on pure principle, I lean against the back of the car and cross my arms over my chest.

"Take the girl to the hospital," he says to Jackson. What girl? "And get rid of him."

Nero grabs my arm and shoves me towards the passenger side of the car. "Do not fucking push me right now, Una." His voice is a low rumble, rolling thunder that signals a storm is about to hit. He shoves me in the car and gets in, wheels spinning past the SUV as he pulls out of the alley. The tension in the car wraps around, pressing on my chest until it's stifling. His anger is a palpable thing, and his silence is ominous to say the least.

By the time he pulls into the parking garage at the apartment, I can't wait to get out of the car. I don't particularly want to be in another confined space with him, but I follow him to the elevator and get in.

When I can't take it anymore, I glance sideways at him. "Are you going to say anything?" I ask.

He cracks his neck to the side and tilts his head back, jaw flexing over and over. "You're lucky I didn't shoot you myself."

"I thought –"

He shoves me back into the elevator wall and slams his fists against the metal beside my head with a loud bang. "You don't get to fucking think," he hisses, blowing hot angry breath over my face. My heart pounds in my chest so hard it's all I can hear. I squeeze my eyes shut and swallow heavily. "You disobeyed me."

My own temper spikes. "I'm not one of your soldiers, Nero. You asked me to do a job. How I do it was not part of the agreement."

He grips my throat the same way he always does when he's mad. "He knew you were coming, and you better believe he would have killed you." The elevator pings and the doors open but neither of us move.

"Those are the risks of the job."
His hand physically trembles against my neck before he shoves away from me and turns his back.

"Damn it, Una." He drags both hands through his hair. I walk straight past him and feel him following me. "I hired you because you're the best. This shit…this is not the best."

I turn on him, jabbing my finger into the center of his chest. "You didn't hire me! You blackmailed me. There's a difference."

His head tilts to the side and he looks at me in that way that has me taking a step back. Of course, he follows. "So, what? You feel slighted so you rush headfirst into a bullet between the eyes?"

"No, I..." I keep moving backwards with him stalking me. "Why do you even care? I didn't compromise you. He already knew it was you." My back hits the kitchen island and he places his hands on either side of me, gripping the edge. "Why do you care?" I repeat. I need to know, because right now, I'm freefalling through the unknown and my stupid little heart is hoping he'll catch me, determined that there must be a reason why he saved me. Meanwhile, my head says he'll stand and watch me hit the ground and smile as my body breaks and shatters in front of him.

He leans in until his lips are brushing so close to my face, his breath caressing my lips as he speaks. "I told you, Morte, you're mine." Then his lips crash against mine. He kisses me like he wants to crawl inside me and consume me, and I let him, because his possession, his brutal need...I want it. No one has ever risked a damn thing for me before, but I know he risked his life coming for me. In his own warped and depraved way, he cares. No one has truly cared about me since I was eight years old. I never knew I wanted or needed it until this exact second. Nero makes me feel safe and the realization shocks me to my core, because he's anything but safe. I don't need protection and I sure as hell don't need a white knight, but I want this savage creature. I want his complete lack of morals, his violence and his need for power and blood. Kissing him back, I tug at his jacket and push it past his shoulders. He shrugs out of it as his lips tear away from mine and ravage the side of my neck. I tilt my head to the side, allowing him more access.

"You make me so damn angry. I want to fuck you until you bleed," he snarls, and I shiver, my breath hitching in my throat. "And this fucking dress." He roughly grabs the skirt and shoves it up, a low groan escaping his throat when his fingers brush all the way up to my hips. I'm not wearing any underwear because the dress is skin-tight. He grips my thighs and lifts me easily. I wrap my legs around him, clinging to his broad shoulders as he moves. He slams me against the wall and one of the paintings sways dangerously. It's nothing but hands and teeth and lips as he drives his point home. My fingers thread through his hair, pulling at the thick strands, wanting more, wanting his punishment just as much as his pleasure. He bites down on my neck hard enough that I actually feel his teeth puncture my skin. I and grab the collar of his shirt, wrenching it apart. Buttons scatter, hitting the tile like rain in a storm, an apt backing for the hurricane that is Nero. Lips slam over mine again, fighting, demanding, taking. His hot, bare skin presses against the inside of my thighs and I'm so desperate for him that I reach between us and yank at his belt buckle. I'm consumed with this unexplainably heightened need to feel him inside me, and he gives me what I want, shoving his pants and boxers over his thighs and ramming his cock inside me. It's like retribution and salvation all at once, pain and pleasure, light and dark, right and wrong…it all blends together until the lines that define us disappear and it's no longer him and me, just us. We are one and the same, the embodiment of each other, two splintered halves of the fractured whole.

His forehead presses against mine and his hand wraps around the back of my neck, holding me there, forcing me to share the same air as him. I grasp his face in both my hands and close my eyes, feeling every rough thrust of his hips, the small spike of pain that comes with having him buried so deep inside me. I listen to every feral groan and staggered breath, and I embrace it all, letting him dominate and own me for just a few precious moments.

The picture on the wall crashes to the floor, the glass smashing and flying across the tile. He only fucks me harder, pounding into me until I don't know where he ends and I begin. I throw my head back against the wall, my mouth falling open on a long moan. His lips rest against my throat, teeth touching my skin but never biting down as he groans. Everything in me tightens, and I cling to him as my body detonates, sending wave after wave of pleasure tearing through my muscles, setting fire to my nerve endings. He growls into my neck, biting down on my shoulder as he thrusts into me harder and stiffens on a long groan.. Bracing his hand against the wall beside my head, he breathes heavily against my neck. My body trembles and my heart thrums in my chest, pounding against my ribs. My fingers drift down the side of his neck as I try to catch my breath, and he pulls back, eyes meeting mine. We stare at each other, saying nothing and everything with one look. His hand grips my neck roughly.

"The next time you do something like that, I will kill you myself," he says, and I smile.

He storms away, leaving me standing there alone.

My hand shakes, my heart hammering in my chest so hard that my pulse thrums against my eardrums, a symphony of fear and heartbreak.

"Please," I beg, lifting my eyes to Nicholai.

His expression softens as he steps closer to me, reaching out and brushing a tendril of hair away from my face. "Become what you were meant to be, little dove." His thumb trails over my jaw, and I close my eyes as a tear slips down my cheek. "Put a bullet in his head or put a bullet in your own," he says harshly. "You cannot live with weakness. Fix it one way or another." His lips brush over the side of my face.

I lift my gaze, staring over his arm at the far wall. "Please don't make me do this," I beg. Tears blur my vision, and I don't care that I look weak.

169

Nicholai looks at me in disgust. "See what he does to you? You are a weapon and weapons don't weep. Make a choice."

The concrete walls of the room press in on me until I can barely breathe. Nicholai's hand slips away from my face and he steps back. My trembling finger rests over the trigger of the gun, and I swallow heavily, hating the fact that I'm so weak. I lift my eyes to Alex, chained to the far wall. His torso is bare, covered in slices that bleed over his skin. Sweat mixes with the blood, coating the chiseled muscles of his body in a crimson glow. His dark hair is damp with sweat and a few loose tendrils fall across his face. I stare into his beautiful green eyes, so full of pain, so full of longing. Longing for what can never be. Longing for a fantasy, a dream, but dreams don't exist in this place. This is where the damned are born and created, shaped and molded until there's nothing left but the cold urge to kill, to take and destroy. I thought I'd found a brief reprieve in Alex's arms, an oasis in this warped version of hell, but I was wrong. Because there is no escape from yourself, from what you've become. Alex made me forget, for just a second. He makes me feel things that I haven't felt since I was taken, since Anna. Love. Kindness.

Meeting his gaze, I tighten the grip on the gun. His eyes are resigned, begging me, but not for reprieve. He's begging me to shoot him. "Do it, Titch." My vision blurs with tears and a sharp pain rips through my chest.

"I love you," I choke. Tears track down my cheeks and a sharp pain rips through my chest.

"Shoot him, Una!" Nicholai roars.

With a ragged cry, I lift the gun, aiming between his eyes.

"Forgive me," I whisper as I pull the trigger. His eyes go wide as the bullet rips through his skull. I scream.

CHAPTER TWENTY-ONE

Nero

The sound of screaming jolts me awake. On a groan, I get out of bed. The second I open my door, Una lets out another scream but it's not coming from her room, it's coming from downstairs. Descending the stairs, I find her on the couch, tossing and thrashing in her sleep. George is sitting bolt upright at the end of the couch, watching her like he's witnessing an exorcism.

"Alex!" she cries, her voice shrill and staggered. A small whimper leaves her lips and she no longer seems like a lethal killer, more like a scared little girl.

"Una." I shove her shoulder but keep my distance because I'm not a fan of what follows when she wakes up. She sits bolt upright, gasping for air as her eyes dart around the room. Her face slowly twists towards me, though I can't clearly make out her expression in the darkness.

"Why are you on the couch?" I snap. I'm tired and this exact moment is the culmination of a line of shit events.

"I..." She stammers over herself and I exhale an impatient breath before reaching for her and yanking her off the couch.

"What are you...?" Throwing her over my shoulder, she squeaks before going rigid stiff. I don't care. I carry her up the stairs and along the hallway into my room before tossing her on the bed. She grunts and bounces on the mattress, landing sprawled. She's still wearing that black dress which is hiked up her thighs, exposing miles of long, toned legs. And of course, I know she's not wearing any underwear.

I drag my eyes to her face, but she won't look at me. She pulls her knees to her chest and wraps her arms around them. I'm waiting for her to bitch and moan at me, but she doesn't. Instead, she withdraws into herself, as if I'm not even in the room. For long moments, nothing but silence reigns between us, and I can almost feel her turmoil from here. I don't care that she has nightmares, because any half sane person in her position would. You don't get to be the kiss of death without seeing and doing horrific things. After a while you'd become numb to it, acts that seemed so monstrous before slowly fade in your mind until they're just normal. Emotions that were once sharp and colorful become dull and grey. No, the nightmares are no concern of mine, but the fact that she always calls for this Alex...that concerns me. When she calls his name, she sounds so tortured.

"Who's Alex?" I ask, staring down at her.

"I told you, someone I killed."

"You've killed a lot of people, Morte, and you aren't screaming their names in your sleep. So, I'll ask again, who is he?" I don't know what it is about it that irritates me. Perhaps because this Alex seems to be the only chink in that impenetrable armor of hers besides her sister. Una doesn't have chinks, and for him to be on any kind of level with Anna, well, he must be important.

"Was. He *was* my friend," she whispers, turning her face towards me. Those indigo eyes hold mine in the darkness, so hard, so sad. "And in a way, I loved him."

"I didn't think you capable."

She turns her face away again and knots the sheets between her fingers. When I'm sure she's going to say no more, she starts talking. "I was fifteen years old and naïve. I thought I loved him, and Nicholai didn't like it, so I was forced to choose between him and myself. I chose me. Killing Alex made me what I am. Nicholai was right to do it. Alex was a weakness, it made me strong." She says the words but they're robotic, as though she's recited them to herself a hundred times.

I knew Nicholai was crazy but even by my standards that's pretty fucked up. When I first bartered her sister in exchange for the job, I threw the threat of Nicholai out there purely on a hunch, having no idea whether or not it would work. But I'd heard stories, had my suspicions.

"And that's why you're here," I say, as a piece of the cryptic puzzle that makes up Una clicks into place. "That's why you haven't found Anna, because Nicholai would kill her."

She slowly nods. "He wouldn't do it out of spite, but he would do it to keep me strong." I can tell she truly believes that. "The strong survive and the weak die, forgotten and inconsequential." She shakes her head. "She'd be better off dead anyway."

"Probably." It sounds cruel, but I won't lie to her. Anna's situation is a fate worse than death.

Her gaze snaps to mine. "She's not like us, Nero. She was good and pure. Promise me you will get her."

I move around the bed, slipping beneath the covers. Her gaze follows me. "Technically, our deal is broken. You didn't kill O'Hara."

She drags a hand through her hair. "Promise me," she pleads. I've never seen her look so desperate. So fragile. Her wings of steel are crumpled and broken.

I sigh. "I intend to buy her. It's the only way to get a slave out of the Sinaloa." Her eyes search my face, seeking the trace of a lie. "But you broke our deal, so now I propose a new one."

"What do you want?"

"I want to know why you have such loyalty to a man who would force you to kill a boy you profess love for. Tell me and our deal stands."

She drops her chin and a lock of white hair falls over her face, shining brightly in the moonlight. "I'll tell you why if you tell me why you wanted your own brother dead."

I smile and press my finger under her chin, forcing her to look at me. "That's not the deal though, is it?" She stares at me, waiting. "Fine, Lorenzo was my half-brother. I hated his father and they both hated me."

"Why?"

"Because my mother was a whore and I was a bastard," I say quickly. "Your turn."

She squeezes her eyes closed and takes a deep breath that has her shoulders rising and falling. "My parents died when I was eight and Anna and I were in an orphanage, until my matron sold me to the bratva at thirteen. They tried to rape me, turn me

into a whore, but Nicholai saved me. He said I was a fighter."
She sets her jaw, and I can see the bloodlust in her eyes. I can
imagine a young Una, small and scared but every bit as
unbreakable as she is now. "He saved me. He taught me how to
fight, gave me power." The way she says it makes it sound like
some guy teaching a little girl to throw a few punches, but I
know better.

"You were one of the bratva's child soldiers." She nods. It all
makes so much sense now. The Russian mafia have always
'adopted' orphans and turned them into soldiers, but Nicholai
Ivanov went one better. He made his own force of elite
assassins. They're feared and spoken of across the world, but
Una is the jewel in his crown, the favorite, the one he calls
daughter. Because he saved her. Because he created her. But as
the pieces fall into place, I suddenly see her for what she really
is. The very qualities that make us human have been torn from
her and though she is indeed strong, she's also irrevocably
broken. Anna is her exception, the ghost of humanity within
Una. It's her lack of humanity that draws me to her though,
because we're both monsters surrounded by people. The
difference between Una and me though is that she's still fighting
herself, otherwise she wouldn't have nightmares. Anna is the
good, the redemption that she's clinging to, and in that sense, I
completely understand why Nicholai would kill her. To do so
would break Una so completely that he would unleash a creature
like no other. She would be perfect. "If you're so loyal to him,
then where does Anna fit in?" I ask.

She shifts on the bed and lies down beside me. "Anna is my
one weakness," she says simply. "But you already know that. I
will do anything I have to for her, even if it means standing
against Nicholai," she says fiercely. Yes, Nicholai has created a
little monster but when you make one so strong, you often lose
control, and I have a feeling that Nicholai's prize dog is about
to bite him.

Anna maybe Una's weakness but Una is fast becoming mine.
I would say it bothers me, but what's the point? She's like a

175

disease that can't be cured, infecting me, spreading and consuming everything until I'm driven mad for her. She's slowly fracturing me, forcing her way inside me until my very cells are forced to evolve and accommodate her, acclimating to this newfound need. She's so much more than just a warm body to stick my dick in. She's the kiss of death, and when I look at her, I see something I've never seen in anyone else; my equal. She's the only one who challenges me, and I find myself waiting for her defiance, craving it even.

For the first time in a long time, I want something other than just power. I want her. She will be *my* jewel in *my* crown. My broken queen.

I wake up to the scent of vanilla and the subtle hint of gun oil. My dick is rock hard and presses against something warm and soft. I open my eyes and tighten my arm around Una's small body. My chest is plastered to her back and her ass is just right there, cupping my cock like it was made for it. I frown because I like the feeling of waking up with her and that bothers me. We fight and fuck, and ultimately, Una is mine whether she likes it or not, but this…this is too…normal. This isn't blurring the line, it's wiping it the fuck away. No matter how I feel about her, I still need her to do a job. We are still Una and Nero, the assassin and the capo. People like us don't get normal, and I don't want it. I pull my arm away from her slowly, torn between needing to step away and wanting to sink my dick between her legs. I get out of bed and get in the shower. The warm spray washes over me and I wrap my hand around my rock-hard dick, stroking over the length and picturing Una's naked body, that look of violence she gets in her eyes when I fuck her. My muscles lock and pleasure tears through me so hard my knees go weak and I have to throw my hand out against the shower wall. This is what she does; she almost brings me to my knees. Almost.

When I get out of the shower, Una's gone. I answer a couple of emails, before going downstairs. I find her sitting at the breakfast bar sipping on coffee. She's wearing yoga pants and her sports bra, and her body is coated in a thin sheen of sweat, I assume from working out.

"I need your help with something this morning." I move over to the coffee machine.

"Oh, you're letting me out?" She snorts.

I move behind her, placing my hands either side of her body and gripping the breakfast bar. My face is level with her neck and I can smell the subtle scent of her sweat mixing with her shampoo. I skim my lips over her skin and she shivers. "I'd happily tie you to the bed and leave you there, but we were set up, and payback's a bitch." I nip at her skin and when I pull away, a twisted smile is on her lips.

"Yes, she is."

I drop Una off and take the long drive to the Hamptons house. I haven't been here much in the last couple of weeks. I've left Gio running the place while I play out my game of strategy. Gio greets me outside the front door the second I get out of the car.

"Any problems?" I ask.

"None." He falls in step beside me as I make my way inside the house which is alive with activity. We called in a lot of guys after last night's shitshow. I'm just waiting for an Irish show of retribution.

We go straight down to the basement and I shove open the old steel door that leads into the main room, the same room that Una watched me set fire to someone in. It's a prison cell for all intents and purposes and a torture chamber when we need it to be. The walls are three feet thick; there are no windows, no escape, and no one to hear the screams. In the center sits a lone figure. His head is dropped forwards against his chest, arms pulled behind his back, wrists and ankles bound to the plastic chair beneath him.

I take the packet of cigarettes from my inside jacket pocket and pluck one out, placing it between my lips and lighting it. Moving slowly towards the prone figure in the middle of the room, I inhale a deep lungful of smoke and hold it.

"Have you enjoyed your stay with us, Gerard?" I smirk, coming to a halt in front of him.

The Port Authority Chief lifts his head, squinting against the bright fluorescent lights. Deep shadows have taken up residence beneath his eyes but other than that his face is unmarked. When dealing with public figures, it's wise not to mark their face. The body…well, that's fair game. He sways backwards and forwards in his seat but says nothing. "You fucked me over, Gerard." I hand in my pocket.

He shakes his head weakly. "I didn't."

"Don't fucking lie to me!" I flick the cigarette towards his feet. "I know you had my shipment seized. I know you spoke to O'Hara and tipped him off. You're not in my good graces, Mr Brown."

"I had no choice!" he wails, voice cracking.

Tilting my head to the side, I release a long breath. "There's always a choice. Now, I'm going to give you the opportunity to make the right one."

"I can't help you," he says, gritting his teeth. "You can't just kidnap me. Someone will notice I'm gone. I have a wife. She'll report me missing," he says desperately, and I smile.

"Like I said, we all have a choice." I take my phone from my pocket and dial Una's number, putting the call on loudspeaker. The ring tone echoes off the concrete walls, resonating around the room.

The line clicks and the sound of a woman sobbing fills the room. "Gerard?" Her breath hitches.

"Hannah!" he shouts, but the sound of her cries cut off.

"Hello, Gerard," Una purrs. "You remember me, don't you?" I can hear the amusement in her voice as she toys with him like a cat with a mouse.

Gerard's terrified gaze meets mine, and I cock a brow. "She's the hot psycho blonde who threatened to take your eye out, in case you forgot. Time to make a choice, Gerard. I want control over all of the docks that Finnegan O'Hara has." I turn my back on him, pacing a few steps away. "And you want your wife safe. I get what I want, and you get what you want. Everyone's a winner."

A bead of sweat rolls over his forehead. "Please don't hurt her."

"Una isn't known for her patience, are you, Morte?"

"I'm feeling generous. I'll count to three." The whimpering in the background escalates to desperate screams.

"One. Two –"

"No!" Gerard cries. "Please, please. I'll do it."

I smile. "That's a good choice Mr. Brown, and I'll remind you now that if you betray me, if you let me down, don't think that I won't go to little Gracie's school or pay your wife another visit."

He drops his head forward and sniffs pathetically. "Please don't hurt them."

"That's all on you, Gerard. I want everything O'Hara had before his unfortunate demise." I pat his shoulder.

"He...he's dead?"

"Guess I forgot to mention that. I thought you needed the proper encouragement to remain loyal. After all, loyalties are so frivolous nowadays." I turn to Gio. "Cut him loose and have him taken back to his wife." I leave the room, placing the phone to my ear. "Okay, you can leave now," I tell Una.

"I was hoping that would be more exciting."

"You can try and make me bleed later if you're feeling that violent."

"Remember you said that." She hangs up and my dick's hard just at the thought of it. The woman has me by the balls.

"Nero." I turn around halfway up the stairs. Gio is standing in the doorway and pulls the heavy metal door closed behind him. "Andre came through." Andre Paro is the guy to know in Mexico, he's somewhat of a broker, liaising between cartels and cutting deals that no one wants to make in person. "I wired a hundred grand to him this morning. He's overseeing the girl's transfer to Rafael as we speak." Rafael D'Cruze is at the top of the Juarez Cartel, and my supplier. I don't fully trust him, but the likelihood of the Sinaloa selling Anna to me is slim. The fact that an Italian is interested in an unknown Mexican sex slave would raise suspicion, whereas Rafael has more weight and respect in South America. If the sale comes from him, they almost can't reject it. Of course, originally, I planned for her to stay with him until Una completed the job, almost like a pay half now half later deal, but well, this is no longer a simple exchange of favors. The lines are blurred, and motivations are called into question. I don't believe for a second that Una would still be here without the leverage of her sister, and I have no intention of giving her Anna just yet, but as each day passes, the plan I had set out seems less and less important. In order to get to the end game though I have to let it play out. I have to let the chips fall and give Una the chance to do the very thing I sought her out for. The plan is what matters, all that can matter, which means Una is still the queen, and valuable as she is, she's still only a piece on the board.

CHAPTER TWENTY-TWO

Una

I t's been a week since Nero killed O'Hara and now here we are, ready to take out the rest of his list. He called a truce and of course they agreed to it, because they're mafia and they believe there's honor among thieves, but they don't know Nero, or they just aren't paying attention, because I had him pegged in one look. For Nero, boundaries don't exist and ethics are laughable. I think that's what makes me want him. I haven't felt truly safe in a very long time, but Nero manages to make me feel protected in a world where I'm the predator, because sometimes, in order to fight the monsters under the bed, you need a monster of your own.

Nero stands in the doorway of the dining room, his arms folded over his chest as he watches me strip down my rifle. My baby, my pride and joy. Actually, that's a lie, because I have twelve exact replicas of the same gun stored in various places around the globe. It's a custom .25 calibre assault rifle. I clean and oil the pieces, going through it methodically, like a ritual. I need this; the calm before the storm. This…being here with Nero; it's throwing me off. Now more than ever I need to cling to my cool indifference, the training that's so ingrained.

I don't look up at Nero, but I hear him move closer. "Nice gun."

I spare him a brief glance. "Thanks." He's wearing a black suit with a white shirt. The jacket is draped casually over his shoulder. His hair is tidier than usual and the confidence he wears so easily looks strained, even masked behind the intimidating stance that he can't turn off. If I'm a chameleon then Nero is a big cat, roaring and baring his teeth, unapologetic about exactly what he is. The irony is, he doesn't even need the teeth. His power is growing, even in the short time I've been here. Sasha has his ear to the ground for me. I've told him I'm working a job for the Italians. Nothing else. But he keeps me informed, tells me about the whisperings of the New York capo so ruthless the rest of the mafia fear him. Marco Fiore has been heard to call Nero a rabid dog, and talk like that will get him killed.

"Nervous?" I smirk.

He tilts his head and whatever lack of confidence I saw a second ago disappears. He circles around behind me, and I fight the urge to turn and keep him in my eye line. I steel my spine and focus on taking a bullet from the ammo box, placing it on the table in front of me. A tremor works over my skin, an awareness of the dangerous presence so close, lingering right behind me. I may fuck him, and to a certain degree trust him, but not completely. Dealing with Nero is like walking on a knife's edge, feeling the cold bite of the blade on the soles of my feet and finding a sick satisfaction in it. He's a dangerous and twisted adrenaline rush, not unlike the same thrill I get when I kill. His fingers brush my neck and my breath hitches as he scoops my hair up in one hand. He yanks my head to the side so hard my scalp burns, but the pain is lost as hot breath blows over my skin, followed by the scrape of his teeth. "Don't miss."

I click a bullet into the chamber. "I never miss."

"Good." He steps away.

Calm. Focus. The icy anticipation of the kill. That's what I need. The images running through my mind at this second are anything but...

CHAPTER TWENTY-THREE

Nero

Marco is already here when I arrive. He sits at the table, a smoking cigar in the ashtray in front of him. He's in his mid-forties, his dark hair is streaked with grey. Marco is one of those guys in the mafia without an official role, yet influential. He's involved in our legitimate businesses, has the ear of Arnaldo…that kind of shit. The mob consists of Made men, soldiers, and the capo controls the soldiers. There are two New York capos and I'm one of them. I manage the family's interests, ensure that the people who pay us are protected, manage the influx of drugs and weapons in and out of my area

. the city. Or at least that's what most people think. The men 've invited to this meeting, the men I want dead, they're the ones who see me for what I really am. I'm someone who can't be put in a box and neatly labelled. What I want goes beyond that. I want power. Absolute power. I will kill whomever I need to, buy the ones I can't and destroy anyone and anything who gets in my way. They see it and it rattles them. As it should. They supported Lorenzo because he was an idiot and idiots are easily controlled. The key to control is to ensure that the people in charge, the people with the supposed power never really have any. Lorenzo may have been the capo, but politics are politics, and even the president has to answer to those beneath him. I don't. I won't, and they see it. It almost seems a shame to kill the few astute men in my organization, but if they're not allies then they're enemies and a wise enemy makes for an ominous one.

"Nero." Marco stands, holding his arms out to the side to embrace me, but it's also an invitation to check him for weapons. I embrace him and he kisses both my cheeks, smiling wide like I'm his best friend. I keep it brief, eyeing the two men he brought with him. He's not carrying but I can guarantee they are. Gio shifts behind me, and I can tell he's thinking the same thing. I brought him instead of Jackson because he's intelligent and calculated. Not rash.

A few seconds later, Bernardo Caro and Franco Lama walk in. Bernardo is the other New York capo and Franco is his savage right-hand with way too much power for my liking. Bernardo embraces me as Marco did, but Franco lingers behind. The three of us take a seat at the table.

"It is a shame you have not invited us to talk sooner," Marco says in our native language. This is at the heart of his issue, the fact that as the new capo I didn't conform to the bullshit customs of paying respect to this fucker. I did it deliberately. If I wanted to make new friends, I'd throw a tea party. I'm much more partial to a bloodbath. Of course, to win any game, you need someone to play against. Marco, Bernardo and Franco are

188

merely opposing pawns. Their presence is necessary in order for me to cross the board and take the king. And take him, I will.

I'm staring straight at Marco when the glass window behind him smashes. Two quick fire shots. His eyes go wide, and he falls face down on the table. I barely have a second to catch up before Bernardo goes down, too. Shots are fired inside the room, and bodies hit the floor simultaneously. And then, silence. Gio stands with his gun raised, having killed Marco's guards. A low gurgled groan sounds from the other side of the table, and I approach Franco where he lies on the floor, clutching a bullet wound in his abdomen.

He glares up at me, blood leaking from the corner of his mouth. "You have no honor," he hisses.

I smile. "Honor is for people who have a line. I don't." I lift my gun and fire one shot at his head. It's done.

CHAPTER TWENTY-FOUR

Una

Staring down my scope at Nero, I focus on the way his lips press together. He appears the image of sophistication and calm, but I can see the subtle flutter of the muscle in his jaw. He's pissed off. Well, I guess I had best get this show on the road before he loses his shit and tries to take all my fun.

Focusing on the back of Marco Fiore's head, I take a steadying breath in then out and squeeze the trigger once to crack the window and again to take him out. The double bang explodes around the alleyway between this building and the one I'm firing on. I've marked every target in the room, but I have to be quick. Bernardo dives for the ground but I catch him in the side of the head. Franco is almost out of sight. I panic and hurry the shot, hitting him in the gut. Fuck. I don't like messy kills, and I certainly don't like to leave any possibility that they might survive. He's out of sight now, so if he's still alive, Nero or Gio are going to have to finish him off. Pausing for a minute, I wait. Nero pops up, because of course, he knows who the shooter is. He's safe. I allow him to approach Franco's body and he says something before pointing a gun at him and pulling the trigger. He stares out the window, and even though I know he can't see me, when I stare down the scope he's staring right at me. I line the shot up and smile as I pull the trigger, hitting him in the shoulder. The impact makes his body jerk before he goes down. What can I say? Something to remember me by when I'm gone.

Smiling, I push up off my stomach, disassembling the gun quickly and putting the pieces back in the case. And my last gift for Nero…plausible deniability. I take the card from my pocket - the queen of aces – and press my lips to the back of the card, leaving a bright red lipstick mark. I throw it on the ground amongst the four spent shell casings. The Italians will come looking, and this is what they'll find. It will either halt their search right there, or put a price on my head.

Exiting the abandoned apartment, I pull my hood low over my eyes as I make my way down the fire escape. My black Mercedes lays cloaked in shadow in the alley at the back of the building and I jog to it. I jump in the car and pull away from the scene of the crime. That's it, I'm done. I took out Nero's guys; I fulfilled my end of the bargain. I'll stay here long enough to make sure he follows through with his end and then… then I'm gone. Anna and I will go somewhere no one can find us.

Freedom has always seemed like such a sweet and alluring prospect and yet now that I'm faced with it, I'm not sure what it really means. Nero is, in a way, a captor, a villain bribing and coercing me to do his bidding, and yet, somewhere along the way he became a dark savior I didn't even know I needed. He makes me feel safe, and in my world, safety is like a rare and coveted gem. For the first time in my life, I'm torn between what I want to do and what I should do, because I've never *wanted* anything.

When I get back to the apartment, Nero isn't yet back. I jump in the shower, throwing on one of his shirts after I've dried off. I've become unnecessarily fond of wearing them.

I'm in his bedroom, sitting on the edge of the bed when I hear the elevator open. The sewing kit is in here, and if he's already been stitched then he'll be so out of it on painkillers he'll have to sleep it off. Gio helps him into the room and glances at me, a calculating look crossing his features.

"You going to shoot him again?" He eyes the pistol strapped to my thigh, and I smile. Nero scowls at me, but it's lost on a wince as he leans against the wall next to the door.

"Would you believe me if I said it was for your own good?" I bite my bottom lip, trying to suppress a grin as I glance at Nero.

"You can go, Gio." The calm in his voice is both terrifying and exciting.

"Nero, you're bleeding."

"Go!" he says with more bite this time.

Gio sighs and throws a hard look my way. "If you kill him, I will hunt you down."

"If I wanted him dead, he'd be dead. The hunt would be fun though." I blow him a kiss and he scowls before walking out of the room. "He is way too serious."

Nero stalks towards me. My heart pounds until it's all I can hear, the beautiful crescendo rising like a wave. He's a walking promise of pain and retribution right now. The white of his shirt is stained crimson, matching the fury painted on his face.

He shrugs out of his jacket and leans over me, forcing me to lean back. His face lingers just inches from mine as he strokes his knuckles over my cheek far too gently. Releasing a trembling breath, I'm poised, waiting. Thump-thump, thump-thump, thump-thump. My heart pounds like the drumbeat in a marching band. His fingers leave a sticky damp trail of blood on my cheek before he drags his thumb over my bottom lip. I can practically taste his blood on my tongue as he touches his forehead to mine and closes his eyes. My entire body coils tight like a spring ready to explode, and every single muscle aches with the tension. Lips brush over mine in the whisper of a kiss and I inhale the familiar spicy scent of him, laced with the metallic twang of his blood. When his tongue caresses mine, I moan. It's a distraction from the fingers inching around me throat, squeezing hard enough to cut off my air. I smile.

"You fucking shot me," he growls.

My smile widens, and his eyes flash dangerously. "Plausible deniability," I recite his own words back at him.

"I should just kill you." A cruel smile twists his lips and I gasp when his fingers tighten, pulling me up to meet him.

"You can't kill your queen."

"I no longer need my queen."

"What will it be then, Nero? Kill me or kiss me?"

"Ah, Morte. Both, always both." He shoves me down on the mattress and his arm locks, his full weight pressing down on my windpipe, completely cutting off my oxygen. He stares down at me with fire in his eyes. And there it is, his fury –pure, unbridled rage. The monster is out of his cage and he's come to play. This is our natural state. Him, with his hand at my throat, me, fighting him every step of the way, only to succumb eventually.

I claw at his wrist, gasping for air through my closed throat. He presses even harder and my heartbeat pounds so fast, the fear consuming me, driving the adrenaline through my veins. I want it, I always want it. Reaching for him, I grip his shoulder and push my thumb against the bloody patch on his shirt, trying to feel the torn and damaged tissue through the dressing that Gio has haphazardly applied. He roars and rears back. Seizing the opportunity, I maneuver him onto his back.

"Play nice," I say, straddling his body and leaning over him. Using the heel of my hand, I press against his shoulder, making him hiss out a breath. With very little warning, he explodes upright, catching me by surprise and shredding the material of his own shirt from my body in a fit of rage. I love that in the heat of the moment he's an unpredictable creature, ruled by his violent nature. His bullet wound doesn't seem to bother him as I wrench the buttons of his shirt open. His lips move over my neck angrily, kissing, biting, sucking down the column of my throat and over my collarbone. He tosses me on the bed and flips me onto my front as if I weigh nothing. I hear the clink of his belt buckle, the rustle of material... My body trembles with anticipation, my skin flushing in goose bumps as I wait for the heat of his touch. Fingers dig into my hips, dragging me across the mattress before he lifts my hips. The hot skin of his chest meets my back as I push up on my hands and knees, his body folding over mine. The steady drops of blood hit my shoulder blade before rolling down my side and dropping on the bed. The red spots mar the pale grey of the sheets beneath it, crimson spreading and staining the fibers. Blood and sex are such a heady combination, the evidence of violence only feeding the desire I have for him. His hand meets the back of my neck and he forces my face down onto the bed. I get no warning before his fingers are pushing inside my pussy, making me bite down on my own arm to stifle a moan.

"So fucking wet. Shooting me does it for you, hey?" He pulls out and pushes back in again.

"I like you angry."

"Oh, baby, I'm fucking angry all right." His fingers leave me, and I barely have time to register any movement before his dick slams inside me so hard I'm winded. A strangled sound escapes my throat as I choke on a pained groan. He doesn't give me a chance to recover before he's pounding into me like he hates me. I smile, relishing in every single inch of his rage. "I'm going to tear you in two before I'm fucking done." And he very nearly does. The entire time I can feel the steady dripping of his blood on my back. I let out a feral growl as he hits a point so deep it feels like he's trying to crawl inside me.

"Yes. Break me, Nero," I beg, hoping for his brand of destruction, seeking a punishment and a salvation that only his unbridled rage can mete out. He drives into me even harder and the pain blends with a deep-seated pleasure, pushing me to a place I've never felt before. My core clenches hard and everything explodes outwards, sending waves of pleasure shooting through every single muscle in my body. His name falls from my lips over and over like a curse, and he stiffens behind me on a roar. When he pulls away, he instantly collapses on the bed. I lie there, desperately trying to catch my breath. That was…uncontrolled. I've spent my whole life chasing control, and distance, striving to be rational at all times, and suddenly, he has me craving the opposite of all those things.

I like walking that fine line, fucking him while knowing we could very well kill each other the second it's over. Needing each other, wanting each other, knowing that we're the last thing either of us should be running towards, or maybe I'm wrong. Maybe we're exactly what each other needs. I embrace Nero, my depraved reflection staring right back at me.

I turn my head to the side, glancing at him. His chest rises and falls in deep swells and a thin sheen of sweat covers his skin. Blood is steadily seeping through the dressing at his shoulder. "You're bleeding," I whisper, brushing my fingers over the sticky, wet dressing.

His fingers wrap around my wrist, the grip bruising. "It's fine. The doctor will be here soon."

I sit up, slowly peeling the dressing away from his skin. The neat bullet hole pumps blood steadily. Normally, it wouldn't be an issue, but it's been an hour since I shot him and now his heart rate is elevated. "I'll be back." I get up and take one of his shirts from his closet. Downstairs, I open my rifle case, plucking a single round from its spot nestled in the foam interior. I then grab the cleaning rod that I left in the dining room earlier.

When I get back to the bedroom, Nero hasn't moved. He lies there with his eyes closed, a red stain spreading across the duvet beneath him.

"I need you to sit up. This is going to hurt." His eyes open and he snorts as he follows my instruction.

"More than being shot?"

"A lot more." He glares at me, and I shrug. "Do you want to bleed out?"

He blinks and it takes him a long second before his eyes open again. Placing the tip of the bullet between my teeth, I pop the head off the casing. The wound is a through and through, and the only way to heal it quickly... well, it's not pleasant but it's worth it. I pull the dressing off his back and place the back of the casing against the bullet wound. Glancing at his face quickly, I take a deep breath and shove it inside. His eyes go wide, and he grits his teeth, snarling.

"What the fuck are you doing?"

"Stop being a baby." I press the cleaning rod into the open end of the casing and push, forcing the casing through the open wound. He growls and I'm pretty sure he's going to hit me before I can get it all the way through. The bullet pops out the front of his shoulder and the bleeding quickens. Nero is swaying dangerously, his breaths becoming fast and hard.

Blood steadily runs down his body, flowing over his muscular stomach until it soaks into the seam of his boxers. Grabbing his jacket off the floor, I take his lighter from the pocket, flipping the top back. He frowns and eyes it through drooped eyelids. "What are you doing with that?" His words are slurring slightly now from blood loss and pain.

"I'm sorry." I've had this done to me and it's the worst pain I've ever experienced. Coming from me, that's saying a lot. I move the flame closer to him, holding it to the edge of the wound. A small spark catches and he roars like a wounded beast. Every single muscle in his body contracts and a vein at his temple throbs erratically before he collapses back against the pillows. He drifts on the verge of consciousness, his chest rising and falling rapidly. By pushing the bullet casing through the wound, it leaves a trail of gunpowder. Light it and it instantly cauterizes the wound, killing any infection and stopping the bleeding. It will heal the wound a lot faster, but it hurts worse than the original bullet.

Picking up his legs, I move them, positioning him on the bed. I take the small syringe of morphine that I left beside the sewing kit earlier and slide it into the vein on the inside of his forearm. Within seconds his eyes close and he's out for the count. Maneuvering his unconscious body enough to put dressings on both the entrance and exit wound is not easy feat. He weighs a ton. I hesitate at the edge of the bed, before telling myself I should sleep with him, to keep an eye on him. The steady rhythm of his breathing lulls me to sleep.

The scene unfolds before me, exactly as it has so many times before. Nicholai stands beside me and thrusts the gun into my shaking hand. The tightness wraps itself around my chest, and the guilt and grief rush up around me until I'm drowning in their murky depths. I look at the far wall, to where Alex is chained; only this time, it's not Alex. Nero stares back at me, his face perfect and unmarked, his hard, muscular torso bare and without a trace of the blood that usually features in this dream.

Nicholai brushes that tendril of hair away from my face. "Become what you were meant to be, little dove." His thumb trails over my jaw, and I close my eyes as a tear slips down my cheek. "Put a bullet in his head or put a bullet in your own," he grates, his lips brushing the side of my face.

I open my eyes and instead of seeing Alex begging me to shoot him, Nero demands that I do so. A small smile pulls at his lips and my arm moves of its own volition, lifting the gun as if I were nothing more than a puppet on a string. Panic starts to bubble up my throat and my breathing becomes frantic as I try desperately to lower the gun. I stare at Nero, tears tracking down my face as I realize what is about to happen.

He stares back at me, a cocky smile plastered on his lips. "Do your worst, Morte."

My finger twitches over the trigger and the bang echoes around the room before his body slumps forward against the restraints.

"Nero!" I scream and fall to my knees.

Jolting awake, I gasp, I can't breathe. My vision is blurred with tears and my entire body is shaking as I struggle for air. Nero lets out a pained grunt and then his hand lands on my face before he falls back against the pillows, breath hissing through his teeth. I swipe angrily at the treacherous tears as I slide out of the bed. All I can hear is Nicholai's voice in my head; *You are a weapon and weapons don't weep.*

"Where are you going, Morte?" Every word he says is strained, and I know how much pain he must be in.

"I'll be back." I take the opportunity to go to the kitchen, grabbing the medical kit. There are various painkillers in there and a couple more bottles of morphine. Grabbing a syringe and needle, I head back to the room. The memory of the dream replays in my head like a bad horror film, and I'm shaken, not by the notion of having the dream, but of the fact that shooting him upset me so much. I can't remember ever feeling such a sense of loss, not even when I killed Alex. I loved Alex, but in a way I always knew it would end badly. We grew up in hell and he was never strong enough to bear the atrocities there. He was too good, too kind, loved too hard and sacrificed too much. Nero, on the other hand, always seems so indestructible to me, so utterly implacable, like a cliff face standing against a hurricane. Nero isn't Alex, Nero is more. And didn't I always know that I was a danger to him, just as he was a danger to me? The dream hit too close, felt too real.

Returning to the bedroom, I sit on the edge of the bed, turning the bedside lamp on. Nero squints against the light as he turns his face towards me. He looks pale, the usual golden tan absent from his skin. He stares at me and I drop my eyes to the bottles in my hand, focusing on opening the syringe packet.

He grips my chin with strong fingers and forces me to look at him. "Don't hide from me, Morte."

"I'm not."

His thumb swipes over the corner of my eye. "You're fucking beautiful when you cry." I squeeze my eyes shut and his thumb trails over my cheek. "Tell me about your dream. You screamed my name. Did I hurt you?" I open my eyes and focus on his lips, because I don't want to look in his eyes. "Tell me what could possibly make *death* cry," he whispers, withdrawing his touch.

"I shot you," I admit.

"Yes, you did," he says dryly, those dark eyes watching me closely.

I shake my head. "I killed you."

"You've killed a lot of people."

"This…" My voice gets stuck in my throat. "This was different. I felt like …like a monster," I rasp. I can't tell him that the reason I felt so horrible is because pulling the trigger damn near tore me apart. I don't want to care for him.

"Because you are. Embrace the monster inside you or become consumed by it. That is the difference between brilliance and insanity, Morte."

He crooks a finger at me. Wordlessly, I climb onto his lap, straddling his thighs. My lips press over his and all the noise in my head goes silent, because nothing outside of him exists for these few seconds. This connection I have to him makes me feel safe, he makes me feel safe, and that scares the shit out of me because people like us, we're never safe. He's dark and twisted but so am I, and I want to bask in his depravity. I want to be held by him and feel protected in the knowledge that he is that which others fear. Pressing my forehead to his, I close my eyes, breathing him in. We both know that whatever this is, it's temporary, but for now, I want to experience something I've never had. Him. This. Us.

When I wake up in the morning, Nero is still out of it. I dosed him up on morphine before we fell asleep last night and his chest rises and falls evenly with heavy breaths. His arm is wrapped around my waist, pulling me tightly into his side. I brush my fingers over the warm, smooth skin of his chest, wanting to stay this close to his blistering heat, because he makes me feel as though I'll never be cold again.

I jump when my phone rings, buzzing against the bedside table like a pneumatic drill. Hurrying to disentangle myself from Nero's hold, I quickly pick it up, glancing at the screen. Shit. Getting out of the bed, I leave the room, quietly closing the door behind me before I answer.

"Nicholai."

"Ah, little dove." He croons in Russian. "I have missed you."

"I've missed you, too." It's more a false of habit than anything, but I do have an affection for Nicholai, a bond of sorts, in as much capacity as I have.

"I have a job for you. Very important, a personal favor for a friend. He requested you." A thousand thoughts rush through my mind, but the main one is that I'll have to leave, but of course, I will. I was always going to have to.

"Where?"

"Miami. Your flight is already booked from JFK this afternoon." Shit, that's fast. "It is an urgent job. You have a forty-eight hour deadline and then your target will leave the country."

"Okay. Do you have an in for me?" Most jobs, I have to do my own reconnaissance, but with only two days, the client usually lays out some form of set up and Sasha does the rest.

"I have Sasha here for you." There's a moment of silence before Sasha's voice comes over the line.

"Your target is Diego Rosso," he says. Diego Rosso is a Cuban weapons dealer with a nasty habit of selling weapons to pretty much anyone who wants to buy them. He's actually number eighteen on the FBI's most wanted list, due to his rather friendly relationship with terrorists in Syria and Iraq. His name has popped up several times over the last few years, and I'm familiar with his network.

"I've looked at his credit card statements and it seems that whenever he's in Miami he sends multiple transactions to an escort agency." He's all business. "I hacked the agency's server and they have a booking tomorrow for one Mr. Julian Torres, an alias of his."

"The girl he booked?"

"I'm sending you her name and address now."

"Thanks." I hang up and linger in the hallway, bracing my back against the wall and pressing the top of the phone against my chin as I think through everything I need to do to tie up here. There is no amount of tying that can make leaving okay though, because, for once in my life, the next kill has lost its appeal. My main concern is Anna. I've done Nero's job, now he needs to do his. I'll do this hit, but I will be back, and I will keep coming back for as long as it takes him to find her. Going downstairs, I pack up my shit. Guns, ammo, cash, the laptop. I can't take it with me, but I'll put it back in the storage locker. I then go upstairs, taking each step slowly before I walk down the hallway. My hand hovers over the handle of his bedroom door, and I almost don't want to go in. I could just leave a note and go, but that would be weak, and I don't do weak.

CHAPTER TWENTY-FIVE

Nero

N ero?" I wake at the sound of Una's voice. She's fully dressed in her black combat pants and long-sleeved shirt. Her hair is loose around her shoulders, and a troubled expression mars her face.

"What's wrong?"

"I held up my end of our deal. I want my sister," she says coldly.

I stare at her for a second, trying to see through her defensive bullshit. "And you'll have her. She's in Juarez with one of my contacts."

Her eyes widen. "You've had her this entire time?"

"Since last week. It will take a few days to get her out of Mexico." I push up off the mattress, fighting the urge to just fucking lie back down as the pain tears through the left-hand side of my body. She stands and takes a step back, crossing her arms over her chest. Keeping my left arm clutched to my body, I climb to my feet and head towards the bathroom, ignoring Una. Every step feels like someone is punching me in the shoulder and Una really isn't my favorite person right now.

"I'll be back in a few days," she says casually. I freeze halfway across the room and slowly pivot. She clocks the look on my face as I approach and raises her chin, setting her jaw defiantly.

"Back from where?"

"Miami. Nicholai called me in for a job."

Fucking Nicholai. "So, the master has clicked his fingers and off you run?"

Her fists clench before she takes a deep breath. Her loyalty to him is unflinching because she knows no better. Nicholai *is* all she knows. "I'm a hired killer, so yes, when someone needs killing, I go."

We stare at each other for a long moment, because I want to stop her and she knows it, but I won't, and we both know that too. "Then go."

"Be careful," she whispers, jerking her chin towards my shoulder.

"Shouldn't I be saying that to you?"

A wry smile pulls at her lips. "I'm the kiss of death."

Unable to keep distance between us, I step forward and wrap my free hand around the back of her neck, yanking her close. "No, Morte, you're mine." My lips brush her cheek. "Remember that." I nip her jaw then step back. Words that neither of us are prepared to speak swirl between us, thickening the air with tension. I turn away and go into the bathroom.

Closing the door, I brace my back against it and wait for her to leave. The second I hear her retreating footsteps fade, I pick up the nearest thing, a bottle of hand wash, and launch it at the mirror. The glass smashes, splintering and throwing my own broken reflection back at me. Pain flashes through my shoulder. She's both literally and metaphorically burned me from the inside out, because I want her to the point of irrationality. A possessive rage clings to the edges of my mind.

I know how Una gets to her clients and the imagine of her kissing another guy, allowing him to touch her, wanting him to bury his face in her neck so that she can render him weak and thrust a knife in his back… I see it all so clearly and it's driving me fucking insane. Una is mine, and she can't outrun that.

Una's been gone for a total of six hours, and as much as I try to work, try not to think about her, I can't. The idea of her on a job plagues me, aggravating me. I know when she seduces a client it's not real, but they don't, they think they have a right to her for a few minutes, and even though she kills them for their troubles, it's not enough.

My phone rings, tearing me from my thoughts. The screen flashes showing a south American number. I pick it up.

"Yeah."

"Nero, I have some information that might interest you."
Rafael. His Spanish accent is slight but distinctive.

"And what is this information going to cost me?"

"Consider it a favor to a friend." We're definitely not friends.
Business acquaintances but not friends. "I hear that you are
acquainted with the mad Russians favorite pet." The irony that
he's keeping said pets own sister and he doesn't even know it…

"What about her?"

He pauses and draws a long breath. "I have heard she's very
pretty, much like her sister. It would be a shame for her to meet
her end." How the fuck does he know that Anna is Una's sister?
No one knows that she even has a sister apart from me, her and
Anna, but of course he has Anna. There's no telling what
information the bastard would try and pry from her. I say
nothing because in this situation words are dangerous. He huffs
another laugh. "Five million dollars is a lot of money."

"Five million dollars for what?" I snap.

"The price on her pretty little head of course. I hear the Los
Zetas sent their best sicario for her. He's in Miami now. I
wonder if the angel of death is as good as they say."

"This favor of yours, is there a price tag on it?"

"Just remember it." In other words, he'll call it in at some
point. "Tick tock, Nero. Run capo, run capo, run, run, run." He
sings before laughing and hanging up.

CHAPTER TWENTY-SIX

I normally love Miami, but I think I'm coming down with something and the heat and humidity aren't helping the nausea that's settled into the pit of my stomach since I left Nero yesterday. The car rolls to a stop on a quiet street beneath the shade of a palm tree and I step out.

Elaina Matthews' apartment is in a small building near South beach. It's non-descript, with a set of iron stairs and a walkway that runs along the first floor. Knocking on her door, I wait, hearing the shuffle of footsteps on the other side.

She opens the door in a tracksuit, a pile of blonde hair scooped up on top of her head.

"Yeah?" Her eyebrows pinch together in a frown.

I could probably think of a hundred reasons to have her invite me in, but my head is pounding, and I can't be bothered with the niceties. Instead, I ram my shoulder into her, pushing her back into the apartment.

"Hey!" Slamming the door behind me, I thrust the needle of the small syringe into her neck, depressing the plunger. She reaches for her neck before her eyelids start to droop. The mixture of Ketamine and Rohypnol works quickly and will knock her out for at least eight hours. When she wakes up, she won't remember a thing.

That takes her out of the equation.

Tugging at the hem of my tiny dress, I take the short walk down Ocean Drive to the Beacon Hotel. The street is packed, and it feels like a carnival. There are people everywhere, street performers, girls in bikinis walking up and down holding up signs for various bars. The sidewalk is littered with tables and chairs as the bars sprawl out into the street. People sit drinking cocktails from glasses the size of my head, the liquid smoking and bubbling like a witch's cauldron. Cars crawl along the beach front, chromed out Cadillacs and supped-up sports cars revving their engines and blasting hip-hop music. It's like a street party, and actually, I don't look even slightly out of place in my slutty dress. The number of people coupled with all the music blasting out of each bar has my senses in overload. I can't help but want to listen and probe the area around me for possible threats. I swear I can feel eyes on me, but I can't sense anything past all the noise. Glancing over my shoulder, I attempt to check for followers. The crowd is so dense, I couldn't tell you even if an attacker were right behind me.

I quicken my pace until I reach the hotel. It's an art deco building, slap bang in the middle of the bars and clubs, and honestly, if I were a wanted weapons dealer, it's a location I would pick. If he needs to escape quickly, he could disappear into the swelling crowd in seconds, slip into any one of ten bars that I can see from here. It's a smart move, but I'm not the FBI, I'm not here to cuff him. He won't be running from me.

Stepping inside, I inhale a breath of the cool, conditioned air. Tiled flooring clicks beneath my heels and I glance up to the curved viewing gallery above. A bar opens up to my right, and I instantly spot Diego. The picture Sasha sent me was a blurred surveillance image, but it's enough. Approaching him, I hop up on the stool beside him and order a vodka without sparing him a glance. The barman moves away to make my drink and I twist my face towards him.

He has that typical Miami look with the linen pants and a white shirt, top three buttons undone. Black chest hair peeks through the gap in his shirt and a heavy gold chain hangs around his neck. His hair is shaved almost to his head. He's just an average-looking guy, I suppose.

"Julian?"

He glances in my direction, holding his glass in one hand and a cigarette in the other. As soon as I inhale the smell, it reminds me of Nero, the scent of smoke and expensive cologne. Diego brings the cigarette to his lips, smiling around the filter tip and making it seem like the dirty habit it really is. Whereas Nero can make the simple act of smoking a cigarette look like a work of art.

"Who are you?" His accent is a strange mix of American, Cuban and Spanish.

211

"My name is Isabelle. The agency sent me." I hold my hand out to him and flash him a blinding smile.

"Where is Elaina?" he asks, suspicion lacing his voice. Shit.

"She couldn't make it. The agency thought you might like me instead." I push as much seduction into my voice as possible and his expression softens.

Eyes skate over my body, locking onto the point where the miniscule dress clings to my upper thighs. Lifting his drink towards his lips, he nods. Jesus, how to make a girl feel good about herself. The barman places my drink on the bar and I take a large gulp of the shit vodka.

"Are you from Miami?" I ask.

He downs his drink and slams the glass on the bar a little too hard. "I didn't come here to talk to you."

I smirk because I'm going to enjoy killing this one. "Of course." I neck the remainder of the vodka. "Shall we?"

Standing up, he surprises me by offering his hand. I take it, my fingers brushing over the thick callouses of his palm, which is good, because then he won't notice how equally calloused my hands are. I can pull on a mask and become anyone I need to be, but once a fighter always a fighter and the evidence simply can't be hidden. My knuckles are thick with scar tissue, the silvery white skin marked from splitting open and healing time and time again. It's given me away once or twice.

I allow him to glide his hand around my waist, fighting my less civilized instincts as he leads me out of the bar. Soon, I tell the angry little demon inside my head. The second he gets me in the elevator, I'm pressed against the mirrored wall with his lips on my neck and his hands on my exposed thighs. The doors open, he drags me out, and I play along, allowing him to force me backwards along the corridor. Jeez, when was the last time the guy got laid? My back hits a door and his hand is practically in my underwear as he fumbles with the key card. This usually wouldn't bother me, my cold detachment allowing me to see it as just part of the job. But today I have to grit my teeth and bite back the bile that's rising in my throat. Just a few more seconds. His lips slam over mine and he shoves me into the room.

The door clicks shut, and the second I'm thrown into darkness, a fissure of unease crawls through me. Something's wrong. "You make a shit whore." No sooner have the words sunk in than his hand slams around my throat, almost taking me off my feet as he throws me into a bedside table. I groan, blinking as my eyes adjust to the faint light drifting through the window. A lamp has fallen to the floor beside me and I reach for it, unclicking the light bulb as he closes in on me again. I get to my feet just in time to ram the bulb into his face. It smashes, embedding jagged shards into his skin. He shouts out something in Spanish as the blood pours down his cheek. I nail him in the kidney and he hits me in the face so hard, I almost go down again. Jesus, who is this guy?

Spitting out a mouthful of blood, I crack my neck to the side before going for him again. For every blow I dish out, he gives me one twice as hard. The last time I fought like this I was in training. This is a fight to the death and we both know it. Launching me onto the bed, he lands on top of me, hands clamping around my throat. He doesn't bother with a gentle easing in. No, the grip is hard enough to break my neck, never mind choke me. I crack him in the side of the temple, but it does nothing. Pulling my mind together, I force myself to think and not panic. *Embrace death.* My right hand is pressed between our bodies, if I can just…I manage to move my wrist enough to drop the silver blade from my cuff, and then I jab him in the crotch with it twice. He roars and leaps back off me. Precious air filters into my lungs, dragging a cough from me as I roll onto my front. He grabs me by the back of my neck and tosses me across the room before following and pinning me against the wall with his forearm across my throat.

"Va a ser un buen premio, ángel de la muerte," he hisses in my face. *You will make a fine prize, angel of death.* Only the Mexicans call me that. What the hell did I do to piss them off? He pushes his whole weight against my throat and my nails rake over his face. I press my thumbs into his eyes and he snarls...BANG! Pain slices across my forearm and then he drops to the floor, dead. I whirl to face a shadowy figure rising from the chair in the corner of the room.

"You're losing your touch, morte."

Nero. What the hell? I hold up my finger and bend over, bracing my hands on my knees as I try and breathe through my battered larynx. Glancing at my forearm I note the bright red line, a bullet burn. Motherfucker. "I had that. And what the hell are you doing here?"

I straighten as he approaches me, dragging his eyes slowly over my exposed body. "Working are we?" Glaring, I tug at the hem of my dress which has ridden up, exposing my underwear.

"Why. Are. You. Here?"

Like a snake, he strikes, fingers squeezing my chin to the point of pain. Anger swirls in his irises like an impending storm and the muscles in his jaw contract irritably.

"Were you going to fuck him?" His voice is a low growl.

"What?!"

"Were you going to fuck the sicario?" he repeats, his tone measured and quiet, which is always worrying. The tension rolling off him is thick and turbulent, a pre-cursor to something much more violent.

"I was going to kill him. Or did that little show down look romantic to you? In fact, don't answer that." That's Nero's idea of perfect foreplay.

"If he hadn't tried to kill you?" Hot breath washes over my face, and I can't help the frantic rush of my heart as his potent brand of lust and fear caresses my senses.

"I really think you're missing the important point, which is that he tried to fucking kill me!"

He tilts my head back with a violent shove, bringing his lips close to my ear. "Listen very carefully, Morte. You can run, you can put half the world between us if you like, I don't care. But you are mine. That pussy is mine. These lips are fucking mine." He pulls back and swipes his thumb roughly over my bottom lip. "Kiss another man again, and you won't like what happens next." My stomach tightens along with his grip. So, that's why he let me take a beating, because he's butt hurt that the Mexican kissed me. It's a job! I'll never understand jealousy.

"Were you following me?" He doesn't answer and I shake my head. "You're crazy." I dig my nails into his wrist, and his forehead touches mine on a deep breath.

"This was a set-up. Someone wants you dead. He's one of the best sicarios the Los Zetas has to offer."

"Someone always wants me dead, Nero." Although I've never had any run-ins with the Los Zetas. At least I can feel better about nearly having my ass handed to me though. Those guys are badass.

His grip on my jaw softens, fingers stroking over my cheek. "Enough to pay five million for the hit?"

My eyes go wide, and I glance at the body. Five million. Jesus. "How did you know?"

"I have contacts." Every time I think I know the extent of Nero's power, he surprises me. "Nicholai put you on this job?"

My mind starts spinning through the web of potential betrayal. "Nicholai would never betray me."

"You're an asset to him. And an asset that is now compromised. If he doesn't want you dead then someone else does, and he's selling you upriver." He steps back and drags both hands through his hair. The beat of music from the street below cuts through the silence that lingers as I try and process the possibility of it all.

"No." I shake my head, scraping my teeth over my bleeding bottom lip. He wouldn't, I know he wouldn't. "He cares about me. He treats me like a daughter."

Nero's burning gaze meets mine, barely restrained anger shining through. "Because it suits him. Do not be naïve. You can't trust him."

No, Nicholai is the only one who has ever cared about me besides Alex. Alex...the boy I shot, the boy he made me shoot. I press my balled-up fist to my forehead and squeeze my eyes shut. If I doubt Nicholai then I doubt everything, every single moment that has led me to this exact point in my life.

"He's using you."

I glare at him, feeling cornered and vulnerable. "Like you did, you mean? And why should I trust you?" My world is crumbling around me. What if it's all just a farce, even Nero?

He tilts his head, his expression cool and impassive. "Because you're mine."

That's it, three words that mean nothing and everything.

"You used me, Nero."

"Yes, and you would do exactly the same, Morte." He's right, I remember thinking the same thing that first night when he mentioned Anna's name. The first rule of negotiation, find something your opponent wants and use it. We're both without morals. We're both born of bloodshed and battle. His knuckles stroke over the side of my neck and my pulse picks up. "You and I are the same, and we would both use everything at our disposal to win. So, let them come. We'll destroy them all." A twisted smile pulls at his lips, and for a moment I feel whole, protected, like I could rely on him. Worse; that I want to. I grab a handful of his thick hair, pulling his face to mine. He kisses me like he owns a piece of me, and he does, because I'm his queen and he's my bloodied king.

CHAPTER TWENTY-SEVEN

Una

We buy a car with cash and hit the road, heading back to New York. Nero's theory is that I'll be safe within his ranks until I can work out who wants me dead, and then…we kill them. That's all we have to go on for now.

Pulling my knees to my chest, I rest my forehead on them. The confines of the car are making me nauseous again. Great. We've only been on the road for two hours.

"You know, you should stay out of this." The pale blue glow of the dashboard casts his face in an eerie light and his lips curl slightly.

"Morte, from the moment I propositioned you, we were tied. If someone is coming after you, it's because of me."

"Which means they'll be coming for you," I finish. He nods. I study his reaction. "You know who it is."

"I have an idea." He glances at me briefly before turning back to the road. "The hit came the day after the shooting. Only an Italian would be annoyed at the death of three other Italians. Arnaldo knows I was shot, but fuck, I'd be suspicious that only Gio and I managed to escape a massacre."

"He helped you with Lorenzo's assassination though..."

"Yes, but he thought I could be controlled."

"And now you're off book and he's suddenly realized that you can't be leashed."

He nods. "You left the calling card. I walked away with a mild injury. If he knows we're working together then as far as he's concerned, I just bit the hand that feeds me, and so did you."

"It doesn't explain why Nicholai called it in though."

He straightens his arms, pressing his back into the seat. "I don't know, but we trust no one until we have more to go on."

"You could still go back. I can run, and he'll have to come after me. He supported you for capo, so to admit that you went against him would make him look weak. He then goes after the kiss of death, and it looks like he's seeking retribution. No one would ever know you were involved."

He huffs a laugh. "Noble, Morte, but haven't you worked it out yet?" He glances at me and cocks a brow. "I live for war."

"What about Anna?" Nero and I may be willing to fight, but I didn't go through all this to save her, just to drag her into a warzone.

"She'll be safe," he says dismissively, and it instantly makes me suspicious. There's not a lot I can do about it right now though. If I don't save myself, there will be no one to save her.

I grip the edge of the toilet and throw up into it. This has to be a new low in my life, facing the disgusting toilet bowl of a rest stop bathroom.

"Una!" Nero bangs on the door, rattling the metal lock.

"Give me a second."
This is the second day of this, and I feel like death. I don't get ill, but I've been feeling awful since before Miami. We're just outside Washington though, so we should be in New York at some point tonight. I hear voices outside the bathroom, and it sounds like Nero is arguing with someone before it goes quiet.

"Sweetheart, you need some help?" a heavily accented female voice asks.

Great. I unlock the door and smile politely.

"I'm fine. Thank you." Her eyes trace over my face, and I'm aware that I look like shit. She's a middle-aged woman with peroxide blonde hair and far too much makeup on. A name badge at her chest that reads; Wendy-Anne. She smiles kindly, and I see a flash of pity in her eyes before she shoves her way inside and closes the door.

"How far along?" she asks.

I frown at her. "Sorry, what?" She glances down at my stomach and I follow her gaze. What the hell is she looking at?

"How long ya been throwing up, sweetie?"

"Uh, a couple of days." This is one of those situations where I kind of want to head-butt her, but the motion would probably make me throw up again.

She presses her lips together in a thin line and glances over her shoulder. "You stay here. I'll be back in a jiffy. I told that fella of yours to leave you be." She winks and then steps out of the bathroom. I have no idea what she's doing but my stomach turns over again and I dive for the toilet.

When she comes back, I'm sitting on the dirty floor waiting for the next round of vomiting. "Here ya go, lovey." She hands me a box and I take it, frowning as I read the front.

"A pregnancy test?" I raise my eyebrows. "I'm not pregnant. I'm sterile," I tell her flatly, handing the box back to her. I've been sterile since I was fourteen, all of Nicholai's Elite are.

"My sister, Eileen, she had them tubes tied. Then there she is, forty years old and knocked up." She shakes her head, pushing the box back towards me. "Ain't gonna hurt nothin' to rule it out." She turns and walks out of the room.

"I'm not pregnant!" I call to her retreating back, but she ignores me and closes the door. I stare at the box for a moment, terrified of it. It's impossible, so this is fine. A little white stick falls out when I open the box. Growing up with guys hadn't exactly leant me to know about anything like this. Hell, I grew up learning how to kill people. This wasn't something I ever even thought of, let alone knew about.

Two minutes has never felt so long. I leave the stick on the counter and pace the short circuit from the door to the sink, almost jumping out of my skin when the door bangs. "Una, we need to fucking go," Nero calls.

"Give me a minute."

This is stupid. I'm not pregnant. I pick up the stick, and the two red lines sit in that tiny little window. I read over the instructions three times. Two lines means positive.

"Una!" I startle and drop the stick, scrambling to pick it up and put it in the bin before I open the door. I hope my expression isn't giving away what I'm feeling right now, because if it is, Nero will think someone has died.

"Let's go." I walk straight past him and out the door. Wendy-Anne smiles at me from behind the till, and I manage a small smile back. This sinking, plummeting feeling has settled into my gut and it feels like I'm walking to my own funeral. This is impossible.

CHAPTER TWENTY-EIGHT

Nero

Pulling back the curtain an inch, I look out over the parking lot of the shitty motel. The likelihood of anyone coming for us here is slim, but I'm still edgy.

Una has a pistol in pieces on the bed, cleaning it. She's been doing it for the last hour, her brows pulled together and her eyes lost and distant. I know it's Arnaldo who's put a hit on her, just as I suspected he would. But when I put this entire plan into motion, I never for a second thought that I would want her so badly. To own Una body and soul. I want to stand beside her and make our enemies bleed. She's no longer a tool; she's the perfect ally, the perfect complement to everything I am. How do you let that go when you know you'll never find it again? Una is my own personal obsession, my weakness and my strength. Together, we're unstoppable.

Crossing the room, I remove the gun barrel she's been cleaning for the last ten minutes from her hand. I place a finger under her chin and force her to look at me. There's a smudge of gun oil on her cheek, smeared over the porcelain skin. Wide indigo eyes meet mine.

"You only clean your guns before you're about to kill someone. Should I be worried?"

She huffs and falls back against the pillows. "It clears my mind." She's wearing one of my shirts again and it pulls up, showing just a flash of her underwear. The sight of her long, bare legs is enough to make my dick hard. Her eyes shift to the dressing at my shoulder. "Come here, let me look at that."

I move closer to the bed and she crawls to me, getting to her knees so she can peel the dressing away. Her fingers are gentle but firm against my skin. The wound still hurts, because that's what happens when someone shoots you and then sets you on fire. I've stopped taking the painkillers because they cloud my mind, and I need complete clarity. "This looks good," she says under her breath.

"No thanks to you."

"It would be much worse if I hadn't used the gun powder."

"It would be much better if you hadn't shot me."

"You know, you're really hung up on that." Her lips quirk into a smile, and I grip the back of her neck, pulling her close. Those indigo eyes drop to my mouth, her lips parting.

"I figure you owe me."

When I kiss her, she tastes of blood and death and everything I want. My free hand slips up her body and beneath her shirt until I'm brushing her breast. Shoving her back on the bed, I crawl between her thighs. Her chest rises and falls erratically, fingers threading through my hair as I kiss over her hip bone and shove the shirt further and further up her body. She's fucking beautiful; toned curves and pale skin, littered with scars, some faded to silver while others are still a rich purple. Her body is a portrait of a hard and violent life, and each and every scar only makes me harder for her.

She yanks at my belt until it comes undone, and then grabs my throat, digging her fingers in on either side of my Adam's apple. When I pull away, she shoves me to my back on the mattress. Then lands on top of me.

"You just love to fucking push me," I growl, grabbing her around the throat. We always end up right here because it's where we belong.

"You know I like you angry." I tighten my grip and a brilliant smile crosses her face. She looks so perfect; innocence and seduction all wrapped up with a fucked up little bow on the top as if she were made for me. When I palm her breast, her body bows, sending white-blonde hair cascading down her back. Those full lips part on a soft moan, and I press my thumb inside her mouth. The little noises she makes and the stroke of her warm tongue nearly make me explode. Sitting up, I bring us face-to-face, wrapping my arms around her until every naked inch of her is pressed against me. To the rest of the world, she's the whisper of death on the wind, feared and revered. And yet here she is, so beautifully vulnerable and trusting in my arms. She feels like all the parts of me I didn't even know were missing, the parts I didn't even want.

The lace of her underwear drags over my cock as she rolls her hips in a move nothing short of pure torture. I have no patience when it comes to her, so I grab the crotch of her panties and tear them away. Her fingers dive into my hair, yanking, demanding. I grip her hips, equally as demanding as I force her down on my waiting cock. The trembling of her body is so beautiful. Her pussy feels like the closest I'll ever get to heaven. She touches her forehead to mine and I close my eyes, feeling her rapid breaths blow over my face. We stay like that for a second, her clinging to my shoulders while I imprison her against me. Her hips begin to roll lazily, and I bite back a groan. I've fucked Una a lot but every time feels more intense than the last. She's like a slow burn scorching everything she touches, and fuck, if I don't want her to incinerate me. I trail my hands up her back, feeling the ancient bumps and welts of long worn scars. And when she comes, it's like art and music blended into one perfect masterpiece. I bite her bottom lip, swallowing her moans as her pussy clamps down on me. It's enough to make me explode inside her and collapse back on the mattress.

I turn to face Una where she lays beside me, but her expression is distant, detached. Something's wrong with her, and I'd say it's the threat of death, but as she said herself, someone always wants her dead. It's more than that. She gets up and goes into the shitty en suite. The door closes behind her and the lock clicks into place.

CHAPTER TWENTY-NINE

Una

My back presses against the bathroom door and I squeeze my eyes shut. This is too hard; being around him is too hard. I thought I could make it back to New York and then figure out a plan, but who am I kidding? There is no plan for this because this is the only eventuality I couldn't possibly have predicted. I stare down at my flat stomach both horrified and mesmerized by the prospect. My head is telling me there is only one option here, that I need to go to a clinic and take care of it. But the heart I never had until a few weeks ago is hesitating, which is ridiculous. It's funny that when something is never even a possibility, you never think about it. And then when it's suddenly thrust in front of you, the reaction you might imagine yourself having never comes. I'm not so stupid as to think that I can have a baby. It's ridiculous. But, I've never done anything good in my life and probably never will. I bring death and destruction wherever I go. I can't stomach the thought of bringing death to something so innocent, something that defies all odds, and it makes me a hypocrite of the worst kind.

A plan starts to form in my mind and it's not ideal, but it's the best I have right now.

"Una," Nero calls from the other side of the door.

"Yeah?"

"I'm going to grab some food."

"Okay."

Now, it needs to be now. Once I'm in New York it will be harder, Nero will be around and if he's not then his men will be. As soon as I hear the motel room door slam, I move. I only have a small bag with me, with just enough clothes for a few days, some cash, a couple of burner phones and one gun. It's enough. For now. I throw on clothes and grab my stuff quickly. My hand is on the doorknob when I stop. I can't just leave him like this. I can't explain to him all the reasons why, but I can give him something.

I take a scrap of paper, letterhead with the motel's cheap looking logo. I hover with the pen over the paper for several moments. How do I say goodbye in a scribbled note? Nothing has changed and yet, everything has. He came for me, put his neck on the line, again, and now I'm leaving without so much as a word. Maybe I should just give him the truth. But then this is Nero. He's not the guy that has babies; he's the guy that puts a gun to their heads when their parents won't do what he wants. He doesn't need to know this.

Nero.

I can't stay with you. I know you would stand by me and fight the world if I asked you to, but this is my war and you shouldn't be a casualty of it. Take your power, live your life. Please keep Anna safe. I'll be back. I just have some things to take care of. Wait for me. Queen always protects king.

Una.

He'll believe that, and he'll let me run. I can't pretend this isn't happening, and I can't just hope that Nero could deal with it. We aren't those people with the white picket fence and the normal lives. We're killers, depraved and motivated by the kinds of things that keep most people up at night. Everything is going to shit all at once. Time and space are what I need to figure it out without burdening him. This is on me, and it's best that way. When you rely on other people it only weakens you, and I can't afford weakness now.

Dropping the note on the bed, I hoist the duffel bag over my shoulder, leaving that run-down motel room without a backwards glance. As soon as I'm on the main road, I stick my thumb out, and it doesn't take long before a guy in a pickup truck pulls over.

"Where ya goin', sweetheart?" he says, tipping his cowboy hat back.

"The airport, please."

I'm now officially on the run. Let the chase begin.

KISS
ME

Kiss of death #2

LP LOVELL

PROLOGUE

My heart slams against my ribs as I stand in the living room of the London apartment, shaking with adrenaline. My fingers ache from gripping the knife so tightly. Something touches my bare foot and I glance down at the pool of blood spreading across the hardwood floor. It creeps around my foot like a river parting around a rock. The blood spreads, spewing from the severed artery of the stranger only a few feet away. I'm an island in a sea of death and chaos. Crimson splatters the walls, spraying over the cheap furniture and staining everything in a way that will never truly wash out. Closing my eyes, I inhale the metallic scent mixing with the lingering hint of gunpowder. That smell is like crack to me. It reminds me that I am death itself.

Five bodies. Five men sent here for the sole purpose of killing me. I've been running for six weeks and in that time, I've been hunted mercilessly. Though, I'd expect nothing less. Five million dollars is an inspirational amount of money, and it's currently the price on my head. I have but one friend left in this world. One person I can trust. Sasha. He helps me stay one step ahead, calling on his contacts so he can warn me when they're coming. But that job is getting harder and harder because I have enemies coming at me from all directions. Sasha confirmed in the last two weeks that it is indeed Arnaldo Boticelli who put the hit on me, just as Nero suspected. So now I have the Italian underboss out for my blood. Nicholai is also looking for me because I defied his order to return to Moscow, and then, of course, there's Nero. I should have known he wouldn't just let me walk away, that he wouldn't be content with my simple promise to return to him. Two weeks ago he turned up here, but it's the apartment on the floor below that I registered under one of my known aliases. This one, I rent cash in hand. No name.

Why rent another apartment under a name I know they'll find? Why bring them here? Because I'm Una Ivanov, and though I may be running for now, I don't hide. If they want me, they can come. I will slaughter every last one of Arnaldo's men if I have to. But a week ago, it wasn't Arnaldo's men that turned up.

The downstairs apartment is rigged with alarms and sensors. The second someone sets foot inside that place, I know about it. The alarm tripped, so I left and went to my spot across the street: a fire escape sheltered in the shadow of a dark alleyway. From there I had a clear vantage point into the apartment, and it's there that I saw Nero. Through my rifle sights I could see the hard set of his jaw, the strain behind his eyes. Of all the people hunting me, Nero Verdi may well be the one I fear the most. You can kill enemies. You can even fight yourself, but you can't fight fate. You can't kill the only person you feel anything for, because as ruthless and violent as Nero is, we're two halves of the whole, hopelessly drawn to one another's darkness. I long for the rush only his brand of fear can possibly ignite. He once told me that I can run, that I can put half the world between us, but I will always be his. I am his, and he is the father of my child. He came here, to London, which makes this more dangerous than ever. He couldn't know about the pregnancy. He's an unpredictable creature at the best of times, but this…I can't even imagine how he'd react. I need time. Six more months to be exact. And then I'll return to him like I said I would.

He has my sister after all.

I blink and glance down at my not quite flat stomach. I have to leave. They took me by surprise this time, snuck in here in the middle of the night. The alarms downstairs never went off. They found me here, in my actual apartment. I can't get rid of these bodies without calling in help, and help will lead my enemies to me like sharks to a fresh kill. I pick up the burner phone I've been using and send a text to Sasha. *Need a clean-up at the apartment for five. Going dark.*

I take a quick shower. The water runs crimson as I scrub the layers of blood from my skin. Wiping the condensation off the mirror, I stare at the reflection. I barely recognize myself and that's good. My once white-blonde hair is now chocolate brown, though the dye is fading in places. I find a Band-Aid and place it over the bleeding split on my cheek. My jaw is marred with an angry red mark and my throat is already turning purple from the belt one of them tried to choke me with. This is England. Gun fights are conspicuous. Luckily for me. It's far easier to take out five guys when they can't shoot you. I throw on a pair of jeans and a loose-fitting hoody, and then I'm leaving with only one bag. I have cash, my knife, several fake passports and a laptop. That's it. I walk the dark streets to the nearby London Underground and head for Victoria Station. From there I'll buy a ticket with cash and get the hell out of here. Maybe I'll go to Ireland, or even Paris, who knows? And the less I know, the harder it is for anyone to follow me. The key to running is to not have a plan, to be spontaneous, and most importantly, to be inconspicuous.

Even I don't know what I'm going to do next, and neither does Arnaldo.

CHAPTER ONE

Una

I hand the guy behind the desk a fake driver's license under the name of Sarah Jacobs. He glances at it and pops it on the photocopier before handing it back to me along with a key.

"N24," he says, his tone bored.

"Thank you." I hitch my bag higher on my shoulder before taking the elevator down to the parking garage. Space N24 is a sleek looking black Mercedes. I throw my bag inside before climbing in and starting the engine. I have no time to waste. In and out.

I pull out of JFK airport and head for the Brooklyn bridge. I need supplies, guns, ammunition, explosives, a bullet proof vest. I debated disappearing into Europe, but I just couldn't stomach the idea of running away from that spineless Italian shit. Nero and Nicholai scare me infinitely more, but Arnaldo is nothing and I'm getting bored of killing his men for him. I'm about to willingly walk into the lion's den so I can kill the pride male and mount his fucking head.

I've broken into Arnaldo's house several times before and I know most of the entrances. Every hidden shadow and camera free nook. I'm going for distract and conquer. Approaching the main gate on foot, I pull my hood up higher, keeping my head dipped and face shadowed. I slide my hands in my pockets, wrapping my fingers around the two grenades and slipping the pins. I drop to one knee and roll them towards the gate. The metal tinkers over the tarmac—the sound such an innocent prelude to the upcoming carnage. I spin around and hunch over just as they explode. Heat hits my back and bits of debris fly past me. There's a creaking of metal followed by a heavy bang as the gate collapses off its hinge. I'm up and running for the woods to the right-hand side of the gateway before the last bits of debris have even settled. Two guards stagger out of the small hut beside the gate and each gets a bullet in the head. I tuck my gun back into my thigh holster and duck into the woodland, following the perimeter wall to the rear of the property.

The back of the house is lit up like the fourth of July, which isn't ideal, but the benefit is it's lightly guarded. There is, however, a guard armed with a rifle usually on the roof. I think the explosion at the gate will be enough to distract the ground security, but assumption is death. I pull myself up onto the wide wall and pause for a second before dropping down on the other side. The pool is in front of me, casting a luminescent blue light across the lawn. Palming my gun, I sprint across the lawn to the nearest shrub, ducking behind it. I'm waiting on baited-breath for the second when an unseen bullet rips through my chest, or perhaps it'll be a head shot and I won't know a thing about it. I hesitate for a second, brushing my palm over my stomach. If I die here today, then so does my baby, and that's…that's a life I'm not willing to sacrifice. This feels like the only thing that matters, perhaps the only thing I will ever do with my life that is truly worthwhile. The problem is I'm backed into a corner with no safe way out. I can't bring this child into the world with Arnaldo on my trail because if I die, then this was all just meaningless. What happens in a couple of month's time when I'm hindered by the pregnancy? When I can't defend myself properly? No, I must do this right now. It's the last chance I'm going to get. I'm Una Ivanov. I will survive, and then I'll disappear like a ghost in the night, have this baby, and get back to doing what I do best. Killing. The child can have a loving family, a chance at normal. It's the best I have to offer it.

With a new-found resolve, I sprint the last few meters to the house, pressing my back to the wall. Honestly, Arnie should really up his security. I slip the backpack off my shoulders and dig inside, pulling out a few blocks of C4. I could have asked Sasha for help, had him hack the security system, and black out the cameras. I probably could have killed Arnaldo without my presence ever even being noticed, but that's not what this is about. I want him to sit in his office and watch his precious house get blown to bits. I want him to witness his men die, one after the other, until he comes to the stark realization that I'm coming for him and there's no one left to protect him. Nowhere left to run. This is about more than just killing him. This is a message: no one hunts death. He's not the first to underestimate me. Of course, he won't be expecting me to come here. Even if it weren't physically suicidal, politically, it's dodgy ground. The Italians might see it as fair. He came after me, so I went after him. Or, they might make me enemy number one, in which case, the entire Italian mafia will be after me. But I have the backing of the Russians….I think. And I'd be lying if I said that I didn't have an unnatural amount of faith in Nero. God knows why. He's a capo in the very same mafia, but he's also their bad boy. A wild card, and, in his own words, I am his. Honestly, he's just as likely to shoot me as side with me, but a girl can hope. And let's be honest, I have an ace up my sleeve, or should I say, in my uterus.

I set up the C4 and move around the corner of the building to blow it. The explosion rips a hole in the back of the house, and I palm my gun, jogging through the carnage and rubble into the building. I shoot at anything that moves, just about making out shadows through the smoke. I point, shoot. Point, shoot. Reload. And so it goes on, until the bodies pile up just as fast as the bullet casings and finally an eerie silence permeates the air around me. The only sound is the steady crackling of fire, backed by the occasional crumbling of the building around me.

I wait a beat before releasing the clips from both pistols and re-loading them as I navigate the desecrated kitchen units. My muscles ache with tension as I move into the hallway. The house is too quiet. This feels too easy. My heart pounds in my chest, my pulse hammering against my ear drums in a mocking beat.

I pause when I hear the tiniest movement from the darkened doorway ahead of me. It's enough. I drop to the floor in the blink of an eye and fire off two shots. I scarcely make it to my feet before I have a gun in my face. I shove his wrist off to the side and shoot him in the gut. He's not dead, but he makes the perfect body shield. Slumping against me, I take his weight, sliding my arms beneath his and firing at four guys who are all coming at me. Bullets hit my friend here and he grunts before falling limp. I stagger under his dead weight and then hear the tell-tell clink of a grenade pin. Fuck. Something hits my boot and I throw the body down on top of the explosive before running for the nearest doorway. I don't make it. A hand flies out, punching me in the throat so hard I'm pretty sure he just collapsed my oesophagus. The grenade goes off, the bang loud enough to make my ears ring. Something wet hits my face and I blink, crawling around on the floor and gasping for air until my vision spots. I make out a pair of boots in my line of sight and force myself to focus, to calm. I drop the small pin blade from the cuff at my wrist and palm it conspicuously.

"Kiss of Death, my ass." The heavily accented voice mocks. I manage to draw a small amount of air into my lungs and move. My hand flashes out and I drag the blade over the back of his ankle, severing his Achilles tendon. He goes down hard, his leg giving way beneath him. "Fucking bitch," he curses before I jam the tiny blade into the side of his neck and yank it towards me. His jugular opens like a tap and blood sprays across the tile floor. Climbing to my feet, I slide the blade back into the cuff and pick up my guns from the floor. Arnaldo's office is on the other side of the house, and who knows how many soldiers he has between me and him.

I'm surprised when I only encounter a handful more guys. I guess Arnaldo's running low on soldiers, seeing as I keep killing the one's he sends me. The mafia are nothing if not arrogant, sitting here in their mansions, thinking no one will dare attack them. His few remaining men go down easily enough and soon I find myself standing outside Arnie's office. The second I open those doors; it's going to rain bullets. He wouldn't have left himself completely undefended. He always has at least two men with him at all times, and given the situation, I'd expect more. I fix my gaze on the small camera just above the door. I know he can see me.

I take two more grenades from my rucksack and lift them to my face, placing my lips against the cool metal as I stare at the camera. A red lipstick mark remains on the metal. My calling card. Fitting, really, in my potentially last blaze of glory. Smiling, I drop the grenades, allowing them to roll towards the doors. I spin away, ducking behind one of the thick marble pillars that adorns his hideously ostentatious hallway. The second they detonate, I'm moving towards the mangled office doorway, guns drawn and bullets flying. A bullet tears through my thigh and I grit my teeth, ducking beside the doorway.

Glancing down, I curse under my breath at the blood running down my leg, soaking my pants. "Come now, Arnie. That's no way to treat your guests," I call.

"You are an enemy at the gates, Bacio Della Morte. You may be revered as a killer, but you will die like a dog."

I laugh. "Maybe, but I sure fucked up your shit on my way out." I back away from the doorway, limping as I go.

"Bricks and mortar..." I take a running start, pain lancing up my leg as I do. When I'm a couple of feet away from the doorway, I drop to my knees. The blood pouring from my leg helps me to slide across the marble floor. I take two shots, before coming to a stop on the other side of the door. A second later and I hear the muted thud of bodies hitting the floor. *Two.* Two bodies. I don't know how many there are though. They could be hiding behind the very walls I now take shelter against.

"Was that bricks and mortar?" I ask through gritted teeth. Resting my back against the wall, I reach beneath my hoody and grab the bottom of my tank top, tearing a thick strip of material away. I tie it just above the bullet wound as tight as I can get it. Closing my eyes, I rest my head against the wall. I know I'm out, but I release the clip on each gun, checking them, just in case I miscounted. I haven't. Fuck. I drop one gun on the floor, keeping a hold of the other. It may be empty, but he doesn't know that. Taking the dagger from my thigh holster, I palm it as I stand. I step into the doorway of the office without hesitation, because perception is everything. Nero can walk into a room full of armed men and completely unnerve them simply because he's so confident, so utterly in control of everything around him. I try to channel his sense of power and entitlement. Arnaldo sits behind his desk, seemingly alone aside from the two dead guards either side of his desk. With a grimace, he lifts his gun and I throw mine at him. It clocks him square in the forehead, leaving him dazed enough that I cross the space to his desk and ram my knife through his wrist, pinning it to the wood. He screams like the little bitch he is, fingers going slack on the gun with severed nerves. I pick up the gun and he watches me, his expression masked in pain. I slide onto the desk in front of him and grab a handful of his greying hair.

"You came after me, Arnie," I tut.

"You aligned with *him*." He spits the words. Blood spreads over the desk, trickling over the edge of the wood and hitting the floor in a steady patter.

"I sell to the highest bidder. He paid more." He paid me with something money can't buy. My sister.

"You're going to die. Your Russian sugar daddy can't help you this time," His fingers wrap around the hilt of my knife. I'm impressed when he wrenches it free from his arm and makes a sloppy dive at me. My palm meets the centre of his forearm and I smile when I hear the satisfying crack of his bone followed by an agonized cry of pain. Men like Arnaldo are not to be taken lightly, but the fact is, they are power players, men who sit behind desks calling shots and rarely killing anyone themselves. When the occasion calls for it, they pull a trigger. He's no match for me and he knows it. I see the defeat in his eyes. The resolve as I bring the knife to his neck. And then I look him right in the eye as I drag my blade across his throat. His eyes go wide and a gurgled choking sound slips past his lips as blood gushes everywhere.

I grip his chin and his fading eyes meet mine. "I don't need help. I'm the kiss of death." I press my lips to his forehead, and when I pull away, that futile last breath leaves his body in a hiss.

I usually feel a small thrill when I kill a target, this time though, I truly feel nothing. Arnaldo was not a mark. He was not a pay cheque. He was not the enemy of some faceless client. He *made* himself my enemy. This was personal. This is what happens when you seek out death. She comes for you. And now, I leave. I just killed the under-boss of the Italian mafia, and there are consequences to that.

245

CHAPTER TWO

Rage. It's my constant companion, driving me to the edge of sanity with each passing day. And Una Ivanov is the fucking cause. I know she can look after herself and she sure as shit doesn't need my protection, but the price on her head is high. High enough to even the odds against her dramatically. If I know anything about Una—the more Arnaldo backs her into a corner, the worse he's making it for himself. It seems he's forgotten who he's dealing with, and if she doesn't remind him of it, then Nicholai Ivanov damn well will. The crazy Russian won't take it well when he hears his favorite pet is being hunted like a dog.

Nothing is playing out the way I planned. She was supposed to be by pawn and instead, she became my queen. My vicious little queen…until she ran from me. What is that saying? You don't know what you have until it's gone? Well, I couldn't possibly have predicted just how much she had gotten under my skin until she left. I should let her go. She's a weakness I don't need. Not to mention the amount of heat that's on her, but every time I think about walking away, about the possibility of her being killed, or worse, surviving…moving on, fucking someone else – I can't. She can't. She's mine and no one else touches her but me.

"Nero," I turn from my spot at the window and face Gio who's standing in the doorway to my temporary office in the London apartment.

"Have you found her?" I ask.

He folds his arms over his chest. "Not exactly."

*****

It looks like something out of a horror film. Five bodies and what looks like the blood of ten. The carpets. The walls. The couch…everything is crimson. I move through the apartment, my eyes skimming over the few possessions Una left behind. There's nothing personal, nothing that would give her away as ever having been here—except the blood bath in the living room. The entire apartment has that nuetral feel of a rental. The en-suite bathroom has a couple of bottles of shampoo, a razor…I pick up the shampoo and open the lid, inhaling. Vanilla. The smell instantly reminds me of her, though it's missing the lacing of gun oil that clings to her. I leave the bathroom and pause in the bedroom doorway, my gaze moving from the bed that I know she was just recently sleeping in to the dead man sprawled on the rug. The hilt of a knife protrudes from his forehead, buried so deep, there's barely any blood. I bend down and yank the knife it free. I inspect the simple yet delicate dagger, smiling as I imagine Arnaldo's kill team creeping up on Una in the dark only to find themselves the victims of a nightmare.

"The cleaners called it in," Gio says, his expression pinched as he leans against the window. We've paid off every possible underground contact we could find, and the cleaners are a good place to start. They're impartial, a third party who will clean up anything as long as they get paid. "She didn't call them though, the Russians did."

"They're supporting her?"

"I guess she isn't leaving them with much choice. They don't want this kind of heat." He waves his hand towards the living room. That's true, but this really was inevitable. Arnaldo keeps sending men after her like she's a bleeding animal with a damn prize hide. Sooner or later she was going to make a mess she couldn't clean up alone. And here we are.

"No, this is more than that. These bodies are at least twenty-four hours old. They're actively helping her. They waited to call it in. They gave her a chance to get clear." I know Nicholai is fond of her, but to help her now would put himself in the firing line. The Russian is crazy, but enough to risk causing a war?

"This isn't her style either. She's clean efficient. This..." he drifts off.

"She's sending a message."

"Message received," he says under his breath. His phone pings in his hand and he glances down at the screen, face draining of color.

"What is it?"

He closes the distance to me and turns the screen. It's an image of Arnaldo's severed head sat on his desk, a red lipstick mark on his waxy forehead. A slow smile pulls at my lips. She did it. Months of planning. Her, her sister...all part of the bigger plan. All part of this. But then he put a hit on her and everything went to shit. I never for a second expected her to walk into Arnaldo's house and take him out. Alone. "She got away?"

"They haven't caught her if that's what you mean. She killed eighteen of his men." I have to laugh.

"We just lost track of her, and she's probably become even more wanted. Why the hell are you smiling?"

We did lose her, for now, but I will find her. "Because she's fucking perfect."

"You're insane."

I'm about to get everything I've ever wanted, except her. I must find her because without her, all the power in the world wouldn't be enough to fill the void left by my vicious little butterfly.

"Let's go back to New York."

I pull the car up next to a stack of containers at the edge of the shipping yard. The early morning sun glares off the surface of the Hudson River and a boat horn drifts on the wind. Gio is practically bristling with tension beside me. "I don't like this," he murmurs. "I don't trust Russians."

"Una's Russian."

"Exactly."

I'll admit that I usually wouldn't agree to this meeting. One call to my phone, a heavily accented voice simply stating a time and place. Nothing more. The only reason I'm here is because that accent was Russian. The only common factor between me and the Russians is Una.

I cut the engine and, for a second, neither of us move. I stare through the windshield at the tall, lean guy resting against the hood of a Jaguar sports car. His blond hair, catches in the light, and sharp green eyes stare unflinchingly back at us. Him and Una could be siblings with their cold, pale features.

I get out of the car, feeling the weight of my gun strapped to my chest. The Russian pushes away from his car, moving like a predator and dancer wrapped into one; calculated and lethal. Just like Una. *He's one of the Elite.* I instantly go for my gun and he tracks the movement like a wolf watching a rabbit with complete indifference and the knowledge that it could end the lesser creature in an instant. Of course, the Elite feel no fear, even when they should.

"Don't do that," he says in heavily accented Italian.

I grip the gun and drop my arm at my side, my index finger hovering over the trigger. "Who are you?"

"Sasha, a friend of Una's."

"Forgive us if we aren't too keen on Una's brand of friend." Gio comes to stand beside me.

"She is more like my sister." His brows pull together as his eyes shift from Gio to me. It's the closest to an expression I've seen from him. "So you are the Italian that lead her to destruction."

"Why are you here?" I ask, quickly running out of patience.

"I do not like you." He narrows his eyes, "but she is dangerous right now. Nineteen Italians is too many. She is the best I have ever seen, but even the best cannot stand against the entire Italian mafia. And I can only help her so much before Nicholai finds out."

"It was you," Gio shifts on his feet. "You called in the cleaners for her."

Sasha nods. "I will do anything for her, but I cannot betray Nicholai, and he wants her back. She killed Arnaldo Boticelli. She went too far. She could maybe run from our father, but not with the Italians hunting her. I cannot protect her anymore. But you can."

I take a steadying breath. "She ran from me. What makes you think I can help her?"

He moves closer until he's standing directly in front of me, those cold, unsettling eyes boring into mine. "We both know that you are not what you seem, Nero *Verdi*. What is it they say? With great power comes great responsibility. I do not know whether you are friend or enemy," he looks me up and down, "but she must have trusted you."

I smirk. "She didn't trust me."

His expression remains unmoved. "She needs help." *Yeah, no shit.* That ship sailed a long time ago. "Get her, and protect her from both your own people and mine. Arnaldo is dead, but revenge is inevitable. Nicholai wants her back, and you have no idea the lengths he will go to for her."

"What will he do to her?" She went completely rogue, helped me do something she never should have for a sister she's supposed to be too cold to care about.

"The human mind is pliant. He can make her forget." He sounds like a damn robot, and I try to remember if Una was ever like this. "He can fix her."

"Fix her?" My fists clench and heat simmers just below my skin, even as a cool breeze drifts across the dockside.

The Russian nods once before turning and walking away. He yanks his car door open, pausing. "I can track her burner phone. I will send you co-ordinates for her destination."

"Wait. Why are you helping her? You're betraying Nicholai for her."

Green eyes meet mine and it's like he's dissecting me. "Because I love her, Nero Verdi." And then he slides into the car, the engine snarling before the car pulls away.

CHAPTER THREE

Una

Paris. The city has an atmosphere unlike any other. The streets are a bustle of activity yet somehow everything always feels so leisurely. I move along the sidewalk, clinging to the shadows of the buildings until I reach the wooden door that leads into the townhouse I'm renting. I was wandering the city a couple of days ago, trying to lay low when I spotted a sign in the window advertising this apartment. My plan was to just stay in Paris for a couple of days before taking a Ferry back to England. A brief trip to throw anyone who might be following me off my trail. But the second Annaliese, the landlady, showed me inside the apartment, I felt a sense of peace I haven't felt in years. It's completely unsuitable. There's only one stairwell, and because it used to be a house there's not even a fire escape from the first floor, but I took it anyway. I guess I just wanted to stop running for a second, hole up and take a breath. Paris is as good a city as any to hide in.

I open the door and drop the small bag of groceries on the kitchen side. The apartment is small; just one bedroom. The windows stretch from the floor to the ceiling and, in a way, it reminds me of Nero's New York penthouse. Afternoon sun spills through the gauzy curtains, casting shadows across the wooden floorboards.

I like it here. I could stay here until this baby is born, and he or she can grow up in Paris, safe from all the dangers of my world. I take the medical supplies from the grocery bag, dumping them on the coffee table before taking a seat. My pocket buzzes and I take out my burner phone, seeing a blank text from Sasha. It's request for a check in. I send him a quick message.

I'm going off grid. I'll be in touch when I can.

I need to remove myself from everything and everyone because even friends can be enemies. I do not doubt that when it comes down to it, Sasha will side with Nicholai. And I'm glad. His loyalty to me is dangerous for him. I shove my jeans down and pull away the dressing that's stuck to my thigh. My haphazard stitching wouldn't be amiss in a Frankenstein film. It was the best I could do with what I had at the time: a pocket sewing kit bought at the local corner shop. It's for sewing on buttons, not closing a bullet hole. The flesh around the stitches is swollen and red, and it hurts like a bitch. I think it's infected, but I can't get any help with it. Any hospital will report a dodgy-looking bullet wound, and all the doctors I'd usually call for this sort of thing are affiliated either to Nicholai or someone else. Granted, the five-million-dollar price tag should have disappeared with Arnaldo—seeing as he's the one who put it there—but I'm worth something to someone. I unscrew the lid from the bottle of vodka and grit my teeth as I pour it over the wound. It stings like a bitch, but it could be worse. A few weeks ago I put a bullet in Nero's shoulder, then laced the wound with gun powder and set light to it. I wish I could do the same now, but that shit is hard enough to do to someone else, let alone yourself. My mind drifts to him and I wonder what he's doing right now. Is he still looking for me? Will he kill me now that I killed his boss? Mafia is supposed to be about family and loyalty, but Nero had his own brother killed. No, something tells me he won't feel an ounce of remorse for Arnaldo's death. But he is a power player, and sometimes in order to gain power, loyalties must be feigned. After all, his power comes from the mafia and it can be taken away just as easily. I promised him I would go back to him, but now I don't know that I can keep that promise. In our world sentiments are cheap, emotions pointless, and loyalties so very easily bought. One act, one moment, one death, and all the pieces on the board have moved. Have they moved so much that Nero and I are no longer side by side, but across the board from each other?

The moment I wake every one of my senses are on high alert. Someone is in the apartment. I sit up and grab the gun from beneath my pillow, flicking the safety off. Darkness swallows me as I creep out of bed, but I freeze at the creak of a floorboard right outside my bedroom door. *Fuck.* I cross the room on tiptoes, ducking behind the door.

My hand tightens around the gun, finger hovering over the trigger. Ready. Waiting. The wall presses into my shoulder blades and my mind hones in, ears picking up on every tiny sound. It must be the Italians. Or worse, Nicholai. If he gets me back, he'll never let me out of that facility, and this baby…I'd rather die. If it were Nicholai though, he'd know that kicking in the door was enough to sign their death warrant. My gaze finds the bedside table where I left my car keys.

The loose floorboard outside my bedroom door squeaks again and I hold my breath. Every muscle in my body coils tight as adrenaline floods my veins. There was a time, not so long ago, when I would simply have walked out there and killed everyone, but that was back when I was the hunter, nowadays, I'm the hunted. There's another step. The door creaks open, hinges squealing in protest. The streetlight outside the window casts a dim haze through the room, silhouetting the arm holding out a gun pointed at my empty bed.

I lower my gun, slip the small blade loose from the cuff at my wrist and pinch it between my thumb and finger like a giant needle. This is the problem with hiding in a city, gun fights draw attention. I creep up behind him, silent as a ghost. My hand slams over his mouth at the same time as I jam the blade into his throat. This little blade has gotten me out of more situations than any gun. It's not big enough to stab someone in the gut or chest, but it's lethally sharp and perfect for opening a jugular. He takes me by surprise and grabs my leg as he goes down, taking me to the floor hard. The gun slips from my grip, sliding a couple of feet away from me. I crawl across the carpet, reaching for my weapon while waiting for the bang signaling my end to echo in my ears. But It never comes. All I hear are the choked last breaths of the man before he hits the floor with a thud. Muffled voices come from down the hall. *Shit.*

I pick up the gun and car keys and bolt for the window. The wood screeches against the frame and the glass shudders as I yank it up. I expect half the neighborhood heard that, including my intruders. Footsteps pound down the hall and I can only hope that the darkness will give me the precious seconds I need to escape. Hoisting my leg over the window, I stare down at the ground two floors below. A few months back, I would have jumped without a second thought, but now—the light flicks on and I panic, throwing my other leg through the gap and balancing precariously on the window ledge.

"Morte." I freeze, hesitating at the sound of that deep voice. "Don't do it," he commands. That trace of an accent makes the softly spoken words sound harsh. I shouldn't look at him, I should just jump. But I do. Glancing over my shoulder, my hands brace against the frame. Nero stands there in his expensive suit with his hair styled in that sexy way of his. Those dark eyes lock with mine and it's like time stands still. I see the threat dancing in his eyes, the promise of violence and wrath, but also want and desire, swirling and mixing into something potent and intoxicating. That power he emits seems to wrap around me, addictive and oh so dangerous, so alluring. I consider for the briefest of moments going to him because I want him to be my savior in a world of enemies, my monster to end all others. But he may be my enemy, I don't know anymore. I can trust no one but myself, and that's hard, especially with him.

The air charges and crackles, his sheer strength of will coming up against my determination to survive at any cost. We are two sides of the same coin, feeding off each other. One singular, chaotic, unstoppable force. His lips pull up at one corner, the smile threatening yet enticing. My heart flutters in my chest as it responds to the thread of fear he instils, now more than ever. He always looks so perfectly put together, as though he isn't capable of killing men in cold blood for nothing more than power. Doesn't he always say that I look so innocent? Both wolves in sheep's clothing.

He takes a step towards me, eyes never leaving mine.

"Don't come any closer." He ignores me and takes another step. I point the gun at his head.

"What are you going to do, Morte? Shoot me?"

"If that's what it takes." I am walking out of here, one way or the other.

His eyes narrow. "You are mine," he says, but words mean nothing when life and death are on the line, and I can't trust him. Another step. "Why are you running? Arnaldo is dead. You said you'd come back to me. Here I am, and here you are about to jump out a window." If only Arnaldo were our only problem.

"Forgive me if I don't trust you." I see one of his men move in my periphery, trying to outflank me. "Remind your men that I have no problem putting a bullet between their eyes."

He holds up a hand and they instantly fall back. "You don't trust me? I'm not the one who ran." He takes another step. He's only a few feet away from me now. I shift my weight forward slightly on the window ledge.

"This has been great and all, but I don't fancy getting caught by your guys down there." I point to the alley.

The ground seems too far away, though in reality I know I can make the drop easily if I just fall into a roll. I glance at him one last time, committing every inch of his perfect face to memory. In a beat, he lunges for me and I push off the window ledge. The ground rushes up to meet me, and my feet hit the street hard. Pain fires up my leg and the stitches in my thigh tear open as I fall into a roll. Rising on one knee, I lift the gun in my hand, pointing it at the window. My other hand instinctively goes to my stomach. I meet his gaze, but its locked on my stomach, on the small but distinctive bump that's protruding between my hips.

I clench my teeth against the pain in my leg. "If you ever felt anything for me, let me run, Nero," I beg. "I will come back to you." And then I'm on my feet and running, every step sending white-hot pain lancing up my leg.

I'm so close to the car I can see the hood peeking out from the shadow of the alleyway. I limp forward, clutching my gun when something collides with the side of my head and my vision swirls. I stagger sideways and feel myself falling. Strong arms catch me as my body buckles uselessly. I'm barely able to make out the blurred profile of Gio's face before everything goes black.

CHAPTER FOUR

Una

When I open my eyes, blinding light assaults my vidion. I try to throw my hand over my face, but I can't. Glancing to the side, I see my hand is bound beside my head, the leather cuff attached to a chain several inches long. My other arm is the same, and both are attached to the bedframe beneath me. *Fucking great.* Nero. That's the last thing I remember. The room I'm in has no windows and a pretty sturdy-looking door, so I'm guessing I'm in a basement somewhere. There's another door half ajar across from me, and I can hear the slow drip of a tap coming from it. My yoga pants have been removed and replaced with a pair of sleep shorts, and the blood-stained shirt is gone. A fresh dressing covers my thigh.

A heavy groan accompanies the opening door as Gio walks in. His usual serious expression masks his face. "How's your leg?"

"Fuck you, Gio. Where's Nero?"

He huffs a laugh as he shakes his head. Disapproval taints the air, and I'm sure Nero's most loyal guy hates me.

"He's busy." Of course he is. Gio takes a seat on the edge of the mattress and places his hand on my thigh, inspecting my leg. The second his skin makes contact with mine, I go rigid tense. *Kill! Kill! Kill!* That sole instinct roars through my head, the impulse so strong and instinctive it hurts not to act on it. I yank against the restraints and the leather bites into my wrists. His hand finally leaves my leg and I sigh in relief, my body going limp.

"How long are you going to keep me tied up like this?" I

His eyes meet mine. "Until I know you aren't going to kill everyone in the building."

"Permanently then."

"Until Nero comes down here and handles you personally."

"You say that like I won't kill him."

His eyes flick to my stomach. "I'd say you currently have the advantage in that fight, wouldn't you?"

I snort. "You give him too much credit."

His brows pull together in a frown. "You should have told him."

Anger spikes through me at his silent judgement. "I don't owe him shit." Regardless of how I feel about Nero, of what he became to me, the fact is: he blackmailed me. He knowingly put me in a situation that placed me right in the crosshairs. I took the theoretical bullet for him. And somewhere along the line he made me feel something for him. In all the chaos, he managed to earn my loyalty without me ever really realizing I'd given it to him, but this is different. This baby is something that I cannot explain to him because I can't even explain it to myself.

"We could have helped you."

"I don't need your fucking help, Giovanni. You forget who I am." My rage rises like a living, breathing thing. Even the cold killer in me is protective of this child when she should be nothing but detached. I'm confused, but driven by instinct and I will kill anyone who tries to harm us.

Gio gets up and steps away from me. "I do not forget, *Bacio Della Morte*." His eyes become hard and unforgiving as he pulls a syringe from his pocket. I jerk against the restraints and snarl as he brings the needle to my skin.

"I'm going to kill you, Gio. Painfully. Slowly."

A small smile touches his lips before the needle pierces my skin and the plunger depresses. He walks out of the room, slamming the door behind him. And then, everything goes black.

When I wake up again, my hands are no longer bound. My shirt is pushed up and the remnants of something wet is smeared over my stomach. The lack of pain in my leg suggests I've been dosed with painkillers. I push to my feet and stagger slightly as the effects of the sedative cling to me. My eyes take in every inch of the room as I cross it, desperately planning. The other door leads to a bathroom, as suspected. It's basic. A shower, sink, and toilet. I turn the shower on, strip out of my clothes, and step inside. Hot water washes away what feels like weeks of grime and dirt, tinging the water a shade of red as dried blood—both my own and others—leaves my skin. I pull the dressing from my thigh and inspect the wound. It looks better, less angry and swollen. Gio must have given me antibiotics. As I stand under the spray, I start to form a plan in my mind. For now, I will wait and see if Nero makes a move. The problem with him is he's frighteningly unpredictable, even to me. In a day or two I will have a clearer picture of what's going on.

Once I'm clean I get out and wrap the towel around me. And then it begins. The boredom. The pacing. After a time, the walls start to feel like they're closing in on me and it's enough to make me want to tear my hair out.

Eventually I hear the click of the lock on the door, and I ready myself to attack, but the second it opens a crack, a gun is pointed at me. "Didn't think I'd come in here unarmed, did you?" Gio asks. "You did threaten to kill me."

I smile coldly. "I don't threaten."

He laughs and signals at someone behind him. Tommy steps into the room, carrying a brown paper bag and some folded clothes. I can't help but smile when I see him.

"Irish," I say. A shy smile pulls at his lips and he holds the bag out in front of him, stretching as though trying to stay as far away from me as possible. I roll my eyes and snatch the bag. He jumps. "I knocked you out one time, Tommy."

"Look, you're scary on your best day. But pregnant? Hormones will make even a sane woman crazy."

I glare at him.

"I swear you have no self-preservation whatsoever, kid," Gio sighs.

Tommy offers me a small shrug. "Sorry, Una, but it's true."

"If you were anyone else..." I've always been fond of Tommy. Maybe it's because he's Nero's soft spot, or perhaps it's because he's managed to stay relatively innocent in this world of corruption. Either way, he's kind of like a puppy that you couldn't bear to hurt. He puts the clothes on the bed and turns around, walking back towards the door.

"Thought you were his valued right hand, Gio. But Nero's got you looking after me like an errand boy."

His lips twitch. "We both know you'd kill an errand boy." The man is nearly impossible to rile, and not for the first time, I wish I was dealing with Jackson.

"True. Where's Nero?"

"He's still busy." His mouth presses into a tight line. And that expression tells me something. Whatever is going on, Gio doesn't approve of it. He backs away and the door slams shut.

What would Nero be doing that Gio doesn't like? That's a stupid question. Everything. Nero is the mafia bad boy, bound by no sense of honor or duty. I've seen enough of their dynamic to know that Gio is the polar opposite. He's all about duty and loyalty. He just happens to be loyal to Nero.

Option one, Nero is going against the rest of the mafia and Gio doesn't like it. Option two, Nero is going against me. The mafia are all about their women and children, so it stands to reason, Gio wouldn't like that either. Shit, I don't know. I'm stuck here, trying to analyze the ethics of men who have none and hoping that the most soulless of them all is trying to help me instead of kill me.

CHAPTER FIVE

Una

I don't know how long I've been in this room, but it's definitely been several days. Every so often Gio and Tommy come in here and give me food—always with a gun pointed in my direction. The longer this goes on, the more suspicious I become. I'm being held like a prisoner. Arnaldo might be out of the picture, but the Italians still want me dead. Probably even more so now, so, it stands to reason that Nero's loyalties have swayed in their direction. The longer I'm kept here, the more convinced I am that he's against me. It's just a matter of time before he hands me over to their new boss. Nicholai might have enough power to get me out of it, but he's the last person I want to save me for various reasons. I'd sooner take my chances with the Italians. At least they protect children rather than turn them into soldiers.

By the time Gio comes in with food, I'm done. He holds the pistol up and I narrow my eyes at him. One of the guys I don't know brings food into the room, but instead of standing at a distance like I have done, I charge him. I'm taking a chance here. I don't think Gio has it in him to shoot a pregnant woman. He'd shoot me without a second thought, but carrying Nero's child? I very much doubt it.

"Una!" Gio shouts at me.

I throat punch the new guy and he chokes, clutching at his throat. I grab him around the neck and pull his body in front of me. "Damn it, Una." Gio glares at me over the guy's shoulder.

"I'm going to make this really easy for you, Gio. You can lead me to Nero, I can snap this guy's neck, or I can take that gun from you and kill everyone in this house until I find that bastard."

Gio inhales heavily, eyes boring into mine. "Fine." He turns away from me and walks out into the hallway.

"Walk," I instruct the guy. He does, following behind Gio. We move up a set of stairs, and then through a door that leads into a hallway. A hallway I know all too well, because I was standing in it only a few days ago. "You have got to be shitting me," I whisper under my breath. Arnaldo's house. We're in Arnaldo's damn mansion? This is not good.

My eyes dart around the hallway and two guys approach us. Gio says something to them and they step to the side, pressing themselves against the walls on either side as we pass. I glance at one of them, spotting the gun tucked into a holster at his chest. I shove my body shield forward a step and he staggers, giving me the perfect opportunity to slam my knee between his legs. In the split second that his groans cause a distraction, I launch myself at the other guy, punching him in the temple hard enough that he sways on his feet. I wrap my arms around him, and yank both his guns from his chest holster. Never have I felt so relieved to have a weapon in my hand. I'm whole again. Complete. Whirling around, I shove the guy to the ground and bring both guns up to face Gio and the remaining man, both of whom now have guns aimed at me.

I smile, loving the thrill of danger that only comes from an impossible situation. "We've been through this before, Gio. You can't shoot me before I shoot you."

His expression is set into a fierce scowl. "Drop the guns, Una." I start inching back along the corridor, my bare feel padding over the marble floor.

"I don't think I will."

"We are not the enemy."

"Well, I feel an awful lot like a prisoner right now."

"It's for your own protection." I'm not sure if Gio actually believes that. He's just honorable enough to think so.

"Protection from who?"

He huffs a deep breath. "Yourself mainly."

"Nice try, but I haven't seen Nero. And you better believe I don't trust that bastard at the best of times." Gio's eyes shift just a fraction of an inch over my left shoulder, and I keep one gun on him while my other arm flies out to the other side, aiming at the newcomer. I don't have to look to know who it is, the turbulent energy is like standing in an electrical storm. Nero.

"You haven't seen me, because I didn't want to see you." I can't help but look at him. Nero looks fiercely powerful in a tailored suit. He's perfect, not one single hair out of place.

Those dark eyes meet mine, always swirling with such beautiful promises of blood and pain. My stomach clenches under his gaze and I fight my hammering pulse, forcing myself to focus. No. He's nothing more than a threat, a potential enemy. I point the gun at his beautiful face, my finger lingering over the trigger poised as though the weapon is a mere extension of myself.

"Trying to keep me prisoner? Big fucking mistake." I hear the shift of footsteps behind me. "I do not need to look at you to shoot you, Gio."

Nero's lips twitch and he looks up at Gio. "Go."

"Nero..."

"Go!" he roars. I hear a disapproving sigh, the shuffling of feet disappearing down the hall before a door closes. And then silence. Only he and I.

Now, I point both guns at him, my teeth clenched as I stare back at the man who once felt like an ally at the very least. A strange sense of betrayal slinks its way around me, squeezing until this horrible splintered feeling settles into my gut. He takes a slow step forward and I press the barrel of the gun against his forehead. We've been here before, in this exact same position— me with a gun to his head and him completely fearless. I was drawn to that confidence, fascinated by it. He instilled this wariness in me which I hadn't felt in such a long time. He stares back at me with a cold indifference, a ruthlessness that makes my heart pound and my breaths shorten. That little fissure of fear calls to me, hypnotizes me. I force it all away, focusing on what needs to be done.

"Who is the new underboss?" I ask, taking the opportunity to gather information. I can no longer trust Nero, and that means getting what I can and getting the hell out of here.

"We need to talk."

I huff a laugh. "You've had several days to talk to me. I'm afraid you're shit out of luck, so answer my question. Who is coming for me now?" My gaze darts to the doors I can see. This is taking too long. I feel wildly out of control and I don't like it at all.

"No one is coming for you. You killed Arnaldo."

"The mafia are like rats. Kill one and two more pop up in his place."

"Una." His hand slowly rises and covers mine. Some of the iciness shifts from his eyes and is replaced by something familiar yet no less dangerous. I allow him to push my hand down until the gun lingers at my side. A sudden wave of exhaustion washes over me. Months on the run have taken their toll, and sometimes it feels like it's never going to end. I squeeze my eyes shut for a second, fighting back the fatigue and the sense of betrayal laced with this strange pain.

"I'm the new underboss," he says quietly. "No one will hurt you."

My eyes snap open. "What the fuck?"

CHAPTER SIX

Nero

She's so fierce. So beautiful. Her once white-blonde hair is dyed a dull brown and I don't like it. It makes her seem so much less than what she really is: extraordinary. She looks tired and thin. Her face is drawn with dark circles lingering below her eyes. And, of course, she's pregnant. I thought nothing could shock me these days. I was wrong. A thousand questions are still running through my mind like a goddamn marching band, and yet, I'm strangely numb, disconnected from it.

She's been locked in the basement for the last three days because I don't know what the fuck to say to her. I'm pissed off that she ran, leaving with nothing more than a note as an explanation. She didn't trust me to protect her from Arnaldo, or at least that's what I thought. Only now I find her, and she's knocked up. It has to be mine. Is that why she left, because she didn't want to tell me? And then, a whole new channel of questions starts. Round and round it goes, but always accompanied by this constant anger.

She follows me into one of the living rooms of the mansion and I go to the corner, pouring out a glass of scotch. I'm about to hand it to her when I hesitate. Pregnant. I drink the whole thing myself. I need it.

Una glances around the room nervously, still clutching both guns in her hands. She looks like she's ready to kill everyone and bolt in the blink of an eye. I'm not letting her go anywhere.

"Why didn't you tell me?" The question comes out sounding like an accusation. She takes a seat on the couch and crosses one leg over the other. She's still wearing only a tank top and a pair of shorts, and my eyes follow the length of her long legs before pausing on her stomach. "I had a right to know."

"Why? So you could tell me to get rid of it? Or perhaps you'd like to play daddy of the year?" She tilts her head to the side, her expression irritatingly blank.

She's right. This was never part of any plan. What would I have said to her? "So instead, you just up and run? You thought: 'Fuck it! I'm wanted by some of the most powerful people in the world, but I'll leave myself completely unprotected while fucking pregnant?'" I don't even realize I'm shouting at her until I stop. The silence echoes around the room, interrupted only by the sound of my own heavy breaths. I never would have wanted this if she'd told me, but now it's not an option. The idea of Arnaldo trying to kill her is bad enough, but I know Una can handle herself. Throw *this* into the situation though, and it's very different.

"I'm always protected. Do not forget who I am." She glares at me.

Her defiance pisses me off. I close the space between us, leaning over and gripping the back of the couch beside her head. She lifts her chin, the corner of her lips curling. Those strange violet eyes of hers meet mine, and the threat of violence swirls in the air like an impending storm. Fuck, I've missed this. I've missed her. After all, what is power without someone to constantly challenge it? My fingers wind around her throat, where they belong.

"I'm not the one who forgets."

She grips my wrist, her nails biting into my skin, and it's here, with this unspoken war raging between us that I always want her the most. I want her brutality and hate, her pain and weakness, but most of all I want her heart, her body, her soul. I want everything that she has to give, and I always will. Time and distance make no difference. She can't outrun me. We are perfect in a way that only two people as volatile as us can be.

I'm angry, but I can't deny the hold she has on me. I never know whether I want to kill her or kiss her or both. I slam my lips over hers, craving her taste. She bites my bottom lip and thrusts her palm into the center of my chest hard enough to push me away. Climbing to her feet, I watch as she circles behind me, her eyes surveying my body like an enemy commander looking for a weakness.

"I don't trust you, Nero."

"I'm not the one that's proven untrustworthy."

She squares up to me. "Tell me…how does one go from a simple enforcer to the underboss in only a few short months?" She raises a brow. "Even if someone were to blackmail an assassin, have her remove all competition and, in turn, have a price placed on her head… Even then, you still couldn't make

275

it to underboss." She tilts her head to the side. "So tell me, *capo*, who did you blackmail to get this gig?"

I slide my hand to the small of her back, pulling her closer. Her round stomach presses against me and I shouldn't care, I certainly shouldn't like it, but there's something incredibly hot about her having my baby inside her. My vicious little butterfly being maternal? It doesn't fit. "Tell me you trust me, and I'll tell you how I got here," I whisper against her ear.

"I don't trust you."

"Well then, we're at an impasse because in order to explain I must tell you something that very few people know. I have to trust you, and that goes both ways."

She pulls away from me slightly, her brows pinched together. "You want me to lie to you?" The last few months have made her wary. Even more so than normal.

"Why do it, Morte? Why run and hide, even after you killed Arnaldo? Why run from me? Why not trust me? Was I not there when shit hit the fan?"

"You caused most of that shit to hit the fan. You don't get to declare yourself a hero just because you tidied up your own mess." She pulls away from me and paces in front of the sofa the same way she always does when she's agitated. "I'll tell you if you tell me why you're the boss," she offers.

Always with the negotiating. "My father—my real father—is the boss."

Her eyes go wide and she halts. "The big boss? Your father is Cesare Ugoli?" I nod and she shakes her head. "Should have known," she mumbles. "And you knew this whole time?"

"Yeah."

Realization blankets her features. "This was the plan. This was always the plan. Anna…it was all for this."

"From the very first moment we met it was all orchestrated for this exact point, for you to kill Arnaldo. For me to become the underboss." Her features harden and I know her well enough to see the precise moment when she locks down her emotions. "But I never expected to want you. By the time you were in danger, I thought I could protect you, but you ran."

She snorts and turns to face me. "I knew what I was getting into. I knew you were an asshole and that you were using me. I agreed to it."

I move closer, forcing myself into her space. She moves away until the wall is at her back and I brace my hand beside her head. "Your turn. Why run?"

Her warm breath caresses my throat. "Because I had a five-million-dollar hit on me and no idea who sanctioned it."

I lean closer, brushing my lips over her cheek. She smells of vanilla and gun oil, and that scent alone makes my dick hard for her. She tries to twist away from me, but I press my body against hers. "If that were it, then why jump out a window after you killed Arnaldo?"

"I…" she stammers, her mouth opening and then closing. Who would have thought the kiss of death would ever be lost for words?

"You are mine, Morte. I would have protected you."

"I need to do this on my own," she breathes, and it might be the most vulnerable I'd ever heard her.

"Do what on your own?" I ask through gritted teeth.

Her eyes squeeze shut and her lips part. She looks so fragile, so innocent, though I know she's not. "I need to leave here, Nero," she almost pleads. A breath hisses through my teeth and my hand slams around her throat again, squeezing the delicate skin. Opening her eyes, she pushes forward into my hold. Her lips caress mine, warm breath washing over my tongue and making my pulse hammers through my veins. "Let me leave, and in a few months, I'll come back to you." I narrow my eyes, trying to decipher her thoughts. "I promise. Queen protects king, remember?"

"Not anymore."

She throws her head back against the wall and bites down on her bottom lip. I've never seen Una look so beaten down, as though she's fought off the world and is somehow still standing. "Please."

"Why? What do you have to do that will take months?" And then it all clicks into place like the gaping hole in an otherwise complete jigsaw. "No." My grip on her throat tightens, until I'm pushing her back against the wall. "No!"

Her fist slams into my stomach. I grunt and press my body flush against hers until our lips are almost touching. "Let me go and have the baby, and I'll come back afterwards."

"Is this what you were planning? To have my kid in some foreign country and just abandon it?" My voice is rising, my temper bordering on rage.

She shoves me. "No, I'm putting it up for adoption! That is not abandoning it."

"Fuck!" My whole body is bristling with rage, and I want to step away from her, but, at the same time, I never want to let her go again. How could she do this?

"What would you suggest?"

278

"If you didn't fucking want it, then why not just get rid of it?" I snarl in her face.

Una stills, her gaze dropping to the floor. "I couldn't. But I won't do this either." She gestures between the two of us. "Look at us, Nero. I can't have a baby. Children need...I don't know...not us."

My anger dissipates and I release my hold on her. Ah, my vicious butterfly. She's so strong, yet so irreparably damaged, so set in her ways. She thinks of herself as a weapon, something trained and unleashed. Nothing more. But she's so much more. She gave up everything to save her sister, a sister she hadn't seen in thirteen years. A sister who, through rigorous training and conditioning, should have become inconsequential. What she doesn't realize is that Nicholai wants her to feel nothing, but she does, and that means he couldn't break her. What Una sees as weakness is proof of just how strong she is. She's right. We are and always will be ruthless and brutal. It's engrained. Instinctual. I know what she's saying is right, and yet, I want something that has never even been a factor until right now. Until it's right in front of me and growing inside her; my dangerous queen.

"You may be damaged, Morte, you may be a killer, but you are not heartless." I cup her cheek, and when she opens her eyes, a single tear skates down her cheek. In the time I have known this woman I have watched her kill without blinking, threaten people without remorse. I have heard her scream such gut-wrenching cries of anguish in her sleep, and witnessed her cry for her sister. I have watched her slowly crack, shattering piece by piece, and with each new splintered part of her I'm pulled further in, drawn to her. But we are who we are. Una must always be my strength, and I hers, because if not we will quickly become each other's weakness. We are equals, but my next words will change that dynamic. "You're staying here. Don't make me force you," I say, before I turn from her and stride out of the room.

279

"Nero!"

I just made Una my biggest weakness, and myself—I just made myself a father. Poor kid doesn't stand a chance, but I will not leave it to be raised by a stranger the way I was.

CHAPTER SEVEN

Una

I pace backwards and forwards in the bedroom that I was shown to via armed guard. Pulling the curtain back an inch, I glance down at the three men standing watch just below the window. And they're facing me. We all know they're here to keep me in, not intruders out, but they could at least pretend. I drop the curtain with a frustrated groan. I will not be held prisoner by Nero. He can go fuck himself. The room smells of him, his cologne subtly clinging to the bed linen. I take a seat on the edge of the mattress and try to think of a way out of this.

I never considered the possibility that Nero would *want* a baby. I guess I never considered it because he was never supposed to find out. And now, he's never going to let me out of his sight again.

The longer I'm trapped here, the more panicked I start to feel. I was running from Arnaldo. I was running from Nero, but mainly, I was trying to stay off Nicholai's radar. The fact is, my child will never be safe as long as it is mine, as long as it is with me. Because of Nicholai. His obsession for designer soldiers started with children of a certain age, around ten years old, like I was. A child is ready to learn how to fight at ten years of age, to be conditioned and honed to a fine blade. He never had any younger than eight, until one of his soldiers impregnated a cook in one of the facilities. I went with him to retrieve the child. I was eighteen then, but I still remember the way he looked at that baby like it was a brand-new weapon in his arsenal. A shiny toy. After that I heard whispers and rumors of babies being bred, of Elite no longer being sterilzed. The younger the child, the more they can be conditioned during their developmental years. Of course, back then I didn't care for the fate of children. They weren't my concern. Truth be told, I still don't. But I care about *my* child. If Nicholai knew about this baby, he would want it. I am, after all, his favorite. I can just imagine the way his eyes would light up if he got his hands on my child.

We're not safe here. Nero and I live in a world plagued with enemies and danger where choices are limited, so it's on me to make sure the only plausible choice is made. When it comes to this, Nero's opinion is inconsequential because he can't possibly understand what Nicholai is capable of.

Of course, now I'm here, and Nicholai will find me. I need to speak to Sasha and see what he knows. I also want to talk to Anna, because despite everything that's going on, I did all this for her, for us. Working with Nero was all so she could be free, but now that she is, I find myself hesitating. I want my sister back but, at the same time, I want to keep her as far from this mess as possible. She's free which is a luxury I will never have. Nicholai will always own me, always want me. Anger, frustration, and fear mix together and have me permanently on edge. I long for the time not so long ago when emotions were a foreign concept to me. These days, I'm an unstable, hormonal mess.

I get up and open the bedroom door. Two guys in suits step straight into my path, blocking the door. One of them is reaching for his gun, and I smirk.

"Really? Touch that gun and you better be ready to use it." I'm irritable and tired, and not in the mood for Nero's wannabe soldiers. The guy's eyes widen but he says nothing. "I need a phone," I say. They both stare blankly at me. "Now!"

"Boss hasn't permitted that."

I huff a laugh. "I suggest you get me a fucking phone or I'm going to break both your noses, and then I'm going to slit your boss' throat in his sleep." I smile sweetly. "Do not test me."

The one that was reaching for his gun steps back, nervously glancing at the other one. "Go," his friend says, jerking his head to the side. The guy turns and walks off down the hallway.

"Wise." I step back into the room and close the door behind me. I do have one ace up my sleeve, and that's pure fear. His men are scared of me, but the question is: who do they fear more, me or him? They might risk a broken neck from me to avoid being disemboweled by Nero. Choices, choices.

I'm starting to get a headache, so I lie down on the bed while I wait. I must have fallen asleep, because I startle awake when someone touches my shoulder. Nero dodges my reflexive strike aimed at his throat.

"Don't do that!" I snip.

He laughs and takes a step away from the bed. "Ah, Morte, I've missed you. Sleeping is so…restful without you."

I sit up and drag a hand through my hair. "What time is it?"

"Late."

I guess I'm not getting that phone. He strips out of his suit jacket and throws it over the back of the chair in the corner of the room. Deft fingers move over the buttons of his shirt and I can't help but follow their trail, watching as the material slowly parts over tanned skin. When I lift my gaze, his dark eyes spark with something dangerously hypnotic. Forcing myself to get up, I head for the en-suite. But before I've even taken a step inside, his hands are on my hips. My body goes rigid for a second, years of engrained conditioning kicking in and demanding that I react before I slowly relax. It's his touch. Nero, my addictive and lethal exception.

The heat of his chest meets my back, bleeding through the material of my shirt. Lips brush over my shoulder and I tilt my neck to the side as my skin erupts in tingles. His hard cock pushes against my lower back. I turn around and step away from him. He cocks a brow and braces his forearms on either side of the door frame as he watches me back away. He's shirtless, and every muscle flexes in a show of power. Tattoos wind down his arms, the ink work wrapping around his limbs like snakes. In his suit, you could almost mistake Nero for something sophisticated, civilized, but it's here, when he's like this that he can't hide. Everything about him is honed and lethal, created for the sole purpose of destruction. I've always glimpsed beneath Nero's veneer, but the closer I get, the more I see. Right now, he's like the devil taking his true form.

My stomach clenches and heat prickles over my skin as he stalks forward, crowding me against the vanity unit. "Don't run from me, Morte." His voice is deep and rough as it works over my senses.

"I'm not running."

He reaches me and lifts me onto the vanity, the icy surface sending a chill over my skin. His broad body presses between my legs until I'm consumed by him, surrounded in every way. With a finger beneath my chin, he forces me to meet his gaze. "You're always running." He swipes my bottom lip and I nip at the pad of his thumb. Darkness creeps across his eyes and that one look is enough to make me shiver in need. It's the promise of something explosive, but I never know which way he'll go. He could fuck me, or he could choke me. He's a thrill ride of the most unpredictable nature.

"Not from you," I whisper. It's a truth and a lie wrapped in one. I want to run from Nero because I want to run *to* him, and that terrifies me.

"Lies. How far would you have gone if I hadn't caught you?" The air crackles with electricity and his anger is almost palpable.

I try to shove him away but it's impossible. "I don't have to explain myself to you." A slow smile pulls at his lips, cold and calculated. My heart thrums in my chest, adrenaline flooding my veins, and I can't help but smile back at him. He's like my own personal high. A shot of adrenalin straight to my soul, reminding me of what it is to be alive, to be human. I grab his jaw and lean forward, brushing my lips over his. "I don't run from you." I bite his bottom lip, waiting the entire time for him to lash out. Honestly, I want it. I live for it.

"No. Me, you fight."

"You make me violent."

His fingers wind into my hair and he wrenches my head to the side, brushing his lips over my jaw. "You make me want to hunt down all who would hurt you and bleed them dry."

Teeth scrape over the side of my throat and my pulse hammers in response. "You can't kill everyone, Nero."

"Fucking watch me," he says as though it were his solemn vow, and I want to believe that it's within his power, within *our* power. His grip on my hair tightens and then his lips crash over mine. I moan as that sweet battle rages between us, the sound of his deep growl like the crashing of steel blades to my ears. Rough stubble scratches over my skin and he thrusts his tongue inside my mouth. Prying his belt open, I slide my hand beneath the elastic of his boxers, wrapping my hand around him. A low breath hisses through his teeth and his body coils tight like a snake waiting to deal a death blow. I work over him, watching him wind tighter and tighter with each stroke. I'm shoved backward until I'm braced on my elbows, my head pressed against the mirror at an awkward angle. He grabs my face, fingers sinking into my skin brutally as he smashes my cheek into the glass. My breaths are nothing more than rapid pants as he brings his lips close to my ear. "You are fucking mine, Morte." He touches his forehead to the side of my face and trails a hand up the inside of my parted thighs. When he brushes over me, a low whimper leaves my lips. I crave this, his touch, his rage, his utter possession.

Two fingers push inside me and I clench my teeth. "Look at me," he groans, hot breath washing over the side of my face. He fucks me with his hand, and I feel so exposed to him, so raw. I both love and hate it. He makes me willingly vulnerable, and I'm so desperately weak for him, yet unbreakably strong.

I almost whimper when he pulls away, only to strip out of his remaining clothes. Nero grips my ass and lifts me, crushing his mouth over mine once more. There's movement and he slides the shower door open before I feel a wall at my back followed by the spray of water hitting my skin. I gasp as the icy cold liquid soaks through my shirt. Nero doesn't hesitate to thrust into me so hard and fast that all the air leaves my body. I feel both invaded and complete. He's branding me, claiming me all over again. Nero and I will never trust each other completely because we know what we're capable of. We are two predators circling each other with a mutual respect. But I want him, and isn't this the most primal of instincts? A simple factor bred into the DNA of every living creature…to be attracted to the strongest of the species. I am the strong, and Nero is the only one who has ever matched me. I want him because I respect and fear him, and that combination is intoxicating. This is attraction and want and need on such a basic ingrained level—it's undeniable.

Hungry, open-mouthed kisses land on my neck and he laps at the water as it streams down my body. I break for him, surrendering and shattering apart as I cling to his broad shoulders. Every muscle strains against his skin as he thrusts into me and stiffens. "Fuck!" His fingers bite into my thighs hard enough that I feel the dull sting of his short nails against my skin. Honey eyes lock with mine, and the silence between us is permeated only by our heavy breaths and the water hammering over tile. "Don't run from me." There's an edge to the way he says it, spoken like an order, but the expression on his face is something I've never seen on him before, desperation.

"I'm not running." I cup his jaw and brush my lips over his. The kiss feels foreign, the gentleness of it jolting me. It's as though we're standing on a precipice. The predators stopping and staring at each other for a moment and wondering if perhaps there is more in this world than the thrill of the kill.

"You will run, Una. I know you that well."

I allow my fingers to trail over his warm skin, dropping my eyes to his lips in the hope that he won't see the truth in them. I've never had a problem keeping my cards close to my chest where my thoughts and feelings are concerned, but Nero sees through me like glass. He's right. It won't be long before I have to run, and I almost feel bad about that because as much as Nero scares me—as ruthless and unforgiving as he is—I actually believe him when he says he would protect me. When he tells me I'm his, I almost want to be. I crave that sense of belonging I have when I'm with him like this, when nothing outside of us exists. But when we step out of this shower, my enemies will still be there. I know without a doubt that Nero is the biggest monster I've ever come across, and I've met some despicable people in my time. There are no lengths he will not go to in the pursuit of what he wants. Add into that an unrivalled intellect

287

and the ability to strategize and manipulate those around him, and Nero is formidable. Yes, he could protect me. He makes me feel safe, but safety is only ever an illusion. The feeling of safety is in and of itself a weakness because it makes you sloppy. If I weren't having his child then it would be the simplest thing in the world to allow myself to want him, to stand shoulder to shoulder with him against all who would harm us. But I am, and I can't explain how this driving need to protect my baby overrides everything else. Nero, me, it doesn't matter anymore.

I wrap my arms around his neck and tilt my chin up, pressing my lips to his. Smiling against my mouth, he bites down on my bottom lip hard enough that I taste blood. Then swipes his tongue over the wound. "I'd almost forgotten how sweet you taste."

He slowly lowers me to my feet, fingers trailing down my body to my stomach. He stills there, closing his eyes as he presses his forehead to mine. I can barely breathe, barely move as he spreads his fingers wide, almost covering the bump. And then, just like that, he steps back and drops his hand.

"I don't like your hair like this," he says, picking up a lock of hair.

"Needs must when you're blending in."

"I prefer it when you stand out."

"So you can see me coming?"

"No, so our enemies see you for what you really are; extraordinary." My stomach clenches at his words. "Dangerous." His fingertips trail my collarbone. "Viscous." Drifting lower, he skims the top of my breast. "And mine," he says, his deep voice drawing the word out. I can't help but take solace in his words. I have never belonged, never had anyone to rely on but me. And even though I know that's wise—I know that relying on anyone but yourself is stupid – I can't help but want the sense of peace that he gave me a taste of before I ran. Even in the midst of chaos, he showed me a glimpse of something that I hadn't experienced since I was thirteen years old. He had my back, and I want that. It's sad; the fairy tale lusting of a girl who has never known anything but death. My head tells me he makes me weak, and my heart wants to lie in his arms for just a little while and rest from the never-ending vortex of death and war that seems to orbit around me.

He places a finger under my chin, pulling my gaze to his. "I will protect you," he vows, almost angrily. "Both of you." I swear he can read my mind sometimes and it bothers me because I should be unreadable.

"I'm tired." I can't think about this right now, and I certainly don't want to make promises to him that I know I'll break. He nods and turns the shower off before wrapping a towel around me. "Don't make me hurt you," I say, scowling at him.

He laughs and I get out of the shower, snagging his toothbrush from the vanity. I raise an eyebrow at him in the mirror, daring him to say anything. He simply smiles and shakes his head, and the second I'm done, he takes it from me, making a slow show of putting it in his mouth. I roll my eyes and leave the bathroom, changing into one of his shirts before crawling into bed. A few minutes later he turns the lights off and climbs in, snaking an arm around my body and pulling me back against him. "Just so you know, if you slit my throat in my sleep, there are guards outside the door and window," he rumbles against the back of my neck.

I glare into the darkness. "I have no weapons."

"You're inventive."

CHAPTER EIGHT

Nero

I wake up in the morning and stretch my arm out looking for Una. The bed is still warm, but she's gone. I check the bathroom first, but she's not there. When I open the bedroom door I find Louis crouched in front of Frank who's slumped against the wall, clutching a broken nose. Blood pours down his chin, spilling down the front of his white shirt.

"Where is she?" I sigh.

Louis flinches when he meets my gaze. "She said she was going to the kitchen."

I swipe my hand over my face and head down the stairs in search of her. The second I step into the hallway, Zeus greets me. George is nowhere to be seen which means he's with Una. Opening the kitchen door, I push aside the plastic dust sheets hanging on the other side. Footprints, accompanied by paw prints, mark the fine layer of dust coating the floor. I round the corner and find Una sitting on the kitchen island in the destroyed kitchen, the dog at her feet staring up at her. She's clutching a mug in her hand and taking marshmallows from a bag beside her. One goes in her mouth before she offers the next to George, completely unbothered by the total destruction surrounding her. The exterior wall is halfway through being re-bricked, and the plastic sheeting covers the gaping hole that leads outside.

"Admiring your handy work?" I fold my arms over my chest and lean against the counter.

She glances at me briefly before turning her attention back to George. "If I'd known it was going to be your house I might have blown more of it up." Her lips pull up at the corner as she strokes George's head. "Or mounted Arnie's head on the front gate."

"You shouldn't be in here. It's not structurally sound." She ignores me and I push away from the wall, approaching her. I glance inside her mug and see hot chocolate, marshmallows swimming in the brown liquid. "Marshmallows for breakfast?" She just shrugs. "And there was me thinking you liked blood in the mornings." I wrap my fingers around her wrist and bring her hand closer, stealing the sugary little lump and wrapping my lips around her finger. Her eyes darken and narrow as she tries to glare at me. "Did you really have to break Louis' nose?"

"If you want me to stay here, then you should probably warn your men what will happen if they touch me. He's lucky it was just his nose," she snaps. I love that she can't tolerate anyone's touch but mine. "Now, I let you off yesterday, but now I want to know where the fuck my sister is."

291

"I told you, she's safe."

"Where? Because I don't see her, and all your best men are here with you, so how can she possibly be safe?"

"Nicholai knows about her."

Her eyes snap to mine. "Says who?" I hesitate and watch her jaw tighten in aggravation.

"It doesn't matter…"

"No, if you know anything about Nicholai, that means you have someone on the inside. Who is it?" She glares at me for long moments. "Who?"

"Sasha."

She presses her hand against my chest and pushes me out of the way, hopping down off the counter. I watch as she paces backwards and forwards a few times, leaving little tracks in the dust. "You went behind my back?"

My temper spikes, manifesting itself with cold efficiency. "You weren't exactly around and he came to me."

"Where is Anna?"

"Mexico."

She slowly lifts her head, and if looks could kill…. "You left her with the fucking cartel?"

"She's with Rafael. She's safe."

She laughs humorlessly and tilts her head back to the ceiling. "It's the cartel. They aren't like your precious Italians. They don't have ethics or a code. They'd sell their own mother for more power. If Nicholai knows about her, she is not safe."

"Even Nicholai won't go to war with the cartel."

"People can be bought, Nero. And Nicholai will pay any price, because if he gets her, he knows he has me."

"No." I move into her space. "No, he does not have you. And if he gets Anna, he still won't have you."

"I want to talk to her." She sounds tired, almost hopeless, and it annoys me, because she doesn't get to give up. She doesn't get to be anything other than the indestructible force I know her to be.

"Come on." I walk us out of the kitchen and close the door behind her. A few of my soldiers linger in the hallway. Una drops her face to the ground as we walk past them. Maybe it's habit, years of hiding her face and not wanting to be recognized, but she can't hide from them. They're my men.

The dogs follow us into the office and I close the door, taking a seat behind the desk. Una perches on the edge, my oversized tracksuit bottoms dangling over her feet. She looks so delicate wearing my clothes, her stomach subtly protruding in front of her, but her body language sings a different song. Her shoulders are tense, eyes surveying everything and taking in minute details. I put the office phone on loud speaker and call Rafael. He picks up on the third ring. "Nero. How are you?"

I'm fond of Rafael. His loyalties are solid, which is why I sent Anna to him. And despite the fact that he's slightly unhinged, his reputation is enough to keep others away from him, and in turn, her. "Good. I need to speak to Anna."

There's a pause. "Nero, my friend. I love that you're a ruthless bastard, but I'm not sure little Anna is ready to speak to you."

"It wasn't a request, Rafael."

He laughs, long and hard, until Una leans over, growling over the phone. "Listen, you *malparido*." Subtle as always. "Put my sister on the line before I come to your shithole town myself and shove my gun down your throat."

He laughs again. "Is that your way of flirting with me, *Ángel de la muerte?*"

Una sighs, turning her fierce gaze on me. "Her foreplay tends to involve knives, Rafael. Now, get Anna."

He laughs, and then, the line goes silent for a few moments. I stand up to leave, but Una's hand shoots out, grabbing my forearm. We both glance down at the spot where her hand is locked on my wrist, and I don't know who's more shocked, me or her.

"What if…what if she doesn't remember?" she whispers, and my chest clenches.

"She'll remember, Morte. You're family."

Her hand slips from my arm as she nods. I grip her chin and place a hard kiss on her lips before leaving the office. Zeus follows me, but George stays with her.

The second I step outside, Gio is next to me. "You know she's going to run at some point, right?" he says.

"I know. Make sure the men are ready."

He nods and peels away. Gio organizes everything so I don't have to. And of course, right now, I'm busy with Una. I know she wants to make sure I never see that baby, and maybe it's wise, but I don't care. She's going to run, and I'll be ready for her, but I've learned never to underestimate Una. You can never have enough men, enough fire power, or enough back up plans when it comes to that woman. Add in the fact that causing her any harm is out of the question, and I'm on edge, terrified she's going to slip away from me. If I lose her now, she'll be nothing more than a whisper on the wind. I'll never find her, and certainly not before she has my baby.

CHAPTER NINE

Una

"Hello." The small voice comes over the line, and my heart lets out a stuttered thump. So many times I imagined what I would say if I ever found her, and yet right now, I've got nothing. Not one word. My mouth opens and closes a few more times as I grapple with foreign emotions.

"Hey," I finally manage.

Silence. I wonder if this is as hard for her as it is for me. But honestly, I hate this because I know what she went through. My life was no cakewalk, but Nicholai was right about one thing. He did make me strong. Anna was relegated to a life where she was continuously made to feel weak, day after day. Month after month. Year after year.

"Thank you for helping me," she says.

"I…you're my sister." And I owe her an explanation, a reason for her suffering. "I looked for you."

"I know. Rafael told me."

"I will get you out of Mexico. I will. It's just not safe right now." I hate that I've managed to save her, but for what? So she can be a pawn to my enemies.

"I'm safe with Rafael." There's a softness to her voice, a fondness. I want to ask her if she's okay, but of course she's not. Anna will never be okay. This entire exchange is awkward because in reality we are complete strangers to one another.

"Okay. Well, I love you." The words feel strange and cold on my tongue. Words I haven't spoken since I pointed a gun at Alex's head and pulled the trigger.

She says nothing, and then the line clicks off. I sit at the very desk I killed Alberto at and grip the arms of the chair hard enough that my fingers start to throb. Raw emotions bubble over and a single tear tracks down my cheek. I let it. A single tear for my sister, for all that we lost, all that was taken from us. A tear for the fact that sheer fate put me here and her there, and what if our roles had been reversed? The irony is that I would never have survived her fate, and she might have ended up in the exact same place anyway. Because had I not fought that very fate so hard, Nicholai never would have pulled me out for training. I want to scream and cry at the world for being so cruel, for stripping us of family and a sense of belonging and making us nothing more than objects. Anna, a possession for nothing more than pleasure, and me, a weapon. We once were a family. We once had each other, loved each other unconditionally. I look down, resting my hand on my stomach. Unconditional love. What would that feel like? What would it look like? The unwarranted adoration of a child. That blinkered ability for someone so innocent to see you through rose-tinted glasses. Isn't that the way I used to see Nicholai, as a savior? Until one day, I suddenly realized that my knight in shining armor was in fact the very monster I needed saving from. For a second, I picture Nero with a tiny baby in his arms, and then, in an instant, that image changes to a teenage boy, his father putting a gun in his hand and forcing him to shoot a boy chained to a wall in a cold, concrete room.

"Una."

I blink and look up at Nero who's standing right across from me. My senses are getting sloppy as my emotions run amuck on me. His eyes drop to my hand on my stomach, and his lips press into a hard line. "You okay?"

I swipe at the tear clinging to my jaw and push to my feet. "Of course." I'm always okay. I can't afford not to be. Especially not now.

CHAPTER TEN

Nero

"You get that shipment here, or I'm going to the Chinese."

"Nero, you ask the impossible. The border…" Fuck me, is it too much to ask people to keep their word?

"Tonight, Max." I hang up the phone and lean back in my chair. Being the underboss comes with its own set of responsibilities, namely, lining the cartels pockets. If they don't get their damn drugs to my city, how the fuck am I supposed to do that? The problem is, they don't really care. Even when the problem is their end, excuses are unacceptable. Arnaldo played nice with them, but I don't bend over for anyone. I'll take my trade elsewhere.

"Boss." I glance up at Tommy standing in the doorway. "Uh, you have an unexpected meeting."

I frown. "No, Tommy. Whoever it is, tell them to go away. Why the hell are you letting people past the gate anyway? We're on lockdown. Get them out of here."

"Well, now, that's not a very warm welcome, is it?"

Tommy stumbles out of the way as Cesare Ugoli strides past him into the office. Three guys step into the room with him, positioning themselves in the corners. Cesare is in his late fifties, but he doesn't look it. Despite his gray hair, there's an edge to him, a quality that you just know not to fuck with. He unfastens the button on his jacket, revealing a waistcoat beneath.

"Cesare."

He lifts a brow. "Not, father?"

This thing between us is difficult. I don't need him for anything other than power. His name holds weight and to be attached to it goes in my favor. Beyond that, I have no feelings towards the man. He left me to Matteo's heavy fist. I don't regret it. Una and I are the same in that sense—the pair of us recognize that we grew up in less than ideal conditions, but we also accept that it shaped us and made us strong. If a bad experience makes you stronger, was it really bad or simply educational? He steps towards me and I round the desk to greet him. He loosely embraces me, kissing my cheek. He's old school, from the homeland. He still speaks with a heavy accent and follows the old customs.

"How can I help?"

Honestly, I don't have the time for niceties right now, and I don't want him here while Una is around. He might be an old man, but he's powerful, and Una did slaughter a lot of his countrymen when she killed Arnaldo. Of course, she doesn't care about politics, and the second he calls her out, she's likely to throw a knife at him. That's all I need.

"I hear whispers, Nero." He steps back and settles into the chair across from my desk. He crosses one ankle over his knee, picking at a piece of lint on his pant leg.

"I wouldn't put much stock in whispers." I take a seat behind the colosal desk and brace my elbows on the wood surface.

"The Kiss of Death," he says, and I still. "I hear she is your whore."

I meet his hard gaze unflinchingly. I could lie. But I don't want to. The mafia will not like Una, but she is what's best for them, even if they can't see it. An organization is only as strong as its leaders. Why have a housewife when you can have a queen?

"She is mine."

His expression shutters, his jaw ticking erratically. "And you know what she has done?"

"I know she played into a plan." A plan that he was all too aware of.

"I don't recall any plan that involved twenty-one dead Italians," he snaps. "Good men."

"Casualties of war, *father*, courtesy of Arnaldo. What did he expect when he sent hit men after her?" I laugh. "She's The Kiss of Death. He was never going to win that fight."

"Arnaldo was a good man. Loyal."

Ah, the bitter irony. "Arnaldo was allowing this organization to stagnate. Is that what you want? To become a relic of the past?"

He leans forward, the movement designed to be threatening. If only I could be threatened. "I took a chance on you."

"And I took a chance on her. She's loyal to me." Sometimes I doubt Una, but when it really comes to it, when it's all on the line, I trust her. She may pretend she's a lone wolf, but I know I have her loyalty just as she has mine.

"She is Russian. And she is one of the *Elite*." He spits the word. "Ultimately her loyalty will be with Nicholai Ivanov. Always. She is a very dangerous risk at best. And even if you had her loyalty, you cannot marry her."

"I'm aware of the customs."

"You are of age. If you are to lead, you must find a good Italian woman."

I laugh. "With all due respect, I wouldn't know what to do with a *good* woman."

"Play with your whore, but do not forget your duty, Nero." Because he did his duty so well, fucking a married woman and leaving her and her asshole husband to bring up the child.

I snap my eyes to his again, all trace of humor leaving me in an instant. "I am not a horse to be put to stud. This isn't up for debate." This could cost me everything, but I won't sit here and act like Una is nothing more than easy pussy. Far from it. I had to work hard for that shit. "It's time the mafia moved into a new age. A strong woman at my side will serve me far better than a subservient one in my bed."

His face starts to redden, and even the men he brought with him start to fidget uncomfortably in the impending silence.

"These are the sacrifices that must be made," he says. "I know this more than anyone."

I stare straight at him. "No."

"No?" His eyebrows shoot up. "You will jeopardize your position, your respect, your culture, all for this woman?"

I push to my feet and round the desk. "If men respect me for the woman I fuck, they are not men whose loyalty or respect I need. Power is earned through deeds and strategy. They see Una as the enemy, but you and I know better." I lift a brow at him. He helped orchestrate the entire plan with Una, for him to shun her now for the very deeds he sanctioned...well, it's very political of him. "If you wanted a puppet, you should have kept Arnaldo."

I rule with fear, and few are more feared than Una. She is like a fabled myth, a whisper on the wind, a tale told to scare children. Only she scares fully grown men. She strengthens our position, but perhaps he is so blinded by his traditions that he cannot see. This is a new world. Keeping women safe and protected is becoming an option we can no longer hold to because there are far too many bastards out there like me who don't care for morals. Do I want the mother of my children to cower helplessly when presented with an enemy, waiting for me to save her, or do I want Una to slaughter them where they stand? There is no choice. Let her be the example. Let her change the way the mafia thinks.

"She is not Italian," he hisses, his face turning an unhealthy shade of red.

"No, she's not. Find me an Italian girl with her skill, her ferocity, and her loyalty, and I will consider her." This is my bargain, because I know he cannot do it. The mafia do not permit their women to fight. And again, as much as the traditions hamper me, they also hamper him.

He pushes to his feet, tugging the material of his jacket tight and fastening the button. "I will be in touch."

I escort him out because I don't want him running into Una on the way. The second the front door closes, she appears from the functioning kitchen that she didn't blow up, a tub of Nutella in her hand and a spoon in her mouth. She leans her shoulder against the doorframe and pulls the spoon slowly past her lips. "Didn't want to introduce me to daddy dearest?" A smile plays over her mouth. A tiny smudge of the chocolate is on her upper lip and it's driving me insane.

"I don't think that would be the safest move."

"Worried he might try to shoot the bastard bearing baby mama?"

She lifts her gaze to mine as I grab the back of her neck and pull her close. Leaning down, I kiss her, swiping my tongue over her top lip and catching the smudge of chocolate.

"Call my baby a bastard again, Morte. See what happens," I breathe against her lips.

"Touchy," she murmurs. "Is this technically the child *of* a bastard, or have you changed that status?" She takes a small step back, biting down on her bottom lip.

"Oh, you just love to fucking push me." I fist her hair and yank her head back hard. The jar in her hand hits the floor with a smash and she smiles like she just won the game. In a heartbeat, she brings a small knife to my throat, pressing it against my skin.

"Play nice," she teases.

"We don't do nice."

She gets that violent glint in her eye. "No. We don't," she whispers as she slices the blade across my skin lightly. I feel the sting, followed by the warm trickle of blood.

"Ah, Morte." I push her back into the room behind her. "I'm going to break you," I promise against her lips.

"So break me."

She shouldn't tempt fate.

CHAPTER ELEVEN

Una

It's been a week, a week of playing nice and behaving. I haven't even killed a single person. I think I'm getting withdrawals. Nero is still Nero. He's still an asshole and, luckily for me, it takes very little to piss him off. Without that, god knows what I'd do for entertainment locked in this damn house. He is different though, more careful. I'm no longer the killer he hired, a disposable body. I'm the walking incubator. I'm Una Ivanov and he's treating me like his baby mama. With each passing day, my anger gets worse and it's probably not helped by the hormones. And as the weeks pass, I will get bigger and bigger, less mobile. I have to be in a safe place for the last two months of this pregnancy because at that point, I can't run. It needs to be now. He's relaxed around me. Maybe he believes I won't try anything. I stand in the bathroom, a towel wrapped around me as I stare at my foggy reflection in the mirror. I finally managed to get the brown dye out of my hair, although I'll probably have to dye it again when I leave.

I watch in the mirror as Nero steps into the bathroom and moves behind me. One hand wraps around my middle, resting over the bump. He's getting bolder, more obvious in his intentions. I shift away and turn to face him.

"I have to go to a meeting in the city today." A small frown line mars his otherwise flawless face. Nero is the image of ruthless grace in his tailored suit. A loose curl of dark hair hangs over his forehead as he tilts his face down to me.

"Uh, okay. I'm not your wife, Nero. You don't have to tell me where you're going."

His lips pull up at one side. "I specifically remember a perfectly good jacket suffering a kitchen knife because I went to a meeting and left you in the apartment."

"That was different."

"The female mind is a wonder." His eyes narrow. "Tell me, how so?"

"Well for one, I wasn't like Moby Dick." I point at my stomach and he laughs. "See, if I were your wife, you'd be too scared of me to laugh."

"Oh, I'm scared of you, Morte." I fold my arms over my chest and he smiles, reaching up and brushing his finger over my bottom lip. "But if you need me to do the romance thing..." He leans in close and skims his lips over my neck, igniting my body. "I want to fuck you so hard."

I snort and roll my eyes. "Romantic."

"Your idea of romance is a knife fight."

"I don't see any knives."

"Ah, that reminds me…" He takes his wallet out of his pocket and pulls something from the coin pouch, holding it up.

"My blade." I take the tiny silver blade from between his fingers, inspecting it.

"I pulled it from some guy's neck in the foyer after your little rampage."

I slide it back into the cuff at my wrist. "Thanks."

"I'll be back in a few hours." He eyes me meaningfully—in other words, don't do anything stupid.

"Try not to kill anyone," I say. "I'd hate to think of you having fun without me."

He brushes his lips over mine and my pulse picks up. "Power isn't bought with mercy, Morte."

"No, it's paid for in blood." I push onto my tiptoes and press my mouth firmly to his, swiping my tongue over his lip. His fingers flinch into my hip.

"A few hours." Then slips away from me, turning his back and walking out the door.

Pressing my fingers to my tingling lips, I squeeze my eyes shut. Now or never. I grab the bag that's under the bed and check through it. I'm limited to only a change of clothes and about a thousand dollars in cash that I found tucked into one of the kitchen drawers yesterday. I move quickly around the room, searching the bedside drawers, the bathroom, the closet. Finally, I drop to my knees beside the bed and bingo. There's a .40 Cal strapped to the bedframe. I pull it away and check the clip before tucking it into the back of my jeans.

The second I step out of the room, Nero's bus boys are in my face. I swipe the legs out from under the big one and pull my gun, pistol-whipping the second. The first moves to get up, but my gun is in his face before he can clamor to his feet.

"I can shoot you or knock you out."

He holds his hands up in surrender. With a swift punch to the temple, his eyes roll back before he's out cold. I shake out my fist, relishing my aching knuckles. It's been so long since I trained, so long since I felt the stinging limbs of a real fight. I miss it.

It's quiet as I make my way through the house. Suspiciously so. I open Nero's office door and slip inside, closing the door behind me. George hops up, wagging his little stump at me. Zeus studiously ignores me as usual. I rifle through the desk drawers until I find what I'm looking for: a set of keys. Either he seriously believes I won't try to leave, or he thinks I'll go on foot. Granted, taking one of his cars will mean he can track me until I can dump it, but, it has its benefits.

George pricks his ears when I turn to leave, trying to follow me. I drop to a crouch in front of him and kiss the top of his head. "I can't take you with me. I'm sorry." He tilts his head to the side and I scratch behind his ear before standing. The garage is at the back of the house, and I manage to avoid Nero's men as I make my way there. Eventually, I'm standing in front of a row of cars. One of them beeps at me when I press the button on the fob. A Maserati sports car. That sucks, considering what I'm about to do to it.

I get in and throw my bag on the passenger seat before revving the powerful engine. It purrs and snarls, making me smile. I find the control for the garage door and it starts to rise, revealing two guards standing on the other side. They frown into the garage, confusion marring their expressions until they make out who is sitting at the wheel of the flashy car. They pull guns and point them at me, but I simply smile and slam my foot on the accelerator. The simple fact is, they won't shoot Nero's pregnant…*whatever* I am. The car lurches forward and they leap out of the way as tire smoke and gravel kick up in my wake.

The driveway is about two hundred yards long, and as I floor it towards the gate, I see men frantically running around. Guns are raised and bullets ping off the hood. I press my foot harder over the accelerator, ducking behind the wheel as I gun it at the metal gate. I meet it with a jarring impact, the screeching of metal on metal and the squealing of tires. The car comes to a halt against the bank opposite the gate, and then the *ping, ping, ping* of bullets sound. I look behind me and slam the car in reverse before shoving it into drive and forcing the ruined vehicle as fast as possible down the road. My heart is pounding as I glance in the rear view mirror, but no one follows me. I need to get off this road, stick to the back roads and then ditch the car. The second I round the corner though, my heart sinks. Two SUVs are pulled across the road, blocking it. In front of them stand Gio and Nero and a whole host of other guys. My foot lifts off the accelerator for a second as I assess my options. The SUVs are blocking the road, but there's a gap between them, probably just big enough to squeeze through…the gap that Nero and Gio are standing in front of. I tighten my grip on the steering wheel and slam my foot back down on the gas. Gio raises his gun and I flinch when he fires at the windshield. The glass shatters, but I keep my gaze firmly fixed on Nero. He's barely a hundred yards away from me now. He lifts a rifle and my eyes widen. I trust none of his men to shoot me, but him? Would he rather kill me than let me go? I don't hear the bang, but I feel the hard thud and stabbing pain of something hitting my chest. I grit my teeth and glance down for a second. A dart is sticking out of my chest, and my head starts to spin. I slam my foot on the brake and yank the steering wheel to the side. The car skids sideways. The sound of screeching tires fills my ears, swiftly followed by the deafening bang of metal meeting metal. Blinding pain rips across my skull along with one thought; run. Fumbling with the door, I throw it open and fall out of the car. My hands and knees meet the tarmac and glass bites into my skin as I try to crawl away. But it's no use. My head is swimming, the fog clinging to the edges of my mind, mocking and taunting me with my own freedom. I pitch sideways, clutching at my stomach as everything goes black.

CHAPTER TWELVE

Nero

❝ Fuck. Fuck!" I roar.

I knew she'd try something, but a car? I didn't expect to have to tranq her behind the wheel of a fucking car. Her head falls back against the tarmac and her arms go limp, falling to her sides. The way she was clutching her stomach scares the shit out of me.

"Get the doctor. Now!" Blood coats her face, pouring from the wound at her hairline and streaking her white-blonde hair red.

I pick her up and climb into the back of the SUV, cradling her against my chest as Gio drives back to the house. I knew she'd try something, so I deliberately left late. Low and behold, I'm barely a couple of miles down the road when I get the call. We pull up to the house. The gate and half my Maserati are all over the road. They've cleared enough of a path to allow us through and Gio pulls right up to the front door.

I climb out and walk through the house to my office where I lay her on one of the sofas. Gio follows a minute later and holds out a wad of bandages and dressings to me. I press them against her forehead, trying to stem the bleeding. There's nothing else I can do.

"She's crazy," Gio grumbles, dragging his hand through his hair in agitation.

"Not like I really expected her to do what she was told."

"Nero, she's pregnant with your kid! You can't give her free reign. She's too unstable." He shakes his head. "She has no sense of self-preservation. She'll kill that baby."

"Enough!" I clench and release my fist before pressing it to my forehead. He doesn't understand Una. I don't agree with her. I can't let her do it, but I see why she honestly believes she's doing the right thing. I get it. I get that she's trying to be selfless.

Gio walks out of the room without another word. He sees things differently. He thinks that women should be protected, children even more so. Una confounds all of that. I brush her hair away from her face, staring at unsettlingly innocent features before my gaze drifts to her stomach. I slide my hand beneath the material of her shirt and press my palm to her bare skin. *Is he or she okay in there? Are they hurt?* I don't know what I expect, a sign or something. I feel nothing. The doctor said the sedative wouldn't hurt the baby, but the car crash…There's a knock at the door, and Gio comes back in followed by the doctor. The older man takes my place and removes the dressing, inspecting her head, "This will need stitches."

"You need to check the baby first."

He opens his mouth to argue but thinks better of it. A machine is set up before he squeezes some gel onto Una's stomach, before rolling the hand held device over her skin. The little screen shows a black and white image, but that sound… the thwap, thwap, thwap of a heartbeat fills my ears and I relax. "Everything looks fine," he says.

I release the breath I hadn't realized I was holding. How can something that was never on my radar suddenly feel so crucial? How can this tiny thing I've never even met, seem like the most important thing in the world? Nothing scares me, but this terrifies me.

I take a seat on the couch across from Una, elbows propped on my spread thighs as I watch the doc stitch her up. She's so still. Too still. Even in sleep, Una is always restless, haunted by nightmares and expecting a strike at any time. The longer I watch her, the more hopeless this situation seems. How do you cage something like her? Wild, deadly, savage. How do you keep a butterfly in a jar without suffocating it?

I want her and I want that baby, but she doesn't want it, so where does that leave us? Will I be forced to choose? Will I have to let her go in order to keep my child? I drag my hand down my face and stand, pacing as the doctor tapes a dressing over her head and stands up. "Keep an eye on her. She should wake up in an hour or so. If she's asleep much longer than that, call me."

CHAPTER THIRTEEN

Una

❝ Oh, my god. My head. I groan as I blink my eyes open. My mind is foggy and disjointed. I panic, trying to pull my fragmented memories together. Nero shot me. I swipe my hand over my chest, trying to feel for a bullet whole, a bandage. Nothing. There's nothing there. I sit up and the room spins in a whirl of colors.

"Careful." Nero's deep voice comes from somewhere in the room. I squeeze my eyes shut and grip the back of the couch, waiting for my surroundings to calm and still.

"You shot me."

"You ran."

My head is throbbing and I reach up, touching my fingers to a dressing at my hairline. I drop my head into my hands and groan. "Why can't you understand this, Nero?"

"I understand. But I don't agree."

"So, you're going to imprison me here until I have no choice? You want me to have this baby, and then what? Just keep it here, next in line to the mafia throne?" I snort. "*If* it makes it that long, of course. We both know you and I have more enemies than North Korea."

"I'll protect you both."

I laugh bitterly and turn my gaze on him. He's sitting with his thighs spread, his elbows braced on them. Dark eyes meet mine, determined, and I know I'll never sway him. "This is the most selfish thing you will ever do, Verdi."

His eyes darken, expression becoming volatile before he explodes off the couch and strides towards me. He leans over, grabbing my jaw in his hand and pulling me closer to him. "Do not fucking push me right now, Una," he says through clenched teeth.

"You don't like the truth, Nero, but this is not one of your power games. This is not a job. This is a child." My child. Our child.

I can feel him shaking as his fingertips dig into my cheeks. "It is not a kindness to take a child from its parents, to leave it, never really knowing who they are. What would you have given to stay with your parents, Morte?" He spits the words venomously.

I tear my face away from him and he straightens, turning his back on me. I've hit a nerve, but so has he. "My parents were good people! And they died. How many families do you think we've torn apart between us, Nero? How many children have we deprived of parents? We are the monsters in this story. We don't get happily ever after's."

He turns to face me. "Even monsters breed, my love," he says mockingly, eyes glinting with that feral edge.

"I won't let you do this just to fulfil your male ego."

"And I won't let you leave just because a kid doesn't fit into your plan." I grind my teeth together and tighten my fists. "If you want to leave after it's born, I won't stop you." The muscles in his jaw flutter beneath his skin. Leave? Would I leave? If this were my only option...if him keeping this baby were the only option, then perhaps I would. Nicholai can never know that I had a child, because he will never stop wanting it. So you see, my options are limited. How did something that was supposed to be simple become so complicated?

The best-case scenario is the baby be completely free of us, but if there were a second option...Nero has enemies, but he can protect himself. My enemies are infinitely more powerful.

"I'll have to," I whisper.

He shakes his head. "Does your job mean so much to you?"

I meet his gaze. Buried beneath the anger and the resentment is a trace of hurt that no one but me will ever see in him. But, then again, I've always been able to read Nero, the same way he can read me. Maybe this is what he needs to think—that I would choose a job over him. I know better than anyone that in the face of dangerous and overwhelming circumstances it's easy to believe that there will be a fix, a way out. Nero isn't used to losing, and, in his eyes, he'll think he can defeat Nicholai. He can't. I could explain it to him, effectively lay out the fact that he is making a choice between me or our child. But I don't want to because I want him to choose this baby. It proves to me that he deserves to be a father. He will protect this legacy with his life, and Nero's protection is fierce and absolute. Meanwhile, I can fall back into the fold of the Bratva and Nicholai will be content because he has me. He'll never even know there was a baby. So, I say what he needs to hear.

"I told you, I couldn't bring myself to kill it, but I am what I am, Nero. I do not want to be a mother." It's partly true. In another world, another time, perhaps I could have been a mother. But in this world, it simply isn't possible. We walk the path in front of us and we can deviate to a degree. We can wish it were different, but eventually we must accept what is.

Nero's hard eyes bore into me. I can practically feel his disgust, his hatred. "Gio," he calls. Gio appears in the room, his usual rigid stance in place. "Take Una to the basement. She is not to be released. If she makes any move to get out, you have my permission to sedate her."

Gio approaches and reaches for me. "Don't." He pauses. I push to my feet and my head spins, I guess from the sedatives still in my blood. My eyes lock with Nero's once more before I turn and leave the office. This is for the best. I've broken his trust and rubbed salt in the wound. When the time comes, he'll let me go to Nicholai without an argument.

Patience is not my virtue. I'm going stir-crazy in this room, and I think it's only been two days. I'm doing press-ups on the ground when the door opens. I ignore whoever just walked in...*seventy-two, seventy-three, seventy-four.*

"Are you supposed to do that when you're knocked up?"

I glance up and watch Tommy take a seat on the edge of the bed, a wry smile on his lips. I carry on, and he waits patiently until I reach one hundred. Bracing my back against the wall, I sit and stretch my legs out. "I'm pregnant, Tommy, not disabled."

Chuckling, he throws a paper bag at me. I look inside and find a sandwich, bought, of course. "Thanks." I take a bite out of it and catch the bottle of water that he chucks next. A scratching comes from the other side of the door followed by a high pitched whine. He rolls his eyes and opens the door a few inches. George slinks through the gap and bounds over to me, his whole body wiggling excitedly. "Oh, hey you." I smile, patting him.

"That dog's obsessed with you." His voice is tinged with just the hint of an Irish accent and it makes me smile. Tommy has always been the one that doesn't fit in with the mafia, but Nero is attached to him, so he protects him where any other Italians would kill him simply for being a half-breed.

"Nero's mean to you. Isn't he?" I kiss the side of Georges nose and he squints like an idiot, making me laugh. Zeus is the loyal one, the guard dog. And I wonder for a second whether in the same way, Nero would be disappointed in his child if it didn't live up to his expectations. No, I can't think about it. "So, what's going on in the free world?" I ask, needing Tommy to just talk about something. Anything.

"Not a lot," he says. "I mean, it's been two days, Una. Not like World War III has started."

I take a mouthful of my sandwich before breaking a piece off and giving it to George. "If you came in here to entertain me, you're doing a shit job."

He lies back on the bed and folds his hands behind his head. "Actually, I'm just supposed to be guarding the door, but I feel bad for ya."

"You going soft on me, Irish?"

He grins at me. "Never, killer."

George pricks his ears and glances at the door a few seconds before it opens. Gio peers inside, his gaze shifting from me to Tommy to the dog before he rolls his eyes. "Nero wants to see you."

"Me?" I ask. He nods and stands back, holding the door open. The second I step past him, Gio presses a gun against my back. "Always such a gentleman, Gio."

"You lost all rights to any nice treatment the second you put that baby at risk," he growls. I'm not one to get angry, but it makes me snap. I spin, planting my boot firmly against the inside of his ankle in a firm kick. He goes down. I land on top of him with my fingers wrapped around his Adam's apple. It won't kill him, but it's certainly not comfortable. He presses the barrel of the gun into the side of my neck as we stare at each other. "You know nothing of my motives, *carogna.* Assume to again, and I will kill you. I don't give a shit how loyal you are to Nero." I get up, swiping a gun from his chest holster as I push away from him. I tuck the weapon into the front of my jeans before he's even standing, and I start walking again.

Tommy lets out a low whistle and whispers to Gio. "Are you crazy? She's Una...and she's hormonal. You, my friend, are suicidal."

"Fuck off, Tommy," Gio snaps at him.

I walk down the hallway and into Nero's office, Arnaldo's office. He's sitting behind that desk and two of his men are standing in front of it, looking at something. The second his eyes lock with mine, something in me hardens, walls erecting themselves, blocking him out. He no longer factors into what must be done. I grab hold of that cold efficiency, embracing the heartless killer within me and holding onto her because I need her right now. The two men move aside and I see a parcel on the desk.

"What is this?"

"It's addressed to you," Nero says, his words icy. And now I see why they all look so concerned. Who knows I'm here? Not many people.

I peer at the package, and then my blood runs cold. My name, is written in Russian. "It could be Sasha."

He tilts his head to the side and I know his mind is spinning through every possibility, every single angle. "Would Sasha send you something?"

I brace my hands on my hips and squeeze my eyes shut. "No." Of course he wouldn't. Sasha and I don't hold to meaningless sentiment. If he wants to give me something, it's inevitably important. You don't mail anything important.

"Open it," Nero says to one of the men. Tommy gently pulls me backwards. Nero gets up and moves around the desk, standing to the side of me. One of his men picks up the package, and I suddenly realize through my fog that they think it might be a bomb. The guy opening it has a steely expression, but I can see the sweat dotting his brow. The paper tears and everyone seems to hold their breath as he peers inside.

"It's okay," he says, removing a small cuddly toy from the package. I frown as he passes me an envelope. It's plain white with no writing on it. Entirely inconspicuous. I open it and take out a card that reads: Congratulations, in Russian. A picture of a stalk is beneath the writing, and it makes my stomach drop. I'm shaking before I even open the card, but the second I see the words, my entire body goes numb.

Little dove,

I hear congratulations are in order.

You have always made me so proud, and now you give me a grandchild, fathered by none other than Nero Verdi.

He will be strong. He will be the perfect soldier.

You must come home now though. Do not make me come for you.

I will see you soon, little dove.

Your loving father,
Nicholai.

CHAPTER FOURTEEN

Nero

I watch as her face goes completely blank and the card slips from her fingers to the floor. I narrow my eyes and wait for her to say something, but instead she just turns and walks out of the room.

"Una?" I go after her. When I round the doorway I see her walking down the hall, her hand reaching for the gun in the back of her jeans. Where the fuck did she get a gun from? She gets to the front door, and my men scramble to there's something about the way she's moving, like a predator hunt, that has me lifting my hand and waving them away. I can't afford to lose good men to her temper.

"Nero?" Gio asks from behind me.

"I've got this. Try and find out where that package came from. I want to know who delivered it," I say without stopping.

I follow Una out the front door and she stalks towards the gate just replaced this morning, after her attempted escape. Again, I wave off my guys and they open the gate, allowing her out. She never breaks stride, never so much as acknowledges them as she walks out the gate and hooks left into the woods.

"Put the entire property on lock down. No one gets within a hundred yards of the gate," I say to the guard.

"Yes, boss. Do you need help?" he asks, glancing after Una.

"No. Give me your gun." He quickly places his gun in my waiting palm, and I follow her into the woods.

Losing sight of her for a moment, I panic, thinking that she's run again, but then I hear a gun shot ahead of me. I take off at a sprint towards the sound of the shot and stop when I reach a small clearing in the woodland. Una stands in the middle, gun raised as she fires at a tree. What the fuck is she doing?

Slowly, I approach her as she fires off round after round, emptying the clip. Her hand drops to her side and silence descends, falling over us like a blanket. I move in front of her. She's standing as still as a statue, even her breaths are barely distinguishable. Her eyes are closed and her expression almost serene.

"Morte?"

Her eyes flash open and there's nothing there. She looks exactly as she did all those months ago: dead, inhuman, emotionless. She tilts her head to the side and it only adds to her animalistic quality. I've always had a healthy respect for this side of her, even as I'm attracted to it. This is the part of her that will sever a man's head without blinking, and if that isn't hot, then I don't know what is. I stroke her cheek gently. Again, her eyes close and she leans into my touch, releasing a long breath. I pull her closer and she surprises me by pressing her lips to mine. Her tongue brushes my bottom lip, and that's when I feel the barrel of her gun press into my stomach. Pulling back, my gaze locks with hers, our faces barely an inch apart.

"Are you going to shoot me, Morte?"

Her expression is blank again, completely indifferent. Damn, she's good. "He's coming," she says, her eyes going distant.

"Who's coming?"

She doesn't answer, so I grab her face, forcing her to focus on me. She presses the gun harder into my stomach. "Who?"

"Nicholai. He knows. He's coming for us." She clenches her teeth and a deep frown etches into her features. "He'll never stop now. There is nowhere I can hide, nowhere I can run. Even if I go to him, it won't be enough. He will want the baby."

"You're not going anywhere."

Her gaze drops to the ground. "All I wanted was to do something good. Just one good thing in a whole lifetime of bad. Have a baby. Give it to a family who would love it. And now…"

I stroke my thumb over her cheekbone. "Now nothing. He will not touch you, do you hear me? Never."

She glances at me, and for the first time since I met Una, I see real, genuine fear in those violet eyes of hers. "You don't know what he's capable of."

"Why does he want a baby?"

"Because we bred him the perfect soldier," she whispers. The words send a chill up my spine, and I really see the kind of life Una grew up in. I knew she was Elite. I knew she was trained from a young age, but I thought Nicholai cared about her in his sick way. This is more than that. This is insanity. "And now...I have no choice. I have to try and outrun him." She takes a deep breath. "I have one bullet left. I don't want to shoot you, Nero, so let me go."

"So shoot me, but you'd better kill me, because if you leave, I will chase you to the ends of the earth." Her jaw tenses and the gun twists in her hand, digging into my ribs. "When are you going to realize that you aren't alone?"

She falters for a second, and steps back. Indecision plays over her features before she drops to a crouch, resting the hilt of the gun against her forehead. "I should have gotten rid of it," she shakes her head. "I was so stupid, so selfish to think that I could do this."

"Morte, you forget who you are, who *we* are. We don't run. I will ask you one more time, do you trust me?" I hold my hand out to her and she glances at it for a second before her gaze meets mine.

"Promise me one thing. If he comes for me, don't let him take me."

"Never."

"I mean it, Nero. If you have to kill me to keep me from him, then you do it."

"Una..."

"You have no idea what he will do to me, what he will do with this baby." She looks so desolate, as though this is her only option, a resigned fate. "I...I will never get out of that place."

Can I promise her that? Could I kill her and my child to save them from that crazy Russian fuck? I see how much she needs me to say I'll do this. "Okay," I say and she nods, slipping her hand into mine as I pull her to her feet. She steps closer to me, pressing her cheek against my chest. I wrap my arms around her slowly, holding her to me for long minutes. "Were you really going to shoot me?"

She pulls away and I release her. "You shouldn't ask questions you already know the answer to." I cock a brow and she rolls her eyes. "It wouldn't have been fatal."

"Reassuring," I mumble, leading her back through the woods.

As soon as we break the treeline, Gio, Tommy, and two soldiers are standing there, guns in hand and waiting. Gio glares at Una and she gives him a one fingered salute before strutting past him, her hips swinging with every step. Tommy peels off and follows her. God knows he's the safest around her.

"Could you stop staring at her ass long enough to tell me what the fuck is going on?" Gio says impatiently.

"The Russian is coming. I want all our best men to be ready to leave in an hour."

"Where are we going?"

"The penthouse. It's impossible to breach, and that makes it the safest place we have." Part of me wants to take Una and run, but I've never run from anything. I feel as though I'm being torn in two. The more primitive part of me, is warring with this new part, this instinct that needs to protect that baby at any cost. But the fact is, Una and I are feared for a reason. She's told me that we can't do this, that our world is dangerous. The irony is that in order to protect that baby, we need to be exactly what we are: formidable, feared and powerful. That, I can do.

Una hasn't said a word, the entire ride from the Hamptons. The second we get into the penthouse, she heads for the stairs. I can tell she's scared. That in and of itself should frighten me. I discuss a few things with the guys. Security, shifts, intelligence on the ground, and then I climb the stairs and push the bedroom door ajar. Light from the hallway spills into the dark room, and I can just make out Una on the bed. George lays beside her, his head resting on her chest as she runs her fingers over the top of his head.

I walk in, and my would be guard dog leaps up, running out of the room. I swear that dog turns into a total rebel when she's around.

I strip out of my suit, and go take a shower. The hot water pummels my tense muscles, but does nothing to help. I'm wound so damn tight. I need to either fight or fuck. When I walk back into the bedroom, Una is lying on her back, staring at the ceiling. Her lips are pressed together in a tight line and she has that determined look in her eye that she sometimes gets. She doesn't move when I get in bed beside her.

"What's going through that mind of yours, Morte?"

"It was all so pointless." She turns her head to the side. "I was willing to sacrifice anything for this baby."

"You would have left," I say, remembering our conversation, her telling me she didn't want to be a mother. Something about it didn't sit right with me. No one goes to that much effort for a life they would happily walk away from.

"As long as Nicholai didn't think it was mine, it would have been safe. So yes, I would have stayed away."

I release a heavy breath. "Una…"

"But the time for selfless acts has passed. He just brought a war to our doorstep." Her eyes lock with mine and she rolls over, dragging her nails over my jaw as she brushes her lips across mine. "I don't know that we can win, but I need you. We kill them all, or we die trying." There's my queen, bloodstained crown in place.

I smile and roll on top of her. "I live for war, Morte."

"Then we slaughter everyone that would do us harm."

Fuck, she's hot when she's violent. I wrench the button of her jeans so hard that it pops off, and then, I'm tugging the material down her legs along with her underwear. Sliding my hands under her ass, I wrench her up and press my mouth over her pussy. A staggered moan leaves her lips as she threads her fingers though my hair, pulling me closer. She rolls her hips, pushing against my mouth as I thrust my tongue inside her. One leg around the back of my neck, and squeezes, choke holding me as she flips me onto my back. Her thighs now straddle my face, her pussy on my lips. I drag my tongue up the length of her as she fucks my face. It's not long before her entire body stills and tenses, long moans slipping past her lips. I love watching her break for me, because I know Una doesn't break. Not for anyone. This right here, is a rarity, a gift that she bestows upon me because she knows I'm strong enough to take it from her.

Her body goes limp and I toss her to the side, getting to my knees and flipping her onto her front. She pants heavily and her skin is coated in a fine mist of sweat.

"I fucking want you, Morte." Gripping a handful of her hair, I pull her up onto her hands and knees, wrenching her head to the side. I kiss up the side of her neck and she trembles. "You're mine," I breathe against her ear. Gripping her hip tightly, I slide into her in one thrust.

Lust and violence swirl between us, mixing with a mutual need to protect the same thing. For the first time, Una and I are completely on the same team and I can feel the power of that. We are one, and we will be unstoppable.

She twists her head to the side and kisses me. She feels like heaven and I will never get enough of her, never grow tired. Everything about her challenges and pushes me, and I crave her. I need her at my side.

My name falls from her lips, and then she's moaning, her back bowing as she pushes back against me. I love seeing her like this, completely vulnerable just for me. She clenches around me and I groan as pleasure fires through my body. I tell her she's mine, but as I come, I know without a doubt, that she owns part of me.

"Fuck!" A groan slips from my lips. We both pitch forward, and I rest my face between her shoulder blades, breathing hard over her damp skin. Eventually, she rolls onto her back. She looks so damn innocent, hair messy, cheeks flushed, and her body swollen with the baby I put in her. I press my lips to hers and work down her chest, sucking one nipple into my mouth as I go. And then, I press a kiss against the taught skin of her stomach. "No baby will ever be more protected," I murmur, glancing up at Una.

She arches a brow. "I think most people just buy a minivan and tape up the electrical sockets."

"We aren't most people, Morte."

Her brows pull together and a small line sinks between them. "Is this what fear feels like?"

"Maybe."

She rubs at her chest. "I feel like I'm unravelling and everything I've ever known is being picked apart a thread at a time. Maybe I'm just not meant for this?"

"No one was ever more suited." She's vicious and dangerous, and I pity anyone who ever tries to hurt her child. She may not be classic mother material, but you only have to look at the animal kingdom to see that the best mothers are also the most lethal ones.

When I wake up in the morning, Una is gone and, as per usual, I have to go in search of her. I find her in the kitchen, standing in front of Gio with a glare on her face. "I'm going to count to three, and then I'm going to snap your neck and leave your body right here for Nero to find."

"I'm not--" Gio starts.

"One." I walk up behind her and kiss her neck before moving past the pair of them in search of coffee. "Two."

"Why are you counting him down?" I squint at her.

She glares over Gio's shoulder. "I want my guns, and he won't give them to me."

I sigh and brace my hands on the kitchen side, waiting for the black nectar to brew. "Gio, I've got this."

He walks away, shaking his head as he goes. He puts up with way more shit than I have any right to ask of him.

"No, you have not *got* this," Una strides up to me, the look on her face promising pain.

"Morte, you and guns…"

She points at me. "Don't you fucking dare. I'm a better shot than any of your shit soldiers. I'm a better shot than you. So how is this going to go, Nero? Are you going to treat me like a prisoner? Your own personal incubator?" She scowls at me, her jaw set into a hard line. "I do not need you, remember that."

She always has to push. I grab her around the throat, pulling her face close to mine, "Don't fucking push me, before I've had coffee." She continues to glare, but makes no effort to get out of my hold. "You are not a prisoner. You are my equal." I shove her away and hand her the key to the armory.

She turns away before throwing over her shoulder. "Actually, I'm The Kiss of Death. No one is my equal."

Damn, she makes me want to hurt her and fuck her. I swear to god, the second that baby is out of her… By the time I've had my coffee, Una is coming down the stairs wearing her yoga pants and a sports bra, with her earphones in. Her hair is pulled into a high ponytail and her hands are wrapped.

"Fancy a round?" she flashes me a wry smile.

"I'm not fighting with you." My eyes drop to her stomach and judging by the look on her face it pisses her off.

"You can just be my punch bag then."

"Anyone would think you just want to ruin my pretty face." I smirk.

"You are far too pretty to be a mafia boss. Sure you don't want me to give you a few scars? Make you look more badass?"

She passes me and swipes her finger over the still healing cut on my neck from last week.

"I have plenty of scars courtesy of you, thanks." Namely the fucking great ugly hole she put in my shoulder. "But just think of it this way, if you ever decide to kill me, my head will make a much prettier trophy than Arnaldo's."

"True." A satisfied grin plays across her lips. Just the memory of Arnaldo's decapitated head is enough to make me hard for her. He found out the tough way what happens when you piss Una off. She's merciless.

I take a step towards her as she backs towards the gym.

"Did I ever tell you how hot I find your extreme bouts of violence?"

She shrugs one shoulder and backs away from me. "Hormones."

"Still hot."

"You're sick," she says as she pushes open the basement door and closes it behind her.

"Says the woman whose hormonal outbursts include blowing up a house and killing eighteen men," I mumble to myself before heading to the office.

CHAPTER FIFTEEN

Una

I pound over the heavy bag again and again until my arms ache and sweat runs down my back. I half expect Nero to come in here and check up on me, but he doesn't and I'm grateful. I need some time to think, to go through everything in my mind. Part of me hates that Nero caught me. That part feels like it's his fault that we're here because he wouldn't just let me run. But then I think: what if we *can* win this? It's pretty unlikely, but what if we could? And there it is—hope. Nero makes me feel things, want things, and I think I'd rather go down in a blaze of glory with him at my side, rather than give my child to a stranger and go back to Nicholai to play his favorite pet again. He reaches too far, asks for too much, and I will kill him or die trying.

When approaching Nicholai, everything needs to be strategic. He doesn't think like normal people. He is the embodiment of the ultimate predator; intelligent, persistent, ruthless, wealthy, and insane. Add all of that together and we're facing an opponent that genuinely frightens me. I've been trained to fear nothing, but it's easy not to fear when the worst case scenario is death. My own death I am not afraid of, but my baby's… Suddenly fear is a very real, very tangible thing, and I don't like it. I don't like the way it settles on my chest and makes the simple act of drawing a breath feel like a chore. I pause and rest my forehead against the bag, drawing deep breaths.

No, I won't let that happen. Even if I fall, Nero will be there. I have to trust that. The path before me seems so clear and yet impossible. The only way Nicholai will ever stop is if he's dead, but can it be done? Can such a key player in the Bratva really be taken down? Maybe, if I can get close enough to him. After all, I am his favorite.

I shove away from the bag and leave the gym, unwrapping my hands as I go. George is lying outside the gym door, but leaps up the second he sees me. My fingers trail his sleek coat as he walks beside me. I turn at the sound of pounding footsteps and watch one of Nero's soldiers go running past me, his hand pressed to his ear piece as he speaks. All I hear is one word: intruder. It's enough to make my heart rate pick up and have me diverting to the armory, a reinforced panic room hidden behind a panel in the dining room. Nero is nothing if not resourceful. I press the key fob into the slot in the wall and enter a code. The door opens with a hiss and I step inside. There's a wall of weapons on one side and TV screens on the other, all showing various cameras in the apartment and building. I glance at each of them, pausing on the lobby. I narrow my eyes at the group of men in suits, all surrounding a single man. Tall and lean, with golden blond hair and a lethal stance. Sasha. Two men lie at his feet, either unconscious or dead. The guys surrounding him are wary, though he seems calm. Typical Sasha. Is he friend or foe now? It's no secret that his loyalty is with Nicholai. But he did approach Nero, and he helped me run. I hesitate for a moment before leaving the room and heading for the elevator. There's one guy standing guard, and he reaches for his gun as soon as he sees me.

"You guys really need to get the memo that I'm not a prisoner," I growl.

"Sorry, ma'am. Boss' orders. No one leaves. No one comes in." I smile, stepping close enough that my bulging stomach brushes against him. "Firstly, call me ma'am again, and I will cut your tongue out. Secondly, think of me as an extension of Nero, because if you disrespect me again, it's not going to go well for you." Shaking, he nods, and I plaster a fake smile on my face. "Now, radio down to those idiots and tell them to let Sasha up."

"Do not touch your radio," Nero's voice comes from behind me, low and commanding.

I turn on him with a glare. "Seriously?"

Nero's wearing only a pair of workout pants, his hair still damp from the shower. "You trust him?" he asks incredulously.

"Of course. It's Sasha." It's not a complete lie. I trust that he wouldn't come here to hurt me, but not that he wouldn't tell Nicholai everything he knows. I don't judge him for it, the kind of upbringing we had, it warps your mind through both fear and conditioning. I felt that same blind loyalty to Nicholai for years, but I had something to hold onto outside of that facility—my sister. Sasha never had that. The closest thing he has to family is me and Nicholai, and I'm essentially making him choose between his father and his sister.

"What if he's here to kill you? Wouldn't he be the perfect pawn? He's close enough to you that you trust him, skilled enough to take you down, and no doubt dispensable, so if I kill him afterwards, Nicholai won't care."

"Sasha's good, but not better than me, let alone when I'm surrounded by half the mob." I roll my eyes. "And Nicholai doesn't want me dead. That's the last thing he wants."

"Una…"

"Please, just trust me. He might have information. He's done nothing but help us so far."

Dark brows pull together and he folds his arms over his broad chest. "I don't like it."

"Acknowledged."

"Don't tell him anything. How did he even know you're here? Does Nicholai know where you are?"

"Capo," I snort, "you own two properties in New York. It's not difficult, plus, Sasha can hack any security camera, anywhere. If he wants to find someone, he'll find them." I jerk my chin towards the camera in the corner of the room. "He can hack through all your firewalls. He's good."

"That's reassuring," he grumbles. "Tell them to bring him up," he says to the guy still standing behind me. He relays the instruction and I wait for the elevator to climb. Nero moves to stand slightly in front of me like my own personal guard dog. On pure principle, I step up beside him, folding my arms over my chest.

The elevator pings and the doors slide open, revealing a wall of suited Italians. Nero's men still don't like me, and most of them either glare at me or ignore me altogether. I don't care, but I worry that their loyalty to Nero might waver since he's fucking the enemy. He and I know that it was retaliation, but even I'll admit that twenty-one dead Italians is hard to explain. And well,

Italians all seem to be linked. Guaranteed, every guy I killed has a cousin or nephew or brother within Nero's ranks, which is always comforting.

The suits step out, filing to either side of the doors and revealing Sasha. His face is steely as always, features severe and angular. A small frown line sinks between his brows as his eyes move from my face to my stomach.

"So it's true," he says simply. I nod and he glances around the room. I can see his mind processing every detail, looking for threats. He's assessing everything, from the distance between us to the way each man is holding his gun, spotting weaknesses, planning, strategizing. I know, because it's exactly what I do when I'm in a hostile situation.

"Why are you here, Sasha?" I ask.

He glances at Nero, and then back to me, his lips pressed in a thin line. "Give us a minute," I say to Nero.

"No."

I turn to face him and he simply stares straight at Sasha, his expression giving away nothing.
"Nero…"

Nero looks at the guys either side of the elevator. "Go." He orders them. "Gio, stay." The men do as instructed, filing away into the apartment and leaving just Gio, Nero, Sasha and me. Sasha's eyes meet mine. I know what he's thinking, that I just thinned out the herd and evened the odds. I step towards him and he closes the distance between us, pulling me into a stiff hug which makes me tense. Sasha and I have never hugged. It's not something you do when neither of you can stand being touched.

"I'm so sorry I helped them get to you. We have to get you as far away from here as possible," he whispers in Russian, so quietly it's barely above a breath. I feel something solid pressing against my stomach and slowly reach down, my fingers brushing over the cool metal of a gun. "Ready?" he asks, body tense and primed for an attack.

"Wait, Sasha." I pull away from him slightly. "I'm not leaving."

"What the fuck is going on?" Nero snaps. I hear the click of a safety being flicked by Gio, and I can feel the aggression pouring off Nero like a living thing slithering over my back.

I hold my hand out to Nero because Sasha, though like my brother, is still a lethal killer. He won't hurt me, but Nero and Gio are simply targets assessed on their threat level. I know this. "I'm not running," I say, in English this time, taking the clip out of the gun he gave me and handing it back to him.

Those jade green eyes meet mine, concern and confusion swimming in them. "Una, he knows."

I nod. "I'm aware."

"Then you know he wants that child."

"I know."

He drops to one knee and swipes a hand through his hair in agitation. We used to take a knee when we were training in the field as a way of strategizing, taking a minute to plan. I follow suit in front of him.

"Where could I even go, Sasha? There is nowhere he wouldn't track me."

"Then…" He sighs. "Then come home, beg him to forgive you. You know he will. He loves you. This…you're just making it worse for yourself, Una." Nero lets out a growl of displeasure behind me and I turn on him.

"Really? Just go to the kitchen."

He cocks a brow, looking at me as if I am another one of his pawns to be commanded. "Forgive me if I don't trust your super killer friend here."

"I swear to god, Nero. Pain, so much pain."

"I thought stress was bad for babies," Sasha says flatly.

I turn back to him and can't help but smile. "Oh, well. Poor kid doesn't stand a chance then." He pushes to his feet, glancing at Nero again. I stand up.

"The Italian is volatile and unpredictable," he says in Russian. "He will get you killed."

"In our world, volatile and unpredictable wins wars," I reply in my native tongue. "He is dangerous and I need dangerous."

"Please come home," he begs. I can see the hint of fear in his eyes, and I know it's not for the baby, it's simply for me because I'm the closest thing to human connection he has. Sasha looks formidable dressed all in black, covered in weapons and wearing the mask of an ice cold killer, but we all have out weaknesses. Just as Anna was mine, I am his, but I don't wish for him to betray Nicholai the way I have. It would break him.

I sigh. "I'm never going back, Sasha. He will do to this baby what he did to us." He will break my child as we were broken. Broken things heal stronger, but for the first time in my life I'm disturbed by the concept.

"Was it so bad?" he asks.

What Sasha can't see is that, despite his many strengths, his life is a sad and pitiful existence. By the time I met him, I was thirteen. He was fourteen, but he had already been in the facility for five years. Maybe Nicholai got me just a little too late, because I never truly let go of the life I had before becoming Elite. Sasha is the living, breathing embodiment of everything Nicholai wanted him to be. His life is whatever Nicholai chooses in that moment because he knows nothing else. He has no freedom, only orders and compliance. And the saddest part of all of this is that he can't see it. He can't see what was taken from him, only the strengths he was given, but they come at a high price. "We were children, Sasha."

"He made us strong, Una. You are the strongest of us, and yet you throw it back in his face." His voice rising slightly before he composes himself again.

"He broke us and turned us into weapons." I take a small step back away from him and closer to Nero. "I've made my choice."

Sasha's eyes flick to Nero, his jaw set in a rigid line. "You think that you are strong enough to protect her from what's coming?" he asks Nero in English.

"With great power comes great responsibility," Nero replies cryptically.

Sasha shakes his head. "You have no idea what is coming. He will go for your weaknesses." His eyes flick to Nero again. "And you have developed many, sister, but I will try to help you."

"Why? If Nicholai finds out…"

"Because you are my sister, and I love you."

"I love you, too." My eyes prickle and I curse these bloody hormones. He turns and gets in the elevator. "But Sasha…" I switch to Russian. "Don't endanger yourself for me. I do not expect to make it out of this alive."

Nero doesn't need to know how low my expectations really are. I throw Sasha the clip in my hand and he snatches it out of the air right before the doors glide shut.

I hold onto those last words between us, because I don't know if or when I'll see him again, and really, Sasha is more like a sibling to me than my actual sister. Sasha and I have always been close, but I didn't think either of us capable of love. Perhaps it's just our own version of it, a mimicked emotion, a sense of attachment we need to name. After Alex, I shunned and feared love as though it were a plague. Loving Alex cost me dearly, and I would do anything to avoid that pain again. To lose someone you care about so deeply is an agony unlike any other, it wounds you, leaving scars that never heal. And then I think: what if Nicholai were to kill Nero? I care for him, I'm invested in him as an ally, as the father of my child, and perhaps…perhaps I love him in a way. Killing Alex tore out my heart, and I don't have much left to give, but I think that whatever twisted, blackened part of it remains belongs to Nero. After all, he is my equal. He's forced me to feel things that I thought long dormant, and I respect him in a way I've never respected anyone else. I trust him, and that speaks volumes.

I turn to face Nero. His arms are folded over his chest and his hair is messy like he's been dragging his hands through it. Gio walks away now that the threat has disappeared.

"You chose to stay," Nero says simply.

I nod, unable to speak the words that are hanging in the air. *I chose you.* If I wanted to escape, I was never going to get a better chance than with Sasha here. All the king's soldiers and all the king's men could not stop the two of us together. On my own, I'm good, with Sasha…we're invincible; Nicholai's best kill team. "Can you trust him?" Nero asks.

"I want to." I want to believe that Sasha would never sell me out. "But you have to understand, the training, it's hard to resist. And the punishments for disloyalty are…" I remember them well. Repeated electrocutions, whippings, water boarding, even injections of scorpion venom that would make you hallucinate.

And when you've seen the things we've seen those hallucinations are not pretty. "He's not the enemy."

He watches me for a few seconds and then nods. "The second he puts you at risk, he is. Do you understand?" I hesitate. "This isn't just about you anymore, Morte. Tell me you understand," he demands, that power he wears so well flexing and rolling like a wave.

"I understand."

I follow Nero to the bedroom where he steps into the walk-in closet. A few minutes later he's wearing dress pants and a shirt to which he is fastening the buttons. I miss his shirtless state, but the devil does wear a suit oh so well.

"Going somewhere?"

He lifts a brow, his expression stoic. "I have some business to handle in the city." Of course he does.

"Don't you have people for that?"

He fastens his belt. "Sometimes, if you want a job done properly, you have to do it yourself."

I flop down on the bed and stretch my arms above my head. Nero's gaze scans over my underwear clad body. "I happen to be very thorough in my jobs." I smile up at him.

"No."

I sigh and sit up. "If I don't get outside soon, I'm likely to maim Gio very badly. I'm sure it's handy if you're right hand has...well, a right hand."

Amusement cracks that implacable mask. "Morte, you are supposed to be laying low."

"That's just it, I'm not sure I want to lay low." I yanks his shirt out of his pants and slide my palm over his abs. "We don't run and hide. Battle lines need to be drawn, capo." His hand wraps around my wrist and he pulls it from beneath his shirt.

Bending over me, he pins both of my hands above my head. His lips are barely a whisper from mine. "And as much as I appreciate your loyalty, Morte, you are not leaving here."

"Equal or prisoner, capo?"

An exasperated breath slips through his lips and, for a moment, we simply stare at each other. "You are the only person in this world that could possibly be my equal," he says arrogantly.

I smile and press my lips to his. I swipe my tongue over his bottom lip, tasting coffee and violent promises. That does it. Grabbing my hips, he yanks me down the bed until he's pressing between my thighs. The scent of his cologne tinged with cigarette smoke wraps around me and I inhale deeply as he bites the side of my neck.

"You do not do anything stupid. You stay within three feet of me at all times." He breathes against my skin.

I smile. "You're forgetting again."

He pinches my jaw between his teeth. "Never." His voice rumbles in my ear before he pulls back and stares at me. "I'm meeting with the leader of the Russkoye Slovo." I roll my eyes. "And you cannot roll your eyes at him, or shoot him, or cut him…"

"Fine. But if you deal with dogs, people will see you as a kennel."

"That makes no sense." He pushes off me.

"It does if you are Russian." I allow him to pull me to my feet. "What deal do you have with him?"

"We'll talk in the car."

"Fine."

*****

The city thrums outside the car window. Car horns blare as we sit in bumper to bumper traffic. I used to hate the city, the towering skyscrapers, the ignorant commuters, the way the people pour down the sidewalks like a river, the smells that taint the thick, putrid air…It's a sensory overload, a nightmare for someone like me.

Music blares through the car speakers. I glance at Nero, and he's pressed into the back of his seat, arm outstretched as he casually drapes his wrist over the steering wheel. He almost looks relaxed, except for the subtle tick of his jaw.

"What's wrong?" I ask.

"Nothing."

I face the windshield again. "Lies."

Neither of us says anything else as we wind through the stop-start traffic eventually pulling up outside an older brick building right by the Brooklyn Bridge. Tall windows are adorned with little flower boxes, and wide stone steps lead to a set of heavy-looking double doors. As soon as the car pulls to a stop, the door opens a crack and a young guy in a suit rushes over.

I get out and Nero throws the keys to him before we walk up the steps towards the door.

Apparently this meeting is, is a formal occasion so I'm wearing a dress and heals. There have been plenty of times when I've had to seduce targets and dress like a woman they'd happily follow to a secluded room. But I feel fake, a blade pretending to be a flower. In some instances, a flower is a good disguise, but in others, you want to be seen as something dangerous and life threatening. A knee length coat goes some way to hiding the baby bump. I know it's pointless now, but showing it just feels like I'm pointing right at a soft spot and daring an enemy to stab me there.

Nero's arm wraps around my waist and he pulls me into his side as we climb the steps. "You look beautiful," he says, amusement in his voice as he twirls a strand of my hair around his finger.

"I have a gun and two knives on me. I will hurt you."

He chuckles as he pulls the door open for me. I glare at him as I pass, but he just stares at my cleavage. "Don't go stabbing anyone. Wouldn't want to get blood on your dress." I'm going to get blood on him in a minute.

We walk straight past what looks like a reception desk. The guy behind it stares at me and I can feel his attention even as we round the corner. Another set of double doors open into a bar. It has that Old-world feel about it with wooden flooring and leather wing back chairs everywhere. There aren't many people in here, but again, everyone stares at me as if I have two heads. Or maybe it's Nero they're looking at.

"Why are they staring?" I say under my breath.

He smirks. "They don't see many women in here."

I glance around again. There isn't a single woman here, and all the patrons are…of a certain ilk. "Brilliant, a gentleman's club. I didn't even know you could still pull that sexist bullshit anymore." Then a thought occurs to me. "Wait, are they going to try and kick me out? Don't they do fencing? Please let me challenge someone to a fight."

"You're blood thirsty today." I snort at that. If he felt like I do right now, entire cities would be on fire.

"You know I'd win." Maybe that's what he's worried about.

"*Morte*. If anyone pointed a weapon at you, I'd be forced to remove both his arms from his body." A fluttering sensation erupts in my chest, even though I absolutely do not need his protection. Still…

"You say the sweetest things."

"Hmm." He places a kiss on my cheek, before guiding me to a table in the corner.

A small man with a greasy comb over sits there, his expensive pinstripe suit out of place and completely cliché. He looks about mid-forties, with an edge to him. His face is lined with evidence of a hard and violent life. But this man is Slovo, and they are bottom feeders, opportunists by nature, but never the ones to take a risk of their own. He lifts a cigar to his lips, squinting through the rising tendrils of smoke as he stares at Nero.

"Nero Verdi, in the flesh," he drawls in a heavy Russian accent.

"Igor," Nero responds.

The man turns his gaze to me. I see the flash of recognition, but he covers it quickly. "And who is this?"

"You know who I am, dog," I snap in Russian.

He laughs. "Well, now I do. You are distinctive, *Una Ivanov*."

Nero pulls out a chair for me, and I sit before he takes the seat beside me. "And you are forgettable in every way."

"Enough with the insults." Nero chimes in, clearly bored.

"I was simply complimenting his lovely suit." I smirk.

Nero's hand lands on my thigh beneath the table, fingertips brushing over the knife strapped to the inside. "Igor, here, wishes to bring guns into our city. Isn't that right, Igor?" I don't miss the '*our*' and neither does Igor. His eyes flick back and forth between us, narrowing. Nero casually slips his pack of cigarettes from his pocket and slides one between his lips before lighting it. The snap of his lighter closing is the only sound as he waits for Igor to respond.

His hand lands back on my thigh and I glance at him. He raises his eyebrows as he inhales a long drag, as though waiting on me to respond. Is this some kind of test? If so, I'm not about to shy away from it.

"That's a big ask." I lean forward, locking eyes with the weasely little man. "But you see, Igor, the lamb does not ask the lion for a favor, when all he offers in return is his own leg to chew on." He opens his mouth to respond. "And I do not want your leg, so tell me, what do you offer?"

Igor places his cigar down and leans back in his chair, rubbing a hand over his chin. After a few moments, Nero clears his throat. "I'm not a patient man."

Igor nods and places his palms flat on the table. "I was going to offer you a new drug, but I give you choice," he says in stilted English. "I can give you drug. Very good, new party drug. All the rage in Moscow. Or..." he lifts one eyebrow, a small smile playing over his lips. "I can become ally."

There's a beat of silence before I laugh. "What could an alliance with you possibly offer us?"

He's the one who laughs this time. "You are with him," he changes to Russian. "Why? I hear that you are wanted, Kiss of

Death. I hear that you killed the Italian under boss, that Nicholai is hunting you. And now I see you here, with him of all people. He seems very…attached to you." He smooth's a hand down the front of his jacket. "So, I ask you, are you loyal to the wolf, or your so-called lion?" *The wolf.* Only the enemies of the bratva call Nicholai the wolf, and it's been a long time since I've heard it.

"I'm here, aren't I?" I revert back to English.

"I do not like Nicholai's pets." Igor's eyes never leave my face. "But I spit on the bratva, and I spit on Nicholai Ivanov." The Slovo are enemies of the bratva. My first solo kill was their former leader in fact. "I offer you my help, Una Ivanov. On one condition: your master dies."

I turn to Nero and he focuses on Igor for a beat longer before his gaze meets mine. "I do not trust him," I say in Italian this time. "I told you, he is a dog, and he will turn tail the second someone offers him better scraps. He'll probably sell us out to Nicholai."

"He will not be close enough or privy to enough information to sell you out, Morte." His lips tilt up, that easy confidence of his pouring off him in waves. He has this way of making me feel as though everything is possible because he's Nero Verdi, and the world would stop turning if he willed it so. "A Russian ally could be useful. His father was killed by Nicholai." I swallow heavily, because Nicholai doesn't make his own kills. He sends his Elite. And now Igor's name rings a bell. Igor Dracov, the illegitimate son of Abram Petrov, the former leader. I killed Igor's father. "He has no love for the man." Nero believes it's a low risk for potential reward, and his calm confidence lends me to having an irrational amount of faith in his decision.

I study Igor. Everything about him looks shifty and I don't trust him. Then again, I don't trust anyone. Except Nero and Sasha. I glance at Nero, and he looks totally at ease, sitting back and letting me make his deal for him. My fingers thread through his and he brings them to his mouth, brushing his lips over my knuckles.

"The Slovo are small and inconsequential," I say. More like a band of rebels than anything else. "How much use can you be to us, Igor?"

He picks up the cigar and places it between his lips, inhaling. "No, the bratva think the Slovo is no threat and that is how we want it. Our numbers almost rival theirs, but I have many people buried in the bratva, quiet as mice. They listen. They see."

"That's settled then," Nero says, done with the conversation.

"Nero…"

"They are well connected, and they are motivated to remove Nicholai. If the bratva falls, then they can assume power."

I narrow my eyes at him. What the hell is he talking about? He turns back to Igor and pushes to his feet. "I accept your proposal. You may move your gun shipment through the city, but keep it clean. If I have to get involved, you won't like it."

Nero reaches out his hand. Igor shakes it before holding his hand out to me. I grit my teeth and take it, forcing back the inner killer pushing to the surface. Whatever he sees in my eyes, it makes him drop my hand quickly.

"Pleasure," Igor purrs, before walking out of the bar.

As soon as we're in the car, I turn on Nero. "The bratva will never fall." The network is enormous, powerful and intertwined into even the government in Russia. It can't be done. Though Nicholai is one of their key players and his death would be a blow; he will soon be replaced.

A knowing smile pulls at his lips as he starts the car. "Of

course not." That's all he says. Damn, the man is so cryptic. He starts the engine, pulling away from the building.

"'Of course' is not an explanation. Care to explain to me what is going through that crazy mind of yours."

"My brilliant mind?"

I roll my eyes. "Nero "

"Fine. Of course, the bratva will never fall, but if we kill Nicholai, they will have to retaliate. Someone needs to take that fall, and I can't bring that back on the family. This has the potential to start a mafia war."

"You want to ally so that you have a scape goat." Damn, he thinks of everything, down the finite details. I can plan a kill to the letter, think of every escape option, every possible thing that could go wrong, but Nero takes that and does it on a massive scale, factoring in key players and entire organizations, gangs, and families. He's never been more attractive to me than he is in this moment, and I don't know if it's a twisted form of bloodlust withdrawal or hormones.

"There is no point in killing Nicholai only to die a few weeks later." His hand lands on my thigh, pushing the material of my dress up until he skims my bare thigh. "I intend for us to survive this, Morte. And you will rule this city with me." The future he speaks of is not one I've allowed myself to think on, because tomorrow is so uncertain.

I laugh. "Not sure your father will approve of that."

He pulls up at a traffic light and glances at me with a twisted smile. "I have a plan."

"Don't you always?"

"Always."

CHAPTER SIXTEEN

Nero

Planning. That's all I've done for the last three days. I've barely seen Una because she's been calling on her contacts in Russia while I've been calling on everyone, anyone who might help our cause. The simple fact is, Nicholai Ivanov is coming for us and we have two choices: hand Una over, or fight. The first isn't an option, which leaves us gearing for a war with a man who has his own personal army and more money, weapons, and influence than God. Not to mention he's insane and obsessed with the mother of my child. Of all the women in the world, I had to want her.

I swipe my hand down my face and look at the blueprints Gio has placed in front of me. I'm sitting on one of the sofas in the pacing backwards and forwards, cracking her neck as though she's about to go on a rampage. Gio flashes me a nervous glance and I smirk. She's decided she hates him, and he's now the target of her rage, of which there's plenty.

"So, the only way in is via the vehicle bay?" He points at the blueprint. Turns out Igor was useful. His people managed to give us accurate plans of Nicholai's military base, not that I think it will do us much good. The only plan we have is to go at him head on.

Una sighs and turns to face us, bending over the coffee table and bracing her palm against the wood. "The base is guarded well. This is the only road in," she says, stabbing the paper with her finger. "It's exposed, with only a tree line on one side. They can see you coming from miles away. There's a guard tower with a .50 Cal machine gun and armor piercing bullets, as well as RPGs. Any unauthorized vehicles are taken out." Gio looks at me, his brows pulled tightly together as she continues. "If you get past that gate, you are left with an impregnable, nuclear blast-proof bunker. And yes, it has only one entrance, and that is the vehicle bay which is heavily guarded by Elite. I could take you out right now, Gio. On my own while carting around a football. You don't stand a chance against one of them, and you are proposing walking into their fucking base, where they live and train, where they will be armed to the hilt." She turns away and resumes pacing, dragging both hands through her hair.

"Do you have a better plan?" he asks. She turns and glares at him. The air buzzes with the promise of blood, and I can practically hear her ticking, ready to go off at any minute.

"Yes! I had a better fucking plan until you two idiots decided to drag me back to New York!" She goes to the window and braces one palm against it, dropping her head forward as she clenches and releases her fist at her side.

"Gio, give me a minute." He gets up, and walks out of the room. The door clicks shut, leaving a tense silence in its wake.

I move over to the window, studying the profile of her rigid back. "Do not make me the enemy, Morte."

She rests her head against the glass and it mists with her breath. "I feel like a sitting duck."

"Perception, Morte. If you think you are a bird waiting for a bullet, then the bullet is sure to find you. We are strategizing, being smart and forming a plan that will actually work. You cannot fight if you believe the war is already lost."

"Nero." Curling her fist against the glass, she lets out a groan. "Your confidence is not going to win this for us." She turns, bracing her back against the window. "You have to go to your father."

"No."

"You are the underboss. We need the backing of the mafia."

"We're talking about a mafia war. And I would be asking him to start it in the name of what? The Russian woman who killed our own."

"We have gone backwards and forwards over every conceivable plan. At the very least, we need the mafia's protection in the aftermath, even if we can pull this off with limited numbers." She pinches the bridge of her nose. "If we kill Nicholai, pin it on the Slovo, and have the Italians protection, we will be safe. The Russians won't want a war either. Without it, we are a bird waiting for a bullet."

I sigh. "You don't understand…"

"You would be asking for his help in removing your biggest competition. Nicholai runs all the guns in North America. That trade is worth millions. Take it." She steps forward, grabbing my jacket in both hands. Her eyes lock with mine, desperation bleeding through her expression. She's scared and I hate it. I hate that Nicholai has my vicious killer fearing for her life and the life of our child. I'm going to end Nicholai Ivanov, but as I look at Una, for the first time in my life, I'm questioning exactly what the price of that will be.

"Morte, there are lines even I cannot cross."

"Fuck politics, Nero. Fuck the lines. You didn't go to such lengths to become underboss, just to simper beneath your father's will." Her eyes drop to my mouth and she leans in, trailing her fingers over my jaw as her lips brush against mine. "Show him why you are the future of the mafia. Show him what real power looks like." She kisses me. "Show him what a man with no lines is willing to do. The Italians may hate me, but they hate the Russians more."

I grab her jaw, tilting her head back until she's looking at me. "They don't hate you, Morte, they fear you. They fear us *because* we have no lines."

Her hot breath blows over my face and a wicked smile pulls at her lips. "Good."

I groan against her mouth, barely a breath away from mine. My vicious queen, so beautifully merciless. I have grown up in the mafia, surrounded by men who will shoot a man in one moment and then preach about their honor and ethics the next. Una and I are the same, she basks in their fear. She likes it. We understand the power of being feared before you've even entered a room, of having your name whispered with both reverence and disgust. I love that about her. We are the new generation, more ruthless, less forgiving, and with a code of ethics that serves us and those loyal to us. Man, woman, or child, if you stand against us, you are the enemy and you will be cut down.

I twist Una's face to the side and kiss her throat, inhaling her vanilla and gun oil scent. "Get changed, put on a dress. We're going to see Cesare." One way or the other, we will pull him to our cause. I'm not above playing dirty. If this is what Una needs to feel safe, then I'll give it to her. Cesare means nothing to me, and Una means everything.

"I hate wearing dresses," she says, scowling.

I smirk, my grip slipping from her jaw and resting around her throat. Her pulse thrums against my fingertips, steady and strong. "My father likes to think of women as something delicate, something to be protected. And you play the innocent lamb very well when you have to, my love." She glares at me and I laugh. "Especially with this." I rest my free hand over her stomach.

"*This* is already making me want to kill somebody."

I kiss her forehead. "Enchant him the way you enchanted me."

"Nero, I tried to kill you and you got hard for it." She rolls her eyes. "That is not enchanting, it's just twisted."

"You like twisted." Grabbing her hips, I lift her, pushing her against the window. Her legs wrap around my waist and my hard dick presses against her.

"I love twisted," she breathes.

I kiss down the side of her neck and she throws her head back against the glass, pushing her breasts towards me. Pregnancy has been good to her, and her chest strains against the confines of her shirt. Sliding the straps down her arms, I suck one nipple into my mouth and she moans, rolling her hips into me. "Fuck," I groan, my cock swelling. I love how she always responds for me, softening and opening up just like the butterfly she is. Grabbing my shirt, she tears it apart. Buttons scatter everywhere, and then her nails are raking over my skin in a burning trail. I hiss and allow her to slide down the front of my body. She removes my shirt while pushing me back toward the couch like a hungry predator. The look in her eyes skates the fine line of lust and violence, both so close. She strips until she's completely naked and so fucking beautiful. Her body is hard, honed muscle, littered with a map of scars, but softened by her full breasts and growing stomach. She shoves against my chest and I fall back onto the couch before she's straddling my thighs. Her movements are aggressive and frantic, and I meet every touch of her lips, every lash of her tongue with the same brutal need, feeding the flames, antagonizing her.

A ragged gasp slips from her as I push two fingers inside her. She touches her forehead to mine and her entire body tenses and trembles as her shaking breaths intermingle with my own. Gripping her throat, I drive into her harder, watching her become totally exposed for me. Her eyes shutter closed on a moan and her skin flushes a beautiful shade of pink. Silvery hair cascades down her back as her hips meet my hard thrusts eagerly. Fuck, she's so perfect.

"Break for me, Morte," I say through clenched teeth.

And she does, moaning and clenching around my fingers, her body contorting erotically.

"Nero," she breathes.

My name leaving her lips in a moment of weakness is so right, so absolute. Her forehead meets mine and I inhale the smell of sweat and sex, mixing with her familiar vanilla scent. She grips my hair and kisses me.

"Now we can go and see your dad," she says, climbing to her feet.

"See, now you just make that sound wrong."

She grabs her shirt and underwear, putting them back on before she heads for the door. "Una, put your fucking jeans on," I snap as she opens the door.

She glances over her shoulder and winks before she walks straight out. "Fucks sake." I yank my pants up and storm after her. She walks right through the lounge where five of my guys are sitting with Gio. I glare at them, daring them to so much as glance her way. They all look away sheepishly, keeping their gazes locked on the floor.

Catching up to her on the stairs, I throw her over my shoulder. "Put me down!"

My palm meets her ass hard enough that she'll be feeling it when she sits down. "You just love to fucking push me."

I drop her in our walk-in closet. "I like you angry."

God, how was I not bored senseless before she came along? "Get dressed."

"I need to shower."

"Oh no." I back her into the chest of drawers, wrapping my fingers around her delicate throat as I bring my lips to her ear. I can feel her pulse racing in anticipation. "You don't get to wash my come off you after that little stunt."

Her eyes meet mine and she bites her bottom lip on a smile. "Now who's dirty? I thought you wanted innocent, contrite, pure…"

"Never." My thumb swipes over her bottom lip as I lean in. "Play the part, but we'll know better, Morte."

Teeth graze over the pad of my thumb and my dick stirs again. "Watch and learn, capo." I step away from her, grabbing a shirt and my gun holster. I walk away before I decide to finish what we started and fuck her.

When I get to the bottom of the stairs Gio clears his throat. "Did you get anywhere with the plans?" he asks. Plans? Oh, the plans.

"We're going to try a different approach." He raises his brows. "We're going to Cesare."

"*We?*"

"I'm taking Una. See if she can't appeal to his strategic side."

He inhales a deep breath. "With all due respect, I think that might aggravate the situation."

"We don't have a lot of choice. I need numbers and political support, Gio." I pull him to the corner of the room. "Nicholai is going to make a play soon. He won't come directly at us, and we can't go to him, not at the base. It's suicide. I think we need to catch him away from his home turf."

His dark brows pull together. "Una could lure him out."

"Suggest that again, Gio, and I'll kill you, friend or not."

He snorts. "Nero, you are facing the impossible. We have to draw him out, and the only thing he's guaranteed to come out for is Una."

"Are you loyal to me or not?"

"We've been best friends since we were fourteen." And he gave up nearly everything to support me. "You know I am."

"Then you are loyal to her and my baby." He stares at me for a beat, then releases a long breath, nodding. His gaze flicks over my shoulder before he turns away, going back to the few men he has gathered. I turn around just as Una comes down the stairs.

"Innocent enough for you?" she asks.

"I'm not sure that's quite the word I'd use," I mumble. She's wearing a gray dress that clings to every fucking thing. That bump couldn't be any clearer if she put a flashing neon sign on it. The material follows the line of her curves and stops just above her knee. She's wearing a pair of high heels and her hair falls down her back in a silver-white sheet. Her infamous red lipstick is firmly in place making her look sexy although it is a blinding reminder of exactly who she is. I'm not sure my father needs any reminders on that front.

She walks up to me and smooths her hand down the front of my jacket. "Come now. You wouldn't want to keep daddy dearest waiting."

CHAPTER SEVENTEEN

Una

"I need to know everything," I say as we sit in yet more New York traffic.

Nero braces his hands against the steering wheel. "You're going to have to be more specific."

"Cesare." My knowledge of Nero's biological father was limited to business acquaintances, political motivations etc. What I needed to know was the minute details that make a person tick.

"He's a strong leader, ruling with a combination of fear and respect. He's of the old ways."

"The mafia do love their traditions," I mumble. The car shuffles forward through the heavy traffic and the blare of a horn rang out somewhere behind us.

"The traditions hamper him."

"Women and children?"

"Amongst other things. When he came to me at the Hamptons house, he expressed his… distaste for you."

I let out a snort. "Nero, I'm Russian. I might as well be the antichrist."

His fingers drum over the steering wheel, a small smirk pulling at his lips. "He wants me to marry a good Italian woman."

I wasn't ready for that. My chest tightens and I glance out the window, trying to dislodge the uncomfortable feeling. "You'll have to at some point." I'd never really thought about it until now, but of course he would. The mafia are all about keeping the bloodlines pure, extending their legacy and protecting their women, their *Italian* women. A good marriage would be strategically and politically wise. I know this. It's the rational, strong thing to do, so why am I annoyed at the idea?

"Morte." Fingers brush my thigh and I close my eyes, swallowing all trace of emotion before I turn to face him. He's pulled over on the side of the busy street and is staring straight at me. I was so lost in thought, I hadn't even noticed the car had stopped moving.

"I'm Nero Verdi. I take what I want." He grips my jaw, his hold hard and unrelenting. "And I sure as shit don't want a *good* woman. I want you, my vicious little butterfly."

His expression is hard and almost angry as we stare at each other. "Nero, you are the underboss. There are rules and customs you cannot simply walk away from."

"I can and I will."

A laugh lingers in my throat but never quite breaks free. "Be serious." He lives for power, pursues it with a lust like no other. To go against the mafia on this… "You can't give up everything you worked for just because I'm having your baby. This isn't…we're just us, okay? No promises. No attachment. We can't—"

"Morte." His eyes drop to my lips as his hold softens, thumb stroking over my jaw. "I love you."

All the breath leaves my lungs and I can't speak. Love. Weakness. Vulnerability. I don't want to weaken Nero, but I think I love him in as much capacity as I have. As much as it terrifies me, it doesn't make me feel weak. The complete opposite. I'm never stronger than when I'm standing next to him. The power in his words washes over me. The sheer exhilaration of being loved by a man like Nero encases me like a steel blanket, impenetrable and warm. I realize that I want his love, perhaps even need it. After all, isn't it love that makes us human? Nero's love goes hand in hand with the very humanity that Nicholai tried so hard to strip me of. He tilts his head to the side, eyes narrowed as he waits for me to say something.

"Does love trump power?" My voice is barely above a whisper.

His lips curl into a smile. "Ah, Morte, when it comes to you, love bolsters power." He pulls me forward and I go to him. When his lips meet mine it feels like more than just a kiss, it's a promise, a vow of something bigger than just me or him. It's us against everything and everyone that would hurt us. I feel the weight of everything he doesn't say in the reverent brush of his lips, his demanding and possessive hold on my jaw. It's a kiss that says he's in my corner, unconditionally. He breaks away and touches his forehead to mine, warm breath blowing over my lips. "King protects Queen now."

And of course, reality comes crashing in like a dam breaking. I wish Nero could protect me, and although I know he can't, I allow him to think he can. It's stupid, but I guess I'm living in my warped version of a dream. Most little girls dream of getting married and living in a nice house. I dreamt of blood and torture. Nero is my version of a fairy tale. Blood soaked and ruthless as we are, this is what we have, and soon it will probably be gone. I told him there is no happily ever after here, that we are the monsters in this story. That's true. Nothing good ever lasts in our world of chaos and death. I wonder if he knows that, or if he truly does think that everything will be okay because he's Nero Verdi and he wills it so.

We pull up outside a townhouse on the Upper Eastside and I get out of the car, staring up at the four-story home on a totally inconspicuous looking street. Flower boxes line the windows and small trees are dotted along the sidewalk. How very upper-middle class family living.

We pull up outside a brick townhouse on the Eastside and I get out of the car, taking in the tree lined side walk and the flower boxes beneath the windows. It's so very…not mafia, and a million miles from the secluded Hamptons mansions of the under boss and capo's. I follow Nero up the three steps that lead to the front door. The ring of the bell echoes through the house on the other side of the thick wood. The door opens on a guy with slicked back black hair and a dark suit. He lifts his chin at Nero before his gaze shifts to me. The scar on his forehead pinches when he frowns.

"She's with me," Nero says. The guy lets us in and closes the door. We're shown up the stairs and to an office at the top of the house. Nero and Cesare couldn't be further apart in their tastes. Nero is minimalistic and modern where Cesare is classic. His office is made up of wooden flooring, leather couches and thick rugs. A bookshelf covers one wall, filled with old books. The room smells of cigar smoke and leather. But where it seems like it should be dark and dingy in here, it's not. Behind the desk is a wall of glass that opens out onto a terrace.

Nero takes a seat and I browse the shelves, spotting some first edition Hemingway nestled in the stacks. I haven't met Cesare in person yet, but simply being inside someone's home can tell you a lot about them.

The door clicks open and Cesare strides in, his face set in a frown. "Nero," he says shortly, barely even glancing my way.

"Cesare," Nero greets him icily.

"This wasn't expected."

"I called ahead."

"Yes, you did. You didn't say you were bringing Una Ivanov with you, though." He spits my name as if it offends him. "I'd rather you didn't invite Russian soldiers into my home."

Nero flashes me a warning look. You could cut the tension in the room with a knife. Rolling my eyes, I walk over to Cesare, placing myself in front of him. "I don't believe we've met." I hold out my hand, but he just stares at me, cool eyes slowly drifting over my body in the form fitting dress. His brows inch up and he glances at Nero, lips pressing into a tight line. "I tell you to do your duty and you present me with this?"

"If it's any consolation, this happened before you decided to claim your son." I know I'm poking a bear with a big stick, but seriously? "Oh and I'm not Elite anymore. Although…I don't recall that being a problem when you needed my services." His eye twitches slightly, but other than that the older man's expression doesn't change. He's good. I smirk and move away from him.

Nero fixes me with a cool look. "I told you, Una isn't going anywhere." I move to his side. His hands are thrust casually in his pockets, and I loop my arm through his, staring Cesare down. I know I'm intimidating, and Nero's terrifying at the best of times. Together we're formidable, even to someone as well versed in power as Cesare. I know it, and so does Nero.

"What you did not say is that she is with child."

I lift an brow. "Surprise?"

He glares at me. "Well done, Nero. You've managed to create an illegitimate bastard with a Russian whore." Nero lets out a low hiss of breath and every muscle in his body tenses.

"That's a touchy subject," I say, trying to hide my delight because I know Nero's about three seconds from nuclear, and well…I like fireworks and blood.

"You will marry an Italian woman and do your duty. I have allowed this to go on long enough." Cesare sneers. "This organization is built on years of tradition, and you shit on it." Nero remains strangely calm, seemingly reining in his temper while I wrestle my own anger simmering just below the surface. My fingers twitch with the urge to reach for the blade strapped to the inside of my thigh.

I move away from Nero and circle Cesare, my eyes assessing him like an enemy, spotting every weakness he has. The way he carries himself suggests that he's had an injury to his right leg. Old, because he's compensated for it. If I were to attack him, he'd have less range of movement on his right side because of it. I glance at Nero and he offers me the smallest shake of his head. "He shits on it?" I tap my index finger over my bottom lip and Cesare twists his head to look at me.

"You know nothing of our ways. You have no honor, no mercy."

Nero sighs. "She's Russian, she kills people. Yes, yes, I'm aware. Now, you are going to accept her as the mother of my child, publicly, to the family."

Cesare laughs, clutching at his stomach before he coughs loudly. "A Russian, with my son. I'd sooner disown you. I will never acknowledge that whore." He stabs a finger in my direction. "And neither will the men. She killed your brothers and you fuck her like her pussy is made of gold. If you marry her, you will lose everything, Nero. Consider that carefully."

Nero's fists clench and this time it's me shaking my head at him. He can't bite. We must always be in control of the old man, maintain the upper hand. "See, this is where we're a little unclear." I take a seat on one of the couches and slowly cross one leg over the other. "Those traditions you were talking about, that honor…" I trail off, smiling slightly. "Do your remaining men know that you orchestrated a hit on your own guys just to get your son in power?" I pretend to inspect my nails. "Do they know that you sanctioned the death of Nero's own brother?"

He snorts. "No one would believe your word, Bacio Della Morte."

"No, but they'd believe mine." Nero circles around the back of the couch and stands behind me.

"Don't waste my time. You implicate yourself as much as anything."

Nero's hand lands on my shoulder. "And?"

My fingers cover his. "You see, Cesare, the difference between us and you, is we don't don a white hat and pretend to be anything other than what we are."

"I wasn't quite raised the Italian way. You can thank Matteo for that. I don't give a fuck about your traditions, and I sure as shit don't care for honor." Nero's voice is low and deadly. "And everyone knows it. I don't have to pretend. You on the other hand… You are the great Cesare Ugoli, a man of honor, a man of the old country."

"The way I see it, you have two choices, Cesare," I say. "You can make me your enemy, or you can make me your ally. I intend to remove Nicholai. I have the skills, the connections, and the benefit of the fact that he wants me back more than anything. And of course, I can bring the Russian gun trade to Nero. Or…"

"Or," Nero growls, "I can make it known that you set up your own men, hired Una and then hung her out to dry, allowing Arnaldo to hunt her like a fucking dog while she was pregnant with your own grandchild."

"And failing that, Nicholai is very welcoming when it comes to men of Nero's skill. He'd do well in the bratva." This time, Cesare's cold expression flickers. I'm bluffing, of course. If he knew the situation with Nicholai, he'd have us over a barrel because handing me to Nicholai would fix all his problems. "Now you've publicly claimed Nero, it would look terrible if he were to work for the enemy."

"You would be lured to that Russian prick by this piece of cunt?" Cesare explodes. And so does Nero. In a shot he's in front of the older man, a gun in hand. I'm quick to grab Nero's arm, forcing myself into his line of sight. I wait for him to shift his rage-filled gaze to me. He stares at me for a beat and then slides the gun back inside his chest holster. Tensions are high, and Nero is volatile at the best of times.

"What do you propose?" Cesare says as he considers his son's reaction.

"You will make it known that Una did not kill those men, that it was Arnaldo, and he set her up as a cover. The hit placed on her was unsanctioned by yourself. The retribution of a lone, pregnant woman will seem fair, and given that he killed his own, it's justice don't you think?" The implication is right there. Cesare sanctioned Nero blackmailing me. He essentially signed the death warrants for the three men Nero had me kill.

Cesare moves over to his desk, taking a seat as he opens a metal box. He takes out a cigar and places it between his lips, lighting it slowly. His lighter snaps shut and the silence that follows is intense. "You would betray me, the family, for this woman?" Ces

"You may have turned your back on your child and the woman you loved, but I will not do the same."

Cesare's brows shoot up before pulling into a deep frown. "And you will risk your position, your name, your life, for this?" His eyes flick to me and I know, he already knows the answer.

"If I have to, then yes," Nero responds without hesitation.

Cesare narrows his eyes at me. "She hones you, like the sharpened edge of a blade. You are more dangerous with her." At least the man saw some sense.

"You may not like me, Cesare, but you hate the bratva. You want their gun trade. I am invested in ending Nicholai. I know everything there is to know about him. I am perhaps the only person capable of killing him. You'd do well to view me as an ally."

He takes another slow inhale of his cigar and the thick smoke winds around the room. "Fine. You do this, Una Ivanov, and the mafia will not accept you, but..." He trails off as though speaking the words pains him. "I will ensure that they tolerate you. Fail..."

"If I fail, I die."

He nods slowly. I get up and walk towards the door. "Morte, give me a moment," Nero says.

Wordlessly, I step outside and brace my back against the wall in the hallway. I miss the days when life was simple. Orders, kills, money. Nothing more, nothing less. There is a certain freedom in having no freedom because you don't have to think. My only thoughts were my next kill, the execution of it, the getaway. My job, my purpose, consumed every waking hour, and I lived for it, until this. I glance down at my stomach which looks like I swallowed a melon. Whoever could have predicted this? In a few short months, Nero turned my whole world on its head, and here we are, blackmailing one mob boss and plotting to kill another. This life is harder and yet easier, because Nero bears the burden with me. I've never had that, and I'm not sure whether it's just setting myself up for failure, but for once, I'm going to do something, not because it's rational or strategically wise. I'm going to do this with Nero despite my brain telling me we can't possibly win, because my heart hopes that we can. The heart is a fragile and unreliable thing.

He walks out of the office a few minutes later, pulling the door closed behind him. "Well, I didn't hear any shots." I study him. "And seeing as you insist on wearing white shirts...no blood."

His lips twist in a smirk that's both sexy and unsettling. "The old man's not dead yet." We walk along the hall and down the stairs, encountering no one on our way out.

"Isn't this place supposed to be well guarded?" I ask.

"Oh, they're watching. They're just subtle about it." He places his hand on the small of my back and guides me from the house. We're in the car before he releases a breath and drags both hands through his hair.

"I don't know why you don't just slit his throat and be done with it." I huff. Cesare does not have what it takes to do what must be done. He is the boss, and I have no doubt he is respected in the mafia, but things need to change. Nicholai has spent years taking and training children all because no one would step in and stop him, and why? Politics. An easy life. No one wants a war. I learned early on that a man can kill in cold blood, and it's no hardship, but until he does things he doesn't want to do, crosses lines that should never be crossed, he has not truly been tested. Life is hard and ugly, and it takes hard and ugly men to rule it. Cesare is a strong leader to those who share his values. Nero has the ability to lead even those who would loathe him out of sheer respect and disciplined fear. That is what it takes to be the king of New York. Nero should take the crown from Cesare's cold, dead body.

"Politics, Morte. All in good time." I'm not cut out for diplomacy.

"Fucking Italians."

"Life with you is always interesting, my savage little queen."

"My life was simple before you dragged me into yours. Kill, eat, sleep, repeat. I meet you and I'm rogue and knocked up within weeks," I grumble. "I haven't even killed anyone in weeks, Nero."

"Okay, but I think that if we work it out to an average, you're probably over your yearly quota." He cocks a brow and clearly thinks he's amusing. "Anyway...we now have what we need from Cesare. We take out Nicholai, come back to New York and we'll have the political protection. The Slovo can take the fall..."

"And we'll live happily ever after." I snort.

"Is there such a thing when I'm with a woman who gets death withdrawal?" He starts the engine, pulling away from the curb. "Look, I have to go and handle something this afternoon. It might involve roughing some Albanians up a little if you want to come?"

I fight a smile. "Are you inviting me along to beat up dodgy drug dealers with you?" His gaze remains fixed on the road as he takes an audible breath, no doubt praying for patience. "How romantic."

"Fine. I'll take you home."

"As it happens, I'm partial to your romantic gestures, capo. Whose knee-caps are we smashing?" His lips pull into a smile, and I wonder if this is what it's like to be normal. Well, almost. He drops the sports car down a gear and we cruise away from the city, heading towards the Brooklyn.

CHAPTER
EIGHTEEN

Nero

I pull up to the old shipping warehouse on the outskirts of Brooklyn. The place is rough as fuck, and I have to leave constant security to guard it, but it's the deal I have with NYPD. I pay them off and, in return, I have to keep the shady shit out of the city. They effectively turn a blind eye, but think of it as the lesser of two evils. The mafia keep their noses clean, have their shit together, and rule with an iron fist. Dodgy blow, street gangs, guns and violence…we keep that shit off our streets, which means the police don't have to. It's a simple fact that if you were to eliminate the mafias and the cartels, anarchy would ensue. That's the corrupt world we live in, the reality of the modern justice system. I'm all too happy to play judge, jury, and executioner.

I pull up to a massive roller door and it slowly lifts, exposing the dingy, dark warehouse beyond. It's empty except for a couple of shipping containers stacked against the wall. My eyes adjust to the dim light cast by a couple of weak strip lights as I pull in. Gio leans against the hood of his Aston Martin, arms folded over his chest as he watches the scene before him. Two guys stand there, fierce scowls on their faces. Jackson is behind them, a gun in each hand pointed at their backs. The rest of Jackson's team are spread out around the empty warehouse.

I get out of the car and go to the trunk, grabbing a metal baseball bat and throwing to Una. Gio's eyes narrow when we approach him and Una takes seat on the hood right next to him. "Nice car."

"Nice bat," he replies.

She twirls the weapon. "Thanks. It's a little more…bludgeon-y than I'm used to."

Shaking my head, I walk over to the two guys, pausing in front of them. I take my cigarettes from my inside pocket and place one between my lips, slowly lifting the lighter to the end. Silence descends through the warehouse and I love it, that pregnant pause, as if everyone in the room is holding their breath. Snapping the lighter shut, I inhale a long draw, holding the smoke deep in my lungs.

"He's such a drama queen." Una snorts and I glance at her. A wry smile pulls at the corner of her lips and she lifts one brow, daring me, challenging. She just loves to fucking push me. Forcing myself to turn away from her, I focus on the two Albanians.

"Do you know who I am?" I say to them. One of them is an older guy, ugly as all fuck with a nasty scar across his throat.

Apparently this one had a brush with death. The other is younger. Both are wearing track suits and have heavy gold chains hanging around their necks. God, it's like something out of a bad seventies crime film.

"V-Verdi," the young one stammers. His friend scowls at him. I nod at Jackson and he grabs both men by their shoulders, kicking them to their knees. The young one whimpers. His entire body shaking as he stares at the ground.

"Yes, I am Nero Verdi." Dropping to a crouch, I rest one arm casually over my thigh and inhale on my cigarette. I toss it towards the young one and he flinches, making me smile. "And you know that means you're in serious shit." I stand again. "Where did you get the drugs you sold in Poison last night?" I ask. Silence. Sighing I turn back to them, cupping my ear. "I'm sorry, I didn't hear an answer."

The younger guy opens his mouth. "We...I..." His friend barks something in Albanian and I throw my head back on a groan. Checking my watch, I turn to Una, crooking my finger at her. She pushes off the hood and Gio rolls his eyes as she sways her hips, bat in hand. My very own little Harley Quinn.

"Gentleman, this is Una. Some call her The Kiss of Death, the Mexicans call her The Angel of Death. You get the point." She swings the bat in loose circles through the air.

The older guy sneers. "You have your woman do your dirty work." He spits on the ground, and Una glances at me.

"Well, now, that's a filthy habit." She strides away from me, heels clicking over the concrete and echoing around the vast warehouse. She barely breaks stride as she swings the bat back and smashes him in the gut. He pitches over on his side, coughing and wheezing as he tries to catch his breath.

"I should mention; she's hormonal." I back up and take a seat next to Gio, watching Una go to town on the older guy. She

381

doesn't touch the younger one, but he breaks a little more with every blow she lays on his friend. She smashes the guys knee caps, as promised, breaks both his arms, his cheek bone, but not his jaw. Good girl.

"You know you two are sick?" Gio comments from his spot beside me.

"Think of it this way, the more hormonal rage she lays into this guy, the less she'll have for you."

He releases a heavy breath and there's a long pause, broken only by the low grunts of pain coming from the man and the whimpering of his friend. "You can't pretend that everything is fine, Nero."

"Do not assume to patronize me on what is coming."

"You're distracting her with mafia bullshit."

I glare at him. "Because if she sits in that apartment and stews on it, she's going to do something stupid. I am buying time and keeping her under control."

He nods towards Una who has her knee planted on the man's chest. He's howling in pain, no doubt from broken ribs. The baseball bat is pressed across his throat and he's gasping for breath. "Looks like you have complete control."

She hisses something at him in what I assume is Albanian. Damn, is there a language that girl doesn't speak? He says something back and her whole demeanor changes. Smiling, she gets off him. She stands up, blood-covered baseball bat in hand, blonde hair loose around her shoulders, and the blood-spattered dress covering her baby bump.

"Did he tell you?" I ask.

"No." She inches her skirt up, then grabs a dagger from the inside of her thigh and throws it, lightning fast. The blade embeds between his eyes and she glances over her shoulder. "He called me a Russian whore."

"Cesare should consider himself lucky then," I say under my breath.

"Fucking hell," Gio swipes a hand over his face, ever the cautious, diplomatic one. He's averse to 'unnecessary blood shed' as he calls it. As though all death should have purpose.

Jackson strolls over and stands beside me. "I think I might need a Russian woman."

I laugh. "They do have a certain….finesse."

"Look, if you two are done getting a hard on for this shit, can we get this over with?" Gio pushes off the hood, waving an arm in the direction of the remaining guy. Una is crouching in front of him, and he's crying.

"Fucking hell, they don't make gang members the way they used to," Jackson grumbles, looking wholly uncomfortable with the entire situation.

I narrow my eyes when Una starts whispering something to him in Albanian again, and then, she strokes his face and its almost intimate. My fists clench and red-hot heat fires up my back.

"Morte," I growl through gritted teeth. She flashes me a wry smile over her shoulder.

"Damn, you two are fucked up," Jackson says.

"Thank you," Gio adds.

A few seconds later and Una stands and turns, walking over to me. "A guy called Camilo Juan."

"That fucking Columbian," Jackson spits. "Rat bastard. What are we going to do with him?" he asks, pointing at the Albanian.

"Let him live," Una says.

I lift a brow, firstly because she's commanding my men, and secondly because she's showing mercy. "Are you going soft, Morte?"

"Oh, for fucks sake, Nero." Gio walks off with a shake of his head before getting in his car.

Una steps between my legs, her hand gliding over my chest, beneath my jacket. "Never." The scent of blood dances along her skin as she presses her lips to mine. Her teeth scrape my lip, and I barely even acknowledge that she's taken my gun until I hear the bang. I pull away from her, and her gaze is firmly locked on me, though the smoking gun in her hand is aimed behind her. The Albanian falls forward, a gaping bullet hole right between his eyes.

"Damn. Una, you have a sister, right?" Jackson asks. I glance at him and he's readjusting himself, a stupid grin on his face.

"A death wish is what you have," I say.

He laughs as he walks towards the Range Rover parked at the back of the empty warehouse.

As soon as I push off the hood of his car, Gio starts the engine and I lead Una to my own vehicle, opening the door for her. That cold brutality of hers brings out the animal in me. I want to fuck her and hurt her, break her and tame her, and I know she'll always take everything I give her and hand it back tenfold. She is perfect and unique and mine. The more time I spend with her, the more I feel the weight of that, as if she's imprinting herself on my dark soul, making herself a vital part of me. I'm not sure whether to fight it or embrace it, but in the end, it doesn't feel like I have a lot of choice. I love her, and for all the power in the world, there are some things you just can't fight.

As soon as I get in the car Una hands me my gun and I tuck it back in the holster. "Feeling better?" I ask.

She leans over the center console, placing a kiss on my cheek. "Much. Thank you. Who knew you were so good at first dates?"

"Technically killing my brother was our first date."

"Yes, because I'm sure that's how they start every great love story, Nero."

"And they say romance is dead."

CHAPTER NINETEEN

Una

I lay wide awake, staring at the ceiling. The lights from the city below illuminate the room in a soft light. Nero always tells me to close the blinds, but I like it. The light reminds me that I'm free, that I'm not in that bunker, buried beneath the earth in the snowy deserted woodland of Russia. The light makes me feel safe and where the sheer amount of people in the city daunted me, it now makes me comfortable. If I were to die here in New York, there would be someone to miss me, people to witness it at the very least. If I were to die in Russia, I would just be another pawn, toppled in a larger game. I never thought anything of it before, never feared death, but I'm starting to think that a person's legacy has meaning. The people we leave behind, if any—that matters. And of course, I'm thinking about this because I'm thinking of Nicholai. I'm thinking of my death.

The bedroom door opens silently and light from the hallway cuts across the carpet. I watch Nero's silhouette as he undresses, throwing clothes on the chair in the corner before he gets into bed. He's been working late again, and I know he feels it just as keenly as I do; the seconds counting down, ticking away. Rolling over, I reach for him, needing to touch him. Funny that his touch grounds me where all others incite me to kill. He turns on his side and rests his hand over my stomach, stroking his thumb in circles over my skin. Warm lips brush my forehead before he pulls me close, tucking my face against his broad chest. I can feel it in the air, bouncing between us: fear. And Nero and I, this is a place where fear has never existed.

"It's been too quiet." My fingers trail up his back, feeling over the hard muscles.

He says nothing for long moments. "Nicholai's just biding his time, probably waiting to see what we'll do."

I know better. I know Nicholai. He waits for nothing, and he always has a plan. He attacks his opponent's weakness, goes for the jugular. It's the intelligent strategy with the least amount of hassle. The simple fact is, if you hold a knife to someone's throat they'll do what you want. He doesn't want to kill me, so he'll try to maneuver me, corral me like a wild horse, backing me into a corner until he has me trapped.

"No, something is coming." I can't shake the feeling that we haven't covered all the bases, that we've missed something glaringly obvious.

"Una, we are here, and you know as well as I do that this tower is nigh on impregnable. All my men can look after themselves. Your sister is buried in the Cartel, well-guarded and well hidden."

"We're missing something, Nero."

"I have a plan."

I sigh and lift my face from his chest, glancing at him. Dark eyes glint in the dim light, and I sweep a stray strand of hair away from his forehead. "Don't you always?"

"I do." He rolls me over, settling between my legs as he kisses over my collar bone. I run my hands through his hair, and I want to believe that he has it all in hand. I want to trust that he can stand against Nicholai, that he can win. I know that I view Nicholai through the eyes of a child, through the eyes of someone who has always bowed to his power and been conditioned to see him that way. But he has not made it to where he is without good reason. Him and Nero are like facing off two monsters and trying to pick the winner. I can't.

"Tell me."

He kisses my chest, looking up at me through thick, black lashes. "Simple. We can't get to him, so we lure him out."

"How?"

"Everyone has a weakness, Morte." He's right, Nicholai does have one weakness.

"Use me."

Any positivity in his expression flees, replaced by a deep frown. "No, it's too risky." I open my mouth to speak but he silences me, placing a hand over my mouth. "I know who you are, and I do not doubt your capabilities, my love. But it isn't just you. Do you trust me?" he asks, releasing my mouth.

"Yes."

He smiles and then his lips work down the center of my chest. He pushes up my shirt, kissing over my stomach. "I won't let anything happen to you," he murmurs against my skin and a wave of emotions engulfs me. I trust him, but I feel this hole in my chest, sheer despair and desperation swirling like a vortex. His plans are loosely formed at best and we are running out of time, I can feel it, like Nicholai's hot breath is skittering across my neck as we speak.

My hand wraps around his neck, bringing his mouth to mine because I need to feel him. I need that sense of invincibility that comes with being held by him, being loved by him. His lips part and I brush my tongue against his. The kiss becomes hard and demanding, and then he's pushing me back down on the bed and sliding inside me. His breaths mix with my own as he fucks me slow and hard, drawing out each and every moan, pushing me higher and higher. And there, in his arms, I find a moment of peace and I know that's exactly what he wants to give me, so I embrace it, I take it. That serenity wraps around me for just a few short moments and I cling to him, wishing I never had to let go of this, but knowing I must. My hands stroke over his muscles as they strain and flex beneath his skin. He's beauty, power, and raw chaos all wrapped up in one man. And he's mine.

I fall asleep in his arms, but even Nero can't keep that empty feeling from filling me.

It's dark, so dark. I'm disorientated, my senses muted and numbed.

"Ah, little dove, you're awake." I turn and Nicholai is standing beside me, his image blurry, but with each blink of my eyes he becomes clearer. His dark gray hair is combed back as always, and his three-piece suit is immaculate, down to the handkerchief in his top pocket that matches his tie. Truly the devil in disguise. "I have a gift for you."

"What gift?" I ask. He turns, and reveals a patch of light on the far wall, illuminating Nero chained against it.

"No," I whisper. I try to go to him, but my feet won't move. It's like I'm cemented to the floor. Nero lifts his head, those dark eyes meeting mine. Blood streams down his torso from several neat and precise cuts on his chest and stomach. "Please let him go."

"Ah, but he is your weakness, little dove. Without him you will become everything you were meant to be." I shake my head and he puts a gun in my hand. I stare down at the weapin, and when I look back up, there's someone else chained to the wall, beside Nero. A boy. About ten years old. His head hangs forward, dark hair messy and disheveled, his small body also covered in blood. He lifts his head slowly. Violet eyes meet mine—eyes identical to my own, but his face... he's the image of Nero. I know this is my child. I know it.

"Shoot one of them, little dove." Nicholai purrs with satisfaction.

"No," I say through gritted teeth. I feel a hot tear slide down my cheek.

"Pick, or I will pick for you."

"Morte," I look at Nero. This isn't like Alex, his expression doesn't beg me to kill him, it demands it. Nero doesn't fear death. I know this, but...but I love him. "Lift the gun," he says calmly. I do. "Good. Now aim it at my head." I do as he says, my hand shaking because my heart demands that I stop. I look at the boy again, a boy I don't know, but I do. In my soul, I know him. "Look at me." Nero's voice lulls me back to him. "Pull the trigger, Morte. Be strong."

"I love you," I tell him as tears now stream down my cheeks.

"I love you," he responds, his expression hard and determined. He nods and I close my eyes, taking a deep breath. My pulse pounds in my ears, the steady inhale and exhale of my own breaths. I place the gun under my chin.

"No!" Nero's and Nicholai's combined cries are the last thing I hear. BANG.

I wake up and bolt upright, gasping for air. Sweat coats my body and my heart is beating so hard I can feel it jolting against my ribs.

"Morte." I swing my gaze to Nero who sits up next to me. He cups my face, swiping his thumb under my eye and catching a stray tear.

"I just...I need a minute." Climbing out of bed, I go to the bathroom and close the door behind me. I turn on the shower and strip out of Nero's t-shirt before getting in. The water does very little to wash away the memory of the dream. It feels so real, the idea of having to choose between Nero, my baby, and myself. And I know that in that scenario, I would choose myself. I shot the boy I loved once, and it broke something inside of me. If something were to happen to Nero...

When I finally step out of the bathroom, Nero has his back propped against the headboard, waiting for me. He doesn't say anything, simply opens his arms and allows me to crawl into them. I'm fragile, as if all the pieces that make up Una Ivanov are slowly splintering apart and being split. Part of me is with Nero, another with Anna, and the last with this baby. Divided, I am weak, but if I weren't divided than I'd have nothing to fight for in the first place, would I? I need to work out a way to be the person I used to be, but with the new motivations I now have. It seems like an impossible task, but I have to do it. I will do it.

I fall asleep to the steady thumping of Nero's heartbeat and the brush of his fingers through my hair. I sleep soundly in the arms of my monster.

CHAPTER
TWENTY

Nero

I lean against the breakfast bar and clasping a cup of coffee. It's early and orange-tinged light of dawn pours through the windows of the skyscraper, painting everything in a tranquil hue. I like this time in the morning, before the world stirs awake. It's as if you're the only person, embroiled in this serene moment of peace, a pause in time before the world starts spinning again and everything that exists in day-to-day life comes pouring back in. And this morning, I need that moment to think.

I left Una in bed sleeping. She tossed and turned all night. Nightmares haunted her well into the early hours. It's been a while since she's had one, but I guess the stress of Nicholai hunting her is forcing them to the surface again. She's so strong, but I see how broken she is. He did that to her. He made her lethal, and in many ways, instilled all the traits I love in her, but for the first time in my life I'm starting to see that strength comes at a price. I want my child to be strong, but I would never want them to pay the price she has. I will win this war with that bastard one way or the other. He broke Una, but I will keep her. I will make her a queen to be feared by all except me. And he will never touch my child.

"Nero." I glance around to see Gio standing in the entrance of the kitchen. It's not even six-thirty and he's here, in my apartment, looking as sharp as ever. I swear he doesn't sleep. "We have a small problem."

He follows me to the living room and I take a seat on the couch, picking up a pack of cigarettes from the coffee table. He sits on the opposite couch and I slide the smokes across the table to him.

"Ziggie," he says simply.

I frown as I light my cigarette, inhaling the satisfying smoke deep into my lungs. "What about him?"

"Jackson went to pick up last night, and it was twenty grand light. He said he'll pay it next week, but..." He lifts one eyebrow as he inhales on his smoke. Fucks sake. Ziggie works Brooklyn, runs a gang down there. For the most part, they're nothing more than ghetto boys and addicts, but they make me good money. Ziggie somehow manages to organize them, a feat that not many could achieve. For that reason, he's useful to me, but this is the second time he's taken it upon himself to borrow money. The problem with dogs like Ziggie is the second you take your heel off their throats, they bite you, even if you are the hand that feeds them. "Jackson roughed him up a bit, but well...you know what he did to him the first time." Yeah, the first time Ziggie stole money Jackson broke both his legs. You'd think that would be an incentive not to have a repeat.

"Okay, go and get him. Call me when you have him. I'll handle it," I say.

Gio nods and pushes to his feet, stubbing out his cigarette in the ash tray. Fucking gang bangers. I don't need this shit right now, but I have to handle it. I'm not about to let my city go to shit while I have the Russian breathing down our necks. Unfortunately, the world does keep turning, no matter what shit is going on.

*****

Ziggie is on his knee's in front of me, hands clasped behind his head. "Look man," he says. "I'll pay you back, I promise." Gio stands to his side, a gun pointed at his head.

I sigh and fold my arms over my chest. "Do I look like a fucking bank, Ziggie?"

"I'm sorry. I'll get it for you tomorrow. Please, please don't kill me." His begging is pissing me off.

"Don't apologize to me when you aren't sorry!" He squeezes his eyes shut, his bottom lip quivering. "You're begging me not to kill you, so you knew the consequences." I drop to a crouch in front of him. "Did you just think I'd let it go?"

"Please. Tomorrow."

My phone starts ringing in the car, but I ignore it. It rings again and I flash an annoyed glare at Tommy who's sitting in the passenger seat. He scrambles to answer it. I turn back to Ziggie and am about to pass judgement when the car door is thrown open.

"Boss." Tommy shouts.

"I'm fucking busy, Tommy. I'll call back."

"But, boss…"

"Tommy!" I roar, turning on him. He goes quiet and drops his gaze to the floor. I know he wants to step away from me, but he doesn't. "It's Rafael."

I frown and step forward, snatching the phone from his hand. "Gio, shoot him if he moves," I say before pressing the phone to my ear. "This is not a fucking good time."

"Anna's gone," Rafael says.

"What? How?"

"I had four men on her. Three were found dead half an hour ago, one barely alive. I've called in scouts from the edges of my territory and put a call out at the border. I'll get her back, but you told me to keep you in the loop."

"Shit. Fucking get her back, Rafael or you and I are going to have a mutual problem in the form of Una."

He hangs up, and I drag a hand through my hair. Once. Just once, I'd like a normal day. The odd drug deal, perhaps a revenge killing, but no. I have to deal with stalker Russians, cartels, sex slave sisters, and last but not least, my pregnant and very temperamental assassin girlfriend.

Gio meets my gaze when I turn around. I take my gun from my chest holster and point it at Ziggie's head. "No..." *Bang.*

Tommy's eyes go wide and he rushes back to the car. "Clean this shit up!" I shout. Gio nods and I get back in the car, reversing out of the abandoned warehouse.

"Is Anna okay?" Tommy asks quietly.

"She better be." Even as I say the words, I know Nicholai must have her. It's just a feeling in my gut, expecting the worst-case scenario. The question now is: how do I restrain Una to stop her from going after her?

When I step into the apartment, Una is nowhere to be found. Zeus comes up to greet me but, of course, George is nowhere to be seen. He'll be with her. I hear a low thud from somewhere, followed by another. I follow the noise to the dining room.

Una is standing on the dining room table, a crossbow raised in front of her. She squeezes the trigger and looses a bolt straight at a canvas painting hanging on the far wall. It lodges bang in the center with the other four that are already there. She's so tiny but she looks so fierce. Her ponytail falls over her shoulder as she tilts her head to aim again.

"That's a thirty-grand painting."

She losses another bolt. "It's ugly."

"It's art."

"I could give George a paintbrush and ask him to replicate it if you like?" She smiles, swinging her hips as she glides to the edge of the table. Grabbing her hips, I lower her to the ground and pull her close.

"I see your aim is as sharp as ever."

"Still better than yours."

Dropping her gaze to my chest, she traces her finger over my tie. I glance down and see the single drop of blood marring the pale blue silk. "What did I tell you about wearing black?" she says.

"It may not show the blood, but it's rather uncivilized."

Her lips twist into an amused smile. "But of course, if the devil didn't look like an angel, he wouldn't be so good at corrupting the innocent now, would he?"

"Hmm." I lean in and graze my lips over her neck, biting her earlobe. "You are very far from innocent, Morte."

"And you are very far from an angel."

I chuckle. "Come and dance around the fire with me, little butterfly."

"I thought I was an ugly caterpillar."

"Never." I kiss her and she wraps her arms around my neck. "Wings of steel, my love." She kisses me back. In the back of my mind, I just know there is a storm coming. Unless Rafael finds Anna in the next few hours, I'm going to have to tell Una and she's going to lose her shit.

CHAPTER TWENTY-ONE

Una

I'm in bed, cuddling George when my phone buzzes, dancing across the bedside table. I glance at the screen and see a Russian number. I assume it's Sasha. Swiping the screen, I press it to my ear. "Hello."

"Little dove." My stomach drops at the sound of Nicholai's voice and I sit bolt upright, my eyes instantly surveying every inch of the room. Each and every instinct I have goes on high alert because if Nicholai can get the number to an untracked burner phone, then surely, he can get to me.

"Nicholai."

"Did you get my card, and present?" he asks, almost joyfully.

"I did." Nicholai does things a certain way. You have to play his game and wait for him to tell you what he actually wants.

"And I asked you to come home, little dove."

"I can't do that." I get up and glance out the window, but of course, even Nicholai can't scale a skyscraper.

"You wound me. But no matter. I told you I would come for you, though, I have had to go to great lengths. I'm not happy with you."

My whole body goes tense as his words sink in. "What lengths?" Silence. "What lengths?" I repeat, my voice rising. I turn around and Nero is standing in the doorway, dark eyes glinting like onyx in the dim light from the city below.

"Una?" A small voice comes over the line. My knees go weak and I squeeze my eyes shut as I brace my back against the window.

"Anna," I whisper, slowly sliding down the glass until I hit the floor. "Are you okay?" I'm aware of Nero moving closer but I keep my gaze fixed on the dark patch of carpet in front of me.

"I think so. What's going on?"

"Just stay calm. Do what they say. I'm coming for you."

There's a rustling sound before I hear Nicholai's voice again. "She looks so much like you, little dove. But you were always so strong, Una. You are the perfect soldier, to be surpassed only by your child." The way he says it like a kid getting excited about a new toy makes me feel sick. "But Anna...Anna is not strong like you, little dove. She will not make a soldier..." He lets that hang in the air between us.

"I promise you, if you touch her, I will tear your heart from your chest," I snarl, the emotions bubbling and swirling uncontrollably inside me.

"Tsk-tsk, I raised you better than that. You have been away too long. It has tainted you. I thought I taught you well enough that love is weakness. Your sister, the Italian, your child…they weaken you, Una. You have become fragile," he spits, anger consuming his voice. There's a pause before he speaks again. "But it is fine. It is fine. I can fix you. Don't worry, little dove. I will make you perfect again. And I will make your child stronger than even you." I squeeze my eyes shut and press my clenched fist to my forehead. "You will come home, and I will set Anna free. You have forty-eight hours, and then I kill her. Tick-tock." The line goes dead and I launch the phone across the room, leaving a dent in the drywall.

I press my palms against my eyes to try and keep from crying, but it's pointless. I'm fucking scared. I'm scared for Anna, I'm scared for my baby and I'm scared for myself because I know exactly what awaits me when I go back there. He will 'reset' me. Months of electric shock therapy, training, waterboarding and reflex conditioning. There is only one way to survive that, and that is to check out, to become numb. No one makes it out of there with a shred of humanity left intact. The mind cannot endure it, and that's why he does it. He doesn't want humans. He wants soldiers, robots, killers without a conscience.

Fingers brush over my jaw, and I drop my hands, meeting Nero's hard gaze. Will I remember him? When Nicholai wipes all traces of emotion from me, will I remember this feeling? Will I even know that I loved him, or will he simply seem like a distant weakness, nothing more than the shadow of a memory? And my child…will I love it? I'm not sure even mother nature can override Nicholai's methods.

He swipes at the tears below my eyes. "You are not going," he says, a growl in his voice.

"He has Anna."

"I know."

"What?" I climb to my feet and move away from him, shaking my head. "Why wouldn't you tell me?"

"Because I didn't know for sure that he had her."

"Fuck!" I drag both hands through my hair. "How did this happen, Nero? You told me she was protected!" I can't help but feel a small sting of betrayal because I trusted him. I believed foolishly that Nero's word, his power, was infinite. And I underestimated Nicholai's reach despite everything I know about him, and that is the bottom line—I should have known. I let my wistful hope cloud my judgement and it has just cost me dearly. I will not let Anna pay the price for my actions. He wants me, not her. She's nothing more than bait. A helpless soul caught in the middle of Nicholai's twisted obsession with me.

"He'll kill her." I imagine all the horrible things he'll do to her, the ways he'll make her suffer, just because I defied him. "I have to go to him."

"No." His voice is deceptively calm. I turn to face him, but he catches me off guard by wrapping his arms around me from behind. One arm goes across my chest, pinning my wrists flush to my body while the other tightens around my waist. "Don't struggle," he whispers roughly in my ear. My heartbeat hammers against my eardrums and my breath hitches.

I fight his hold, but his arms are like steel. "Nero…"

"I won't let you do it, Morte." His breath touches my neck. His hard body is unrelenting. "You don't get a say when it comes to the safety of our baby."

I take a deep breath and compose myself. "You don't understand. He'll kill her and then he'll just keep coming. He will. Never. Stop."

"Una…"

"You said we were equals."

He hesitates, and a low groan slips past his lips. "This is different. Your head isn't clear when it comes to Anna."

"Do you trust me?" I twist my head towards him and his cheek presses to mine. Ragged breaths slip from his lips and I can almost feel his desperation like a living breathing demon in the room. He's scared. Nero is scared.

"Morte…"

"Do you trust me?" I repeat.

"Yes."

"We have to control it."

"What?"

I struggle to get free and he reluctantly releases me, though he looks ready to pounce again at any moment.

"Nicholai thinks he has the upper hand, and we have to let him think that, lull him into a false sense of security…" His dark eyes lock with mine. I see that urge in him, the need to lock me up and throw away the key. I have to make him see. "I know where he'll take me. You can come for me."

"You're not fucking going!"

"I have to!" He takes an ominous step forward, and I shuffle back. "If I go, he'll think he's won. I can…I can get close to him, take him out from the inside," I say in a rush. "It's the only way."

"No," he growls.

"Just hear me out. And try to be objective."

"I can't be objective when it comes to you."

"And that is why Nicholai will win, because he does not love, he does not feel. He has no weakness."

He cups my cheek, forcing me to look at him. "Love is not a weakness, Morte. It is strength." I wish I could believe him, but with so many people I love on the line, I don't feel very strong.

"I am his only weakness," I say slowly. "I'm the only one who can do this, Nero."

His jaw tenses and he sighs heavily before getting to his feet and walking away from me. "No, I have another plan. Get dressed. We're expecting visitors." And then he's heading out of the room, dismissing me completely.

*****

I sit on the couch in Nero's office while he makes several calls. I'm staring at a laptop screen, but I can feel his eyes on me. My leg bounces erratically. The walls of the room feel as if they're pressing in on me. All I can see in my mind is that broken image of Anna before Nero found her and bought her. I see the thin and broken girl being raped on a web cam for the sick entertainment of depraved men. Would Nicholai do that to her? Will she survive that again?

Eventually I can't take Nero's burning stare anymore. I decide to leave and go in search of some coffee. I'm standing at the breakfast bar, trying to calm myself, when the ding of the elevator reaches me. The second I hear the distinctive lilt of Spanish accents, I'm storming through the apartment. I recognize Rafael D'Cruze from all the years that Nicholai would make us learn every influential leader, capo, boss or even dirty politician.

Four men are with him, and they're all talking quickly to Nero and Gio. I storm in their direction and, at the last minute, they glance my way.

"Ah, shit," Gio mumbles, just as I swing for Rafael, slamming my fist into his jaw.

One of his men moves, and I yank a gun from the back of my jeans and point it at his head. "I will shoot your worthless, sack of shit ass where you stand."

Rafael rubs his jaw and raises his brows, glancing at Nero. "She always like this?" Nero shrugs one shoulder before shifting to stand beside me.

"They're here to help," Nero attempts to assure me. I'm not assured.

I glare at Rafael, meanwhile the guy in front of my gun shifts slightly. "Loco puta," he mumbles. I pistol-whip him across the bridge of his nose and he staggers back, clutching his now broken nose. Nero clears his throat to cover a laugh.

"You lost my sister."

Rafael sighs and swipes a hand over his face. "Do not think that I take this lightly. The Russians killed three of my men and shot another." There's an edge to him, something dangerous, and usually I'd take note of it, but today, I'd sooner just kill him.

"I don't give a fuck about your men! She was supposed to be safe with you." Nero promised me she was safe and I hate that he did because now I can't take his word.

"She was heavily guarded and in one of my houses that only

my closest men know about."

"Well then, it looks like one of your closest men is a rat, Rafael." I glare at the men beside him. I never should have left her with other people. I may put her in danger, but I'm careful, Nero is careful. He keeps only his most loyal people close. None of Nero's men would have sold her out, but outsiders can easily be bought, and Nicholai has a lot to offer as payment.

"They shot my brother," one of the guys behind him says as though I give a shit.

"I. Don't. Care. If I were you, my only concern would be the fact that *my* sister is gone." I glance at the guy who spoke. "Do you know who I am?" He glares back at me. I step around Rafael and stand toe to toe with the man. "If I don't get her back, I'm going to come to Mexico and end your entire fucking cartel."

"O-kay…" Nero wraps an arm around my waist and pulls me back against his chest. "They came to help." I shrug away from him and pace the length of the room. I feel like I'm hanging by a thread, my emotions swinging like a pendulum and this close to snapping, but I won't do it in front of these men. Leaving the foyer, I go into the darkened living room and move to the window. My mind is this foggy swarm of emotions and nothing is clear.

They must have a rat. But what if they don't? What if Nicholai paid Rafael for Anna and this is all just a set up? Pressing my hand to my stomach, I squeeze my eyes shut. A floorboard creaks behind me. I know it's Nero without looking. Lips skim over my shoulder and I lean into him. The touch that once left me so conflicted now feels like the only real thing in my life. And, in the midst of complete chaos, he's the only one I can rely on.

"We need help, Morte." His arm snakes up the front of my body before his fingers loosely wrap around my throat.

I trace the length of his forearm and grip his wrist, twisting my head to the side. "What if they're working with him? We can't trust them."

His lips press against my temple. "No. You don't have to trust them, you have me." I turn in his arms. Dark eyes, hard and determined, locked with mine. "Let me handle it." Warm breath skitters over my lips, the subtle scent of mint and cigarette smoke swirling around me. "Promise me you won't do anything stupid. Tell me we're together on this." He sounds so oddly vulnerable and it breaks my heart a little. It's a promise I know I can't keep, but I make it anyway.

"Always," I whisper. He grips my face and kisses me hard, lips moving over mine as though he's trying to stain my very soul. Little does he know, he irrevocably imprinted himself on me a long time ago. Whatever plan Nero is trying to come up with, he's grasping at straws, I know it. He knows it. Otherwise he wouldn't be trying so desperately to bring me to get me in line. Nicholai has us backed into a corner. Checkmate. The game is over, but Nero refuses to accept it, because of what he stands to lose.

And isn't this the way this was always destined to go? Everything has come full circle and I'm right back where I started with him; me and Anna. Nero and I could no sooner run from this than we could fate itself because we orchestrated it. Every move we've played has brought us here. We fight, we kill, it's inherently twisted into every fiber of our DNA, and this is the price we pay. Normality is a distant wish, a dream that we can't quite grasp. I want to grasp it though, more than I've ever wanted anything in my life, but I won't sacrifice people along the way. I won't sacrifice Anna today only for Nicholai to play another hand and catch me tomorrow. No, this has to end. I'll let Nero plot and plan. I'll go along with it for his sake, but I have my own plan.

"Come. We have to talk to them," he says, taking my hand and leading me towards his office.

Gio sits beside Rafael on one of the couches and once again, the blueprints are on the coffee table. Truthfully, I'm not sure Nicholai will even have Anna there. That's his main base, but he has others, and of course, I know the layout of that base intimately. Logically, he would take her elsewhere, but then he told me to come to him. That is where I'd go, so maybe she is there.

Nero moves to the corner of the room and pours out a glass of whiskey. He looks more worn than usual, with shadows lingering below his eyes. He swallows the whiskey in two gulps and turns his attention to the plans. I take a seat next to him, and his hand lands on my thigh possessively. They discuss everything, but I barely hear them. They're flogging a dead horse. Anna isn't getting out of that base unless he willingly lets her walk out the gate. And the only way he's doing that is if I walk in.

Rafael gets up, swearing in Spanish as he stalks to the side of the room and slams his hand against the wall. Nero leans into my side, whispering in my ear. "I think Rafael is in love with your sister." Rafael and my sister. I clench my fists and one hand instinctively reaches for the blade strapped to my thigh, my fingers brushing over it. Another reason for me to hurt him, taking advantage of my abused and broken sister. Nero chuckles, covering the blade with his own hand. "Such a vicious butterfly."

I push to my feet. Everyone tenses, expecting me to do something, but instead I simply brush past Rafael, glaring as I leave the room. I check my watch. I have forty-five hours and nine minutes before I have to be in Russia. I go straight to the armory and open the door to the panic room that also houses all the weaponry. Checking the cameras, I see that Nero and the Mexicans are all still in the office. I grab a .40 Cal and a spare clip and shove both in the back of my jeans with my 9mm. Next, I open all the drawers, glancing over the various bullets until I see what I'm looking for. There are two tiny silver canisters tipped with needles. I take them, shove them in the pocket of my hoody, and leave the room. As I step out of the dining room, I bump into Tommy. He startles and clutches at his chest.

"Jesus, do you have to creep around in the dark?"

"It's just me," I snort.

He glares. "You do realize that makes it worse?"

"You are such a pussy."

"No, I just have a self-preservation. You haven't killed me yet, so…"

"I haven't killed you because I like you."

He smiles wide. "I'll take that as a compliment."

Tommy has this innocence about him, a side that's managed to remain untainted by the darkness that surrounds him. I tease him, but I hope he never loses it. I hope he always see's the light in the dark, no matter the circumstance. "Never change, Tommy."

He frowns. "Are you okay?"

I nod and walk away from him, unable to dwell on the people here; on the life I have or could have had. Instead I go to bed, sliding one of the metal canisters beneath my pillow. I'm ready, organized. I have everything I need to do what must be done, and so, I lie here, my stomach churning horribly. By the time Nero finally comes to bed, my emotions are completely fraught and burnt out.

He slips beneath the covers, and glides his hand around my waist. "Morte," he whispers.

"Yeah."

"Are you okay?"

Not even a little bit. "Yeah."

"I have to ask because Rafael is still alive." I can hear the amusement in his voice.

"As soon as this is done, he's fair game." He not only loses my sister, but he made a play for her.

His lips brush my neck. "I'll even hold him down for you."

"I thought he was your friend."

"I don't have friends, morte. I have pawns, and when they fail me, they lose favor." God, I love how utterly heartless he is. I turn over and thread my fingers through his hair, pulling him to me. I press me lips to his, needing to feel him, craving his strength and brutality and everything that makes him so inherently feared by all who hear his name. I want my monster. His tongue brushes against mine and I moan into his mouth, raking my nails over his neck.

I get to my knees and straddle his body, our lips never breaking apart. He sits up and wraps his arms around me so tight that it feels as though he'd never let me go. His lips drift to my neck, warm and hard, demanding yet giving. I scratch my fingers through his hair and cling to him, wishing that I could pause time and remain here, safe in his arms. I've always been alone, always fiercely independent, but having him has made me realize what it is to have someone. To be protected. And once you've known that…I have a feeling to be without it is its own form of cruel torture. His hand slides between my legs and a breath hisses between his teeth when he realizes I'm not wearing any underwear beneath his oversized t-shirt. Fingers press against me and he groans against my throat on an open-mouthed kiss.

"So fucking wet, Morte."

I wrap my arms tightly around his neck and close my eyes when he pushes inside me. Every time with him is a shameless claiming, complete possession laced with something so raw and real that I almost feel as though I can't breathe without it. Nero always feels like the very essence of life, right on the ragged edge at all times. He shifts beneath me and then his fingers are replaced by his cock pushing against me. Hands grip my hips, guiding me down over him slowly. It's so intense. So all consuming. What was once a bloody battle now feels like the sweetest surrender, the melding of two war-torn souls embracing each other's scars. My hips roll over him and his breath stutters, arms pinning my body to his. Pleasure fires through me and I throw my head back on a low moan. Our lips meet and the frantic kisses slow, growing deep and drugging. This tension hangs in the air between us—all the words neither of us can say—and I wonder if he knows? Both his hands cup my face and he tilts my head back, sliding his tongue across mine, push and pull. Back and forth. I think of leaving him and my chest tightens because it's the last thing I want. But this isn't our reality? This right here is a dream, a life we have no right to. I see that now, and as hard as it is to let go of dreams, at some point, we must wake up. He pushes up against me, staking his claim on me, marking me in every way.

I try to erect the steel walls that I need to protect myself, but my heart remains painfully exposed. His movements become slow and teasing. He's so deep, he's practically a part of me. A slow wave of pleasure builds and then crashes over me, rolling on and on. I press my lips to his, squeezing my eyes shut as a tear tracks down my cheek. He stiffens beneath me, his movements becoming jilted and brutal as he groans my name over and over.

"I fucking love you." He touches his forehead to mine and I inhale the scent of him: cigarettes and whiskey tinged with mint.

"I love you," I whisper, pushing him back on the bed. Our eyes meet and he strokes the curtain of hair away from my face. I see his feelings reflected right back at me, the kind of

411

obsession that consumes absolutely. Ours is a love that burns so hot and bright that it destroys everything in its path. Separate, we are strong, but together we are unstoppable. And I'm about to separate us. I hate it, but I do what must be done. I must believe that what we have will transcend time and distance. I'll need him, even if it's just the simple thought of him.

Closing my eyes, my hand slides beneath the pillow. I almost hope he stops me because I don't want to do this. It breaks my heart to betray him. I kiss him gently, allowing my lips to linger over his. My fingers wrap around the small canister and I think of Anna. In a lightening quick move, I jab the dart into the side of his neck. He stills and I pull back, meeting his shocked expression. "I'm sorry." My voice breaks as the tears now pour freely down my face.

"Una, no," he rasps. His hand wraps around my throat, and I do nothing to fight him off as he squeezes hard.

Instead of pulling away from him, I push closer, kissing him. My tears spill onto his lips. "I love you, Nero. Trust me." His eyes start to droop, and his hold loosens. "One day, I will return to you." His eyes roll back in his head, and I kiss him one last time before I slide away from. I throw on a pair of black jeans and a hoody before I grab the bag I left under the bed. I spare Nero one last glance, and then, for the second time, I leave with his scent still clinging to my skin and the taste of him on my lips. Only, this time, it feels like I just ripped out my own beating heart. This time there is so much more at stake.

I move through the apartment, careful not to make any noise. I can't let Nero's men dart and catch me again. Nero will literally chain me in a basement somewhere and never let me out. I slink through the living room and pause when I hear a loud click. Freezing, I slowly shift my gaze to the couch. The bright red end of a cigarette glows in the darkness and I can just make out Rafael's features. I reach for the gun at the back of my jeans, wrapping my fingers around it slowly. If he tries to stop me…

"You are going to him." His voice is low and deep.

"Do not try and stop me. I do what I must."

He leans forward, allowing the cigarette to hang loosely from his fingers as he props his elbows on his thighs. "You will sacrifice yourself for her?"

"Yes."

"And your child? You will sacrifice your child for her?"

I clench my teeth, fighting down the spike of anger. "I thought you...felt something for her."

He sighs and pushes to his feet, moving toward me. He's a massive guy and the predator in me takes him in warily. "Yes, but Anna would never wish you to sacrifice an innocent child, *Angel*."

"I have a plan."

He takes another slow drag of his cigarette. "Ah, you and Nero and your plans."

"This one doesn't involve Nero."

"How do you know the Russian will release Anna?"

I pinch the bridge of my nose. "I don't." I feel like I'm free-falling, trapped in a hopeless situation. But Nero always says life is just a giant chess game. All I have to do is position key players. "I need you to do me a favor," I say. He nods. "If he doesn't release Anna, bargain for her return. Once he has me, he doesn't need her. Let him put her to good use elsewhere."

"Bargain what?"

"You have access to a port..."

"Yes."

"Offer him the use of it. Getting arms over the southern border is the easiest access point into America, but the cartels won't allow the Russians any foothold."

His brows lower over coal black eyes that glint in the darkness of the apartment. "That would cause problems."

My gaze darts towards the top of the stairs. I don't know how long that tranquilizer will work for. I'm guessing he went on the lighter side of the dosage for my body weight. Nero weighs more than twice what I do. "Look, it won't be for long. Anyway, Nicholai is not one to break his word. I think he'll let her go."

"You are his favored pet, *Angel*. And you have proven unruly. He has the means to control you, do not think that he will give that up easily." I nod. "Go. I did not see you."

"Thank you."

"And Una..."

"Yes?"

His eyes drop to my stomach, a pained expression crossing his face. "Be safe."

I turn away from him and head for the elevator, palming both my guns as I descend into the parking garage. When the doors glide open, I expect to find half an army down here, but there's only two guys in suits. Both have cigarettes in hand and are staring at me blankly as though they just received a surprise guest. I charge the first guy, pistol-whipping him hard enough to knock him out. The second goes for his gun, and I kick his legs out from underneath him, nailing him in the temple with my fist. My eyes dart over every shadowy inch of the parking garage before I get up and jog towards my motorbike still parked where it was left all those months ago. It coughs and splutters as I turn the key, but eventually roars to life. If there was no army of Nero's men before, there will be soon. I place a small earpiece in my ear and swing my bag onto my back before I'm wheel spinning out of the parking garage. My phone rings, buzzing in my pocket. I press a button on my ear piece and Billy James' voice comes over the line.

"Where am I meeting ya?" he says in his thick southern accent. Billy is a pilot who has gotten me out of some dicey situations. He's very good at forging the necessary paperwork for bogus flight plans.

"Teterboro. I'll be there in about half an hour," I shout over the roaring engine of the bike.

"Yes ma'am." He hangs up and I drop the bike a gear, sending it hurtling towards the George Washington bridge. I may be away from Nero, but I never underestimate his power or reach. New York is his city, and as long as I'm in it he can catch me. I don't know what scares me more now, Nicholai or what Nero will do. He's going to be so pissed. I wish I could have explained this to him, but he won't listen to anything rational when it comes to me or the baby. Nicholai taking Anna has forced my hand, but it also made me realize there is nowhere we can run. We could fight, but he has us outgunned in every way. He got to Anna, and that means he can get to me, so I'm taking control. I'm taking a page out of Nero's book and playing it smart, being strategic. I will end this, one way or another.

When I pull up to the runway, the guard takes one look at me and waves me through. Again, Nicholai's reach is far. This is one of the runways we use to move in and out of the country unnoticed. The Elite are ghosts, and ghosts fly under the radar at all times. The Americans need never know of our existence, not even aliases if it can be helped.

I drive the bike over to hangar six and park it in the corner, pulling a tarp over it. I have no doubt that Nero has a tracker on it, but I'll be long gone by the time he finds it. Billy leans against the steps of a small private jet, thick arms folded over his gut and a cigarette hanging from between his lips.

"I thought you weren't supposed to smoke around jet fuel," I say dryly.

He smiles, taking the smoke and flicking it across the hangar. I roll my eyes. Jesus, this is what happens when you employ a redneck to fly you around. I shove a stack of bills into his hand and climb the steps.

"Well ain't you cheerful tonight, blondie? Ya know, I dropped everything to fly you."

I stop at the top of the steps. "Very kind of you. I'm sure that ten grand helped."

He sniffs as he walks up the steps. "Ain't gonna hurt." That's what I thought.

I take a seat on one of the leather chairs and lean back in it, bracing my head against the headrest. My stomach is churning with anticipation. I wish I could turn back, I really do, but I push those thoughts aside and focus on the part of me that's been lying dormant. I search for the girl that experienced too much too young, that saw horrors and did things her own fragile mind couldn't comprehend. The girl who became a monster. I need that girl again. That girl was broken and unfeeling and she missed out on so much, but she was capable of taking down Nicholai. It's so easy to just slip into that dark place where fear and pain do not exist. That place is easy, but it's also dangerous. I could easily lose myself there and forget what I'm fighting for. The memory of Nero, of what we have…Nicholai will try to strip me of it. Nicholai always told me that love is weak, forced me to shoot Alex, the boy I loved, just to prove it. But he's wrong. Love can make you stronger than ever, because the fact is, Nero and I are stronger together than we are apart. And with him at my side, we are a force of nature, a fucking hurricane. Nicholai has no idea the kind of hornet's nest he is kicking. I know Nero will rain hell down on Nicholai in every way he can, and my capo can be quite inventive. This is a war on two fronts.

Several hours later and the plane bumps onto the runway. I managed to sleep a little but it was interrupted with violent dreams of blood and torture. As soon as the plane comes to a stop, I stand up.

"There's a jacket there for ya," Billy shouts from the cockpit. I pick up the winter jacket tossed over one of the spare seats and put it on. I hadn't even thought of that, and, of course, Russia is freezing.

"Thanks!" I shout back and descend the steps. My boots leave footprints on the snowy runway. The freezing wind bites at any exposed skin, making me shiver violently. I'd forgotten what real cold feels like. Moscow is like an apocalyptic hell in winter. We've landed in another private airport on the outskirts of the city, and now, Nicholai will know I'm here. He has spies everywhere, but this is a bratva entry point and is constantly watched. I pick up my pace, jogging to the gate that exits the airport and ducking beneath the barrier. The airstrip is right in the middle of a small town, again, so that it can be easily monitored. I make my way down one of the side streets and glance over my shoulder quickly before stopping outside an old, run-down looking garage. The paint is peeling from the door, and the hinges sit at a strange angle as the rotted wood sags heavily. Taking my bike keys from my pocket, I select a small rusted key and unfasten the iron padlock, wiggling the lock before it finally releases. I have to heave my entire weight behind each door to push it open and reveal an older model Jeep Cherokee. All over the world, Sasha and I have safe houses, storage lockers full of supplies, cars. This is one of Sasha's.

I go to the back and feel inside the tail pipe for the key, then unlock the door and slide behind the wheel. Thick clouds of fog swirl in front of my face as I turn the ignition over and the car coughs. A low whirring comes from the laboring engine before it begrudgingly sputters to life. This is it, the final leg of my journey, and as I pull out onto the dark Moscow streets, it feels very much as though I'm driving right into the gates of hell.

Minutes drift into hours, and I think of Nero. Glancing at my phone, I note the blinking red battery. I think about it for only a moment before I'm dialing his number. It's stupid and sentimental, and I know better than anyone that I have no room for sentiment—but just one last time.

"Una." His voice is strained and tight, laced with a rage that would make grown men shrink back in fear.

"Capo," I whisper.

There's a beat of silence. "You're in Russia."

"I know you don't understand, but…"

"Turn the fuck around, right now. Wherever you are, stop. I'll come for you."

A stabbing sensation takes up residence in my chest. "I can't."

"You would do this? You would hand him our baby?"

He sounds so hurt, and behind all that rage I know he must be in agony. My eyes prickle with unshed tears again and I bite my lip angrily. "Please trust me. I have a plan. You will have the baby."

There's a pause. "But not you?"

I say nothing for a moment. "I promised I would come back to you in one way or another." Even if he only gets a piece of me, that baby will be all the best pieces. The untainted ones.

"Morte, please…" His voice breaks, and I squeeze the steering wheel tight until my knuckles turn white.

"I love you," I tell him.

"Una…" I hang up and a lump lodges in my throat. Emotions threaten to bubble over, but I lock them down. I shove them into a deep, dark recess of my shattered heart, and erect a steel wall around it. That is where Nero will live until I can see him again, or until I die. He'll remain locked behind impenetrable steel because the Una that Nicholai wants, his little dove, she cannot love.

After hours of driving, I turn down a desolate track that's barely noticeable in the thick snow, but I could find this road with my eyes closed. In the same way that a bird always knows where to migrate, this is instinctual. I once called this place home, after all. A wall of snow rushes at my headlights as I follow the tree line. Eventually, a bright spot of light becomes visible in the distance. The closer I get, the brighter and bigger that singular light becomes. I stop the car right in front of the eight-foot tall chain-link gate. Razor wire looms ominously, the jagged edges casting shadows through the light.

I cut the engine and close my eyes, resting my forehead against the steering wheel. This is it, the moment it all ends. I hear the rickety clicking of the gate sliding back and when I open my eyes, two figures are standing in the gap, the snow eerily billowing around them. My numb fingers reach for the door handle, and bitter-cold winds rips through me. I force myself to stand and face the two men in front of me, refusing to show fear because fear is power.

"I'm here to see Nicholai," I shout over the raging winds, reverting to my native tongue.

A rifle is pointed at me and the guy on the right jerks his head behind him. Their faces are covered, leaving me unable to make them out. I walk towards the small concrete building buried in the snow. The roof is a curved dome and, to the unsuspecting eye, it looks like nothing more than an old aircraft hangar, but it sinks well below the earth and is an impenetrable maze of tunnels built to withstand nuclear attack. Nicholai is nothing if not paranoid and insane.

They pause outside the door to the vehicle bay. One of them pats me down, removing the single .40 Cal from the back of my jeans before pushing me forward. The door opens in front of me. A rifle is jabbed into my back and used to shove me forward a step. The first part of the bunker is the vehicle bay, and standing there, between the SUVs and snow mobiles, is Nicholai. His hands are folded in front of him. His wool coat layered over a pristine suit. He looks so utterly flawless and so out of place in this frozen hell. The irony is that he is, in fact, perfectly placed. The heartless devil presiding over his kingdom of torture and control.

"Little dove," he breathes, his face breaking into a wide smile.

Even though every muscle in my body is tense, readying to fight, I remain stoic. I fully acknowledge the threat in front of me. And it's strange, because although I've been away for several years, I have always viewed Nicholai as a father figure, someone who helped me, who made me strong. I knew he was flawed. I knew it was hard and ugly, but I accepted it. I was loyal to him. Until now. Until he wants my child. Because suddenly, the things he did, his methods and his motivations, are not justified. And it isn't until now, until it's *my* child he wants, that I see that so clearly. Nicholai is not my savior, but my persecutor. I now see him as the sick and twisted creature he is.

He steps closer, reaching a hand towards my stomach. I growl and twist away from him. "Where is Anna?"

"She is safe."

"You will release her immediately."

420

"My sweet little dove." He grips my jaw on a maniacal laugh. "You are nothing here." He squeezes until pain radiates through my face. "You are only what I made you. You. Are. A disappointment."

"Let Anna go." I wrench my face away from him and drop to a crouch, kicking at the legs of the man with the gun. He hits the ground with a thud. I pop up with his gun raised and pointed in Nicholai's direction.

"Ah, you see..." he tucks his hands in his pockets and walks a few paces to the right. "You always were the best, Una. Better than anyone else." Icy-blue eyes meet mine. "You made me so proud."

On some silent signal, figures emerge from the shadowy recesses of the garage. At least twenty or so, all armed, all Elite. They won't be as good as me, but I can't take twenty.

"Will you kill me, little dove?"

"Release Anna."

"I would have. But you continue to insult and dishonor me at every turn. So, I will not give you honor. Your sister will stay here. Perhaps she will motivate you." I had a feeling he would do this, and it makes my task here infinitely more difficult. Two figures move in on either side, one pointing a gun at my head, the other aims the gun at my stomach. Looks like Nicholai is making them as ruthless as ever. Left without any choices, I drop the gun and hold my hands up.

I'm led through corridors that I could navigate with my eyes shut, shivering violently as the concrete walls of the underground fortress seem to emit cold like the inside of a refrigerator. I'm locked in a cell on the very same wing I stayed in when I first came here. Nicholai saved me from the clutches of would be rapists only to bring me here and have me locked up. I stayed here for weeks. The guards wouldn't talk to me. I was deprived of sleep, food, beaten…and after weeks, Nicholai 'reappeared', telling me he'd had to leave me. I was thirteen. I'd lost both my parents, been torn from my sister, nearly raped…he seemed like a savior to a little girl who had never had one. And what did I have to do in exchange for his kindness, his respect, his adoration? I had to be strong. I had to be the best. I had to kill. And as long as I did those things, I believed I had his love. I think I needed it because despite him beating it out of me, despite him forcing me to shoot Alex…isn't love the only real motivator in this world? As humans we crave it, need it, and will do almost anything for it. It is our ultimate and unavoidable weakness. I sold my soul for the love of a man who uses the adoration of helpless children to build an army.

CHAPTER
TWENTY-TWO

Nero

The second she hangs up the phone, I'm fighting back blinding rage. I try to call her back, but the line has been disconnected. How could she do this? I launch the phone across the room with a roar. Gio is standing silently beside the door, arms folded over his chest and a frown pinching his features. Jackson is sitting on the couch. I called him in because I don't want Gio's rational, diplomatic advice right now. I want blood. I want fucking war and Jackson will give it to me.

"She's only twenty miles from the base," Gio places an iPad on the coffee table. A small red dot blinks in and out on a map. When we first caught Una in Paris, we knocked her out and I had the doctor place a tracker in the back of her neck. She'd never notice it, and I'm hoping the Russians won't be looking for trackers on her. "Even if we could get to her, Nicholai will have ground forces that close to the base. It would be a suicide rescue mission."

I'm completely helpless and I can't stand it. I tell myself this isn't over, that we can still fight, but damn it, she surrendered without even telling me. And she went behind my back, so I have no plan, no way of getting to her. She cut me out and now I'm left standing on the outside while she takes my child into an impregnable base with a guy she's openly admitted is crazy.

"Find a way of contacting Sasha," I tell Gio. He's good with computers and hacking shit. I'm sure he can find a way to get a message to the guy. He may well be our only way of contacting Una now. Gio nods and leaves the room.

Jackson glances at me. "What are you thinking?"

"Get your guys together and contact Devon. I want them ready to go tomorrow morning. We're going to burn everything Russian to the ground. You want a fucking rat, you smoke him out." Devon is my other New York capo, loyal and lethal. None of the guys will need asking twice when it comes to fucking up the Russians.

"On it." Jackson gets up. I pour out a glass of whiskey and he hesitates in the doorway. "We'll get her back, boss." Then he leaves.

I hope he's right, or I'll bring the bratva to its fucking knees with my wrath. After all, without her, without my child, what do I have to lose?

I stand in front of the inconspicuous looking brick building on the Lower East Side, settled between two restaurant chains. A passerby wouldn't look twice, but I know better. Leaning against the hood of my car, I lift a cigarette to my lips, inhaling a thick cloud of smoke. My mind constantly drifts to Una, wondering what he's doing to her. It's those thoughts that feed my rage, like constantly pumping oxygen onto a blazing inferno.

Jackson comes around the corner of the block and casually strolls over to me. "Might want to step back," he says with a wicked smile. We round my car and duck down behind it. A couple of his guys use the car parked behind mine to take cover. Jackson hands me the primitive looking cell phone. I hold down the one for several seconds, and then, the street behind us erupts. The bang is so loud it makes my ears ring. Windows blow out on the nearby buildings, and heat weashes over me

Jackson throws his head back, laughing manically. "Roasted Russian anyone?"

I push to my feet and watch the inferno of flames engulf the small brick building. The fire spreads, reaching for the restaurants on either side. People run down the street screaming while others stagger out of the restaurants. No one leaves the Russian club, and that's because Jackson rigged it with enough explosives to bring down a building twice its size. Low and behold, the roof suddenly caves, sagging inward before collapsing in a flaming pile. A secondary explosion makes the ground tremble. I round my car, climbing into the driver's side. The window is smashed from the explosion, but I don't care. This is just one of twelve different attacks happening all over the city. Nicholai thought he could just take what's mine, that there would be no consequences, well, this is the consequence. I do not care for repercussions. What more can he do to me? He has taken everything, and I will see that Russian fuck bleed out all over the New York concrete, even if it's not his blood.

I call Cesare as soon as we're a few streets away from the blast. "Nero," he says when he picks up, his voice coming over the car speakers. Jackson stares out the window, deliberately trying to look as though he isn't paying attention.

"Nicholai has Una." My voice sounds far calmer than the white-hot rage that's burning me from the inside out. "This is a courtesy call. Perhaps now would be a good time to call your Russian contacts."

"What are you going to do?" he asks carefully.

"I've already made a start, but I'm going to burn everything the Russians have to the ground. You tell them that for every-fucking-day my woman and my child are not with me, I will kill a Russian woman and child."

"No. You go too far. She is Russian! She is Elite."

"I never told you about what Nicholai has planned for my child, did I?" Silence. "He's going to turn it into the ultimate soldier, raised from birth to be a weapon for the bratva."

He clears his throat and I know that as much as he hates Una, he hates the idea of a child of Italian blood- his blood- fighting for the enemy. "Let me call Dimitri. I can reason with him." Dimitri Svelta, high up in the bratva with links in the Russian government. He's as corrupt as they come, but corrupt I can deal with. Nicholai's outright insanity cannot be reasoned with.

"The bratva have allowed Nicholai to do this for years. He has built them an army."

"I can speak to them about the child, but she is Russian, Nero," he says, as though she belongs to Nicholai, a piece of property to be bought and sold.

"She is mine. That baby is mine. And I wasn't asking permission. This is what I will do. Stand against me and I will unleash your secrets, old man. Try to stop me and you will make yourself the enemy. Pass the message along to Dimitri." I hang up and lean back in my seat, slamming my foot over the accelerator.

"So we're at war?" Jackson asks.

I nod. "A war the likes of which the Russians have never witnessed." I glance at him. "I ask you to walk into a bloodbath. Are you with me?"

"As if you even have to ask. I'm the only fucker who might almost be as sick as you." He snorts. "We'll get Una back. You're a damn site more manageable when she's around. I mean, I'm down with the blood and bodies, but Cesare is probably shitting on himself right now." He laughs and I shake my head.

Cesare had better pull through, because right now, I'd take his fucking head without blinking.

CHAPTER TWENTY-THREE

Nero

Gio sits in the passenger seat, and I can practically feel the tension coming from him. I usually acknowledge his advice, after all, he is a Made man born and bred. He knows what it takes to hold power in the mafia, but right now, I don't give a fuck about the mafia. I'm going to use every inch of power that I have to get Una back.

We pull up at the shipping dock and I get out of the car. The briny smell of the harbor hits me as Gio comes to stand beside me. We make our way towards the small maze of shipping containers in the center of the shipping yard. That constant rage is beating away at me, consuming everything in its attempt to fill the gaping void left by having Una torn from my side. The hinges creek loudly when I open the door of the dark blue container, the paint peeling off the iron beneath. The single light bulb rigged from the ceiling casts a harsh yellow glow over the inside of the container. Jackson and Devon are here, both their faces set in a stony mask. Jackson nods to me when I enter. Devon is young for a capo, and unlike Jackson's hulking bulk, he could be a businessman, a young banker or something of the nature, except for the fact that he's a bloodthirsty little shit. Gio is my second because I've known him my whole life. He has morals, and he's the only person that can possibly rein me in when I go too far, which is often. Jackson and Devon are my capos because they have none. Jackson moves to the side, revealing two figures huddled against the back wall, one clutched in the arms of the other.

"Bring them," I say, taking my gun from my holster. Jackson grabs the woman by the arm and drags her to her feet. She immediately starts crying, heaving, desperate sobs as she reaches for the child. Devon grabs the kid. They're both shoved to their knees in front of me.

"Take the bags off."

Jackson yanks the bags from their heads and they both blink. The woman is probably in her late thirties. Her face is tear-stained and her dark hair is matted to her cheeks. The kid is a teenager. Despite having pissed on himself, he's not crying, though his bottom lip trembles. They're the wife and son of a bratva leader here in New York, and that's unfortunate for them.

As I look at them, I know I should feel something, because even for me this is bad. These people are complete strangers to me. They didn't take Una. They don't want to take my child. And perhaps, as I look at this kid I should be thinking: what if this were my child? But I don't. I feel nothing but cold fury. I think of nothing but sending Nicholai a message loud and fucking clear: I will keep coming for you, and I will spill innocent blood until the streets of New York run red.

I lift my gun and Gio shifts beside me. "Nero, please…"

I glare at him. "Do not question me."

He swipes his palm over his face. "You are crossing a line you can't come back from," he pleads, eyes flicking between me and the woman in front of me. She turns, pulling her child into her arms as she cries.

"In war, there are casualties, Gio. Until I get Una back, this is fucking war." I lift the gun and pull the trigger. Maybe I'm every bit as bad as Nicholai. I don't care.

CHAPTER TWENTY-FOUR

Nero

Ten days. It's been ten days since Una left and seven days of mercilessly killing Russians. I'd say that the blood weighs heavy on me, but it doesn't. Cesare has begged me to stop. He doesn't have the stomach to make the hard decisions. He believes that this can be solved with words and tact. The simple fact is, battle lines must be drawn in blood.

With Rafael's help, I've managed to fuck up the bratva's drug and gun supplies. This will be a war of attrition and I will starve them out if I must. Without their drugs and guns, the bratva will soon be scrambling around, desperate for money. It stands to reason that the life of one woman and one child is not worth complete anarchy. What's left of the bratva here in New York are reaping my wrath and they're running, retreating to Russia because the Italian underboss has declared war.

Nicholai has no weaknesses, and Una is his obsession, so he'd never give her up. The only ones who can force Nicholai's hand are the rest of the bratva, so it's them that I now press.

I lift the glass of whiskey to my lips, downing the burning liquid before I refill the glass. It's two in the morning and I can't sleep. Instead, I sit at my desk staring at my laptop screen. At the tiny red dot on a blueprint. Una's tracker. It hasn't moved from the same room in Nicholai's base for the last nine days. Is he holding her prisoner? Or did they find it? What if she's dead? I clench my fist on the desk in front of me. No, she can't be.

I lift the glass to my lips again when my phone beeps. Frowning, I glance at the screen and see it flashing with a security warning. The fire exit door has been breached. A slow smile pulls at my lips because I know exactly what that means. Nicholai finally got my message. There's no one in the apartment other than me. Gio was staying here, but I sent him back to the Hamptons because I couldn't take his bitching anymore. I have two guys on the lobby and two on the parking garage, but that's it. Una isn't here to protect anymore, and I want them to come.

Opening my desk, I take out the .45 Cal that I keep there, checking the clip before I slide it back with a resounding click. My .40 Cal is strapped to my chest. If that isn't enough, then I'm fucked anyway.

I switch off the desk lamp and plunge the office into darkness. The glow from the city below allows me enough light to make my way to the door. My shoulder blades press flush against the wall beside the door, and I wait. I hear nothing, but of course, if they're Elite, I wouldn't. Eventually the door handle to the office slowly lowers. My pulse drums rapidly as adrenaline floods my system. The second someone opens the door I aim through the gap and pull the trigger. A body hits the floor, and if there are more, I've lost the element of surprise.

Moving through the doorway, my eyes dart everywhere, searching for a trace of movement. Something brushes my leg and I swing my gun downward, only to find Zeus, his sleek black coat camouflaging him with the shadows. I spot a shadow at the top of the stairs and I shoot, barely able to see if the shot hit home before I hear footsteps in the lobby. Without hesitating, I tell Zeus to stay, and then I'm striding towards the lobby, allowing the anger bubbling beneath the surface to manifest and boil over. They take Una and now these fuckers are in my house. A bullet cracks past me, grazing my ear with a sting. I stand in the entrance to the kitchen with a clear line of sight right through to the lobby. My reflexes act without my consent, and I fire off two shots, downing two bodies. My muscles ache from the strain of being so tightly bunched, panting breaths coming in sharp pants.

I round the corner and a silhouetted figure steps in my path. We both raise our guns at the same time, freezing in place.

"Nero," the familiar voice greets me.

"Sasha. I should have known. I told her you couldn't be trusted."

"Do not talk to me of Una," he says, his voice void of emotion. "You bring about her ruin."

"Why is that?" I ask. "Because she no longer wants to be a member of the boy's club?"

His jaw tenses for a second, and then he's dropping to a crouch and sliding his gun across the floor. I frown in confusion and mimic his action. I barely have time to blink before he punches me, hard. I stagger back a step, but he's right there again, swinging at the other side of my face. A smile pulls at my lips, as I duck and nail him in the gut. He doesn't even flinch before he kicks my legs out from underneath me. We fall to the floor trading punches and blows until every part of my body is screaming in agony. The taste of blood on my tongue is its own high, and it makes me mad with a kind of violence I haven't felt in years. I straddle his body and punch him in the throat. He chokes before he jabbing me in the kidney, then in the temple. Dazed, I tilt sideways, and then he's on top of me, hands wrapped around my throat. I hit him in his ribs, stomach, back. Everywhere, but he's locked on like a python and my oxygen is now dwindling. Jesus, he's like the damn terminator. In one last ditch effort, I grip his elbow tight and shove against his shoulder. I hear the satisfying pop of his shoulder dislocating and his small grunt of pain. His fingers go lax and I take the opportunity to shove him to the side, crawling away from him. My vision blurs as I slump against the wall, watching as he climbs to his knees and smashes his arm into the side of the breakfast bar to relocate his shoulder. Eventually he collapses against the bar. And here we sit, the pair of us breathing heavily, bruised and bleeding.

"You fight well," he says.

"Thanks." There's a beat of silence. "Is she still alive?"

He turns his head towards me, and I can just make out his blank expression. "Of course."

I know he's not going to say anymore and aggravation creeps in. "So you were sent to kill me."

"I volunteered."

I smirk. "Well, perhaps they should have sent more men." I gesture towards the two dead bodies sprawled in my lobby.

He tilts his head back against the wall. "She begged me to intervene, to stop Nicholai from sending a team after you."

"This is you intervening?" I snort.

436

He says nothing for long seconds. "Do you think she loves you?"

"I…yes."

"She used to be different, you know? Before Alex. They were best friends. She loved him. I saw the way she looked at him, like he was the only thing that made her happy. She was sixteen when Nicholai made her shoot him." Jesus, that's fucked up, even by my standards. "She was not the same after that. I never saw her happy again."

"Is that what it is to be Elite? Would you kill her if he asked you to?"

He hesitates. "No."

He'd defy an order for her. And that's when I realize… "You love her."

"She makes me happy." It's such a simple statement, almost innocent, which is not a word I would ever associate with Sasha.

"She loves you as well, Sasha. She refused to believe that you were the enemy."

"And you make her happy." He sighs heavily. "I don't…I don't want to take that away from her, but I have a duty. I have orders."

"What if you didn't?" He tilts his head to the side. "What if Nicholai didn't exist? What if you didn't have orders? What then?" His brows pull together as though the question perplexes him. "If you love her, Sasha, help her. Help her baby. My baby." Desperation leaks into my voice, and I'm sitting forward because I realize that this might be my only shot, my only chance to help Una.

Pushing to my feet, I limp over to him. He gets up, clutching his arm to his side as we stare at each other. "She once told me that together, you and her were the best." He nods once. "Then be the best, but fight for a cause. Pick a side Sasha." I bend down and pick up my gun, handing it to him. I'm trusting him because Una trusts him. That damn woman has me doing stupid shit for her.

He takes the gun and stares at it for a second. "You would die for her?" he asks.

"Of course."

A deep frown etches into his features and then, with a sigh, he turns the gun around and shoots himself.

CHAPTER TWENTY-FIVE

Una

I don't know how long I've been here, or even where I am. Restraints keep me strapped to a bed, and my head is spinning as my mind fogs with sedatives. A hand strokes over my hair, and I blink against the bright overhead lights, trying to focus on the blurry figure in front of me.

"Little dove, it's time." I recoil away from the voice, trying to twist my head to the side.

"Time?" My voice is raspy and barely audible.

"Time to meet your baby." What is he talking about? He steps to the side and a woman replaces him. The prick of a needle meets my arm, and then she's gone. Nicholai takes my hand in his and strokes my cheek. I manage to focus on him, on his icy blue eyes. A soft smile touches his lips. "I am so glad you are home. This will all be over soon, and I will make you strong again." Tears threaten and I squeeze my eyes shut. "Any minute now," he says.

My eyes fly open when my stomach tightens like a steel band. "What's happening?"

"You are having your baby, little dove. He will be stronger than even you."

Panic settles over me. "No, I can't. It's too early."

"Shh, shh, you've been sleeping for weeks. You will be fine. I would not let you die, little dove. You are too precious." He strokes over my hair again, and then stands, kissing my forehead before he leaves the room.

I've never felt less fine in my life. Weeks. I've been here for weeks. My plan...my time is up now. This baby is coming, and once it's separated from me, my task becomes infinitely more difficult. I can only imagine the terror Nero is raining down on everyone. My midsection clamps down again, every single muscle going rigid tight. I grit my teeth and my body contorts, but only so far because my wrists, ankles, and chest are pinned to the bed. Oh, god. He's going to leave me here to have this baby on my own.

The door opens again, and Sasha walks in the room. I've never been so happy to see him. His posture is stiff, his face set in a grim expression.

"Sasha." He stops beside me, body bristling with tension. I notice one arm is tucked against his chest in a sling. "What happened to you?" His other fist clenches tight. He says nothing for a moment. "Sasha?" I can just about reach my fingers out and brush his hand. He flinches before his eyes meet mine.

"I had a run in with the Italian."

My heart plummets into my chest and my pulse races. If Sasha went after Nero, one of them must be dead, and Sasha's standing right here, so… "Is he…?"

He shakes his head. "He lives." I relax my head back against the bed, breathing out a sigh of relief. I need Nero to live. He is my reason, and I must cling to that. "But he has declared war."

"Of course." It's Nero. He lives for war. I have to trust that he can win this one.

There's a long beat of silence before he speaks, his voice quiet. "I'm sorry, Una."

"What for?"

"I should have…You shouldn't be here."

"Where's Anna?" I ask.

His lips press together, eyes shifting around the bleak, grey room. "She's here. She's safe."

My stomach locks up again, and I drag in a sharp breath, tightening my fists until my nails bite into my palm.

"Where?" I grit out when it passes.

"She's being held in one of the cells."

"Please, Sasha." I want to help Anna, I do, but I have to trust that Rafael will do as I said and bargain for her. "I need your help."

441

"I cannot help you." His voice is strained, green eyes guarded. Sasha is ruled by duty, and I know the likelihood of him going against it for any reason is slim, but I have to try.

"The baby," I whisper. "You have to get it out, take it to Nero."

He braces his hands on the edge of the bed and drops his head forward. I clench my teeth under the next wave of pain. "You must let this go, Una."

"Sasha…"

"No!" He slams his palms down on the edge of the bed, glaring at me. "No more, Una. You were the one who failed in your duty. You never should have been working with Nero Verdi, let alone sleeping with him. You brought this on yourself." His blond eyebrows pull together tightly. I fight back tears. He was my last hope. My only hope. It seems I have lost everything. My sister is imprisoned. My baby will be a soldier. My brother hates me. And Nero; I sacrificed Nero in the hope that Sasha would do this for me. Nero always said that Nicholai failed to break me, but now, as my body tries to purge the child from within, I realize that I'm about to find myself more alone than I ever was before.

Is it better to have loved and lost than never to have loved at all? I think it would be better if I had never met Nero, never found Anna because the emotional pain is far worse than anything physical.

"I understand," I say, turning my gaze from him and focusing on the ceiling. He remains in the room, but I ignore him, even as the pain progresses over the next few hours.

When the agony reaches an all-time high, the door opens. A guy in a white coat walks in along with two women in scrubs. Nicholai lingers behind them, walking to me slowly. They release my ankles and bend my legs, spreading them. I'm in too much pain to focus on what they're doing as they stare between my thighs.

Nicholai strokes my hair, a small smile on his lips. "You know, childbirth is said to be the most painful thing a person can experience." Another contraction grips me and I pitch off the bed, tugging against the restraints and fighting back the urge to scream. "Do you remember what I taught you, little dove?" I don't answer him because I can't. "I taught you that pain is in the mind, and so, you will have no drugs." He strokes my cheek, kissing my forehead gently. "You will bring that child into this world, and you will let it be a reminder that you are Una Ivanov. That child will be torn from you, and with it, this disease, this weakness that you have allowed to infect you. The pain will both punish and cleanse you." I can't truly process his words because another wave of blinding agony washes over me. And he's right, this is the worst pain I've ever experienced. I have been shot, burned, cut, drowned, but this…it feels like my body is being split in two, shredded apart one piece at a time.

"Push, push, push," one of the nurses says. And I do, I push, and a scream breaks past my lips as my nails embed deep in my palms. Nicholai smiles wide and then turns away, leaving the room. I collapse back on the bed and my eyes drift closed. I wish Nero was here. Warm fingers thread through mine, gripping tight, and when I open my eyes, Sasha is there.

"You can do this, Una. You are the strongest person I know." I'm not though.

It seems to go on forever, until one sensation blends into the next and all I feel is a pain so intense, it seems to pulse with my very heartbeat. Another wave of pain grips me, so strong that my vision dots. "Push!" I find the last vestige of strength I have and push with everything in me. Almost instantly, the pain lessens, my body relaxes, and I slump back against the bed. I just want to close my eyes and drift away. And then, I hear a noise that makes my heart stutter in my chest. A cry so small and delicate, so out of place in this concrete hell. The doctor places this tiny thing on my chest and I glance at it, at him. His pink skin is covered in blood, but he's perfect. In a single heartbeat, my entire world tilts on its axis. Everything that I thought mattered suddenly no longer does, just him. My baby. I try to touch him, but my hands are still restrained. With him right here, right in front of me, the reality of our horrible situation hits home hard. Tears track down my temples and I wish more than anything that I could hold him.

"Sasha, please," I whisper. I hear his ragged sigh, and then he lets go of my hand, glancing towards the door before releasing the leather cuff. I hesitantly place my hand on the tiny baby's back and clutch him to my chest, pressing my lips to his head. He lets out a small cry and I pull him closer to my neck. "Thank you."

The door opens, and just like that, I know. Nicholai stands off to the side, a smug smile on his face. "He is perfect, little dove."

I spread my fingers over his tiny body, wishing it were enough to keep him clutched to me, but this was always a losing battle. I know that the only way to save him is to let him go. But my heart can't handle it, and this need unlike anything I've ever felt is raging inside my head, screaming at me to hold onto him, to never let him go.

The nurse pries him away from me, and a fresh wave of tears flow freely. I don't even have the will power to stop them. He's wrapped in a towel and handed to Nicholai who coos at him like a proud new father, but he's not Nicholai's child. He's Nero's. He's mine.

"Thank you, little dove," he says, and then he walks out of the room, taking my baby with him. Pain and heartbreak like I've never felt consume me, and this horrible noise echoes around the room. It takes me a few seconds to realize that the sound is me. It's the sound of a heart shattering. It's the sound of a mother losing her child.

*****

I allow the dark waters to surround me, to become as a soothing embrace. For the briefest of moments, I consider just opening my mouth and inhaling. The pain in my chest is this constant ache and part of me wishes I could just cut it out, but I can't, I won't because it reminds me that my child was real. And that is the very reason that I must survive at any cost.

My lungs start to burn and my fingers twitch, a nervous reaction, my body screaming at me that this is not good. Pain is all in the mind, and fear is nothing but pointless emotion, so I force it back the way I was trained to. The hand wrapped around the back of my neck wrenches me upright and I drag in a lungful of air. Nicholai stands across the water tank from me, arms folded over his chest as he frowns at me. Moving closer, he studies me, assessing every little detail, every tiny reaction.

His lips twist into a small smile. "You think you hide it so well, little dove."

"Hide what?"

He strokes the back of his hand over my cheek, tilting his head to the side. "The fire in your eyes. The anger. You hate me now, but in time, you will see. I do this because I love you. I will make you strong again, and then everything will be as it once was." I clench my jaw and nod. "But first, I must remind you of what you are. You are a creature of my making, little dove, and I will break you over and over until you remember it, until you know nothing else." A tremor of fear works through my body and goosebumps dot my skin. I know he'll do exactly as he says, and I know I'm not strong enough for it. I thought I could do this, but being here—I remember why I became his creature. Simply because it was easier. If you let go of your soul, you can't feel it being decimated one piece at a time.

"Now, take her to level six," Nicholai says dismissively before I'm marched out of the room. Level six is where they perform

445

all the electro-shock therapy. It's been two days since I gave birth and my body is already screaming from the trauma of it, but this is what I must endure. The quicker he gets this over with, the better. I just hope I don't break because even at full strength and with my emotions in check, Nicholai's methods push the mind and body to a place it should never have to go.

CHAPTER TWENTY-SIX

Nero

It's cold as fuck. I'm sitting in a car with Gio in the passenger seat, and we're parked at the side of a narrow country road that's halfway hidden under the cover of the forest. Snow falls all around us, and even though I can see my breath in front of my face, we can't turn the engine on.

The deal I made with Sasha was vague at best. He would help me. Help Una. But I had to stop the killings, lay low and wait for him to contact me. So, I agreed, and he went back to Russia with an authentic looking bullet hole in his shoulder. It hasn't been easy. It's been weeks and everything has been eerily quiet. Doing nothing has felt like a slow torture.

Sasha's message was simple. A set of co-ordinates and a time and date, along with the instruction to stay out of sight until the time is right. That was it. I don't know what we're waiting for, or when that right time will be, but we have ten minutes until whatever is supposed to be happening will happen. Of course, the co-ordinates were for just outside Smolensk, near the Russia and Belarus border.

I'm on edge because we're in Russia. I can only hope that means Una has somehow escaped. The ten minutes come and go, and I'm getting more and more agitated when we see a set of headlights round the corner. We've been here for nearly an hour and I haven't seen one car on this road. The car passes us and pulls into a shallow shoulder before it cuts its engine.

Gio glances at me. "Sasha could have been a little more informative," he remarks.

I keep my eyes locked on that car. No one gets out. It just sits there. And then, a few minutes later, another set of headlights. A truck. It slows as it approaches and pulls into the shoulder behind the car. The doors of the car open and two guys get out, both armed with rifles.

"I guess this is it," Gio says.

I take my gun from its spot on the dashboard. "Go in fast and hard. They won't be expecting us." He nods, palming his gun as we get out. The powdery snow silences our footfalls. We follow the tree line until we're right across the road from the truck. Two men have gotten out of it and the group of four are approaching the back of the vehicle. There's the loud clatter of the roller door being lifted, and then I hear it, a tiny cry coming from the back of that truck. The cry of a baby. I'm running across that road before the men have even really registered it. I shoot two of them before a rifle is pointed my way. Gio is right behind me though, taking them out. I get to the back of the truck and look inside. It's dark, but I can make out shelves, stacked with weapons, boxes of ammo and supplies. And in the corner, the source of that tiny cry. I jump inside and get out my phone, turning on the torch. There's a black duffel bag hidden behind crates of explosives. I can't think about that now though. I unzip the bag, and there, wrapped in several blankets is a tiny baby. My baby.

I pick up the scrap of paper that's tucked into the blanket and read over the messy writing.

I cannot help Una, but she will be fine. Look after her son. He is her happiness.

I swallow the lump in my throat and scoop up my baby, my boy, holding him to my chest. I owe Sasha a debt that I can never repay. Jumping down from the back of the truck, I meet Gio's gaze. A soft smile pulls at his lips as he glances at the bundle of blankets screaming in my arms.

"She did it," he says.

"Yeah, she did." Now I can only hope that this wasn't a sacrifice. As I hold him in my arms, I've never loved Una more. I need her. He needs her. I will protect our son with my life until she comes home. She promised me.

"Blow up the truck." I step over bodies as I head back to the car.

CHAPTER TWENTY-SEVEN

Una

My back hits the concrete floor with a thud that resonates through my bones. The guy presses his knee into my chest and lands three blows to my face. I lift my guard, but it's no use. My muscles are weak from being in an induced coma for so long. My body is soft and still recovering from the baby I had only a week ago. But this is what it is to be Elite, pain and suffering, because weakness is not tolerated. Nicholai is proving a point, and punishing me.

"I thought she was supposed to be the best," my opponent says, grunting as he goes for another punch. A few of the other Elite snicker under their breath. The kid's arrogant and lacking in respect. I allow him to land two more blows on me, leading him into a false sense of security before I break cover and summon all my strength, punching him in the throat. His eyes go wide and he coughs, trying to suck in a breath through his collapsed trachea. I shove him off me and his face starts to turn purple.

Climbing to my hands and knees, I spit a mouthful of blood onto the concrete. Normally, I would relish in being back on this concrete, fighting with newly trained Elite, because no one else can provide me with a good fight. But right now, every single part of my body hurts. My face is swelling and I'm pretty sure my nose and cheekbone are broken. The ribs on my right side throb painfully and my knuckles are split open to the bone. This is what it is to meet Nicholai's standards.

His shiny dress shoes step into my line of vision, and then he crouches down, much the same way I've seen Nero do when he wants to drive home the fact that he is the one with all the power. His finger presses under my chin and he lifts my face. I make a conscious effort to wipe all trace of thought or emotions from my expression as I look at him through swelling eyes.

"You were once the best, Una." Disappointment paints his features. I say nothing and he simply shakes his head before walking out the door. Sasha is leaning against the wall beside the doorway, thick arms folded over his chest. His brows pull together in a tight frown as he pushes away from the wall, moving past me. As soon as he stands in front of them the Elite all stand to attention.

"Adam, get back in line," he snaps, and the kid who just beat the shit out of me gets to his feet, clutching at his throat. "Take note. You underestimate her because you see her as weak, and she is right now. But…" He steps back until he's beside me. "Una Ivanov is the only soldier to ever be awarded the name Ivanov. She is feared by men much more lethal than any of you. By all means, take advantage of her weakness, it is what a good fighter does, but do not disrespect her. Even at her weakest she still bests you, Adam." I bristle at the fact that he is continuously calling me weak. "Dismissed." They peel away, heading to the barracks at the back of the training room. He turns and looks at me, eyes touching on various points of my body, assessing injuries. "You've gone to shit."

"I just had a fucking baby," I growl, even as I know it's no excuse. Not in this place.

He sighs and tugs at the neckline of my tank top, revealing an ugly bruise that I know is settling into the deep tissue of my shoulder. I'm pretty sure I've torn a ligament as well, but honestly, between the broken bones and concussion, it's the least of my worries. "Come on." He heads for the door, entering a code on the pad before stepping into the corridor. I follow him to a door down the hall. When he opens it, I want to turn around and walk back out. "Sasha," I groan.

He whips around, a stern expression on his face. "This is day one. If you don't shape up fast, he's going to let them kill you, Una. You will only get back into his good graces if you become what you were. You must be the best."

He's right. I know he's right. He goes to the enormous metal tub and turns the water on before going to the steel chest freezer in the corner and scooping several buckets of ice into the water. Stripping out of my clothes, I step up to the tub and take a deep breath before I throw my leg over the side. The easiest way to do ice baths is to do it fast, so I quickly step in with both feet, sucking in a sharp breath before I drop below the water.

"I think I'd rather have the electrocutions," I say through tightly clenched teeth. The freezing cold only adds to the throbbing pain rippling over every inch of skin.

"You'll go numb in a minute." He sits on the edge of the metal tub. Sasha and I have been naked around each other so much, I don't think he even notices. "Has Nicholai mentioned anything about your child?" he asks, causing an entirely different kind of pain to settle deep in my chest.

"No. Why?" Green eyes meet mine and he hesitates for a second. "Why? What's happened to him, Sasha?"

"He has been taken. Nicholai can only surmise that it must be a mole, someone Nero Verdi has paid off."

I think about that for a second. What if it isn't Nero? "Why does he think it's Nero?" His eyes dart around the room and I know what he's thinking, nowhere is safe in this place. Everything can be heard.

"Your Italian has been making quite the nice little bloodbath. He declared to Dimitri that for every day he did not have you and his child, he would kill a Russian woman and child. Though he stopped after I tried to kill him. We can only surmise that he fears the repercussions of his rash actions." I fight a smile. Nero fears nothing and would welcome repercussions. Sasha made a deal with him. It's the only plausible explanation. Which means Sasha helped get my baby out of here. He lied when he said he wouldn't help me.

I sit up in the ice bath and pull him into a loose hug. "Thank you," I whisper against his ear.

When I pull back, he nods. The idea that Nero has our baby, that he is safe, has that ache in my chest diminishing. And without it, the physical pain feels like an easy burden to bear. Now I must focus on my mission here. I must immerse myself in the Elite again, become the best, earn their respect, and then, with Sasha's help, I am going to bring Nicholai down, surrounded by the very soldiers he trained.

"Okay, get out. We're going to train," Sasha says.

No pain, no gain, right? This is going to be plenty painful.

CHAPTER TWENTY-EIGHT

Una

I close my eyes and grit my teeth, waiting for the touch to come. My entire body is trembling, demanding I react. I've been here before, back when I was trained, but that was to purpose, for a reason. This…this just feels like punishment and slowly, piece by piece, it is shredding my humanity.

I hear the shifting of feet. A palm slams around my arm, the cool metal of the glove touching my skin before unloading a massive electric shock. *Kill, kill, kill.* It's my only thought, over and over until I can comprehend nothing else. My mind shuts down, completely blank. I react, instinct overriding everything. It's as though I'm watching a TV, watching someone else break the man's arm and snap his neck with such force that his lower jaw comes almost completely loose. Another Elite moves towards me and I watch as I go hand to hand with him. He raises a gun and I shove his wrist to the side, snapping his arm until the gun is pointed at his own chest, then I squeeze the trigger twice, ending him. Another starts to approach…

"Enough!" Sasha's voice booms through the room and I swing my gun in his direction, then at Nicholai standing against the far wall. "Una, drop the gun." It's Sasha. I try and force my body to obey, my fingers to release the gun. My hand shakes. He moves closer until the barrel of the gun is against his chest. "Una, look at me." I look at him and he wraps his fingers around the gun, careful not to touch me. I slowly release the weapon and stagger back a step. Squeezing my eyes shut, I try to force the red mist from my mind. Dropping to a crouch, I press the heels of my hands against my eyelids. "You push her too far," Sasha says.

"I give her what she needs," is Nicholai's cool response.

"She will break. Her skills are unparalleled, but if you break her mind, she will be of no use to us. If you wish to punish her so, just shoot her already."

"You forget your place," Nicholai growls.

"I train the soldiers. And she is my best." I hear the heavy steel door open and then close again. "Una." I open my eyes and glance up at Sasha who is towering over me. The floor around him is covered in blood. And two mangled bodies lay at the center of the mess. "Go and get cleaned up." He jerks his head towards the door and I stand, walking numbly down the hallway.

I can't take much more of this. He's been doing this for a month straight, forcing me to endure and kill. Instinct and lack of conscience are what make the perfect killer. Touch conditioning hones in on the most primal of instincts, forcing the things that make us fundamentally human from our mind, and without that, emotions—affection, love—they are all

456

inconsequential. He's turning me into an animal and there's nothing I can do to stop it.

CHAPTER TWENTY-NINE

Una

One month later

I grip the smooth length of wood, wrapping my fingers around it. Vadim stands across from me, his arms braced wide as he grips his own bo staff. A small smile touches his lips as he watches me. He's a few years younger than me, but he's good.

I shift to the left and he does the same, mimicking my movements. Suddenly, he breaks away, coming at me. The two sticks crack against each other, moving so fast that it's nothing more than a series of clicks. He strikes forward, but reaches too far. I maneuver to the side, slam my stick across his shoulder blades, and step on his foot, sending him crashing to the ground. I move to the side of the improvised ring, cracking my neck to the side. Sasha remains close, his hands clasped tightly behind his back as he watches me. He has grilled me constantly for weeks, and finally, my body is what it once was. To attack and kill is again as instinctual to my muscles as breathing. I hear Vadim get to his feet, and then he's rushing me. I smile. Stupid boy. Sasha's eyebrows raise a fraction and I crack the wood over my knee. In a split second I whirl and launch the splintered piece of wood like a spear. It hits Vadim in the shoulder so hard that he ends up on his back on concrete. I stare down at him, clutching at the piece of wood protruding from his mangled shoulder. That familiar sense of satisfaction washes over me, power and the sheer thrill of violence are like a drug.

"That wasn't a fair fight," he says, panting.

I offer him nothing as I place my boot on his chest. "There is no such thing as a fair fight. Use the weapons you have. Be smarter than your opponent." I lift one eyebrow and grab the wood, yanking it out of him. He grunts in pain, squeezing his eyes shut. "And be grateful I aimed for your shoulder and not your throat."

Sasha comes to stand beside me, waving over someone to help Vadim. "Take him to medical."

The room fills with the sound of a slow clapping and both Sasha and I turn to see Nicholai walking across the training area, a wide smile on his face. "Ah, little dove, you have become yourself again. So merciless." He smiles. "I have a job for you both. It seems Rafael D'Cruze would like your sister, little dove." I give him no reaction. He hasn't mentioned Anna since I've been here, and he hasn't mentioned the fact that he is no longer in possession of my son. Perhaps he wants me to think that he is. After all, the easiest way to keep the mother's loyalty is if you hold the child. Or perhaps he thinks he's rid me of such loyalties. Maybe he has. Truthfully, Nero, the baby...it all seems like some distant lost dream that I can't quite fully remember, but that feeling of having him for only a brief second is branded on my heart, in my soul, even if my mind forgets.

"He offers some much needed trade, now that the Italian has made it very difficult to move anything in and out of America." His jaw clenches and his eyes flash angrily.

"You are meeting with him?" Sasha asks.

"Yes, and you will both come with me, but first." A twisted grin pulls at his lips. "He does not believe that Anna is still alive. He wants proof of life. You will go to her, little dove, and you will cut off her little finger. She has a tattoo on it does she not? A slave number."

"Okay."

He tilts his head to the side, as though waiting for more of a reaction from me. I know he's looking for any sign of weakness, but he won't find it. I have steeled myself and prepared a long time ago for the fact that both Anna and I will probably die in here. Is it a fair sacrifice? No. But I can't save everyone, and I'm tired of trying to. If taking her finger buys her freedom, then it is a small price to pay.

"Go with her, Sasha." Nicholai hands me the key to her cell. "I want to trust you, little dove, but I will be watching. Always." He strokes my cheek and my body locks up, the urge to kill him roaring through my head like a drum beat. It's worse than ever before. The thought of human touch makes me feel sick now. Bloodlust pumps through my veins like pure adrenaline. I have to fight with every last shred of my restraint not to lash out.

He smiles and drops his hand, signaling us to go. Sasha walks beside me, and we wind down corridors until we come to the elevator. I can feel Sasha's eyes on my face as we descend, but I refuse to acknowledge him. I remain cool and calm, distanced. It's just a finger.

When we're outside her cell, I expect to feel something, a hint of anticipation or fear, but I don't. I feel nothing. The door opens and I see her huddled in the corner of her bed. Dirty blonde hair hangs in her face. A plain gray hoody and tracksuit bottoms seem to make her look paler, more sickly. Of course, this is the first time I've actually met Anna face to face since we were children. Those deep blue eyes slowly meet mine, and I see the slightest spark of hope in them. For a second, I am that thirteen-year old girl, clinging desperately to my eight-year old sister as they try and drag me away from her. I see the tears tracking down her little pink cheeks and it jolts me for a moment. But I force all those thoughts and feelings back. Right here, right now, she is nothing to me.

"Hold her down," I say.

Sasha goes over to her and pushes her down on the bed. "Una?" her voice is small and broken. I take the knife from my thigh holster and grab her wrist, forcing her palm flat against the thin mattress. "Una, please," she whispers, tears now pouring down her face.

"Lie still. This will be over soon," Sasha tells her.

I steel myself and bring the razor-sharp blade down on her finger quickly. The blade bites through bone and she screams. Blood soaks into the mattress beneath her, and I grab the blanket, wadding it up and pressing it against the wound.

"Hold this," I instruct her. She clutches it with a shaking hand as hysterical tears pour down her cheeks. I pick up the finger and walk out of the room, unable to look at her. "Get someone to stitch that," I say to Sasha.

I stand to one side of Nicholai and Sasha stands on the other. Across from us, Rafael is flanked by two of his own men. The snow is melting now, and a layer of slush covers everything. We're on the roof of an abandoned parking deck, and everything around us is bleak and gray, reminiscent of the Russian winter.

Rafael's eyes meet mine and I stare back at him, giving away absolutely nothing. His expression becomes pinched and his shoulders hunch with tension before he glances back at Nicholai. "I offer you reasonable terms, but I want proof of life."

Nicholai throws his head back on a laugh. "You are demanding for a nobody," he says arrogantly. Rafael is a powerful cartel boss, but Nicholai thinks himself a god surrounded by his Elite. "Here." He reaches into his pocket and throws something to Rafael. A plastic Ziploc bag, and in it, is Anna's finger.

The Mexican's dark brows pull into a frown as he stares at the plastic bag in his hand. "Is this a joke?"

"Of course not. See, it is fresh. Just cut this morning." Nicholai spreads his hands to the side.

"This is not proof of life," Rafael growls, and there it is, painted all over his face. He loves her. Where it once annoyed me, I now only see it as foolish because he does nothing to hide it. He exposes his weakness and Nicholai will exploit it.

Stepping closer to him, Nicholai grins. "On my honor." He places his palm to his chest. "Una cut it off herself."

Rafael's gaze swings to mine. "You did this?" he asks, his voice laced with clear accusation as he holds up the bag.

I fight with the urge to defend my actions. I can't seem too invested to Nicholai. "You wanted proof of life. Now you have it. Her finger for her freedom seems like a good trade to me." I keep my voice completely flat and indifferent. His eyes shift from me to Nicholai and back again. I see him piecing it together, trying to comprehend the woman he sees now with the woman he once met.

"She loves you," Rafael snarls.

"Love is weakness, Rafael." I cock a brow and step closer to him. "After all, look at you here, brokering non-advantageous deals, all for my sweet, little sister."

His lips pull into a small smirk, his expression otherwise shuttering before he looks at Nicholai. "Do we have a deal?"

Nicholai's head tilts to the side. "We do." I want to breathe a sigh of relief because Rafael just bought Anna's freedom. Nicholai's pieces are slowly being taken off the board, one at a time. With Nero, Anna, and my son out of play, soon it will be just him and me standing toe to toe.

CHAPTER THIRTY

Nero

I wake up to a sound, barely a whisper of noise over the baby monitor before it cuts out. My heart leaps into a sprint and I reach for the gun on the bedside table. I've always been twitchy, but having a baby, it's the kind of stress I can't even begin to explain. And seeing as Dante is wanted by that mad Russian fuck, I take no chances.

I silently leave my bedroom and stalk down the hallway, only to find George curled up right outside the nursery door. That's weird. Frowning, I carefully push the door open. The night light illuminates the shadow of a hooded figure in the room. I lift my gun and point it at them until I realize they're holding Dante, then lower it a fraction. They might as well be clutching my fucking heart in their arms. The figure turns around, and violet eyes crash into mine, eyes I see every time I look at my son. Una. My pulse rises and I release a breath that I feel like I've been holding for months. She's exactly the same and yet different, harder. A purple scar runs across her cheek bone, marring her otherwise smooth milky skin. Dark shadows linger below her eyes. She's thinner, harder with absolutely no evidence that she ever carried the baby in her arms.

"Hello, Nero." She clutches Dante tight to her chest, one hand resting lightly over the back of his head. Her eyes flick from my face to the gun, still pointed at her. "Are you going to shoot me?" I want to trust her. I want to believe that she's come back to me, but something makes me hesitate. It's been five months since she left, and four since Sasha sent Dante to me. Nicholai wouldn't just let her go. I want to trust her, but I can't trust anyone when it comes to my son, not even her.

"Why are you here?" Fuck, it's hard to be cynical with her.

She glances down at Dante and rests her cheek against his head, closing her eyes for a second. "He's so perfect," she breathes before her eyes flash open to meet mine. She moves over to the crib and gently lays Dante down. Her fingers grip the edge of the crib and her head drops forward. "I was sent to kill you and take my son. It's a test of my loyalty."

My pulse speeds and my fingers tighten around the gun. "And where is your loyalty?"

When her eyes meet mine, they're cold, but buried beneath the surface in the part of Una only I can ever see, are layers and layers of pain and torture.

"With him," she whispers, glancing over her shoulder into the crib. And like a crack ripping through a pane of glass, she breaks. Her chin drops to her chest and she grips the edge of the crib so hard, her knuckles turn white. I move closer to her and the dim light reveals tears glimmering on her cheeks. She presses her palm to her chest, rubbing at it absentmindedly. "My loyalty will always be with him."

"Morte." I reach out to her. Her entire body locks up before she sidesteps me, holding her hand out.

"Don't." Her eyes go wide, and she shakes her head. I approach her again and she backs away like a wild animal. "Nero, I don't want to hurt you."

"I'm always your exception, Morte."

"This is different. He…" A sad smile touches her lips. "I'm not sure I can come back from it this time." And fuck if that doesn't kill me a little bit. What the hell did he do to her?

"Come." I jerk my head towards the door. She hesitantly follows me out of the room and into my own. She's tense, primed as though she's about to attack, and as much as I don't doubt her loyalty to Dante, I won't risk provoking her around him. Her fingers clench and release repeatedly. Her movements are jerky, and it's almost like watching a junkie on a come down.

Four months since she had a baby and her body is as tight and honed as it was before, every inch of her shaped into the perfect weapon. She has tight black jeans on with a gun strapped to one thigh and a knife to the other. Her hood covers her blonde hair, just the way it was when I met her. I can almost pretend for a second that no time has passed at all and we're right back where we started, me and her. Enemies and allies. Wanting to both kill and fuck each other. But, of course, everything has changed. Now we have a baby, enemies, and I love her.

I linger in the middle of my room, fighting the urge to go to her. "Talk to me."

She goes to the window and stares down at the city lights below. "What did you call him?"

"Dante."

"Dante's inferno," she whispers. I walk over to her slowly. "Nero. Please." Her voice trembles and the muscles in her back tense. "I can't control it."

I brush over the narrow strip of exposed skin at her hip. My fingers barely make contact with her skin before she strikes, punching me in the gut twice and slamming her foot against the side of my knee. My back hits the floor and she's right there on top of me, the knife in her hand, the blade pressed to my throat. She's breathing heavy, eyes wild in a way I've never seen before. It's like she's not even here.

"Morte."

Her teeth clench and the blade bites against my skin. If I touch her again, I think she's going to slit me open and leave me to bleed, so I do the only thing I can. I fight. Bringing my arm inside hers, I knock her hand to the side and toss her off me, landing on top of her. Her legs go around my waist and she squeezes tight, pressing on my kidneys hard. She punches me in the jaw twice before I manage to pin her wrists above her head. She thrashes and snarls like something possessed, as though she's in physical pain. "Una, look at me. Look at me!" Her eyes snap to mine, savage and turbulent. "Focus on me, remember me."

She throws her head back and a ragged cry slips from her throat. "Please," she begs. Fuck, why do I feel like I'm hurting her? What the fuck did he do to her?

"Morte, I'm not going to hurt you. I love you." Tears slowly trickle down her temples and I gently touch my forehead to hers, inhaling that familiar vanilla and gun oil scent of hers. She stills, her body occasionally convulsing as though I'm electrocuting her. I hate this. I hate that he's done this to her. I hate that she willingly allowed him to do this to us.

Slowly, carefully, I touch my lips to hers. She stills, her lips parting slightly. I kiss her harder and she bites my bottom lip. When I pull back and she manages to free one hand, punching me again. Motherfuck. I grab her by the throat and pin her to the floor. There was a time when we were always like this, when love was a war, and the only way to get past her defenses was to fight her. Maybe we just need to go back to square one.

Her eyes flash between wanting to kill me and wanting to kiss me, and in its own sick and twisted way, it's hot. "Always so strong, Morte," I breathe against her ear. "But you will break for me, the same way you always do." My fingers tighten on her throat and she grips my jaw, raking her nails over my face hard enough to draw blood. I hiss out a breath and yank her hoody over her head before flipping her onto her front. "Tell me you want this," I say.

She rests her head against her forearm. "I don't want to hurt you."

"Ah, but I live for your brand of violence, my love." I remove her knife and gun. "Do you trust me?"

There's a beat of silence. "Yes."

"Good." I pin her down by the back of her neck and she goes fucking rabid. Once again, she bucks and snarls, her fingers clawing at the carpet as she tries to break free. The strap of her tank top slips from her shoulder and I press my body over hers, brushing my lips over the exposed skin. She continues to fight me, and I keep on holding her, even as her breaths grow ragged, and her muscles tighten. I kiss up the side of her neck, over her back. It takes a long time, but slowly, bit by bit, she relaxes, and I loosen my grip on her. I trail my hands over her sides and slowly push her tank up, watching her every reaction as I kiss up her spine gently. She shivers, and I smile, gripping her hips and flipping her over again. Her eyes meet mine, still wild, but calmer, more in control.

"What will it be, Morte? Kill me or kiss me?"

"Both," she whispers, that single word so tormented. "Always both." Fuck, I missed her. I slam my mouth over hers, and she clings to me, her body softening under my touch. Nicholai will never have her. Una is mine, and she will always be mine. He may think her a weapon and, in many ways, she is, but this right here, this is something she gives only me, and I will remind her of it a thousand times over if I have to

She reaches down, tentatively gliding her palms over my body. Her hands are once again, calloused and rough, and it makes me groan. My vicious queen, scars bared. I nip at her jaw and she twists her head to the side, allowing me more access. I yank the button of her jeans open, dragging them and her underwear down her legs. She watches me, a hint of violence in her eyes, the threat lingering just below the surface.

"Are you thinking about all the ways you'd like to hurt me?" I smirk. She opens her mouth to speak, but I grab her around the throat, pulling her close until our lips are touching. "You can't. You've already done your worst."

Her eyes close, brows pulling together in a small frown. "I'm sorry." I push her back on the floor, and she reaches for my boxers, shoving them down my thighs. She holds onto me tightly, as though she's afraid to let go, and when I push inside her, she's right there with me, enraptured by every second. There are so many elements to Una, I'm not sure I'll ever truly know all of them, but as I stare at her, I feel like I know her better than I know myself. And I want all of her. Every beautifully fucked up part. She is perfectly ruined. My vicious little butterfly, my savage queen, my love.

She throws her head back on a moan, and I swipe my tongue up the column of her exposed throat. Her body bows towards me, hips rolling with every thrust. She feels like home, like everything is right as long as we have this, as long as I have her. I fuck her slow and deep, and I watch her fall apart for me the way she always does, baring herself to me. The lioness exposing her jugular. Her body tightens and her nails claw down my back in a burning trail. I grit my teeth because she feels so good and it's been so long. She lets out a long moan. I drop my head forward, kissing her and growling against her lips as I come. "I will always be your exception," I say through heavy breaths.

"Always," she whispers. "I love you."

I lift my face from her neck and lock eyes with her. "You are mine, Morte. He will never have you."

CHAPTER THIRTY-ONE

Una

I jolt awake and take a moment to realize where I am. Neros' bed. Sleeping next to him almost seemed like a dream to me. The first whispers of morning light trickle through the darkness, painting the room in tones of gray. I glance over at Nero, his dark lashes casting shadows over his cheekbones. His face is something I thought I had committed to memory, and five months isn't that long, but I had started to forget just how beautiful he is. A stray lock of dark hair falls over his forehead and it makes him look a little unruly.

The slightest noise comes from somewhere in the house and I turn away from Nero, silently climbing out of bed and leaving the room. I go to the nursery and open the door, walking over to Dante. He's wide awake, his stumpy little legs thrashing around as he stares up at me with eyes the exact same shade as my own. His head is covered in a downy layer of dark hair that's sticking up in every direction. Smiling, I lean down and scoop him up, bringing his tiny body against mine. It's as though every frayed nerve, every broken facet of me all comes together, healing under his innocent touch. He makes me feel whole. He gives me purpose. I kiss his soft hair, inhaling the scent of him, a smell that is unlike anything else in this world.

We go downstairs and I hold him while I make coffee. George lingers around my feet, wagging his tail excitedly. I open the fridge and stare at bottles of formula. There's some kind of machine sitting on the kitchen side, but I have no idea what to do with it. A wave of sadness hits me because I've missed all this. I don't even know how to care for him. Dante makes this noise and then he's crying, well, more like wailing.

"Shh, stop. It's okay." I'm frantically glancing around for something that might make him stop when Nero appears in the doorway, his thick arms folded over his bare chest and a small smirk on his lips.

"He's a grouchy fuck in the mornings."

I hold Dante out to him, and he takes him from me. I smile at the two of them with matching bed hair. Nero and I are naturally drawn to each other's blood thirsty nature, but he's never been sexier than he is holding that baby.

"What does he want?" I ask.

"He wants what all guys want, to eat and take a shit."

I wrinkle my nose. "Gross."

"Or in his case, he shit his pants and now he's not happy about it. Isn't that right, dude?" Nero lifts Dante, shaking his head at Dante's little, scrunched up, squalling face. "Be back in a second. Can you put a bottle in the machine for a few minutes?"

He disappears and I'm left staring at the contraption, feeling completely useless.

A little while later and Nero comes back, handing me Dante again. I take him and Nero smiles down at him before he goes to that stupid machine, putting the bottle in it. I move closer, taking note of how it works. His lips pull up in a wry smile. "Guns are much easier."

He reaches for me, gripping my hips and pulling me between his legs. My muscles bunch and tighten reflexively, but it's nothing compared to my usual reaction to being touched. He strokes my hair back off my face and I tentatively scratch my nails over the stubble of his jaw. His lips brush the inside of my wrist and my skin tingles in response. The small but intimate contact feels like a fire after I've been living in the freezing cold. He steps closer to me, pressing Dante between our bodies.

"I missed you, Morte."

I missed him as well. More than I can say. I tilt my chin up, brushing my lips over his. He kisses me, trailing his fingers to the back of my neck and pulling me close. This feels right and strong. It feels like everything I'm fighting for. Dante starts to fidget, letting out a high-pitched squeal. I pull away from Nero and glance down at the tiny person.

"Way to cock block me kid." Nero turns around and removes the bottle from the machine. He splashes a bit of milk on his wrist and then hands it to me. "All yours."

I take a seat at the breakfast bar and cradle Dante in one arm, holding the bottle in front of him. He sucks loudly and I can't help but smile as I watch him.

"This is the way it should have been," Nero says quietly. I look up at him. He has his elbows braced on the breakfast bar, clasping a cup of coffee as he watches us.

"How did you do this? Where did you learn how to take care of a baby?"

"Tommy's mom has been helping." He shrugs. "And the rest, you kind of learn as you go." To think there was a time when I thought he wouldn't want a baby, when I was going to deprive him of being a father. In the tiny glimpse I've had of them together, I can see that Nero is an amazing father. It brings me more relief than I can say. If I fail to kill Nicholai, if I die, Dante will have everything he needs in Nero.

"I don't want to leave him."

"Then don't." Something dark and volatile crosses Nero's eyes. "Stay here. Turn your back on this idea."

"Nero, it's been five months. I gave up the first four months of Dante's life so that I could keep him safe and remove Nicholai. I'm so close."

He puts his coffee down and places his palms flat on the breakfast bar. The muscles of his torso flex and roll as he shifts, the ink on his arms seeming to dance over his skin with every move. "We are stronger together. Look at what he's done to you!"

"I just need more time."

"Do you know what it's like? Not knowing what he's doing to you? Not knowing whether you'll come back alive?"

"You forget who I am." I say the words, but the assured arrogance I once spoke them with is gone. Any pride I once harbored in who I was is long gone.

"No! I do not fucking forget. But by the time he's done with you, will I know who you are? Will you?"

"Yes," I respond. Nero and I, we are unbreakable. The things Nicholai has done to me...Nero should be nothing more than a distant memory. Dante, more like a dream. I should have been able to kill Nero and instead, he brings me back, he grounds me the same way he always has.

"You are his prize toy, and if he thinks he can't have you, no one will."

I put the nearly empty bottle down on the counter. Standing up, I round the bar and hand Nero Dante. He takes him, throwing a dish cloth over his shoulder before pressing his palm to Dante's back and hugging him close. Never did a man look so out of place and yet completely at home with something so fragile in his arms. My son in the arms of my monster. There's nowhere else I'd rather him be. "Please trust me, Nero." I push up on tiptoes, kissing him quickly and then the back of Dante's head. "I am his weakness. I blind him."

"If anything happens to you, I will slaughter the bratva piece by piece until there is nothing left." That violence I love so much swirls in his eyes, threatening to spill over.

"I have a plan. I need your help."

"Ah, Morte, tell me what you need and it will be done." Of course it will, because he's Nero Verdi. Nicholai thinks himself invincible because no one can stand against him, but I haven't unveiled my secret weapon yet. I haven't unleashed my monster. Nicholai has no idea what we are capable of.

The entire drive from the airport to base, I think through the plan in my head. This will work. This has to work. Part of me wants to turn around and go back to Nero, to let him face this fight with me, but I can't. I have risked everything to take Nicholai down, and I will succeed, or die trying. This will be the legacy that I leave my son.

They allow me straight through the compound gates and when I pull into the vehicle bay, Nicholai is there, waiting. His hands are clasped behind his back, his suit as immaculate as ever.

"Little dove. I see you are disappointingly empty handed," he says as I approach.

I force myself back into that cold unfeeling place as far away from Nero and Dante as possible. "The child was not there."

"Oh? And is Nero Verdi dead?" Those ice-cold eyes fix with mine, looking for any minute trace of deception.

"Verdi has sent the child away for protection." The lie slips easily from my lips as I stare unblinkingly at him. "I gained his trust to ascertain information. He is not dead. I may yet have use of him."

He tilts his head, and it reminds me of a predator assessing prey. "He is in love with you."

"Yes."

"And he believes you in love with him?"

"Yes."

"And where is the child?"

"With Rafael D'Cruze."

"He sent the child to your sister." He laughs, clapping his hands together. "And what did you tell him, little dove?"

"I told him that he needs to forget me. I said I would ensure the child's safety but that this is my place." Have I always sounded so robotic and cold?

"Good. This is good." There's an edge to his voice, and I know he doesn't trust me. If I were any other soldier he would have put a bullet in my head the second I came back. Nicholai would have written anyone else off as defective. I'm only standing here because of his favor.

"Do you know the exact location of the child?"

"Yes. He is being kept in Rafael's compound near the border," I relay the location Nero and I picked. "But we must move quickly. I do not think he trusts me."

"You and Sasha will assemble a team. You will go to Mexico and retrieve the child. Kill Rafael D'Cruze. And kill your sister." He lifts a brow to drive the point home.

On a nod, I start to turn away.

"And little dove?" I pause. "I will come with you to Mexico. I do not trust you to do what must be done." If he weren't so blinded by his obsession with me, he wouldn't trust me at all. Perhaps in his own twisted way he loves me. After all, they say love is blind. He wants so badly to believe that I am once again his loyal, favored daughter, that he ignores what is right in front of him. How could my loyalty possibly be to him when my child is out there? If he had children, if he knew what that love feels like, Nicholai would not trust me. But his obsessive, sick version of love leads him to his own destruction. It will be me, his precious daughter who rips out his heart.

I'm so close I can almost smell his blood tinging the air. The game is so nearly over.

CHAPTER THIRTY-TWO

Una

Humid heat clings to my skin, wrapping around me as Sasha and I make our way to the car. He gets in the driver's side and I hop in beside him. Three Elite climb in the back with rifles in hand. The sun is just starting to drop below the ragged horizon of Juarez in the distance. The address we're going to is Rafael's mansion, a few miles outside of the city.

Nicholai insisted that we land and go straight in before anyone could get word of our presence to the cartel. The city is a mess of graffiti-covered buildings, pothole filled roads, and general disarray. This is cartel country, where the daily number of murders is higher than some countries have in a year. These streets may look like a city of people going about their business, but it's a war zone with the cartels continuously fighting for ground.

Our convoy of cars winds through the streets that lead out of the city, dropping into a valley that runs between the ragged dusty hills of the Mexican countryside. We come to a stop on a dirt road about a mile from Rafael's main gate. We get out and go to the back of the car, arming ourselves with weapons. Sasha's gaze meets mine and he gives me the tiniest nod.

Altogether we have twenty Elite, which is more than I hoped Nicholai would bring, but I'll roll with the punches. Nicholai gets out of the car behind ours, his suit no less appropriate for the dusty desert of Mexico than it is the icy expanse of Russia. He glances around his assembled soldiers, all clad in black and armed to the teeth. "Your mission is to go into the compound and retrieve the child. Kill everyone." Cold eyes meet mine, and I know he's making a point, because everyone includes Anna. "Do not fail me," he says without looking away from me.

We turn and start jogging towards the compound. Sasha and I are running point. The rest of the soldiers follow us. The sun beats down on us and sweat trickles down my back as we make our way up to the villa. As soon as we near the perimeter fence, we take cover behind a small rise of earth.

"Guards," Sasha says to me.

One of the others hands me a made-up rifle and I pull the stand down, resting it on the top of the ridge. Staring down the sights, I line up both guards, focusing the crosshair just to the left of the first guy's shoulder. I have to be accurate here. Deep breath in, hold, squeeze—squeeze. Two shots fire off in quick succession and both guards go down. The shots have more cartel soldiers rushing towards the gates, and I fire at them too, watching them drop one by one.

"Move," I shout. Sasha leads the band of Elite to the front gate, breaching the compound. This is where it gets complicated. "You two," I signal to two of the Elite. "With me." Sasha nods as he continues on with the rest of the group. I take the two and split off, moving through the house until I find the stairway that leads to the first floor. Reaching in my front pocket, I quickly screw a silencer onto my gun. My senses attune to the two men walking behind me; every muted footfall, every drawn breath. We reach the top of the stairs and walk down the hall, passing a couch scattered with cushions. I whirl around, yanking the knife from my thigh holster and throwing it at the same time as I grab one of the cushions, shoving it against the face of the guy on the left. I knock him off balance just enough that he staggers to the wall. I spot the flash of steel and bow my body away from him just as I press the gun against the cushion and pull the trigger. A muted pop sounds. The tip of the knife nicks across the skin of my stomach before his body falls to the floor. I sigh at the blood seeping through my tank top and before retrieving my knife from the other guy's skull.

Following Rafael's instructions, I find the last door at the end of the hall. Rafael's office. He's not here, but the windows have a full view all around the compound. My mission right now is simple: remove the Elite and clear the compound. I tried to persuade Sasha to turn them, bring them to our side, but it was too risky. We couldn't let anyone know that we weren't with Nicholai. Elite loyalties run deep where he's concerned.

I glance out each of the windows until I spot the group of four Elite crossing the courtyard, guns raised. Resting my rifle on the windowsill, I line up the shot. All four of them are down within two seconds. All that training, all those years of fighting, and they didn't even have the dignity of a decent death. They died as they lived, as cannon fodder for a mad man. Six down. Fourteen more to go.

CHAPTER THIRTY-THREE

Nero

I drum my fingers over the steering wheel and glance at the clock on the dashboard. Gio fiddles with the buttons for the air conditioning, tugging at the collar of his shirt. The sun glares off the hood of the car and I squint into the rear-view mirror at the car parked behind me. On cue, a cloud of dust kicks up from the valley below us. I pick up the binoculars and watch the convoy of black Range Rovers wind along the empty desert road, their tinted windows hiding their occupants. They pull over to the shoulder and all the doors open, soldiers clad in black climbing out and arming themselves. Sasha and Una stand at the head of what must be twenty Elite.

"Fuck, that's a lot of Elite," I murmur, a wave of unease creeping through me. It's too many.

"How many?" Gio asks.

"Maybe twenty."

"I'll go tell Rafael." The door opens and hot, dusty air fills the cabin.

I adjust the binoculars and smile when the back door of the second Range Rover opens and Nicholai Ivanov himself steps out. Una said he would come, but I didn't believe it. He's known for his sharp intellect and his strategic skill, but this—coming here—surely he's not that arrogant? He's completely exposed, ripe for the picking. Even with his Elite…this is cartel country. And, of course, he couldn't possibly predict what Sasha and Una are about to do to his precious Elite, or maybe he could have, if he weren't so obsessed with Una and the idea of having her child. It's exactly as she said; he's blinded by her. He'll never even see her coming.

The band of Elite disperse, heading up the hillside and leaving Nicholai alone with only two Elite to protect him. Stupid. So very stupid. The door opens and Gio gets back in.

"He's here. Only two guards with him," I say.

"This seems too easy."

I toss the binoculars in the glove compartment. "I'm not sure whether it's a trap, or he really is that sure of his force."

"It seems to go against his nature, but then he did come deep into Rafael's territory once before to get Anna."

This is too good of an opportunity. Sasha would have warned us if they'd brought more force. Una might be kept in the dark, but not Sasha.

"Lets go." I glance in the rear-view mirror, meeting Rafael's hard gaze as he sits behind the wheel of the car behind. Anna is beside him in the passenger seat, despite me telling him that Una wouldn't like it. Apparently, he thinks she's safest where he can keep an eye on her. If only Una were so easy to control. I start the engine and pull away, sending the Hummer down the steep hillside, kicking up dust and rubble in its wake.

I give it to Rafael, he has all the best kit. Armor plated Hummers with mounted .50 Cal gun's on the roof. One of his men is hanging out the sunroof, ready to open fire on the Russian and his beloved soldiers. He has instructions not to kill Nicholai though. Una deserves that honor.

As soon as we're on flat ground, we're flooring it towards the parked Range Rovers. The two soldiers move in front of Nicholai, firing bullets at the car. Shots ping off the hood and I slam my foot over the accelerator. When they realize that their bullets aren't doing shit, they run for the car, ushering Nicholai inside.

Gio reaches back and taps the knee of the guy with the big ass gun. He opens fire, the bullets leaving golf-ball-sized holes in the body work of one of the parked Ranger Rovers.

"Damn, I need one of these cars."

"Might be a bit conspicuous in New York," Gio shouts over the deafening *bang, bang, bang* of gunfire. The Range Rover screeches away, heading into the desert, and I follow. Rafael pulls up beside me. Bullets spray the back of the Range Rover, shattering the glass and tearing holes through the body work until one tire explodes. The car veers violently to the side, fishtailing before skidding sideways and tipping. It rolls over several times before coming to a stop on its wheels again. Palming my .40 Cal, I throw the door open. Gio and Rafael fall in beside me. I shoot the injured Elite slumped against the steering wheel. The other one already looks dead. Rafael goes to the back door, bracing his hand over the handle as he watches me. With a nod from me, he wrenches the door open and Nicholai falls out of the car. I'm sure he's dead, before he groans and attempts to crawl across the floor.

If it were up to me, I'd tie him to the tow bar and drag him back to that villa for Una to end, but he might die on the way and she needs to be the one to kill him. He has taken more from her than anyone. I kick him in the gut hard enough that he lands on his back, gasping for air. His suit is covered in dust and blood trickles from his nose, pouring down his chin.

"Nicholai Ivanov." I smile and yank him from the dusty ground. He sways and Gio grabs his arm, holding him up. "How the mighty have fallen."

"Nero Verdi," he says and then laughs. "And Refael D'Cruze. You both reach too far. You will die before you reach the border."

Rafael laughs, toting a rifle over his shoulder casually.

"Who's going to stop us?" I raise a brow and cup my ear, tilting my head. "I don't hear anything. Oh, wait. That's because no one is coming. You are all out of allies, Nicholai."

His teeth clench. "I need no allies. I have an army. My Elite will end you, and your child will be mine."

My fingers flinch, wanting to grab my gun. Instead I punch him in the gut hard enough that a breath wheezes past his lips. Gio holds him up and I cup the back of his neck, bringing my lips to his ear. "Your Elite are dying as we speak. Killed by your own...your best. After all, you did make Una quite formidable." I step back and his cold eyes flash with rage.

"I made her strong. I made her the best..."

"You fucking broke her!" I shout, my temper spiking before I manage to fight it back. "But you're right, Nicholai. You made her strong." I search that soulless gaze and notice the drop of seat that rolls down his temple. "Strong enough to put an end to you."

A sick grin spreads across his lips. "Una is mine. She will always be what I made her."

"That's where you're wrong. Una is mine. And you're about to see what happens when you try and take what's fucking mine." I nod at Gio and he drags him towards the car before I break my word and kill him right here. Gio shoves him inside next to our gunman who is now sitting on the back seat, pointing a pistol at him.

Rafael comes to stand beside me, a smile pulling at his lips. "I can't wait to see this."

My vicious little queen will finally get her revenge.

CHAPTER
THIRTY-FOUR

Una

The distant sound of gunfire fills the house, but I don't know who's winning. The simple fact is, a band of Elite are not easily taken down. The office door flies open, and I swing my gun towards Sasha. He frowns at me, impatience written all over his blood-spattered features. "Come.'

I push to my feet, swinging the rifle over my shoulder. We descend the stairs and I follow him out of the villa. The cobble stone courtyard is surrounded by flowers, and the scent of night jasmine catches on the hot desert breeze.

Rafael's guards that I 'shot' come to stand with us as the main gate is opened, allowing two Hummers to cruise into the courtyard. The windows are completely blacked out, heavy duty guns mounted on their roofs. Sasha is rigid beside me and I can practically feel the tension pouring from him. I know this is hard for him. His loyalties aren't as black and white as my own.

The passenger side door to one of the hummers opens, and Nero climbs from it. He's wearing gray suit pants and a black shirt, open at the collar. With his Ray Bans and his perfect face, he looks like he should be in the pages of a magazine rather than here, in a cartel compound, participating in a mafia war. Gio gets out of the driver's side and Rafael climbs out of the other car, followed by Anna. Her long, blonde hair catches in the wind, and she folds her arms over her body, staying close to Rafael's side. I lock eyes with my sister, and she offers me a small smile. Apparently, I'm forgiven for cutting off her finger.

"Now that everyone's here..." Nero opens the back door of the car and drags out Nicholai. His suit is rumpled and dirty as though he's been rolling around in the dirt. His nose is bloody, and the man who always seemed so strong and invincible is now very far from that reality.

I'm seeing it with my own eyes, but it doesn't quite seem real. We put this plan into play, but I always thought that he would somehow see it coming, that he would outmaneuver us the way he has done to so many others. But he was blinded by his own desperation, his own demented obsession, and in the end, it was his obsession with Dante that brought him to this point. He broke his own rules, and instead of going after a vulnerable, helpless child from an orphanage he chose the child of two of the most feared people in the world. Stupid.

That icy blue gaze of his meets mine before shifting to my side. "You," he says to Sasha, voice layered in accusation and disappointment. "I gave you both everything."

Me, he wanted to trust, but didn't quite. Sasha...well Sasha was the unfailingly loyal, prodigal son. Until he watched me— the best of the Elite—fall. Until he witnessed my love for Dante. It changed him. So, when Nicholai asked him to gather intelligence on whether my son was indeed in Rafael's possession, Nicholai never doubted it. It was too perfect.

I take a deep breath and step in front of Sasha, knowing that this weighs more heavily on him than it does me. "You gave us nothing. You took everything." I feel nothing but cold indifference as I approach him, aware all eyes are on us. Nero's presence is the strength I need, but he leans against the car, standing back, allowing me this.

I circle Nicholai, kicking him hard enough to send him to his knees. Grabbing his jaw, I force him to look at the four bodies of the fallen Elite I shot, scattered haphazardly over the courtyard. "Do you know why you are here, Nicholai?"

He says nothing, fighting against my hold. I grip the top of his head and threaten to snap his neck. "You are here, on your knees, because you were arrogant. You believed yourself invincible, protected by your army. Protected by your children." Releasing him, I walk over to Sasha who hands me two knives. They clatter to the cobblestones when I toss them in front of Nicholai. "Pick them up." I crack my neck from side to side as I pace a few feet towards Nero and back again. "Fucking pick them up!" I shout when he doesn't respond.

"So you can kill me and call it a fair fight?" he says.

A low rumble of laughter comes from Nero. "Nothing could make that a fair fight. You will die, undoubtedly."

"You took my child from me and then forced me to fight some of your best only days later." Anger is threatening to consume me and the urge to just shoot him in the face is strong. I squeeze my eyes shut, remembering the moment he turned his back on me, leaving me strapped to a bed while he walked away with my baby. "So now you will fight your best, Nicholai. You will know what it is to fight for your life."

His eyes meet mine for the briefest moment and then his jaw clenches. I smile when he grabs the knives and charges me. No finesse, no skill. My feet remain planted until the very last second, when I catch his arm and twist it behind his back. The satisfying crack of bone rings out over his roar of pain. The knife slips from his grasp and I catch it, slamming it deep into his shoulder. His pain echoes in my ears, his screams a symphony of sweet revenge.

He spins, slashing wildly with the remaining knife, his movements nothing more than the desperate efforts of a man who knows his fate is sealed. I easily divulge him of his remaining blade, imbedding it into his other shoulder. And the screams grow, higher and higher, reaching a crescendo the likes of which I've never heard with a clean kill. This is not clean. Killing has always been an easy skill for me. I enjoy it because I'm good at it, but it's just a job. I don't make my victims suffer. This…this isn't a job, and I want him to suffer like I've never wanted to hurt anyone before.

He sways on his feet, blood pouring from both shoulders as he glares at me. "The Bratva will hunt you, little dove," he says through a grimace.

"I don't think they will. After all, with you dead, their guns and drugs will once again run freely." I grasp the hilts of both blades, yanking them out and slicing them in front of me, lightning fast. His stomach splits open in a cross from ribs to hip. He collapses to the ground, gasping and twitching like a dying fish.

I crouch down next to him. "Goodbye, Nicholai." My blade finds home in his throat, deep enough to sever the spinal cord. That final tell-tale breath leaves his lungs and I fall back on the ground, staring at his lifeless body. Lifting my face, I look around at all the people watching, all the people he hurt. Families ruined, children broken. This was what he deserved. This was justice. And finally…I'm finally free.

EPILOGUE
Nero

One month later

A plume of smoke rises as I extinguish my cigarette in the ash tray. I push up from my desk and turn off the lamp. I've been up late dealing with the fallout of Nicholai's death, handling Cesare and the Russians. It seems they're willing to call it quits if we let them trade their guns in our territory. Cesare agreed to it, so for now I have to go with it…at least while the old man still breathes.

I climb the stairs and check in on Dante the same way I always do on my way to bed. Tonight though, I find Una sitting in the armchair in the corner of the room, Dante cradled in her arms.

Her dark clothing blends with the shadows as though she were born from them.

I didn't even hear her come in. Her and Sasha went out for a job earlier, a 'quick hit' as she calls it. Once a killer, always a killer. They get paid well and it feeds her bloodthirsty nature. But fucking Sasha will not use the elevator because he says, and I quote: It's an ambush waiting to happen. In a private elevator. He insists they use the stairs and has somehow bypassed my alarm. He and Una move like ghosts, so I never know when either of them is going to just pop up.

Una's knuckles are split open. Blood splatters adorn her neck, streaking through her white-blonde ponytail. My bloodstained queen, cradling her innocent child. Dante's cheek is pressed to her chest, lips parted as he breathes heavily. One step is all it takes to have a .40 Cal pointed at my head in the blink of an eye. Of course. Una's palm covers the side of Dante's face as though she would protect his ears from the gun shot.

"Are you ever going to stop pointing guns at me?"

She tilts her head to the side before tucking the gun beneath the cushions again. "Don't creep up on me like that."

"It's not creeping." I carefully take -more like pry - Dante from her. She lets him sleep on her every night, even though he sleeps just fine on his own. My guess is she's making up for lost time. I lay him in his crib, and he doesn't even stir. He sleeps like the dead, and I hope he always does. I hope he never has a care in the world. With Una for a mother, he'll always be protected, sheltered from the dangers of this world.

"You can't sleep in his room for the rest of his life, Morte."

"Watch me."

I laugh. "Come on."

She gets up, glancing longingly at Dante before she finally follows me out of the nursery. She whistles for George and he trots up the stairs before curling up right in front of Dante's crib. That damn dog is almost as attached to him as he is to Una. She insists he sleeps with Dante for protection. What the fuck that dog is going to protect him from, I don't know.

As soon as our bedroom door closes, I pick Una up, pinning her against the wall. Her fingers thread through my hair, tugging hard as I kiss down the length of her neck, groaning as I inhale the scent of vanilla and gun oil mixed with the metallic twang of blood. It's fucking hot. I still when I feel the cool kiss of steel at my neck and pull back, cocking a brow. A twisted smile plays over her lips. "Don't do it," I warn.

Those violet eyes flash, lust and violence roaring to the surface. Without breaking eye contact, she drags the blade along my collar bone. I hiss out a breath as she brings it to her lips and licks the blade.

"Oh, you just love to fucking push me." I yank her away from the wall and throw her on the bed.

She smiles because she's just as fucking depraved as I am. My perfect match, my other half, my vicious little butterfly. My broken, savage queen. There's no one else who could possibly stand beside me but her.

"I love you," she says, her eyes bright and cheeks flushed.

I press my forehead to hers. "I fucking love you, Morte."

She may have started as a pawn in a game, but now, she is the crowned queen. She is that which I treasure most. She is my happiness. Even monsters can find a happily ever after.

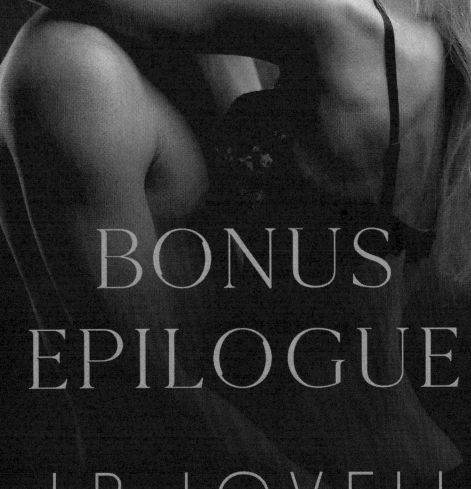

BONUS EPILOGUE

LP LOVELL

EPILOGUE

Two Years Later

Bitter wind whips around me. The snow beneath my knees melts, soaking through my jeans as I focus through the binoculars at tonight's mission; a non-descript grey building hunkered within the other snow-covered businesses in the commercial district. It's just a few miles outside Moscow, almost hiding in plain sight. From the outside, it looks like a pharmaceutical supply company. It's a good front, a reasonable excuse for the guards on the door, but I know they're Elite from the way they're dressed. This facility isn't a military base though. Our intel suggests it's another lab. This isn't where soldiers are trained, it's where they are created. My son may have been an obsession for Nicholai, but little did we know that the idea of breeding soldiers was not a new one. We've already shut down two exactly like this one.

Two years, and every time I think we've destroyed all the Elite bases, another pops up. Nicholai is long dead, but the bratva weren't willing to let go of his legacy. A lot of the facilities simply moved below ground. My guess, his Elite army were an attractive prospect to someone. The bratva certainly isn't short of power-hungry madmen.

Sasha's voice crackles over my coms. "Move. Now."

Lowering the binoculars, I shift my stare through the sights of my rifle. Two quick shots and the guards are down. One more takes out the gunman on the roof. Then Sasha moves in with a team of Italians we picked specifically for these jobs. Nero doesn't give a shit about rescuing children, but he does care for dismantling anything left of Nicholai. For me, this is personal. I swing my rifle over my shoulder and push to my feet, cutting across the empty top level of the parking deck. Three flights of stairs down, and I'm crossing the quiet street beneath the orange glow of a street light. With the businesses all closed for the night, my boots crunching through snow is the only sound in the eerie silence of deep winter. As soon as I'm inside the building, the steady pop of gunfire greets me. Bodies already litter the floor in the lobby, and I skirt around them on my way to the elevator at the opposite side of the room.

It descends several levels before the doors open on carnage. More bodies, gunshots, blood.

I find Sasha in a control room just off the main corridor, hunched over a computer, hacking their data systems. It's the easiest way to document everything and trace the women and children being kept here.

"I just need a minute to get through the firewall," Sasha mumbles, his fingers flying over the keyboard.

"Hurry it up. I want to go home."

He spares me a cold glance. "Yes, you have a wedding to prepare for."

"No, I've just been here freezing my ass off for a week already." And I miss Dante. And Nero.

"You're going soft."

I ignore him, because he's right, instead stepping out of the room.

Moving down the corridor, I clutch my gun. The cinder block of the walls gives way to glass. I stop beside the window, staring into a room full of plastic cribs, all lined up in rows. As soon as I push open the door, the high-pitch wails of babies crying filters in. There was a time when the noise would have irritated me, now all I can think is that I've never heard Dante cry like that. He's never had to. I've seen enough security footage from these facilities to know how they operate. These babies are left here, expected to be soldiers. Their basic needs are met, but they're never held, never comforted, and it cracks my cold heart. Even Nero doesn't truly understand my misplaced morality when it comes to the job I've tasked myself with.

I pass the cribs, each child wrapped in an indistinctive white blanket which somehow strips them of all identity, and I finally come to a stop beside the crib in the far back corner. The baby's face is red, mouth open as though trying to cry, but only a hoarse sound comes out. An identification number, 213, is printed on the tag around a chubby ankle. Sex and date of birth. Female, only two months old. The urge to soothe her pain is a poignant jab in my chest. Scooping the child up, I bring her to my chest and after a few seconds, she quiets. I wonder if Nicholai ordered these children deprived of human touch from birth. It would make the touch conditioning more effective. The thought has me pressing my palm firmly against the baby's back.

"You'll be okay, little one." When I glance at her face, I still. Indigo blue eyes blink up at me; the exact same shade as Dante's. Something stirs in my chest, this unexplainable pull, a knowing... My pulse rages against my eardrums so hard, I barely hear Sasha approach.

"Una, you need to see something."

I know exactly what he's going to say. I can feel who and what this baby is to me. Words get stuck in my throat before finally coming out in a strangled rasp. "I know."

He holds an open file in front of my face, the identification number 213 is printed at the top of the page. And there's only one other detail I can focus on. Mother: Una Ivanov. Father: 001011. Just a soldier.

"I..." I look to Sasha, unsure what to do, what to feel. She's mine, biologically at least. But I knew that, was drawn to comfort this child before I even picked her up. It shouldn't shock me. This is what Nicholai did, and even now, his effects are still far-reaching. He harvested eggs from my own sister when he had her. We found her daughter, Violet, in a facility last year. It stands to reason that he'd do the same to me. I was in a coma for weeks before I had Dante. They could have done anything to me, taken anything from me. But in two years, we've never found a child of mine. I had hoped... I don't know what I hoped. That no child of mine would ever suffer in a place like this. How many of my children could be out there?

"Do not think about the possibilities, Una." Of course, Sasha knows exactly where my mind is going. He's logical like that.

My arms tighten around the child. "Let's go." I stride from the room, Sasha following silently. We have teams in place to handle everything. The children will go to orphanages. Raphael and Anna will take in and help the women who have been trafficked, and the facility itself will be destroyed, bringing me one step closer to ending the nightmare that embodied my entire life.

I press my lips to the little girl's downy head. "I promise, no one will ever hurt you or abandon you again, *sladkiy*." It's a promise I will keep if it kills me, and I have no idea where that will leave me with Nero. All I know is, I owe this child a life.

When the plane lands in New York, Tommy stands waiting on the runway. A briny scent drifts off the dark waters of the Hudson River, and what once seemed so foreign, is now a reminder of home. As instructed, Tommy put a baby carrier in the back of the SUV. I don't miss his confused expression as he opens the door and waits for me to secure the child.

"Did you tell Nero?" I ask before I close the door and head to the passenger side.

He sinks behind the wheel and shakes his head. "You told me not to."

"Good."

"Is this one of those things where I don't tell him and he kicks my ass?"

"No." I turn my attention to the window, watching the New York city skyline pass in the distance.

"I'm not even going to ask," he grumbles.

My stomach clenches with nerves as we creep toward The Hamptons. Nero and I are supposed to be getting married in three days. We're happy, we know who and what we are. We have Dante. And I'm about to throw a huge wrench in the works because Nero only likes his own child. He hasn't softened at all where anyone else's are concerned.

After half an hour of driving through the darkness, Tommy pulls through the guarded front gate of the mansion that was once Arnaldo's. The house we now call home. Light spills through the windows, illuminating the perfectly manicured lawn.

The baby is still sound asleep as I remove the carrier from the backseat and make my way inside. I don't generally feel fear, but as approach Nero's office, it's very real. It's fear of the unknown, of potentially having to make a choice.

When I step over the threshold, Nero looks up from his desk, the phone pressed to his ear. His gaze shifts from me to the carrier at my side.

"That's fine, Gio," he says. "Let me know what you decide." Then he hangs up, tossing the phone on the desk. "Morte. I missed you."

I remain near the door, stumbling over the words I should say. When I don't move or speak, Nero pushes to his feet and approaches, brows tightly knitted together. "What's wrong?"

I meet his dark gaze when his fingers brush my cheek. "She's mine."

The words settle on his face before his attention drops to the tiny creature sleeping, so blissfully unaware of how messed up her short life has already been.

"I won't abandon her." My voice is stronger than I expected, despite what feels like a ball of jagged thorns in my gut. I didn't carry her the way I did Dante, but she's no less my child. I feel her, like part of my soul. But she's not Nero's child, and he's beyond sentimental charity. "It's a lot to ask. I understand if—"

He cuts me off with a kiss, lips lingering over mine. "Don't you know yet? You could ask me for the world, Morte, and I would hand it to you on a silver platter."

"This is different."

"I had considered this might happen. Given Nicholai's obsession with you. He used your own sister to create a child…" Of course he'd thought about it. This was Nero. He had a plan for everything. "So, ask me."

"She's not yours, Nero." It's the harsh reality, a brutal truth.

"What's yours is mine, and what's mine is yours. Isn't that what marriage is all about?"

Jesus. It's not like I brought home a stray dog. I brought home a baby with zero warning. "Just like that?"

"As I said, I've considered the possibility for a while. Trust me when I say, a father is not biological. So, ask me, Morte."

"Will you be her father, Nero?"

"Of course." A smile pulls at one side of his lips. "A wife and two kids. I'm becoming positively civilized."

I place the carrier down and grab his face, kissing him hard. I couldn't love him any more in this moment. He might have been the villain to everyone else, but to me and our children, he was a blood-stained hero. "Just when I think I know you, you surprise me, Capo."

"There's very little I wouldn't do for you, my vicious butterfly." He pulls me close. "What are you going to name her?"

"You don't want any input?"

"Well, I did name Dante without you."

"You did." I look down at the little girl's downy white hair, the same as mine and my mothers. "Tatyana. It was my mother's name."

"A beautiful name. And I'm sure she'll be just as beautiful and deadly as her mother. God help us all." He releases me. "Now, put the baby to bed. I missed you, my soon-to-be wife."

I snort. "Stop."

"Oh, you don't want to be my wife anymore?"

My arms wind around his neck, fingers raking through dark hair. "You know how I feel about your bullshit mafia formalities."

His lips whisper over my neck. Teeth scrape my skin. "But you make such a ruthless queen of said mafia."

A high-pitched cry has him stepping away from me and glancing at the floor.

I wave a hand toward Tatyana. "Your new princess calls."[MOU1]

His brows pull together as he crouches down and scoops Tatyana from the carrier. "Fuck me, I'm not cut out to be a girl dad." He looks genuinely concerned, and I have to fight a smile. Poor kid has no idea what she's in for, but he'll certainly protect her. I stand by the fact that the formidable and violent Nero Verdi is never more attractive than with a baby in his arms. "Come on, *Tesoro*. Let's see if we can get you some formula."

"Nero."

He pauses at the door. "Yeah?

"I love you."

"I fucking love you, Morte." He leaves the room. Tatyana's cries rise over the sound of his footsteps as he retreats down the hall.

It's a strange thing, to have had your life mapped out before you, only to have someone step into your path and divert it so violently you can't remember what it was ever like to be without them. Nero is a dark and twisted reflection of myself. My soul mate if there is such a thing, the father of my children. My monster. Forever.

*****

Thank you so much for reading Una and Nero's story. I hope you loved them! If you'd like to read Una's back story, keep reading for Make Me, Kiss of Death #0.5

If you'd like to read Anna and Rafael's story, **HATE ME** is available HERE.

MAKE ME

Kiss of death novella

LP LOVELL

Author note: This book is set in Russia. All characters are Russian and therefore they would be speaking Russian, however, for obvious reasons, the book is written in English.

Warning: The characters in this book are between the ages of thirteen and sixteen. Some scenes are violent and dark in nature. Please be aware.

CHAPTER ONE

13 years old

"She has fire in her soul and grace in her heart."- Unknown

Life has this way of dealing you a crap hand. You might be born into a loving family, you might have a shot at being something, and then it all falls apart. Your parents die in an accident with no living family to look after you and you end up in a place like this, an orphanage. It's just me and my little sister, Anna, now. In the blink of an eye, I was no longer protected and loved. I became the protector at the tender age of eight. Five years we've been in this place, and I've learned how to survive, because as much as this is supposed to be a place that takes care of children, that definition is apparently open to interpretation. I've learned though…the only person who will ever look out for you, is you.

Sitting on the floor of the cupboard, I wait for the kitchen staff to leave. I hear to clanging of pots and pans being put away before the lights power down, depriving me of the tiny sliver of light I had to see by. Waiting until I hear the clicking of the lock, I leave my hiding place. My stomach growls at the thought of food as I tip toe across the kitchen and open the pantry door. Spotting a loaf of bread, I swipe a couple of slices and two apples, before quietly closing the door again. The trick is to not take too much and risk them noticing. Getting in here isn't hard, it's the getting out that's difficult. The kitchens are in the basement and with the door locked the only way out is through a tiny window that leads above ground. I find a spare cloth and use it to wrap my stash up like a parcel. Jumping up on one of the steel work units, I reach for the window and jerk the old latch hard enough to get it loose. It opens with a loud creak and I wince, hoping that the matron isn't lurking around. I've been stealing food from the kitchens for months. I know she knows, but she just hasn't caught me yet.

The Russian government pay orphanages such as this a basic rate per child, for their food and clothing and general care. I guess the matron saw an opportunity. Like I said, the only person you can rely on is you, and she's definitely looking out for herself. She likes to think of us as cattle, if you can cut the cost of keeping each child, then you increase profit. Our food is rationed to just one meal per day, and clothing is passed down from older children to younger ones until the material is so thread bare that it's disintegrating. Anna gets stomach cramps and feels dizzy due from lack of food sometimes, so I steal some for her. Not enough that it would be noticed in theory, but around here, everything is noticed.

I push up on my hands and drag myself through the window. My shirt catches on the rusted metal frame and I hear the material tear. Shit.

I wriggle my body, and the irony of the fact that my starvation has made me skinny enough to steal food and escape through the kitchen window is not lost on me. As soon as I'm clear, I reach in and swing the window back in place. The groaning of the hinges and click of the latch is loud, and I freeze, pressing myself against the wall of the building as I hold my breath. My heart pounds in my chest, the danger of being caught giving me an adrenaline rush. I start running again, making it across the small courtyard before I push up the window that leads to mine and Anna's room. We share it with two other girls, but they don't really talk to us. One of them made Anna cry when they arrived a few months ago, so I told her I'd cut her hair off in her sleep if she ever looked at her again. They both refuse to even look at me or my sister now. It's not like I threatened to kill her or anything. They're not the only ones. The other children steer clear of us. We don't make friends. We don't have to, because we have each other and that's all we need.

I throw my leg over the windowsill and drop down on the other side. Anna sits bolt upright, pressing herself against the wall.

"Shh," I whisper, placing my hand on her leg.

"You scared me," she breathes.

"Who else is going to come through the window?" I keep my voice low as I turn around and slowly slide the old sash window back down. I know it must have woken the other girls up, and that they see me disappear some nights, but they say nothing.

I kick off my shoes and pull back the covers of Anna's bed, climbing in. She shuffles closer to the wall, making more room. I'm supposed to sleep on the top bunk, but I can't remember ever actually sleeping up there for an entire night. Anna has nightmares and if I don't sleep with her, she wakes up screaming.

"Here you go." I place the small package on the bed and unwrap it, revealing the two slices of bread and two apples. Anna picks apart a piece of bread, placing small pieces in her mouth. It saddens me to see my little sister take her time, savoring a piece of bread. *A piece of bread.* It wasn't always like this. Our parents were good people. They took care of us, loved us. Anna was only five when they died, and she can't remember them at all. I'm left alone with the memories of a life that could have been, the ghosts of a better time, and the horror of how they were torn away. I don't see things the way I used to. I learned quickly that tears don't help anything and wishing things were different doesn't make it so. I prayed and begged, and soon I also realized that if there was a god, surely he would help me, help us. No one will help us. It's up to me. I will get us out of here one day. I will protect Anna and make a better life for us.

"I'll save the apple." Anna smiles brightly and puts one apple under her pillow before she lays down. I lay beside her and stroke golden hair behind her ear. Those sapphire blue eyes of hers stare at me, so wide and innocent. I wish I could protect her from everything, but it's getting harder and harder. The matron already hates me because I defy her, and now she has it out for me. I just hope she doesn't manage to catch me stealing food.

I kiss Anna's forehead. "I love you, bug."

"Love you." Her eyelids grow heavy and her breathing evens out. I let the sound of her soft breaths lull me to sleep.

I wake up when something collides with my face, the sound of skin meeting skin ricocheting around my skull. My eyes shoot open and I immediately flinch away from the matron. She stands with one hand on her hip and an apple in the other.

"Come with me," she says with a sickly sweet smile on her face. Anna huddles against the wall and I can feel her shaking.

"It's okay," I tell her.

I know what's coming and I don't want Anna to see it, so I get up and follow the matron out of the room. She leads me to her office on the other side of the orphanage and opens the door, stepping inside. I close the door and stand there, gaze fixed on the worn brown carpet.

She whirls around and back hands me across the face so hard that the blow sends me to my knees. Spitting a mouthful of blood onto the floor, I bring my hand to my split lip. She towers over me, her face set into a cold mask. The matron looks like a school teacher with her grey hair pulled into a twist and her knee length skirt, topped off with a cardigan. Yeah, she looks like a nice older lady, except she's not. This isn't the first time my face has had a run in with her hand.

"Stealing food!" she shouts. "Ungrateful. You are ungrateful and spoilt. I've been too lenient on you, Una Vasiliev." I say nothing and she points at a chair. "Sit." I sit and she shouts for someone to come in. I hear the door open but don't take my eyes off her. Whoever just walked in comes up behind me and binds my wrists to the arms of the chair, then they move away. I start to panic, tugging against the restraints.

"What are you doing?" I ask, my voice hitching.

"Teaching you discipline." She places a cigarette to her lips, lighting it. I've never seen her smoke before. The look on her face as she approaches me is full of venom.

"You will learn your place, Una. You are nothing and no one, an unwanted orphan. Say it!" She shouts in my face, spit flying from those thin, cruel lips. That cigarette hangs between her fingers and the smell of tobacco wafts around the room. I stare back at her defiantly, refusing to break, refusing to acknowledge what she wants from me. The rough wood of the chair bites against my bare thighs, exposed by the shorts I'm wearing. The leather belts that secure my wrists to the arms of the chair are worn, but they still chaff against my skin, leaving my skin raw when I fight against them. The matron likes the children here to be well behaved and easy. I'm not. I know what they have planned. I refuse to accept this fate and above all I refuse to accept it for my sister.

517

"I will teach you your place, girl. Remember that you deserve this." She takes the cigarette and stamps it into my shoulder. It hurts, really hurts. I grit my teeth, biting back the scream that's trying to work its way up my throat. The scent of burning flesh fills my nostrils and I gag against the smell of my own melting skin. A twisted grin forms on her lips. She enjoys my pain, so I fight against my own instincts. I lock my jaw and steel my spine, staring her right in the eye. This isn't my first time taking her abuse, and it won't be the last. Her punishments went from a few pink stripes with a belt across the backs of my thighs, to crimson bleeding stripes across my back and several punches to the face that involved a chipped tooth or two. Of course the more she's given out over the years, the more resilient I've become. So resilient that I can pretend that this doesn't make me want to scream and cry. It's not even the pain that makes it horrible, it's the fact that every time she hurts me, I'm reminded that I really am alone, that no one will come and protect me. She stares me down and I stare right back, spitting another mouthful of blood at her feet. One day, I will kill her for every horrible deed that she has ever done. But I have to survive long enough to do it.

CHAPTER TWO

"Everything in life is temporary." – Unknown.

I stare at the crack that runs across the old tile floor. My heart is beating fast and I cling to Anna's hand in an attempt to stop myself from shaking. The other children are lined up either side of us, each one wishing a hole in the ground would open up and swallow them. Anything to escape notice. Their shallow, panicked breaths only remind me that I'm not safe, that we're not safe. Anna's nails bite into my palm, and sweat slicks her skin, making her tighten her hold on my hand. I try to block out the sound of heavy footsteps as a pair of boots slowly cut into view, disrupting the small patch of tile I'm focused on. I swallow heavily and squeeze my eyes shut, praying to any god that might listen that he'll keep walking. As always, my prayers are met with a mocking silence. I flinch when cool fingers touch my chin.

"Open your eyes, girl." I bite back the whimper trying to make its way up my throat and open my eyes. The face in front of me is one that is branded into my mind, the nightmare that every child here at the home wakes up screaming to in the middle of the night. I know him only as volynshchik, it's from a children's story. The Volynshcik is a man who would lure children from their parents using a magical pipe. Only this man doesn't lure children from their parents and he needs no pipe. He takes the children who have no parents, the abandoned and the unwanted, the desperate and the neglected. But no amount of neglect could possibly be more frightening than the whispers of his name, the tales of what happens to the children he takes…well, buys. Because the matron not only starves and beats children, she also sells them.

On the outside The Volynshcik looks like any other man, short cropped hair, slightly greying, a face that isn't particularly memorable, but it's his eyes that have me shaking in fear. His eyes are completely void of life, more animal than human.

"This one's pretty." He says with a sick smile, never taking those icy eyes off me. "How much?"

The matron steps forward, her hands folded behind her back. She narrows her eyes at me before addressing him. "She's no good as a whore."

He snaps his gaze to her and she recoils, dropping her head. "I didn't ask if she was."

She glances at me out of the corner of her eye. "She's unruly. She can't be broken." She presses her lips together. "We tried." I glare at her and hatred crawls over my skin like insects. I rub my free hand over my left arm, hiding the burn marks she branded into my skin only a few days ago.

A twisted smile pulls at his lips as he turns to me. His eyes drag over my body in a way that makes me feel sick to my stomach. "How old?"

"Thirteen." The matron replies.

He grips my jaw tight enough that I know it will leave a bruise. Those cold eyes bare into mine and despite the debilitating fear gnawing at my gut I stare right back at him. He laughs, startling me. "I'll take her." No, no, no, no. He leans in close, blowing vodka scented breath over my face. "And I will break you, child." He presses his lips against mine so softly and it's more terrifying than if he'd struck me. I slam my eyes closed again, fighting tears. "I promise."

*****

All I can hear is the frantic pounding of my own pulse in my ears. This can't be happening. Anna wraps her arms around me, the sound of her sobs muted to an agonising moan as she buries her little face in my chest. Her tears soak through my shirt, wetting my skin. I can't think. All I can do is hold onto her tightly and hope that something or someone will save me, save her. I'm not scared for myself, I'm scared for my baby sister, alone in this place, alone in the world. She's only ten years old. She needs me.

A rough hand lands on my shoulder, yanking me back away from her grasp. "No!" I shout.

The matron stands behind Anna, holding her in place as she reaches for me, her cries becoming so tortured that I feel my heart breaking. The image of her becomes blurred as the tears fill my eyes.

"Let go!" I thrash against the man but he applies more pressure on my shoulder until it feels as though my bones may physically crumble under his grip. "Anna." I sob. I fight him every step of the way, refusing to go quietly. An arm wraps around my throat and I tuck my chin, sinking my teeth into his forearm.

"Fuck!" He releases me and I fall forward onto my hands and knees. I'll crawl to her if I have to. A scream makes its way up my throat when strong fingers wrap around my ankle. I catch sight of my sister, her sweet face red and tear stained. Then something hits the back of my head and everything goes black.

Chapter Three

"Innocence is like polished armour; it adorns and defends." - Robert Bishop

Blinking my eyes open, I groan and flinch back against the bright fluorescent lights over head. My head is pounding and my body feels stiff and achy. All at once, everything comes rushing back. Anna. I panic, sitting bolt upright. The motion makes my head spin and my vision dip in and out. All I can see is concrete. The walls, the ceiling, the floor, all grey and bleak. No windows, no anything. I'm laying on a fashioned bed, hanging from the wall via two chains. It's a prison cell. I notice a security camera set into the corner of the room above the door, the red light on it blinking. I pull my knee's to my chest and wrap my arms around them, fighting back tears. I squeeze my arms tighter in an attempt to stop the violent shaking of my body. Anna and I have never had it easy, but we at least had each other. Only now, I'm here, and she's still there at the mercy of that evil woman.

And me...I've heard stories of The Volynschik. The children he takes are never seen again. A tear tracks down my face and I swallow around the painful lump in my throat. I jump when the door screeches and then opens. The second I see him, the fear grips me so hard I think I'm going to be sick. A horrible smile pulls at his lips as he comes to a stop a few feet away from me.

I curl into an even tighter ball, trying to make myself smaller. Another man walks into the room, lingering by the door.

"Hello, child. My name is Erik." The Volynschik has a name. I drop my gaze to a spot on the bed directly beside me. I don't want to look at him and I don't want him to look at me, to see me.

"She's pretty." The other man says in a way that makes me shiver in fear.

"Why do you think I brought her back?" He laughs. "Stand up, girl." He barks, but I don't move. I can't move. My limbs are locked in place. I yelp when he reaches for me, grabbing a handful of my hair and dragging me off the bed roughly. My knees collide with the concrete floor and pain ricochet's up my legs. His boots are right in front of me. I want to get as far away from him as possible, but I stay still, staring at the floor as tears track down my cheeks steadily. He drops to a crouch and his calloused fingers grip my jaw, forcing my face up. I slam my eyes closed and he laughs.

"Close your eyes all you like. Do you remember what I told you?" I say nothing, but feel his hot smoke scented breath on my face. "I promised I'd break you." He whispers. The words trigger something in me and animal instincts kick in. I wrench my face away from him and scramble backwards, pushing to my feet and pressing myself against the wall in the far corner of the room. His laughter echoes around the small space and a frustrated cry leaves my lips. I'm not getting out of here. Two grown men, against me, a girl. He's going to break me and probably kill me, or worse, make me a whore. I know all about these things, the places they send girls my age. I'd rather die.

His laughter cuts off and he storms across the room, reaching for me. I lash out at him, but it's a pathetic attempt. Gripping the top of my t-shirt, he tears it apart, straight down the middle. I yelp and curl in on myself, covering my body from him.

"She hasn't even got tits yet." His friend says, spitting on the ground.

Erik grabs my hair, pulling my head back so hard that I cry out as I'm forced onto my knees in front of him. He steps close and pulls me into him until my cheek is pressed against his crotch. "I don't mind." He laughs. Bile burns the back of my throat and I fight the impending panic that makes me want to curl into the foetal position and just blank it all out. For a few seconds my mind tells me to just accept it, that this is what I must do to survive, but the second the thought crosses my mind, I recoil from it in disgust. I snarl and lash out, punching him between his legs. His hold on my hair becomes so painful that I scream, but then he lets go. Staggering back, he sucks in ragged breaths, cupping his crotch. I know it will be short lived, but I bask in the small victory for a second.

"You little bitch! Hold her." It all happens at once. The concrete floor hits my back. Hands grab at my arms and body, pinning me down. I scream and my nails rake over skin. Erik's body falls over mine like a lead weight and hot breath blows over my face making me wretch. I kick and lash out and when it does nothing, the tears blind me. He pulls at my jeans so hard my entire body jerks and he'd drag me across the floor if it weren't for the other man holding me down. He throws my jeans to the side and I try to pull away, to curl my bare legs closer to my body. Fingers wrap around my ankles, wrenching them apart. A sickening grin works over his face and it feels as though someone has a hold of my heart, squeezing it in their fist. He reaches for my cotton panties and I manage to work one arm free, swinging at him and slapping him across the cheek. My palm meeting his cheek sounds like a thunder clap in the room. His hand slams around my throat and he snarls in my face, spraying spit over me. I gasp for breath, bucking my body uselessly. He rolls his hips between my legs, groaning as black spots dot my vision.

"Enough!" The voice comes from the doorway and Erik stills. The guy holding me down releases me as if I'm on fire. "Get off her." The voice says. Erik flashes me one last glance and pushes to his feet. I sit up and scramble backwards into the corner of the room, holding the tattered pieces of my shirt together as I pull my knees to my chest. I don't want to be here. I want to be anywhere but here. Pressing my face against my knees, I close my eyes. I imagine I'm back at the orphanage with Anna sitting next to me, her sweet smile on her face.

Something brushes my knee and I whimper, lifting my face. A man crouches in front of me. He has dark hair with a few gray streaks at his temple, and eyes the same colour as a stormy sky. He wears a suit with a waist coat beneath his jacket and a red tie knotted neatly at his throat. A small smile touches his face and his eyes meet mine, watching me for so long that I have to look away. He doesn't try to touch me though. Slowly, he reaches inside his jacket pocket and takes out a lollipop, offering it to me. I frown, confused. I don't trust him and I don't take it from him. He shrugs and takes off the wrapper, popping it in his mouth before he slides his jacket off his shoulders and slowly drapes it around me. I grab the two sides and pull them together, covering my entire body inside the material.

"What's your name?" He asks. I don't respond, and he lowers himself to the ground, sitting on the dirty concrete in his nice suit, propping his back against the bed. All I can hear is him sucking on the lolly. "My name is Nicholai." He stretches his legs out and crosses one ankle over the other. "Nicholai Ivanov."

"Una." I whisper.

"You're strong. A fighter." He says, holding the bright red lolly in front of his face and inspecting it.

"Please let me go." I whisper, fighting back tears. "I want to see my sister."

He tilts his head to the side, rubbing a hand over his chin. "It's the strong that survive in this world, Una. And the weak…they die, forgotten and inconsequential." I sweep my hair back behind my ear and he tracks the movement. "I can offer you the greatest gift of all, little dove. I can make you strong."

"How?"

A smile pulls at one side of his mouth. "I can make you a warrior." He stands up and offers me his hand. "If you survive…and I truly hope you do, little dove."

I put my jeans back on and Nicholai leads me up a set of stairs into what looks like a normal house, except it has a prison in the basement. There are lots of women here, most of them wearing nothing but their underwear. They all smile at Nicholai, some wave or blow him kisses. Men with guns stand in doorways, and they all bow their heads as he passes them. I cling to his hand. I don't trust him, but I trust them less. After all, isn't Erik one of them? And Nicholai saved me from him.

When we step outside one of the men call to him and he turns around. "I'm taking this one." He places a hand on top of my head and I want to shrug out from under his touch but I don't.

The man looks at me and an amused smirk appears on his face. "That one?" He laughs. "Boss…"

"Borris, do I look in need of your opinion." The hand falls from my head as he steps forward, staring at the man. He's still sucking on that lollipop, and he releases it with a pop. He says nothing, just stares.

"No, boss." He mumbles.

"Good." He presses a hand to my back and starts walking me in the opposite direction. "Come, little dove."

He walks to a black sports car and holds the door open for me. I get in and he leans across me, grabbing the seat belt and fastening it before closing the door. I have no idea where he's taking me but it has to be better than staying here with Erik. I don't have a lot of options right now.

CHAPTER FOUR

"Life - the way it really is- is not a battle between bad and good, but bad and worse." - Joseph Brodsky

 e drive over night and eventually I fall asleep. When I wake up, the night sky is turning to gray. The radio is turned down low and Nicholai taps his fingers on the steering wheel, humming along with the song. I focus my gaze out the window, shivering just at the sight of the snow clinging to the ground. I wrap my arms around myself, snuggling into the enormous suit jacket that hangs from my shoulders.

We drive down a long deserted road, lined with trees that give way to the forest. Their branches slump heavily under the weight of the snow, which glows in the darkness, reflecting the moonlight. It looks enchanting and scary, yet somehow peaceful. Eventually we pull up to a tall gate, set into a chain link metal fence, topped with razor wire. I can't see what's on the other side as a flurry of snow crosses the path of the headlights. A single guard with a rifle approaches the window. He looks freezing, huddling into his puffy jacket as a stream of misted breath leaves his lips. Nicholai rolls the window down and a flurry of bitter cold air rushes in, making me shiver. He barely glances at Nicholai before running to get the gate like a frightened mouse.

"Who are you?" I ask so quietly I'm not sure if he really heard me.

He tilts his face towards me and a small smile touches his lips. "I'm Nicholai Ivanov."

"What do you do?" I rephrase.

He sighs. "I do lots of things, little dove. You will learn all about it very soon. You're going to work for me."

I swallow nervously and the car pulls forward again. "Doing what?" I whisper.

"I'm not sure yet, but train hard, fight as if your life depends on it and maybe you'll become everything you could possibly dream of." He smiles. The car stops and I finally tear my gaze from his gray eyes. My door opens from the outside and a man in gray, blue and white military uniform stands on the other side, waiting for me. I shoot a worried glance back to Nicholai. "I will be back for you very soon, little dove. Remember what I said. Fight." The soldier grabs my arm and pulls me from the car. I want to cry at the freezing cold air biting at my cheeks. The door slams shut behind me and the engine revs before it pulls away, wheels spinning and spraying snow everywhere.

I'm alone, miles from my sister and once again terrified of the unknown situation I'm about to walk into.

"Move." The soldier thrusts the barrel of his gun into my back and I fall forwards a step, scrambling to get away from him. The building in front of me looks like some kind of military base, like a hangar of sorts, buried amongst the snow as though it's a part of the landscape. It's well hidden and apparently guarded. Where the hell am I?

I don't know how long I've been here. Another concrete room, another prison. Nicholai never came back. There are no windows in here and I have no idea if it's night or day. My captors bring me food three times a day, and that's my only measure of time passing, my only form of routine, but I'm starting to think that's unreliable. Sometimes it feels as though the meals are only five minutes apart. I think I've been here for ten days. I think. They leave the lights on all the time, which makes it difficult to sleep, and when I do fall asleep, they wake me up. They shout at me for no reason and tell me they're going to kill me. Sometimes they simply drop food inside the door and leave, others they come in and beat me for no reason.

I'm tired and confused, and my entire body aches. I just want it all to end. I live in this constant state of apprehension, trying to guess what's coming next, but whatever I think they're going to do, it's always wrong. Why would Nicholai do this to me? He betrayed me. I trusted him. That was my mistake. Trust. Why would he bring me here? But then, why wouldn't he? If there is one thing I've learned in my short life it's that people are inherently evil. They want to hurt others, and they want you to be weak and vulnerable so you're that much easier to prey on. I wish I could say that I was strong, and in the orphanage I was. For Anna. This is different. The matron couldn't kill me. These people can and they will. I see it in their eyes. I find myself becoming paranoid, waiting for the day that they open that door, put a gun to my head and pull the trigger.

I jump when the door clicks open. The same guy as always steps inside with a tray of food.

"Please." I beg him. "I can't take any more." I've resorted to this, to begging. Even if they kill me, it has to be better than this, than the torture. I fear death but I fear this more, this unending cycle, the waiting, the not knowing. And what if they never let me go? What if I'm to just stay here, enduring this forever? What if it gets worse and they try to rape me like Erik was going to? Did Nicholai pluck me from one hell only to thrust me into a worse one. At least Erik spoke to me. These men don't. And you don't realise how much you crave human interaction until it's gone, until you spend days with only your own thoughts for company.

The guy places the tray on the floor by the door and walks out without speaking a word. I'm ready to scream, to bash my head against the wall, anything, anything but another minute in this place. I don't know how long passes but the door opens again. I remain on the bed, staring at the ceiling. There's no point in trying to talk to him, because he never talks back. I learnt that quickly.

"Little dove?" I turn my head at the sound of the voice, convinced that my ears are deceiving me. "I am sorry I could not come sooner."

Tears prickle my eyes and I sniff them back as I sit up on the bed. He smiles warmly at me, but I don't move. I can't. It's a trick. I'm sure of it. I place my back to the wall and tuck my legs up.

"Come now, don't be like that." He coos.

"You left me." I say in a hurry.

Still he smiles. "Unavoidable I'm afraid. But I'm back now." He moves into the room, coming closer. I don't know him, and he brought me here, he put me in this concrete box...but I haven't spoken to anyone in so long ...

"They hurt me." I say hoarsely.

"I'm sorry." He takes a seat on the bed next to me. "I'm here now. I missed you." He strokes my dirty tangled hair back away from my face, tucking it behind my ear. "I won't let anything happen to you, little dove." He cups my face in both hands, stroking his thumbs over my cheeks that feel permanently damp from tears that never seem to stop falling. For the first time in what feels like weeks, I feel safe, and I know Nicholai is the only person I can trust. The only one. He cares for me when no one else does. He'll protect me. I throw my arms around his neck and he pulls me close. I inhale the scent of cigarette smoke and although I should hate it because of the matron, I don't. It reminds me of him, of his jacket. It reminds me that he saved me. "My dangerous little dove." He coos. I cling to him and he simply holds me, making me feel protected. I haven't felt protected since my parents died. "Are you ready?" He asks.

"For what?"

He pushes me back and looks at my face. "To become strong."

CHAPTER FIVE

"The trust of the innocent is the liars most useful tool." -
Stephen King

Nicholai walks ahead of me, striding down the grey concrete corridors. I don't see anyone else here, and it makes me jumpy. The echo of our footsteps has me glancing around nervously. Eventually he stops outside a door and turns to face me, a smile on his face.

"You have five minutes. There are fresh clothes for you." He gestures with his arm for me to go inside. I glance at him briefly and then open the door. The floor beneath my  is tile and I can hear the steady echo of water dripping. Showers. There's a vanity shelf on the left hand side with some folded black clothes. Five minutes he said. I strip out of my dirty jeans and the t-shirt they gave me on my first day here. It's freezing cold and my teeth chatter as I shiver violently. I turn on the water in one of the showers and it's cold, but I don't have time to wait for it to heat up. He said five minutes and I don't want to risk him coming in here to drag me out. I jump under the cold water and almost scream when it touches my skin. It heats up quickly though and I swear, hot water never felt so good. There's a soap dispenser on the wall, and the gel soap smells like cheap toilet cleaner, but I don't care. I rub it into my hair and over my body, washing it off until the water runs clear and I feel clean. I want to stay in that heat all day but I can't. By the time I'm dried and dressed I already feel more sane, as though I've physically washed away the effects of my imprisonment. I'm dressed in a long sleeved black shirt and what looks like combat pants of some description.

When I step outside Nicholai checks his watch. "Good. Lets go." Where we're going, I don't know, but I follow anyway.

He walks ahead of me to the end of the corridor where he once again stops in front of a door and gestures for me to go ahead of him. It makes me suspicious, as though he wants me to go first and face what may be on the other side. I know it's ridiculous. If he wanted to hurt me or kill me, surely he would just do it? But I can't shake the paranoia.

I place my hand on the heavy steel handle and push down. The hinges squeak loudly as I push it open into a small corridor with another door in front of us.

"What is this?" I ask.

"Your new home." He says quietly. There's a key pad on the left hand side, and he leans around me, entering in a code.

When the door opens, I stand frozen. He pushes me inside and the door bangs closed behind us, the heavy metal bang echoing around the vast room. A loud buzz sounds around the room, signalling the fact that we're now locked inside, imprisoned. I panic and turn around, colliding with Nicholai's chest. His fingers wrap around the top of my arm and he spins me away from him so hard that I nearly fall. He holds both my shoulders, forcing me to look at my surroundings. The room is vast, and

536

for the most part it's an empty space. Every available wall is covered in weapons. Guns and knives, cross bows and swords. There are targets on the far wall and heavy punch bags hanging in the centre of the room. The worst part though is the worn concrete beneath my feet. The grey is stained with blood, turning it a strange shade of brown with streaks of red in places.

Nicholai moves in front of me, bending at the waist and bringing himself eye level with me. He puts a hand in his pocket and takes out a lolly, offering it to me with a flourish and a smile. I take it from him with shaking fingers, watching him take out another one and unwrap it.

"I want you to meet someone. Sasha!" He shouts and pops the lolly in his mouth. A figure shifts from the shadows, moving over the ground so gracefully, his footfalls are nothing more than a whisper. He stops just to the left of us and stands bolt upright with his hands clasped behind his back. He can't be much older than me, although he's at least a foot taller and heavily muscled, despite having that gangly teenage look about him. His golden blonde hair is cropped short, and his clothing is all black, a long sleeved shirt and cargo pants much the same as mine. Green eyes remain firmly fixed ahead and I actually find myself looking, trying to spot what he's looking at on the far side of the room.

"Sasha, this is Una." He spares me a brief hard glance, but says nothing. "She will be joining you and your comrades in training." Again his eyes flick to me, lingering just a little longer this time.

"Nice to meet you." I try for polite, but immediately feel stupid.

There's an awkward pause before Nicholai speaks again. "Sasha is one of my brightest. I have high hopes for him as I do for you." He assures me. "He will look after you, won't you, Sasha?"

He claps a hand on the boys shoulder and he nods stiffly. "Yes, sir."

Nicholai smiles around his lollipop. "Good. This makes me very happy. Make me proud, little dove." He winks and then heads for the door.

He's leaving. Of course, I knew he would, but panic rises in me. I don't want him to leave. What if they put me back in that cell? He's the only one I can trust here. I start to move towards his retreating back, but Sasha wraps a hand around my mouth, using it to wrench my body back against his. His fingers dig into my jaw hard enough to bruise. My breaths become erratic and I struggle against him. He holds me easily though, and I watch as Nicholai flashes me one last look over his shoulder before walking out the door. As soon as it's closes Sasha releases me. I wheel around and stagger away from him, keeping my eyes firmly fixed on him as I back away.

He sighs and narrows his eyes impatiently. "Grow up, or you will die."

"Where is he going? Why am I here?"

"He goes wherever he likes. He's the boss, and you're here because he thinks you have what it takes."

"What it takes for what?"

"To be one of his elite." He steps closer to me, tilting his head down until I can feel his breath on my face. He cocks one eyebrow. "A killer. An assassin." He says the words quietly, for effect. He's trying to scare me, and it's working, but I refuse to show it. A killer? Strong.

"An assassin." I frown, breathing the word.

He eyes me up and down before shrugging. "Well, you are a girl, but if Nicholai wants you…" He turns and starts walking away. "Keep up, and try to make it through the first week. He asked me to watch you. I'd rather you don't die."

I run after him and he pushes through a door, exiting the room. There's yet another concrete corridor with the harsh fluorescent strip lights flickering above our heads. He opens a door and steps aside, allowing me to walk in front of him. The second I step inside, four sets of eyes stare at me. I drop my gaze to the ground and wait. I'm not sure what for.

"This is Una. Nicholai brought her personally. Try not to be assholes." They stare at me as if I have two heads. There are four sets of bunk beds in the room and the four guys are sprawled across different ones. No windows, only the harsh lighting.

"But...she's a girl." A dark haired boy spits the word as if it's dirty.

A laugh comes from one of the others, a tall boy who has no shirt on. "He's never seen one before."

Something gets thrown and then they act as if I'm not even here. I release the breath I'd been holding and Sasha jerks his head, gesturing for me to follow.

"This is your bunk." He points to a metal locker. "Your locker. It has a set of basic kit in it, although it won't fit you. Breakfast is at five and training starts at six." He turns his back and crosses the room, taking a seat on one of the lower bunks.

"Don't mind him. He's taken one too many punches to the head." I look up at the topless guy. His forearms are braced against the bunk above mine and he ducks his head, flashing me a blinding smile. He's the dark haired, brown eyed poster boy for good looks. My eyes linger a beat longer than they should on his muscular torso, and I blush, trying to look anywhere but at him.

"Um, thanks?"

"Alex."

I nod. "It's nice to meet you, Alex." I glance nervously towards Sasha, expecting him to shout at me for talking to Alex, but he's not even paying attention.

Alex follows my gaze and smirks. There's something about him, an easiness that feels misplaced. This place already feels like a tomb, a concrete tomb no one knows about, a place where children are trained to become killers apparently. I will die here. I'm almost resigned to that fact, and yet…Nicholai brought me here. He said he has faith in me. Maybe I can do this. Maybe I can be strong. Maybe I can become someone feared, because fear garners respect. I want that. I want to be powerful. For some reason I want to be worthy of Nicholai's hope, his faith. I want to make him proud.

It's not until the lights are turned off and I'm laid on my back in a dark room with four boys that it finally dawns on me…this is it. It has to have been nearly two weeks since I left the orphanage, and in those two weeks, I've been locked in my own personal torment. Not once in this entire time though was there ever a fixed end point. Honestly, I thought they would kill me, but if they didn't…if they didn't then I had just a slither of hope that they would send me back to the orphanage, back to Anna. Now, that's gone. This is the end point, this is where I will live or die. The only way I might see Anna again is if I impress Nicholai enough and become what he wants me to be. That isn't happening any time soon.

I allow myself to think of her, something I avoided while in that cell. She must be having awful nightmares right now. I miss her so much. Tears prickle behind my eyes and then start to fall in a steady stream. I press my hand over my mouth to quiet my ragged breaths and squeeze my eyes shut, willing myself to get a grip but I can't. I hear the aggravated sighs of more than one of the guys in the room. They must think I'm some pathetic girl who won't last two minutes. I probably won't. I don't know how long I lay there trying to smother the sound of my own tears but eventually the springs on the bunk above me groan and I just make out a pair of legs in the dim lighting before Alex jumps to the ground.

I sniff and sit up, watching as he sits on the edge of my bed. "You keep crying like that, titch, and these guys are going to hammer you in the ring tomorrow." He whispers, and I can make out his brilliant grin in the darkness.

"I'm sorry." I keep my voice low.

He sighs and lays down on the bed beside me. "We were all there once. Come here."

I frown at him. "What are you doing?"

He grabs me and yanks me close to him, wrapping his arms around me. "I'm tired. Go to sleep."

I lay there, my body tense. Why is he doing this? I'm instantly suspicious of any form of kindness, because well…it's a rarity in my life. No, it's like he said, he's tired and I'm keeping him up. That's all. I finally relax into his warmth. He remains on top of the blanket, the thin material dividing our bodies. It's freezing outside, but Alex is in only his workout pants and a tank, seemingly untouched by the icy air. His breaths even out pretty much immediately and I focus on him, on the steady pounding of his heartbeat next to my ear, the rhythmic draw and release of his breath. The sounds lull me to sleep.

CHAPTER SIX

One year later. 14 years old.

"A child is an uncut diamond." - Austin O'Malley

Alex's fist collides with my jaw and I stagger backwards, spitting out a mouthful of blood. He's got at least forty pounds on me, and three extra years of training. He's good. He throws another punch and I duck, popping up and catching him in the kidney. The hit doesn't do much, but I can see the pain written on his face and it gives me a smug sense of satisfaction. I'm the girl, the one who was supposed to be a whore. Nicholai's favourite. They taunt me, and make it known that they see me as no threat here in the ring, but all it does is make me even more determined to prove myself. Alex throws me to the ground and I smile, because this is where I'm best. I manage to twist my body and wrap one leg around the back of his neck. I see the moment he realises his error and he tries to get up. He lifts me clean off the matt, and slams me back down.

I smile at him as I hold onto my ankle, squeezing against his artery until his eyes roll in his head. I maintain it until he passes out, his entire weight falling on top of me. I lay there on the mat, panting and trying to catch my breath. My ribs scream in protest with every breath and I can feel my jaw swelling already. James, our trainer comes into view, hovering over me.

"Good." He shoves Alex's unconscious body off me with his foot and turns away. He doesn't think that a girl should be here, training with his soldiers, especially an under fed scrawny girl. His praise is hard earned but all the more valued for that very reason.

Nicholai was right when he said he'd make me strong. This, right here, it feels like a purpose. It makes me feel as though when the monsters come for me, I can fight them, and come they will, because they always do eventually.

Sasha appears over me and offers me his hand. I take it and jump to my feet. "Anyone would think you're adverse to blood." He murmurs under his breath. His green eyes meet mine and he cocks a brow. I know what he's thinking, that I'm squeamish. This is not the place to be squeamish. We're soldiers, assets. They train us, condition us to become numb to everything, particularly blood, violence and death. I'm fine with blood. We fall back in line beside Sunny and Adam, the other two guys in the unit. They don't like me and I don't like them. We don't talk to each other at all.

"I just don't like unnecessary mess." I say flatly. Why draw blood when you can disable an enemy without it?

"You're such a girl." He whispers. I want to hit him but I don't.

Alex groans from his spot on the floor. James is crouched beside him, wafting a pot of smelling salts under his nose. He coughs and waves James away.

"God, that smells like shit." He looks up at me and smiles. "You're getting good at that, titch." He pushes to his feet and walks over to us, shaking his head. I glare at him but say nothing else as he falls in line beside me. I hate when he calls me titch in front of the others.

James stands in front of us, meeting each of our eyes in turn. He lifts a finger and points at me. "You underestimate her because she's female!" He shouts before stepping up in front of me. "And you must learn to use that to your advantage." His lips curl slightly at the side and it makes the long scar that runs diagonally across his face, sink into his skin. James is the kind of guy that would scare the shit out of even the most hardened soldiers, but he's a great trainer. He told me the first day I was here that he didn't want me to be the best. He wanted me to kill the best. "Dismissed!" He shouts.

We break and head for the showers. The days here are gruelling and it doesn't seem to matter how used to it your muscles should be, they still ache at the end of every day. Our days consist of training in everything from fighting to shooting and general physical fitness. Then there's the mental side as well as the educational. I'm learning English, Italian, Spanish, and German. We also learn tactics and strategy, because it's not enough to kill a target, first you have to get close and then you have to have an escape plan. Everything here is like a mental and physical assault, retraining your body and mind to see the world in a completely different light. James often tells us that to be the best you must expect the unexpected and be prepared for any eventuality. Preparation at knowledge is key to survival.

I step into the locker room and strip out of my sweaty training gear. I'm the only girl here, and well, this facility isn't exactly geared to having girls. I get no special treatment, including when it comes to the communal showers. I gave up on modesty a long time ago. Being naked is just par for the course, and I don't have time to be shy about it. The guys don't care, although Alex is getting increasingly weird about it, as it is Sasha now I think about it. I walk into one of the open shower stalls and turn on the water. As usual it takes a few seconds to heat up. I've learned to like the few seconds of cold. It's like a jolt to my body, reminding me that I'm alive. As soon as the heat kicks in the warm water soothes my aching muscles. When I turn around I find Sunny glancing in my direction. Even after a year we barely talk or acknowledge each other, and he relishes in trying to make me uncomfortable. His eyes drop to my chest and I glare him. My attention is drawn to my left when I hear a low growl. The shower stalls are separated by dividing partitions which cover the average adult from mid thigh to shoulder. Alex is at the stall to my left and his gaze is firmly fixed on Sunny, the muscle in his jaw ticking as he stares at him. The tension is thick in the air and I find myself glancing between the two of them.

"Una, get out." Sasha says quietly, appearing in front of me and holding up a towel like a wall, blocking me from the rest of the room. His face is serious and his eyes keep subtly flashing towards Alex. "Now." He growls.

I roll my eyes and snatch he towel from him, stepping out from beneath the hot water.

"It's just skin, guys." I grumble, mainly in Sunny's direction. "I have no idea why you're being so weird about it." None of them say anything so I take a deep breath and leave the bathroom, heading back to the dorm. I throw on a pair of work out pants and a tank top - all in black of course – and head to the cafeteria. Sasha and Alex are normally with me, but they're apparently busy having their strange boy moment with Sunny. I attempt to drag my fingers through my hair, but the wet strands are tangled together hopelessly thanks to their lack of any kind of actual washing. Magda, cooks all our food in the cafeteria. She's a nice lady, but mute. She hands me a tray of food and I smile and thank her. The food here is good, lots of meat for high protein and carbs for energy. It's a far cry from the rations in the orphanage. Once again my mind flashes to Anna and I almost immediately slam the door shut on it. I think of her and feel guilty for leaving her alone, I then feel bad, so I refuse to allow myself to think of her, which makes me feel even more guilty. The entire thing is best just left alone while I'm here, unable to do anything about it. It's a pointless thought process that does nothing but hurt me.

I'm halfway through my food when Sasha and Alex finally walk through the door. Sasha has a serious look on his face which isn't abnormal, but Alex strolls along behind him, grinning at me and showcasing a nasty split lip. I sigh and fold my arms in front of me on the table, waiting for them to sit. Sasha sits across from me and Alex sits next to me.

"Jesus, Titch, you're like a hoover." He smirks, nodding at my tray. Adam and Sunny walk in and I instantly hone in on Sunny's swelling left eye and bruised jaw. He's also walking slightly hunched over. Alex is a brawler, irrational, hot headed and when he hits, he does maximum damage.

"You got in a fight with Sunny. Why?" I ask him. Sasha drops his eyes to the table and some of the humour disappears from Alex's eyes.

"He had it coming." He says, and I don't miss the violence in his tone.

"Alex, you'll get in trouble." He'll get in more than just trouble. Everything about this place is based on discipline. There are strict rules, because honestly, when you put teenage boys together, trained in lethal combat, you expect it. Fighting goes against everything they want and it's punished severely.

His hand lands on my leg and he squeezes above my knee. "I'll be fine, titch." I frown down at his fingers on my thigh and when I look up, Sasha is giving me a strange look. What is going on with them today? I push to my feet and pick up my tray. "Where are you going?" Alex asks.

"I'm not hungry." I scrape off my tray and hurry out of the room before he can say anything else. I don't like the tension. I don't like the way that Alex is acting, and I don't like the way that Sasha keeps looking between us.

I go to the dorm and throw myself on my bed with a huff. I lay on my back, staring at the rusted frame of the bunk above me. Closing my eyes, I listen to the silence. It's rare and peaceful. I jolt when something brushes my cheek. I must have fallen asleep. Alex is sitting on the edge of my bed and a frown line sinks between his brows as he stares down at me. His fingers brush over my cheek as his eyes search my face.

"Why are you looking at me like that?" I ask quietly.

A smile pulls at his lips and a frown disappears. "Are you mad at me, titch?"

I roll my eyes. "Don't answer a question with a question."

He smiles wider. "So you are mad at me." A lock at dark hair falls over his forehead and those dark eyes meet mine, that twinkle that is all Alex in them.

"Why would you fight with sunny?" I sigh.

The frown comes back and he drops his eyes to the spot beside my head. He twirls a piece of my hair around his finger until the white blonde strands cut into his skin. The silence stretches on until he finally snaps his gaze back to mine again.

"He was looking at you."

"Uh, it's sunny. He's a dick. He only does it to try and annoy me." Alex takes a heavy breath. "It's not a big deal." I reassure him.

He drags a hand over his face and refuses to look at me again. What the hell is wrong with him? "Titch, don't make me say it." He groans.

Sasha walks in and his eyes flick between me and Alex. "What is he going on about Sasha?" He always gives me straight answers. "Why did he fight with sunny?"

Even Sasha looks uncomfortable. "Look, Una, you're a girl." He raises his eyebrows and I sit up on the bed, glaring at him. "And…" He clears his throat.

"And you're living, sleeping… showering with guys." Alex finishes.

"This is a problem because…"

Sasha rolls his eyes. "Jesus, Una. Sunny looks at you like he wants you." He raises his eyebrows.

"You don't look like a kid any more, titch." Alex mumbles awkwardly.

Oh my god. I can feel the heat creeping up my neck until it takes over my face and reaches my hairline. Both of them are refusing to look me in the eye, although Sasha is less obvious about it. It's true that in the last year, with a proper diet I have finally filled out from my formally skeletal form. My hips are fuller and I now have breasts, but it's not like they're enormous! Certainly not big enough to be gawking at.

"You're right, sunny is a dick." Alex says, as though trying to somehow make this better. I can't even look at either of them. This is mortifying.

A few minutes later Sunny and Adam walk in. Silence falls over the room and the tension feels like a physical weight pressing in on me. I can feel every eye focus on me, so I get up and go to my locker, taking out my gloves. I'd rather be anywhere but here right now, and so even though I'm tired and my muscles ache, I go to the training room.

I pound the heavy bag, feeling the weight of it against my knuckles. Each punch ricochets up my arm, making my limbs ache even more. I press through it until my hands hurt and my arms go numb.

"Careful, killer." I turn and find Alex lounging against the wall. He's shirtless as usual, wearing nothing but his workout pants. His hands are thrust deep in the pockets of his pants and his ankles are crossed one over the other.

"What do you want?" I turn my back on him and throw another round of punches at the bag. I still when I feel his hand on my shoulder. He wraps his arms around me, one around my waist and one over my chest. I can feel the heat of his bare chest burning through my tank as he presses against my back.

"I'm sorry." He breathes right next to my ear. "I didn't mean to upset you." He presses his lips into my hair and it's something he's done a thousand times before when he's crawled into my bed at night. I never thought anything of it. It's brought me comfort at times I felt alone and lost. It's Alex. He's my best friend. But this suddenly feels different. The gesture doesn't feel like the simple act of one friend comforting another. This is their fault, him and Sasha. They just had to bring up the boob thing and make it weird. I take a deep breath and lean back against his body. He towers over me and his thick arms wrapped around me have always made me feel as though nothing in this world can touch me. I turn around and press my cheek against his chest, listening to the steady beat of his heart. That rhythmic thump, thump, thump has soothed me to sleep many times. His hand cups the back of my head, stroking over my damp hair.

"You didn't upset me." I sigh. "Boys are idiots."

He laughs. "I won't argue with you."

I pull my face away from his chest and look up at him. "You still didn't explain why you hit Sunny." I whisper. "I can take care of myself."

He tilts his head back and releases a heavy sigh. "I don't like him looking at you."

"Why?" I say, so quietly I'm not sure if he even hears me.

He brings his gaze back to mine, narrowing his eyes impatiently. His arms tighten around my body, and he stares at me for so long, time seems to stand still as I get lost in his eyes. And the way he's looking at me, he's never looked at me like that before. He brings his face closer to mine and my breath seizees in my chest. My stomach tenses, fluttering with something strange. This is Alex, my Alex, the boy who holds me when I'm sad, defends me when I don't need defending and kicks my ass for my own good. He taught me to throw a punch, how to reassemble a gun in under ten seconds. Right now though, he feels like none of that and all of that. I can't explain it. He feels like something foreign and yet warm and familiar, safe. Those dark eyes of his burn into me as though he can see into my very soul. And then they drop to my lips, lingering there. I'm both embarrassed and curious at the same time. I feel the blush blossoming over my cheek bones. My breath hitches and his arm leaves the small of my back. He brushes a strand of hair away from my face, and my eyelids flutter closed. My heart leaps into the sprint and my skin tingles under his touch. Calloused fingers trace my jawline and warm breath blows over my face before his lips brush over mine in a feather light caress. I freeze, unable to move, unable to breathe. He kisses me. Alex kisses me. I'm too confused to react. His lips are softer than they look, and his fingers trail down the side of my neck leaving tingles in their wake. When he breaks away I open my eyes and drop my gaze to the worn concrete floor beneath my feet.

"Una..." He starts, but says nothing more. I finally lift my eyes to his and in this awkward tension seems to linger between us. "I'm sorry." He stammers.

I shake my head. "It's okay." Or at least I think it is. Honestly I'm not really sure myself. His arms are still wrapped around me and the embrace that felt simply friendly a few moments ago now feels like something else.

"It will be lights out soon." He says, stepping back and holding his hand out to me. I take it and his fingers thread through mine as he leads me back to the dorm room. Sunny and Adam glare at us as we walk in. Sasha makes a deliberate effort to ignore us.

I get changed and climb into bed. Alex hoists himself up onto his own bed and then the lights go out. The darkness wraps around me, hiding everything, but it's here in the quiet of the dark that I hear and see the most. My lips tingle and I press my fingers against them, remembering the feel of Alex's kiss. Why would he do that? I've never thought about being kissed before. I mean, it's not as if there's an awful lot of room for fairy tales in my world. Kisses and boys… those are the things told in the Disney films I used to watch when I was young, before all this. Things from a different place, a different time, things that don't belong here. Alex and Sasha are my best friends but James has always told us we are disposable, which is why we must be the best. Anything less and we die. I know all of this, having willingly embraced it in order to be strong, to make Nikolai proud. And yet, Alex has always been my safe place. In his arms, hearing his carefree laugh, I can almost pretend that this isn't our life, that we are just two normal people, a boy and a girl. I want that. I want to be strong, but I wish I didn't have to be. I wish that this world wasn't so messed up that I need to be.

I'm still awake what feels like hours later. I can hear the heavy sleep drawn breaths from the other guys in the room and the god awful snoring coming from Adams bunk. The springs of the mattress about me creek, and then Alex's leg appear, hanging over the side of the bed. Is he going to get in my bed? Do I want him to? Wait, why wouldn't I want him to? He's always done it. The kiss, that's why. I don't get much choice because he doesn't ask. He simply hops down, his feet hitting the ground so lightly that they make no sound at all. He tugs at the edge of the blanket and I find myself shuffling over, making room for his ever broadening frame in the tiny bed. He gets in next to me and says nothing. I turn on my side and stare at him, he stares back and I can just make out his eyes, twinkling in the dark. After a while he smiles, his brilliant grin standing out against the darkness.

"Why are you smiling?" I whisper.

"Because you're beautiful."

I blush and tuck my chin, focusing on his chest. "Don't be stupid."

"Nothing stupid about it." A light feeling creeps through my chest and my stomach clenches. He wraps his arms around me and pulls me close, kissing my forehead. His lips linger on my skin for several moments before he props his chin on my head. I breathe in the familiar scent of him, and sigh on a contented breath. He holds me like that and strokes over my hair until I drift to sleep.

CHAPTER SEVEN

"One of the keys to happiness is a bad memory." - Rita Mae Brown

"Breathe in. Pause. Feel your heartbeat. Slow it, control it. Now squeeze the trigger." I stare down the scope, focusing in on the metal target shaped like a person. I apply pressure on the trigger and the rifle explodes. I watch as it hits the target right on the centre of the head. I look up at James who is standing over me, looking through his binoculars at the target two hundred yards away. He glances down at to me, his expression unreadable.

"Good." One word. He moves down the line checking on Sasha to my right.

"Good?" Alex laughs from my left. I glanced at him and shrug. Guns I can do. I like the control, the precision. It's not about strength or bodyweight. There's something about the distance of it as well that I find appealing. I'm not squeamish, though I admit that I'm scared of having to kill someone with a knife or something. It seems so brutal and unnecessary. Guns are clean, methodical, distanced. I fire a few more shots and then James taps my shoulder.

"Go work the bag." He says and I almost groan. I hate the bag. Instead though I get up and do as he says, working at pounding the bag for the rest of the morning.

*****

I grunt when my back hits the mat and Sunny lands on top of me. His legs straddle my body and his fists pound against my forearms as I block him from connecting with my face. He laughs manically and it pisses me off but I refuse to break my guard. He'll falter soon. He's arrogant and he assumes I'm weak. He pauses between punches and his left shoulder drops slightly. He's tiring. I break and strike out, taking one in the jaw from his right hook, but punching him in the throat at the same time. He chokes and his eyes go wide. His weight shifts backwards slightly and I punch him in his junk. I hear the collective groan of pain from every guy in the room right along with Sunny. It's like he's been shot with a stun gun. His entire body goes rigid and he pitches to the side. I roll to my feet and walk over to him. I should probably be above pettiness but I'm not. I hate him. I swing my leg back and land a good kick to his kidney before James shouts at me.

"Just making sure he stays down." I smirk

Alex dips his head, hiding his smile as I fall back into the line. Sasha stands vigilantly beside him, his expression stoic and serious as always.

"Alex, Sasha, you're up." James points to the two of them and they strip out of their shirts, coming to stand across from each other. We call it the ring but it's really just a designated section of the training room that we fight in. There are no ropes, and certainly no soft landing. If you go down it's on the cold, hard concrete, and let me tell you, it hurts. Sunny has finally limped back in line just as Alex and Sasha stand off against each other. Sasha has a better technique, but Alex has this brutality in the way he fights. They're pretty evenly matched and James always pairs them. I can see why. If Alex took on more of Sasha's technique, and Sasha took on some of Alex's fire, they'd both be unbeatable.

They rain blows down on each other until both of them are bloodied and bruised. Neither seems to have the upper hand. I've watched them trade punches like this for hours before. In the end, James calls time on it and calls us back into line.

He starts talking, but my attention turns to the heavy buzzing sound of the main door opening. I glance towards the door, watching a figure step into the room. I have to fight a grin when I see Nicholai standing, watching us. I don't see him often. He drops in every now and then to check up on us.

"Dismissed." James barks.

The others head straight for the showers, throwing a few glances at Nicholai. They whisper about him, they fear him. When I first came here they would speak of him, telling me that he's the big boss of the Russian mafia. I know very little of the mafia, or the bratva as they call it in here. They say that Nicholai is a powerful man, and I suppose he must be to train his own soldiers. They also say that he's a bad man but it all depends how you define bad. To me, he's one of the only people who has ever cared about me. No matter his deeds, that is what I will always think of when I see him. When I look in his eyes I can only see his kindness, and I can only feel gratitude. The boys all call him sir and only speak when spoken to. I'm not the boys. I jog over to him where he stands talking to James. He looks his usual immaculate self in his suit and tie. His greying hair is swept back and he's clean shaven, the sharp planes of his face stark against those stormy grey eyes of his.

"Nicholai!" I grin.

"Una!" James shouts, scolding me. I flinch against the bite of his voice, but Nicholai holds up a hand, silencing him.

He turns his attention to me and smiles. "Little dove. I have missed you." He croons.

"I missed you too." He reaches out and brushes his thumb over my bruised jaw. "James tells me you are doing well."

I shrug one shoulder and smirk. "For a girl."

He laughs. "Oh, my precious little dove…some of the greatest men in history have been brought to their knees by a woman. You will slay them with your looks, woo them with your innocence and end them with a bullet." He winks. "Perfection." I blush and drop my eyes to the floor. "I came because I have a job for you."

I frown. "A job?"

He nods. "A protection detail."

"Sir, they are not ready." James interrupts.

Nicholai sighs before reaching beneath his jacket and un-holstering his gun. James tenses and I hold my breath for a second, waiting for something to happen. He stares at James the entire time as he turns the gun and hands it to me. I tentatively wrap my fingers around the hilt allowing my index finger to brush the trigger.

"Shoot the targets, little dove." He points at the targets on the other side of the enormous concrete room. They're maybe fifty yards away from where we stand by the door, but this is where I excel. We train ten hours a day and hand to hand combat is where my sheer lack of strength lets me down, but with a gun in my hand I'm the best. I lift the gun, flicking the safety off. I glance down the sights, take a breath and fire one bullet after the other in quick succession. A perfect bullet hole sits in the centre of each target when I'm done. I flick the safety back on and hand the gun back to Nicholai. He's looking at me with narrowed eyes, a strange smile on his lips. He turns and claps a hand on James' shoulder.

"You are too modest James. One year and she's a prodigy in the making." The muscles in James' jaw twitch erratically but he says nothing. "Get Sasha for me, please." James stalks away and Nicholai smiles down at me. "Very impressive." He jerks his chin towards the targets.

"I like guns." I tell him, and he laughs.

"You are a blessing to me." He strokes a hand over my head and I swallow a lump in my throat.

"I…" I'm cut off when Sasha walks over to us. His back is straight, his posture tense, the same way it always is when he's around Nicholai. Sasha says that my familiarity with Nicholai is disrespectful. Nicholai doesn't seem to think so.

"Sir." Again, Sasha stares straight ahead, not even looking at either of us.

"I have a job for the pair of you. Come." He enters a code into the key pad beside the door and it buzzes open. I haven't been past that door since I arrived here a year ago. Everything from sleeping quarters to shower facilities and cafeteria is all contained within this one wing of the facility, cut off. We live, sleep and train together, just the five of us. Of course I never talk to Sunny or Adam, so really it's just the three of us. Sasha is like my brother, and Alex…Alex is my best friend. I've found a sense of belonging here, but it doesn't mean it isn't hard.

We're made to fight until we're bleeding, battered and bruised and barely able to stand. And beyond the physical is the mental. We're made to sit and watch hours and hours of footage of people being killed. A fifty calibre bullet will blow a mans entire head off and a grenade will completely tear a body apart. They never tell us why, simply force us to watch the gruesome scenes. The thing is though, I don't find them so gruesome anymore. Normality is whatever you make it, and this is my normal. Every single facet of my life is structured towards death and destruction.

Nicholai leads us down a corridor until he comes to a room with a heavy steel door. This room doesn't have a key pad, but a sensored screen which he presses his thumb against. It beeps and the door releases. My jaw drops when I step inside. I've never seen so many guns, from hand guns to sniper rifles.

"Suit up. Take whatever you need." He holds his arm out, inviting us into the room. Sweet.

I pick up a holster, fastening it around my waist and picking up a 9mm and a .40 cal. I check the clips on both and grab two spare clips. I find a dagger and thigh holster, strapping that to my leg.

I walk back out of the room and Nicholai wordlessly hands me a jacket that he seems to have acquired from nowhere. "It's cold outside."

Sasha takes the other jacket and locks eyes with me for a moment. If this is a gun toting activity then I can't help but wonder why he isn't taking one of the other guys. They're much more experienced than I am.

"Come. We're late."

CHAPTER EIGHT

"We're not in Wonderland anymore, Alice." – Charles Manson

I sit in the back seat next to Sasha, watching the outside world pass by my window. Nicholai is in the front and a man I've never met before drives the big SUV, winding down the snow covered drive, away from the compound. A blur of forest flashes past the window and I remember seeing that same row of snow capped trees when Nicholai brought me here. That memory feels as if it belongs to someone else, another girl from another time. That girl was vulnerable and scared. I'm still vulnerable, still scared, but of different things. I've always wanted to ask Nicholai about my sister but something always stops me. Call it instinct, but I don't think he'd like it. I wonder how she is. I hope that she's okay.

"This job...you are a protection detail." Nicholai says without turning around. "I don't expect trouble, but be vigilant and if they make a wrong move, shoot to kill." He turns in his seat and taps a finger between the eyes driving the point home. He slams the clip into the bottom of a colt .45 and shoves it into a chest holster as he turns back around. "Stay close at all times in a marked formation."

"Yes, sir." Sasha responds.

"Yes, sir." I say more quietly.

I have practiced, shot at more targets than I can possibly count, but this is different. These are people. I flash Sasha a nervous glance and he simply shakes his head slightly, gritting his jaw. Don't ask questions, simply follow orders. We're soldiers, and that's what soldiers do.

We pull up in what looks like a disused factory of some sort. The man who was driving removes a large holdall from the trunk and then disappears. I take a gun from my holster and palm it, feeling the weight of the metal resting comfortably in my hand. Sasha's eyes sweep over the darkened yard and Nicholai simply stands there, unwrapping a lollipop and putting it in his mouth.

"This way." He starts walking towards one of the buildings and pauses in front of a side door, allowing Sasha to go in first. My heart is pounding too fast as I scan the shadows, waiting for someone to jump out.

A hand brushes my shoulder and I jump. "Calm, little dove. Remember your training." Nicholai purrs.

"Clear." Sasha shouts.

We go inside and walk up a set of iron steps that lead to a walkway that overlooks the factory floor below. It's a good vantage point with a clear view of all the exits. Nicholai opens the door to a small office. There are papers littered everywhere, and the place looks as though it hasn't been used in years. He flicks a switch and an emergency light casts a low glow throughout the room. He takes a seat behind the cheap looking desk and kicks his heels up, still sucking on his lolly.

"Sasha, stay outside. Una, come stand behind me." I do as he says and move behind him.

We don't have to wait long. "Three of them coming in the entrance." Sasha says a few minutes later.

"They're late." Nicholai grumbles, pushing to his feet.

Sasha steps to the side of the door, allowing them in. They're big and burly, all of them dark haired and dark eyed with tanned skin. They wear suits, giving the impression of businessmen, but they're not. The way their eyes shift around the room, focusing on me and then Nicholai puts me on high alert. I can see the outline of their guns fastened against their chests and it has my fingers lingering over my own.

"Nicholai." One of them says with an accent. He glances at me and smirks. "You bring children to fight your battles now?"

I can't see Nicholai's face, but I see the way the muscles in his back tense, though he seemingly ignores the comment. The conversation switches to Italian, and although I am learning the language, I'm nowhere near fluent. I think Nicholai says something about money. The guy doing the talking frowns and whatever he's saying, he's not happy. The other two remain tense and alert.

I catch Sasha's eye briefly before glancing back at the guy on the left. He keeps staring at me and a twisted smirk pulls at his lips as he drags his eyes over my body. It makes my skin crawl, but I remain still. Suddenly Nicholai slams his palm down on the table, and it seems as though everyone has a gun in their hand in an instant. It seems Nicholai has quite the effect. I bring the .40 cal up, pointing it straight at the pervy one's face. His gun is pointed at Nicholai.

"Careful now, sweetheart. Wouldn't want to hurt yourself." He says in broken English. My English is a lot better than my Italian.

Nicholai holds his hands out, trying to calm the situation. I can't take my eye of the guy in front of me, but something happens on the other side of the room. I hear a cry of pain, the crunching of bone. It's going south. I see the guys finger twitch over the trigger which is pointed at Nicholai and I react. I shoot. The bullet hits him between the eyes and his head snaps backwards before his body follows suit. My mouth falls open and I drag heavy lungfuls of air into my body. I killed him. Adrenaline floods my veins and my hand trembles around the gun. I killed him. Holstering the weapon, I push to my feet. The guy who was talking is hunched over the desk, a blade slammed through his hand, pinning him there. The other guy is on his knees in front of Sasha, and Sasha has a gun rammed against the back of his skull.

"You owe me fucking money!" Nicholia growls, in Russian this time, getting in the mans face. "And yet you add insult to injury by trying to kill me." He's still sucking on his lollipop. Leaning over the desk he presses down on the hilt of the knife. The man grits his teeth and bites back a pained groan. "Big mistake, my friend." He shakes his head and then nods at Sasha. The gun shot seems deafening, and I watch as the man that was on his knees falls forward, a hole blown in the back of his skull. "I don't like traitors." Nicholai says calmly before he yanks the blade out of the mans hand and slashes it across his throat. A warm spray hits me in the face and chest and the man falls forward, choking and gasping on the desk as blood pours from his neck. It spreads over the wood beneath him until it's running over the side, pitter-pattering on the carpet in a steady flow. This is what we're trained for. Death and destruction.

Nicholai pulls into the base, and the car sits idling outside the building. Sasha gets out and I open the door.

"Little Dove?" I pause and he turns in his seat, smiling at me. "I am so very proud of you. You are ready for the next stage in your training." I frown but again, say nothing. "You will be magnificent. Your name will be feared, the whisper of death on the wind." He breathes, a look of awe crossing his features. Something uncomfortable winds around my chest, but I swallow it down. "It will be hard, but you must endure. You must survive. Be strong, little dove. Take the gift I am offering you."

"I will." I say quietly before getting out of the car.

An escort takes us back to the training wing.

My mind is flashing like a faulty film reel, only it's the same image, over and over again. My bullet. That man's face. No amount of videos can prepare you for that. The dorm is empty when we get back. Sasha wordlessly drops his kit and heads for the showers. I just... I need a minute. There's a two-foot wide gap between my bed and the wall. I wedge myself into the corner, and pull my knees up to my chest. I stare at backs of my hands, resting against my thighs. They are literally covered in blood, tiny splatters dotting my skin in a fine mist. I thought I was ready, but death, the reality is a far cry from the ideal. I imagined that I would simply pull the trigger and it would be no different to firing at one of those human shaped metal targets. I don't know what I expected to feel. I guess I never thought about it. In the heat of the moment, when faced with the possibility that he might kill Nicholai I simply reacted. There was no thought or reason to it. It's the exact second after you've pulled the trigger that your mind starts to over analyse. Nothing could prepare me for the blood, for the light leaving his eyes, the deafening bang of the gun signalling the end of his existence. There was something brutally humbling about it, the reminder of how fragile human life really is. It was horrifying, but more worrying, there was a strange thrill in taking his life. I've never felt more powerful. I've never felt stronger. What would Anna think of me now? Would she see me as strong, or would she see me as a monster? In the space of eighteen months I've completely changed. The life I had was no walk in the park. Starvation and abuse were daily factors that I thought so awful at the time. It was the childish notion of a girl whose life was a battle of bad and good. This life is a battle of bad and worse. There is no room for good, only survival. Only strength. Only what must be done. In my world, humanity itself is a weakness, and right now I feel as though I'm barely holding onto mine. It's like I took a run and jump off a cliff, willing to become this killer, only I changed my mind halfway and now I'm clinging to a small ledge, clinging to the basest form of what makes us fundamentally human. Why though? What has humanity ever done for me? Why do I feel so guilty?

"Una." I peer up at the sound of Alex's voice. He's standing on the other side of the bunk, his arms braced against the frame as he focuses on me. I can't even look at him. Alex, regardless of the brutality he's seen still manages to be good. He smiles when he shouldn't be able to, laughs when anyone else would cry. Maybe he's broken too. Maybe he's too uncaring to be bothered by the things that should affect us. Or maybe he just manages to maintain his humanity while being here. Maybe he's just stronger than the rest of us. He moves around the bed and comes to a stop in front of me. I watch as he drops to his haunches and those deep brown eyes move over my face.

"You look like something out of a horror movie, titch." I slowly bring my eyes to his, waiting for some kind of disgust or judgement. It never comes.

"I killed a guy."

He sighs and props his back against the wall, stretching his legs out beneath the bed. He places his hand on my knee and his thumb strokes rhythmic circles against the material of my cargo pants. "That's kind of the point of being an assassin." I nod. He's right. Of course, this is ridiculous. "You're allowed to care though. It doesn't make you weak."

I look at him and I'm worried he sees me for what I am, what I'm becoming. Alex is too good for this place. He still see's me as the innocent, broken girl who walked in here, but she's long gone and I wonder if he knows that? When he opens his arms, I go to him, wrapping myself in him. I bask in his warmth and inhale his familiar comforting scent. The blood and the death slowly ebb away until I can't feel them any more. He presses his lips to my forehead, lingering against my skin for long seconds, despite my blood covered state. For a few moments I bury myself in him and allow him to take me somewhere else, somewhere that isn't the cold, grey walls of the dorm. I pretend that we're that boy and that girl, the ones we could have been. Normal. Not monsters and killers.

CHAPTER NINE

Six months later…15 years old

"Let it define you, let it destroy you, or let it strengthen you." – Unknown.

The hand presses on the back of my neck, pinning me beneath the water. I try to hold my breath, but my pulse is beating erratically, and the harder my heart beats the more desperate my lungs become for air. I'm pulled up and I drag a burning breath into my lungs. Torture is as much a part of my daily routine now as fighting and killing. My body count is now at twelve. Twelve kills in only six months. I go between working for Nicholai and being here, trained, tortured. Each day is a test of endurance, a battle of the mind over basic instinct. I always win. But the water…the water is it's own brand of fear. I've been electrocuted, cut, burned, beaten, but none of them bring you as close to death as water.

James stands in front of me, the other side of the water tank. His arms are behind his back as always, and the black material of his military style jacket pulls tight over his chest. He grimaces at me and the scar that runs diagonally across his face sinks into his skin making his expression twisted and deformed.

"It's here, at the limit of death, when you think you have no choice but to give up, that the strong are separated from the weak." He nods and I'm thrust back into the water. Again I panic and flounder and again I'm brought up. "Embrace death, only then can you conquer it." He growls, and I'm forced under again.

This time, when I reach the point of no oxygen, they don't let me up. My lungs burn and a rabid kind of desperation claws at my mind. It's here, at the precipice of death where it's impossible to think rationally. It's here where the mind can no longer battle the body and the unbridled instinct to survive will kick in. I hold out and hold out, until finally I can't anymore. My body shuts down and my mind closes in on itself, refusing to let me open my mouth even though I need to. The pressure grows and grows until I feel as though I'm about to explode. I open my mouth and inhale, only the air never comes. Water rushes into my lungs and I panic, but it's accompanied by a strange kind of relief. I've always been scared of dying, but as my body desperately tries to work through it's distress, my mind is at ease. There's nothing I can do, and a strange kind of peace comes with that knowledge. Everything goes black.

I wake up and choke, sitting up and coughing up water. My lungs feel raw and strained. I'm laying on the floor next to the water butt. James is hovering over me and the guy who held me under water is crouching at my side.

"Congratulations, you just stared death in the face and won." James says. I don't feel like I won. "Embrace death, Una. Become her. Only then will you not fear her." He walks away and the other guy gets up and follows him. I sit there, my lungs burning as I continue to cough up water. When I finally stand

and leave the room, I find Nicholai waiting in the hallway. He's leaning against the wall, sucking on a lollipop as usual. He reaches in his pocket and offers me one, but I shake my head. Another ragged cough works up my throat that seizes my entire body. My lungs are trying to purge the water and I know from experience it will take days for them to do so.

"You are doing well, little dove." I like Nicholai's praise. It makes me feel like all of this is worth it, like there's someone routing for me. We start walking down the corridor and he wraps an arm around my shoulder, pulling me into his side. "Do you know why I do this to you?" He gestures at me. "The electrocution, the drowning, the pain…" I shake my head and I'm not sure I want to know. "It is not because I like your suffering. Quite the opposite." His expression looks genuinely pained for a second before he continues. "I will tell you a story. There was a man who once trained a dog. Every time he fed the dog he would ring a bell. Soon, every time he rang the bell, the dog would drool, whether he received the food or not. The response was conditioned." I glance up at him, a frown on my face. "Humans are much the same. We are naturally conditioned by our own minds. When you are thrust into the water, your mind panics, it is conditioned by it's own need to survive. I want you to be able to over-ride your own mind, little dove. To do this is to have absolute power." He smiles wondrously. "How strong you will be to conquer death and fear. And more so, with certain training, you can make anything instinctual. Conditioned behavior." He shakes his head. "The mind is an amazing thing."

Is it even possible? To have no fear, not even of death itself…I'd be like a robot.

571

CHAPTER TEN

"The best protection any woman can have is courage." -
Elizabeth Cady Stanton

I stand with my hands at my side. Igor, one of the new enforcers lingers behind me. I can sense him, his every breath, his every movement. Nicholai once said to me that someone could be conditioned, but I couldn't understand the full extent of that until I started to experience this particular brand of it. Deprived of all human touch, except for pain. Conditioned over several months to only ever feel pain at another's touch. The kill reflex, Nicholai calls it. Alex is my only exception, but his innocent caresses are not enough to over-ride the hours and hours of daily torture. My mind is no longer my own. It's like I've been programmed. Igor shifts his weight and I remain still, bracing. I know what's coming and I want to react, every muscle demands that I do so, but that's not part of the exercise. He touches my arm and an electric shock rips across my body. The second his hand leaves me ingrained instincts kick in and I have him on his back, my fingers wrapped around his Adam's apple, in an instant. Kill, kill, kill. My finger nails dig into his skin, drawing blood as I cut into his flesh. I want to rip his throat out. He chokes and attempts to hit me but I grab his head in both hands and slam it into the concrete. Kill, kill, kill... it pounds through my brain like a drumbeat. I can't fight it. I feel his skull crack against the concrete and blood pools around his head, crawling across the bleak grey floor, staining it. Eventually hands gripped my arms and again, their touch...kill, kill, kill. I snarl and fight until they finally release me. I turn in a crouch and face Sasha and James, panting heavily. James maintains his cold expression while Sasha flashes me a knowing, almost pitiful look. He knows what it's like because he's going through it too, except Sasha can't even bare to wait for the shock.

"Little Dove." I glanced to the left where Nicholai stands, watching. He's been here a lot more recently. He watches the training sessions and always speaks to me afterwards. The look of pride in his eyes always pulls me through. It makes this worth it. I am strong and he sees it. "You make me so proud." He smiles and steps towards me. I allow him to get within two feet and then I step backwards.

"Don't." I plead. I don't want to hurt him. I don't trust myself not to. He offers me a sad smile and hold his hands up, coming to a halt.

"This is just part of the process, to make you the best." He assures me. The best... it seems like an unimportant notion now, but I understand. This is my purpose.

"Sacrifices must be made, little dove."

I look across the room, locking eyes with Alex. His expression is serious. It's been a long time since I saw the lightness and laughter in his eyes. The training has broken him down, but he still offers me a small smile. Nicholai dismisses me and I feel all eyes on my back as I walk away. I've become the circus freak, more animal than human. Feral. Wild. That's what happens when you're stripped of your fundamental morals and programmed to become a monster.

I go to the door and sit on the floor, bracing my back against my bed. It's just the four of us living here now. Sonny broke under the first round of touch conditioning and was taken away. I don't know where. Sasha walks in the room and spares me a brief glance, grabbing a towel and heading for the showers. We used to be so close, but of course that couldn't last. Friendship is a form of dependence, and dependence is a weakness. Now we're simply two people who understand what the other is going through, but are too consumed in our own torment to help each other. He passes Alex on his way out. Alex comes and sits to my side. He wraps his arm around me. They've made it so that I can't stand human touch, but it's different with him. He's Alex, my Alex. His touch could never evoke fear and I could never harm him. I lean into his shoulder and feel his warm breath blowing through the strands of my hair.

"That's getting harder and harder to watch." He murmurs. I hate seeing Alex go through it as well, but of course he reacts the way he always does in a fight and comes out swinging.

I tilt my face up so I can see him. "It's necessary." I know he doesn't agree with me and he doesn't understand my loyalty to Nicholai. Alex was the son of a bratva soldier, his destiny mapped out from youth. He's been here since he was ten. He knows nothing else. He doesn't know what it is to feel weak and helpless. He will never understand my gratitude to Nicholai. This is hard, of course it is. If it were easy everyone would be the best and not everyone can be the elite.

"I wish it weren't." His eyes dropped to my lips and he lifts his hand, stroking his fingers down the side of my face. This is still the spec of warmth in my cold and calculated world. The only time that my mind is silent, peaceful. Alex is my safe harbour. He wraps his hands around my waist and pulls me until I'm straddling him, sitting in his lap. He pulls his knees up, cradling me between his strong body and his thighs. His hands cup my face and me touches his forehead against mine until we're breathing each others air.

"I love you, titch." He whispers and I squeeze my eyes shut, fighting back the wave of emotion. I love him, but saying it out loud feels too real. The two halves of me fight, one side telling me this is weak whilst the other clings to Alex with every fibre of her being. A stray tear falls onto my cheek and he presses his lips over my skin, catching it. "Don't cry."

I don't want to talk or think about things, so I kiss him. His lips brush over mine and I close my eyes, finding comfort in the sweet caress of his mouth against mine. Everything stops for a moment. He is the calm in a world of chaos. A breath of cleansing air in a toxic atmosphere. Without him I couldn't survive here. The strong survive, but he is my strength.

"First to draw blood wins." James says, gesturing Alex and I forwards. I step out of line and into the open space otherwise known as the ring. Alex stands across from me, a smirk on his lips. When I step to the left he mimics it, always keeping a distance between us. I palm the blade in my hand, wrapping my fingers firmly around the hilt. I wait for him to move and he does. I've watched Alex fight and fought him myself enough to know that he is skilled but impulsive. When you're outmatched by fifty or so pounds, patience is key. Brawn won't get me anywhere here. He rushes me, and I duck, swinging my blade towards his thigh. I never make contact. He blocks the hit, going for my arm. I roll and come up behind him, jabbing my elbow into his lower back. He grunts and then huffs a laugh. Arrogant bastard. I swiped his legs out and he goes down hard. I'm straddling his body with a blade at his throat before he can blink. He grins, biting down on his bottom lip. Blood. They want blood. I lightly flick blade over the base of his neck, barely scratching the skin. A thin line of blood wells, and I push off him quickly.

"Good." James says to me before turning to Alex.

"Arrogant, messy, undisciplined. Disappointing." Alex climbs to his feet and says nothing as he falls back in line. I feel bad, but the truth is, Alex always holds back when he fights me. He leaves his guard open, his attacks are messy. He pretty much hands me and the win. And when I take it, I make a concerted effort to do you as little damage as possible. I don't know why that is. I care about Sasha just as much as I do Alex, but when we fight it's like a bloodbath. He's ruthless and I'm brutal. I'm bruised for weeks afterwards.

Nicholai comes to stand next to me as we watch Sasha and Adam fight. He's been for the last two days.

"You held back on the boy." He says without taking his eyes off Sasha.

"Why cause more damage than necessary?" I ask, twisting my head towards him. "He's one of your assets. I don't want to break your stuff." I smirk and he lets out a low chuckle.

"Break him all you want, little dove. He's disposable. They all are, except you...and Sasha." The words make me sick to my stomach but I make sure it doesn't show on my face. He touches my shoulder and I flinch, the voices roaring to life in my head. Kill, kill, kill. It's like a curtain descending, blinding me to anything and everything else. "Control it. Breathe. It is an advantage to have such reflexes over an enemy, but you must be stealthy. You are a killer, but you must be like the Oleander flower, beautiful, delicate to look at, but deadly. I will give you the weapons, little dove, but you must control them, hide them. Unleash them only when needed." He lets go and I release the breath I had been holding. "It appears this training is working a little too well. It is curious though…you do not tense when this boy touches you." He jerks his head towards Alex and I'm instantly alert. He can't know about Alex and I. He wouldn't like it.

"How so? If he touches me it's to strike me, and I strike back." A smile pulls at the corners of his lips and he says nothing else, instead, taking a lollipop from his pocket and unwrapping it before putting it in his mouth.

He knows.

CHAPTER ELEVEN

"Perhaps the unattached, the unwanted, the unloved could grow to love as lushly as anyone else." - Vanessa Diffenbaugh.

I'm jolted awake and I'm confused for a few seconds, but then my eyes adjust and I see the man standing beside my bed, pointing a gun at me. I react without thinking, years of training kicking in seamlessly. I grab his wrist and divert it away from me before twisting my body and landing a kick to his gut. He coughs and doubles over. I'm standing over him holding his own gun to his head when something hits me in the chest. My entire body seizes and then goes completely numb. Two men carry me from the room. I try and call Alex's name, but I can't seem to find my voice. Nothing seems to work, as if my brain has been cut off from the rest of my body.

I'm dragged down a long corridor and down a set of stairs before I'm dumped on a cold floor. I groan and rub over the spot on my chest where two spots of blood are blossoming, making my tank top sticky. Taser prongs. There's shouting, a door being slammed and then the soft stroke of fingers on my jaw.

"Little dove, wake up." I groan and manage to climb to my feet. I freeze when I see the figure chained to one wall of the empty room. Alex. His torso is bare, covered in slices that bleed down his stomach. Sweat mixes with the blood, coating the chiselled muscles of his body in a crimson glow. His dark hair is damp with sweat and a few loose tendrils fall across his face.

"Alex." I whisper his name and he lifts his head slightly. Tears prick at the backs of my eyes and I bite the inside of my cheek to stop them. "What is this?" I whisper, unable to bring myself to look at Nicholai, because the truth is, I know what this is. This is why I hid my feelings for Alex from him.

Nicholai circles around behind me before moving to stand right beside Alex. He grips Alex's jaw and twists his face to the side, forcing me to look at the bruised, bloody mess. "This boy, you have an affection for him, no?"

"I…" I force myself to look at Nicholai. "Please." My voice breaks slightly. "He's my friend." A stray tear tracks down my cheek and I let it fall.

Nicholai rushes towards me. "Shhh, shhh, little dove." He wipes away the tear and cups my cheek. "I will help you." He's going to help Alex? "You see, this…love, it is such a crippling weakness."

"No." I shake my head. He removes his gun from the holster and takes my hand, forcing my numb fingers to wrap around the hilt.

"I do this for you, little dove." He steps to my side and I stare down at the gun.

My hand shakes, my heart hammering in my chest so hard that my pulse thrums against my ear drums, a symphony of fear and heartbreak. I know what's coming. Of course I do. How stupid I was to think that I would get to have anything good.

"Please." I beg, lifting my eyes to Nicholai.

His expression softens and he reaches out, brushing a tendril of hair away from my face. "Become what you were meant to be, little dove." His thumb trails over my jaw and I close my eyes as more tears slip down my cheek. "Put a bullet in his head, or put a bullet in your own." He says, his voice suddenly harsh. "You cannot live with weakness. Fix it one way or another." His lips brush over the side of my face.

I lift my gaze, staring over his arm at the far wall. "Please don't make me do this." I beg. Tears blur my vision and I don't care that I look weak.

Nicholai looks at me is disgust. "See what he does to you. Make a choice."

The concrete walls of the room seem to press in on me until I can barely breathe. Nicholai's hand slips away from my face and he steps back. My trembling finger rests over the trigger of the gun and I swallow heavily. I lift my eyes to Alex, chained to the far wall. I stare into his beautiful eyes, so full of pain, so full of longing. I know beyond any doubt that I love Alex. He's my sanctuary, my safe harbour. Alex is the good in a world of evil, the beautiful light in the ugly darkness. To kill him is to kill any remaining good in me.

I meet his gaze and tighten the grip on the gun. His eyes are resigned, begging me, but not for reprieve. He's begging me to shoot him. "Do it, titch. Shoot me." Oh, god. My heart shatters.

"I love you." I choke. Tears track down my cheeks and a sharp pain rips through my chest.

"Shoot him, Una!" Nicholai roars.

With a ragged cry I lift the gun aiming between his eyes.

"Forgive me." I whisper on a sob and pull the trigger. His eyes never leave mine as the bullet rips through his skull leaving a hole in his forehead. His body slumps forward, his arms pulled taught against the chains. The steady flow of blood hitting the concrete is the only sound I hear.

For long moment I just stand there, staring at Alex's body. Inside I'm screaming, crying, sobbing. My heart is fracturing into tiny pieces, shattering and crumbling to dust. I'm breaking, collapsing in on myself and the pain is so intense I'm not sure I'll survive it. I don't think I want to. My lungs seize and my heart splutters in my chest. I hear the gun clatter to the ground, falling from my numb fingers.

I mourn for the boy I loved, for the girl I used to be, a girl who never would have done this. I just killed the best person I know, the only person who truly cared about me besides Nicholai, and it was Nicholai who put the gun in my hand, he who forced me to this. Alex cared enough that he begged me to shoot him instead of myself. And I'm enough of a monster that I did it.

"Little dove. Una." I lift my gaze to Nicholai, and as I look at him, something inside me snaps. The pain, the noise, it all stops. I stop. I cease to feel. It's like a switch flips in my mind. Everything that made me who I was blinks out like a broken light bulb. The numbness that ensues is peaceful, easy. I embrace the cold detachment with open arms, revelling in the darkness. After all, don't monsters live in the dark?

CHAPTER TWELVE

Nicholai

"The world breaks everyone, and afterward, some are strong at the broken places." – Ernest Hemmingway.

I smile. There she is, my perfect little dove. So strong, she's always been so strong. She killed the boy, rid herself of her weakness, just like I knew she would. I see it, the exact moment when the light leaves her eyes. All the emotions that make us humans so weak, extinguished in the blink of an eye. Those wide violet eyes of hers look up at me. I stroke a strand of her white blonde hair back behind her ear.

"So perfect. You make me so proud." She blinks slowly. "You are like the daughter I never had." To watch her fight is like poetry, to see her kill is art, a dancer spinning her craft on the great stage. She will be exquisite. The perfect death for any man who might find himself on the wrong end of her gun. "From now on you will be Una Ivanov, my daughter in name." I lean close and press my lips to her forehead. She tenses but makes no other move. "And your name will be whispered in fear, little dove."

Yes. Innocent and beautiful and deadly. She will be that which men both covet and fear equally. My Oleander flower. A Kiss of death.

Thank you so much for reading Nero and Una's story! Do you want to know how Cartel boss, Rafael fell for rescued sex slave, Anna Vasiliev?
HATE ME available now on Kindle Unlimited.

If you would like to know what happens to Sasha in life after the Elite, LOATHE ME is available now on Kindle Unlimited

Dear Reader

Thank you for reading!

I love all my books, and all my characters, but I adore Una and Nero. They are my perfect characters, so awful, but so perfect together.

Seriously though, thank you. Without you, all of this would be pointless. So thank you for one-clicking. Thank you for reading my work, and thank you for being awesome.

If you would be amazingly kind and leave a review, I would be so grateful. Leg humps would be owed.

THE AUTHOR

Sign up to LP Lovell and Stevie J. Cole's newsletter and stay up to date: Join the Mailing List

Lauren Lovell is a ginger from England. She suffers from a total lack of brain to mouth filter and is the friend you have to explain before you introduce her to anyone, and apologise for afterwards.

She's a self-confessed shameless pervert, who may be suffering from slight peen envy.

Other books by LP Lovell

She Who Dares series:

Besieged #1

Conquered #2

Surrendered #3

Ruined #4

Collateral Series:

Hate Me #1

Hold Me #2

Have Me #3

Touch of Death:

Loathe Me #1

Leave Me #2

Love Me`#3

Wrong Series:

Wrong

Wrath

Wire

War

Standalone:

Absolution

Rebel

Dirty Boss

The Pope

The Saint

The Game

No Prince

No Good

Website: https://www.lplovell.co.uk

Facebook: https://www.facebook.com/lplovellauthor

Goodreads:
https://www.goodreads.com/author/show/7850247.LP_Lovell

Amazon: http://www.amazon.com/LP- Lovell/e/B00NDZ61P

Printed in Great Britain
by Amazon